THE
SILENT SPIRIT

THE
SILENT SPIRIT

Margaret Coel

BERKLEY PRIME CRIME, NEW YORK

THE BERKLEY PUBLISHING GROUP
Published by the Penguin Group
Penguin Group (USA) Inc.
375 Hudson Street, New York, New York 10014, USA
Penguin Group (Canada), 90 Eglinton Avenue East, Suite 700, Toronto, Ontario M4P 2Y3, Canada
(a division of Pearson Penguin Canada Inc.)
Penguin Books Ltd., 80 Strand, London WC2R 0RL, England
Penguin Group Ireland, 25 St. Stephen's Green, Dublin 2, Ireland (a division of Penguin Books Ltd.)
Penguin Group (Australia), 250 Camberwell Road, Camberwell, Victoria 3124, Australia
(a division of Pearson Australia Group Pty. Ltd.)
Penguin Books India Pvt. Ltd., 11 Community Centre, Panchsheel Park, New Delhi—110 017, India
Penguin Group (NZ), 67 Apollo Drive, Rosedale, North Shore 0632, New Zealand
(a division of Pearson New Zealand Ltd.)
Penguin Books (South Africa) (Pty.) Ltd., 24 Sturdee Avenue, Rosebank, Johannesburg 2196,
South Africa

Penguin Books Ltd., Registered Offices: 80 Strand, London WC2R 0RL, England

This book is an original publication of The Berkley Publishing Group.

FIRST EDITION: September 2009

Library of Congress Cataloging-in-Publication Data

Coel, Margaret, 1937-
  The silent spirit / Margaret Coel.—1st ed.
      p.   cm.
   ISBN 978-0-425-22976-7
1. O'Malley, John (Fictitious character)—Fiction.   2. Holden, Vicky (Fictitious character)—Fiction.
3. Wind River Indian Reservation (Wyo.)—Fiction.   4. Women lawyers—Fiction.   5. Arapaho
Indians—Fiction.   6. Murder—Investigation—Fiction.   7. Domestic fiction.   I. Title.
   PS3553.O347S55   2009
   813'.54—dc22   2009014625

PRINTED IN THE UNITED STATES OF AMERICA

10   9   8   7   6   5   4   3   2   1

For Jim and Mary Seels

ACKNOWLEDGMENTS

One of the great pleasures of writing a novel is the opportunity to meet so many interesting and wonderful people who are willing to share their expertise and experiences and offer suggestions that, without a doubt, make the story better than it otherwise might have been. I thank them all for their generosity.

Jim Seels for suggesting a novel featuring Tim McCoy, for providing key books and articles on McCoy, *especially Tim McCoy Remembers the West: An Autobiography with Ronald McCoy*, and even DVDs of *The Covered Wagon* and several McCoy silent films, and for taking the time to show me around Hollywood and Cahuenga Pass. I could not have had a more enthusiastic and well-informed guide.

Robert Pickering, PhD, forensic anthropologist and deputy director of the Buffalo Bill Historical Center in Cody, Wyoming, for good-naturedly extending advice on arcane forensic matters to a neophyte such as myself.

Merle Haas, director, Sky People Higher Education, Northern Arapaho Tribe, the Wind River Reservation, for her encouragement and friendship and for sharing pertinent information on Tim McCoy.

Todd Dawson and Doug Walker, FBI special agents in Lander, Wyoming, for their generosity in taking the time to speak with me and help me navigate the thickets of procedural matters.

John Horton, district supervisor, Wyoming Department of Probation and Parole, in Lander, Wyoming, for advising me on ways in which his department works.

The Reverend Thomas J. Holahan, CSP, vice rector of Santa Susanna Church in Rome, for allowing me to read his "Rome Diary" and giving me a sense of an American priest's experiences in Rome.

Carl Schneider for proving to be a compendium of information about all sorts of matters.

Fred Walker for advising me on various types of guns.

For Virginia Sutter, PhD, a member of the Northern Arapaho Tribe, for her ongoing encouragement and friendship.

Karen Gilleland, Bev Carrigan, Sheila Carrigan, Philip F. Myers, Carl Schneider, and my husband, George Coel, for reading the manuscript and making the many suggestions that enhanced the story and left me deeply in their debt.

Long hair has never returned,
So his woman is crying, crying.
Looking over here, she cries.

—Oglala Sioux "kill song," from *Black Elk
Speaks* by John G. Neihardt

*Hollywood is a town that must
be seen to be disbelieved.*

—Walter Winchell, about Hollywood in the 1920s

1

THE HITCHHIKER LOOMED out of the brightness. A large figure standing at
the side of Seventeen-Mile Road, huddled in a bulky jacket, a black
cowboy hat pulled low, left in a cloud of snow from a truck speeding
past. He held out a gloved hand like a policeman stopping traffic. Father John O'Malley pressed on the brake pedal. He could feel the tires
on the old Toyota pickup grappling for purchase in the snow. "È il sol
dell'anima" came from the tape player on the seat beside him. Snow
had fallen during the night, and now the snow drifted and sparkled
like diamonds over the road and the flat, open land that ran into the
blue sky all around. The second Friday in February, the Moon of Frost
Sparkling in the Sun as the Arapahos marked the passing time, and the
sun was as bright as an August day.

Father John had passed the hitchhiker before the pickup skidded to
a stop. In the side mirror, he watched the man lope across the snow,
pulling a backpack off one shoulder. The passenger door swung open
and the hitchhiker stuffed himself onto the seat, waves of cold folding

around him, specks of moisture spattering the dashboard, and the faint, sour odor of sweat invading the cab.

"You see that truck go by?" he shouted. "Pulled away like I wasn't standing there freezing to death."

Father John recognized the man. Kiki Wallowingbull, about twenty-five years old, and at least ten of those years spent incarcerated—juvenile detention, tribal jail, state prison—for drug possession and distribution and probably a list of other offenses. Father John had met him a couple of years back, before Kiki was sentenced to the state prison for selling drugs in Riverton. He knew Kiki's grandfather, Andrew Wallowingbull, one of the Arapaho elders. Andrew had never lost faith in the young man. "One of these days, he's gonna get himself straightened out," he'd told Father John more than once.

"What's that?" Kiki looked down at the tape player.

"*Rigoletto*," Father John said. "You like opera?"

"You gotta be kidding."

"Where you headed?" Father John eased the pickup back into the lane. The truck had disappeared down the white road ahead.

"Hollywood," Kiki said.

"Hollywood?" Father John glanced over at the man with the bulky jacket bunched up around his ears, knocking his hands together on top of the backpack. "That's a long way."

"Just get me to the highway." There was a sharpness in the voice, a lashing out. "I'll catch a ride to Rawlins, hop a freight to LA," he went on, a little softer now, staring straight ahead, as if he were reading the rest of it off a teleprompter. "Used to listen to them trains goin' by. Sounded real loud and clear when I was inside. Made up my mind I was gonna ride one out to Hollywood and take care of some business, soon as I got paroled."

"How long have you been out?" Father John said.

"Long enough. Why do you care?"

"The parole officer knows you're leaving?"

"No reason for him to know what don't concern him."

Out of the corner of his eye, Father John could see Kiki swiveling his head about, glancing from one side of the road to the other like a hunted man. Desperation rolled off him like sweat. He had counseled men like Kiki. Wound up tighter than a spring, ready to snap. Anything might set them off.

He said, "LA's a long way to go on business." He was thinking that the drug pipeline ran from Mexico to LA, and from LA all the way to the reservation.

"I'm done with drugs if that's what you're worrying about," Kiki said. "I'm going to LA for my grandfather. I owe him big time. He deserves to know what happened to his father."

Father John shot another sideways look at the man. "What do you mean?"

"You heard of the Shoraps that was in the old cowboy-and-Indian movies?"

"That was a long time ago." Father John had read about the Arapahos and Shoshones from the reservation who had gone to Hollywood in the 1920s and acted in some of the silent Westerns.

"Had to have long hair to get in the movies," Kiki said. "Otherwise they didn't look like real Indians. Some of 'em were old buffalo Indians, still dreaming about the Old Time when they hunted the buffalo before they was sent to the rez." He pounded one gloved fist against the other. "They had to dress up in costumes and hop around some campfire 'cause some director says that's what Indians do. Everybody forgets what happened."

"What are you talking about?" Father John looked over again. "What happened?"

"My great-grandfather got killed, that's what happened." He kept pounding his fists, as if he were beating a drum. "Charlie Wallowing-bull, Grandfather's dad. Only Grandfather never knew him, 'cause he was born after Charlie left the rez with the rest of the Shoraps, thinking they was gonna be movie stars. Three hundred of 'em went off to be in *The Covered Wagon*. All of 'em came back from Hollywood, except Charlie. Grandfather says his mother kept waiting and waiting. Waited for twenty-five years, sure he was gonna come back 'cause he wasn't ever gonna leave her and his kid. Everybody said he'd walked away, went to Mexico or someplace. But Grandfather says he knew the truth from the minute he was born. Some things you know in your bones. He wasn't ever gonna have a father 'cause his father was dead."

The thrum of the tires on the snow and ice filled the silence. A sign as large as a billboard rose at the side of the road ahead: St. Francis Mission. How easily he had settled back into the old routines after the six-month sabbatical in Rome, Father John thought, as if he knew the routine in his bones. It was the way things were. Breakfast this morning at the senior center with several of the elders, and in thirty minutes, the monthly meeting with the social committee would get under way at the mission. A dozen pickups would pull into the mission grounds and park around Circle Drive.

He had left Rome the previous Wednesday, a cool morning with a thin sun struggling to break through the cloud cover and the roar and exhaust of motor scooters and the bleating horns of square-framed cars filling the streets, and a persistent, hurried buzz running through everything. Twelve hours later, the small plane that he had boarded in Denver was circling Riverton, the pilot unsure of whether to attempt setting down in the blizzard. Then, finally bumping across the runway, plunging through snow and ice. He had wanted to laugh out loud with the sheer joy of coming home.

"You expect to find out what happened to your great-grandfather?" he said.

"I'm gonna find out who killed him, if that's what you mean." There was a snarl in Kiki's tone, a residue of bravado probably left over from long days and months in prison.

"How about I buy you breakfast?" Father John drove past the entrance to the mission. "Then I'll drop you on the highway wherever you want." He was thinking that Lucy Running Bear, the high school girl he had hired to help out in the office, would take detailed notes at the social committee meeting, assuming some kind of emergency had come up, and in a way it had. A young Arapaho with a backpack and chip on his shoulder, hitching rides and catching a freight train to Hollywood to find out what had happened to his great-grandfather somewhere back in the 1920s.

"How about a drink? You being the Good Samaritan and all."

"I don't drink anymore," Father John said. "I'll buy you a cup of coffee."

Out of the corner of his eye, he saw the young man shrug and let out another muffled laugh. "What the hell," he said.

THE RESTAURANT IN Riverton was a collection of tables and booths arranged on a green-tiled floor with traces of icy footsteps and melting water. Moist smells of bacon and fresh coffee wafted over everything. They sat at one of the booths in front of the plate-glass windows that looked out over the parking lot with snow-covered vehicles scattered about. Across the lot, thin lanes of traffic ran along Federal Boulevard.

Kiki bent over a stack of pancakes, pushing pieces around in a pool of syrup until the white surface of the plate showed through, washing it all down with cup after cup of steaming coffee that he refilled from the brown plastic container in the center of the table. From time to time he glanced around at the other tables or pitched sideways and stared out the plate-glass window. And all the time talking on and on about the old movies, the silent Westerns, the Arapahos and Shoshones playing the Indians. Real Indians acting like Indians, he said.

Father John finished the two slices of toast that he had ordered, pushed the plate aside, and refilled his own cup. "How did they get to Hollywood?" he asked.

Kiki took another gulp of coffee. "Rode horses down to Rawlins, took the train. Only they went to the Utah-Nevada line where they was filming *The Covered Wagon*. After they got done making the movie, some of 'em went to Hollywood to promote it. My great-grandfather was one of 'em, only he never come back."

"They took the horses?"

Kiki lifted his shoulders in a half shrug that was like a twitch. "Got paid more if they brought their own ponies. Tipis, too. Cowboy from these parts, white man name of Tim McCoy, set up everything. Went around the rez talking to the longhairs and buffalo Indians, told 'em how there was good money in making movies, and how they needed real Indians 'cause they were tired of slapping brown makeup on a bunch of white men that didn't know a pony from an elephant and kept falling on their asses. Didn't take much talking, Grandfather says. Those old buffalo hunters was happy to get off the rez. You watch the movie and you can see how happy they was. They're supposed to be looking fierce and mean, but they look happy, like they was making more money than they ever knew existed and all they was doing was being themselves."

"What's your plan?" Father John asked.

"You think I don't got one?"

"I think you do. That's why I asked."

Kiki stuffed the last forkful of pancake into his mouth and chewed for a couple of seconds. "I been doing a lot of thinking. I got it figured out what happened. All I gotta do is fill in the names, find out who was responsible." He sipped at the coffee, eyes narrowed into brown slits, staring over the rim, locked on some movie unfolding in his head.

"You think someone was responsible for your great-grandfather's disappearance?"

"Disappearance?" Kiki let out a loud guffaw. Specks of coffee flew over the table. "I told you. Somebody killed him. I been listening to Grandfather's stories all my life. I been talking to some folks, putting it together, one piece at a time until it all started to get real clear. He was a good actor, Charlie was. You ever watch *The Covered Wagon*?"

Father John shook his head.

"Best-looking guy in the movie. He's the Indian all the important white folks talk to, like he's as important as they are. Rest of the Indians, they're riding around attacking wagon trains. But Charlie, he's smart, he knows what's going on. Everybody listens to him. It's sad how the bad guy kills him." Kiki shook his head a moment, as if the movie were a sign of Charlie's fate. "He was a real good actor. Could've won one of those Academy Awards if they'd been giving 'em then. Could've stayed on in Hollywood, kept on making movies, moved the family out to California. I could've grown up like one of them Hollywood rich kids."

"Why would someone want to kill him?"

"You think they was gonna let some Indian get to be a big movie star that everybody looked up to?" Kiki threw his head back and stared up at the ceiling a moment. "Changed everything when Charlie got killed. My great-grandmother, Anna was her name, went to work to take care of her boy, put some food on the table. Worked like a man in the fields, driving the rigs, baling hay, only she was a little woman with a baby strapped on her back. Took whatever work she could get just to keep her boy alive. Worked herself to death, that woman did. Grandfather said when she died there wasn't nothing left of her, just a sack of bones and swollen fingers. Cataracts so bad she couldn't see nothing."

He dropped his head, squared himself at the edge of the table, and locked eyes with Father John. "You believe in justice?" he said.

"It's an imperfect world, Kiki."

"What kind of answer is that? You believe in justice is what I want to know."

"I believe in justice, but justice isn't always possible."

"Oh, yeah? Well, you're wrong about that. I say it's about time we got some justice for what was done to the family. Changed everything, ruined Anna's life, ruined my grandfather's life. You know how hard he had it? Going off to war, getting shot up in the Pacific, laying in a hospital bed for eight months, then coming back to the rez and trying to find work. Only there wasn't no work on the rez, and nothing for

Indians anyplace else. You know what that's like? My own dad grew up feeling hungry all the time. So he started drinking, 'cause you know what? You ain't so hungry when you're drunk. Runs his pickup off a cliff, him and Mom inside, and it wasn't no accident. He got fed up. Couldn't take it anymore."

"Listen, Kiki." Father John clasped his hands and leaned over the table. "You can't change the past. You can't make things right."

Kiki refilled his coffee cup. For a long moment, he stared at the steam curling over the rim. Then he said, "I thought about doing that."

Father John was quiet.

"Driving off a cliff. I mean, it'd be easy. Then I thought, no way. Why should we keep paying for what Charlie's killer did? I figure Grandfather's got a right to know why his father never came home and why everything got changed. He's got a right to some kind of justice."

"How do you expect to learn the truth in Hollywood?"

"It's a storytelling place, right? That's what they do in the movies, tell stories."

"There's no one left from the 1920s," Father John said.

"Stories are still there, I figure. Somebody knows what happened. Some old white geezer waiting to die heard the story and knows what happened. All I gotta do is find him." He was staring at Father John. "What?"

Father John realized he'd been shaking his head. It was the Arapahos who talked about the past as if it had happened yesterday, every detail in place, the weather, the jokes, the way an ancestor had walked and laughed. "You're putting a lot of trust in the ability of white people to remember the past," he said. He could still see the perplexed look on the faces of the students at the Jesuit prep school in Boston where he had taught American History, as if history were a foreign country they saw no reason to visit. He had tried to make history come alive, to help the students understand that it was important. Every semester, one or two students seemed to get it, and he had been content with that. That was success.

He left Kiki where Gas Hills Road peeled off the highway, a blurred figure in the brightness, backpack hanging off one shoulder, obsessed with the past, Father John thought, as if he had exchanged one addiction for another. Traffic was light, judging from the faint tire tracks in the snow. It could take a while for him to catch a ride. Before Kiki had gotten out of the pickup, Father John had fished a folded fifty-dollar bill out of his blue jeans pocket. Money left over from the sabbatical in Rome. There hadn't been any reason to use it until now.

2

FATHER JOHN DROVE through the tunnel of cottonwoods that separated Seventeen-Mile Road from St. Francis Mission. Snow blew off the branches and showered the windshield. Ahead the mission buildings around Circle Drive glistened in the sunshine, remnants of the past that remained rooted in place while the rest of the world had moved on—the yellow stucco administration building, the white church with the spine that seemed to sway against the sky, the old stone school that was now the Arapaho Museum, the redbrick residence, the traces of concrete foundations—ghosts of buildings that had once existed.

All of it familiar, he thought. He had spent six months in Rome, helping out at St. Ignatius's parish and spending long hours in a velveted, brocaded conference room inside the Vatican Library discussing ways to bring the Christian message to indigenous people around the globe. At the table were priests from Africa and India, South America and Central America, the far reaches of Siberia, and he, the only priest from North America. He would close his eyes and see the mission, the

scratches on the old wooden doors at the entrance to the administration building, the paint peeling at the corner of the church, and the
light glowing in the stained glass windows in the evenings.

He parked in front of the administration building and watched
Walks-On in the rearview mirror bounding across Circle Drive, a red
Frisbee clutched in his jaws, snow billowing about. The dog was on
him as he got out of the pickup and Father John patted his head and
told him to drop the Frisbee. Walks-On pirouetted a couple of times
on his single hind leg before depositing the Frisbee at Father John's
boots. He picked it up, tossed it into the field, and watched the dog
chase underneath, snatch the Frisbee out of the air, and lope back. It
was a game they always played. When he came home, Walks-On was
waiting, the beat-up, cracked Frisbee or an old, half-peeled tennis ball
tight in his jaws. He had bought him a new Frisbee and a good rubber
ball before he'd left for Rome, but Walks-On preferred the old, familiar toys.

They were alike, Father John thought, two strays no one had
wanted. The golden retriever puppy with the crushed leg in the ditch
out on Seventeen-Mile Road that first winter Father John was at St.
Francis, and the alcoholic priest fresh out of rehab, still recovering, not
quite whole. He gave the Frisbee a hard toss, sending it to the far side
of Circle Drive. Old Father Peter had taken a chance on him. And he
had brought the puppy home after the vet had removed his hind leg—
a three-legged dog he called Walks-On. In an odd way, he thought, the
name seemed to fit both of them.

Walks-On came running back, the Frisbee clamped tight, wagging
his tail, the joyous look of expectancy in his eyes. Father John sat on
his heels, patted the dog's head, and scratched his ears. "We'll play
later," he said. He couldn't resist tossing the Frisbee one more time before he started up the concrete steps in front of the administration
building.

A rectangle of sunshine bathed the corridor inside, nearly obliterat-
ing the black–and-white portraits of past Jesuits that lined the stuc-

coed walls. The old wooden floors squeaked under his boots. His office was on the right, the door always open. He had hung his jacket on the coat tree and sat down at his desk when he heard the clack of footsteps in the corridor.

Lucy Running Bear darted into the office, barely breaking the rhythm of her footsteps. She was pretty, he thought, seventeen years old with the look of a child still about her, black hair that ran over her shoulders, a silver ring in one nostril, and red nail polish. She plopped a stack of messages on the desk, then proceeded to give him a running account: they missed him at the social committee meeting, but he shouldn't worry. She kept detailed minutes. Ada Longfellow had a baby boy last night; Johnny Yellow Feather fell on the ice and broke his hip and was in Riverton Memorial; Muriel and Ernie Whiteman needed an appointment for counseling.

"And by the way," she said, giving him the intent scrutiny he used to give students who arrived late for class, daring them to come up with a plausible explanation, "Jack Many Horses and Blanche Curfey are still in the hospital, in case you were thinking about visiting."

"On this afternoon's schedule," he said. Even with an assistant priest, there was always so much to do—visit the old and sick, counsel parishioners, oversee social programs, Alcoholics and Gamblers Anonymous meetings, religious education and confirmation classes. The daily Mass, the weekly confessions. But there was no assistant priest.

Then, yesterday morning, Lucinda Running Bear had appeared in his doorway. There he was, trying to straighten his desk, locate his files, and settle himself back into his office that had been taken over for six months by Father Ian McCauley, and there was Lucinda, sprawled in a side chair, squeezing a tissue and patting at the moisture on her cheeks, going on about how her daughter, Lucy, had dropped out of high school. Which would only lead to trouble, and wasn't that a fact? She was at her wit's end. What could she do? Would he talk some sense into her?

Not two hours later, Lucy sprawled in the same chair. A pretty girl, even with the blue tattoo of a snake that ran up her right arm—her medicine, she told him when she caught him looking at it. There was a mixture of innocence and defiance about her, as if she could will herself older and more experienced than her seventeen years. High school was boring, she said; she was never going back, no matter what her mother said. What did her mother know anyway?

He had offered her a job. She blinked at him several seconds, disarmed, he'd thought, bereft of the ammunition she'd brought along. All the arguments dissolved into nothing. He could use some help, he told her. The filing cabinets were a hopeless jumble. The printer was out of ink, and he hadn't been able to find the surface of his desk beneath the clutter. He needed someone to answer the phone, greet the drop-ins when he wasn't there, which was a big part of each day, work on the computer—bulletins for Sunday Mass, agendas for meetings of the social committee, ladies sodality, men's groups, the schedules for the ushers, and the Sunday drum groups. An endless list of minutiae that kept the mission running. He would pay her what he could; he was sorry, but it wouldn't be much. He had expected her to refuse.

A job? she said. Sure, she could use a little money.

Now he thanked her for the messages. The girl seemed to have thrown herself into the job, and she was certainly organized. As soon as she had pivoted about and headed back down the corridor to her office, he had called Muriel Whiteman and set up a counseling appointment for later this afternoon. He returned the other calls, then went back outside and cut new tracks through the snowy field enclosed by Circle Drive, Walks-On running alongside. As soon as he opened the door to the residence, the dog raced past and skittered down the hallway toward the kitchen. A spicy smell drifted through the sounds of running water, the clank of metal and glass. He tossed his jacket and cowboy hat onto the bench and followed Walks-On into the kitchen.

Elena stood at the sink, swishing dishes in soapy water and laying them in neat rows in the rack on the counter. "A little early for lunch," she said, throwing a glance over one shoulder. She was somewhere in her seventies, although she had never volunteered her age. "Old enough to know something," she would say whenever the matter came up. She was half Arapaho, half Cheyenne, a short woman, barely reaching his shoulder, with tight curls of gray hair, the rounded face of the Cheyenne, the fiery determined eyes of the Arapaho, and a white apron cinched around a thick waist.

"Just had coffee and toast." Father John pushed a chair out from the table with his boot and sat down. He had eaten a bowl of oatmeal, two pieces of toast, and a cup of coffee this morning before he'd gone to the senior center. Two more cups of coffee there. Coffee and toast in Riverton.

"You'll get a paunch on you, you don't watch out," Elena said, turning around and facing him. She was so like his mother, the way he remembered her when he was a kid, cooking dinner in the tiny kitchen in the corner of what passed for a living room in the daytime and his and Mike's bedroom at night. The flat sat above his uncle's saloon on Commonwealth Avenue in Boston. He could still close his eyes and summon the faint odors of whiskey and beer and the muffled shouts of laughter and the clink of bottles that floated up the narrow stairway and seeped through the flat. And his mother, piling plates high with mashed potatoes and hard-fried hamburger patties and canned peas, fussing over him and his big brother. It was the image he held on to, before the last years when she no longer knew either of her sons.

"What do you know about Kiki Wallowingbull?" he said.

Elena was quiet a moment, wiping her hands on the apron. Finally she stepped over to the table and sat down. "Why're you asking?"

"He was hitching out on Seventeen-Mile Road this morning, and I picked him up. He's on his way to California."

"That's good news." Elena clasped her hands across her middle and sat back. "Let him sell his drugs and raise hell out in California. We don't need the likes of Kiki Wallowingbull in these parts."

"You think he's still dealing?"

"You think wolves turn into lambs?" Elena shrugged. "I'd say he's doing what he's always done, causing trouble, giving his grandfather all that heart trouble. Wonder the old man's still walking around. Raised that boy themselves, him and Mamie, after their own son drove his pickup off a cliff, him and Kiki's mom both drunk inside. Andrew and Mamie took the boy in, wasn't about to let him go to some foster home where nobody'd love him or teach him the Arapaho Way. That's the kind of thanks Andrew gets for all the trouble. Kiki don't want to live the Arapaho Way. So what's he doing, going off to California?"

"He wants to learn about his family."

"That's a laugh. He never cared about family."

"Maybe he's trying to change, make up for the past."

"In California?" Elena laughed. She started to push herself to her feet, then sat back down hard. A shadow of comprehension crossed her face. "You telling me he's looking for his great-grandfather? Went to Hollywood to be in the movies and never come back?"

Father John nodded.

"Nobody cares about that anymore." She turned partway in the chair and gazed at the window for a long moment. An invisible film might have been flickering across the glass. "People here used to be proud of all those warriors, and women, too, that was in the cowboy-and-Indian movies. They used to say, 'We showed 'em what real Indians was like, not those painted-up white boys and girls with feathers on their heads. Real warriors riding over the plains and fighting for our lands. Real Indian women taking care of things and cooking the food. Made everybody proud, 'cause the movies showed that we were people living in villages and hunting the buffalo. When the white men came, we had a right to protect what was ours.' "

Father John waited a moment before he said, "I think Kiki's trying to make up for the trouble he caused. Give something back to his grandfather."

Elena gave him a long searching look. "Maybe he's on the run from trouble here," she said. "Might be California's a good place to hide. All them people out there, he figures he can get lost." She gripped the edge of the table and pulled herself to her feet. "I've known that boy since he was no bigger than a grasshopper, and I'm telling you, there's something off about him. Always has been, ever since his daddy drove off that cliff. Left him full of anger. It's like a hot oil bubbling inside him. I wouldn't believe nothing he said. If he's going to California, I say good riddance."

She swung around, marched back to the sink, and plunged both hands into the soapy water. Then she looked back. "You gonna be here Sunday?"

"Far as I know." He never knew from one day to the next where he might be. He was the interim pastor at St. Francis Mission for a while. The provincial might call today, and tomorrow he would be on his way again, but he was here now. That was what he tried to hold on to.

"Good," she said, bent into the task of washing the dishes.

Father John headed back down the hallway, pulled on his jacket, and grabbed his hat. He let himself out the door and retraced his own tracks through the snow. There would be a feast after Mass on Sunday to welcome him back. A surprise; he wasn't supposed to know. But he knew his parishioners would hold a feast. It was the Arapaho Way. He had wanted to tell Elena that the whole idea made him uncomfortable, that he preferred to slip into the old routine as if he had never been gone. But how could he tell her he didn't want the women to go to all the trouble of preparing a feast that he wasn't supposed to know about?

VICKY RECOGNIZED THE determined thud of Adam's footsteps in the outer office before the knock sounded on the door. Then he was in her office. She kept her eyes on the computer screen, but in her peripheral vision, she saw him walking toward the desk, black hair slicked back, broad shoulders and dark, handsome face with the faint scar on his cheek.

They were partners: Vicky Holden and Adam Lone Eagle, attorneys at law, the black letters on the pebbled glass door said. An Arapaho and a Lakota with an office on the second floor of a beige brick building that fronted Main Street in Lander, a short distance from the border of the Wind River Reservation where she had grown up. Spacious and neat, everything in its place, with polished desks and upholstered chairs and yards of muted gray carpeting, and a secretary and an associate lawyer on the payroll. Sometimes she felt as if she had landed on the far side of the earth.

Adam settled into the chair on the other side of the desk. She could feel him waiting. Still she took her time before lifting her eyes from the lines of black type and turning toward him. The brief she'd been writing had to do with tribal water rights and whether the Arapahos and Shoshones should develop a plan to sell the water they owned to a town like Riverton, located within the reservation's exterior boundaries, but not part of the reservation. The tribes could compete with the water consortium that had supplied water to Riverton for years. A very important issue, Adam had said after last week's meeting with Lawson Newman, the tribal water engineer. And in the tone of his voice, she'd heard the capital letters: VERY IMPORTANT. The kind of case that mattered, that would make a difference for her people, the Arapahos. The kind she and Adam had agreed to take on. They would go forth, do battle on behalf of important issues. But why did the issues feel so empty, so devoid of flesh and blood, lacking the people who used to wander into her office, brown faces long and worried, muffled voices asking if she could help.

"You know what the state courts said in the Bighorn Decrees," Adam said, launching back into the conversation they'd had this morning. "The tribes are prohibited from selling water off the reservation. I think we have to advise the tribes to back off. They have no legal justification."

"Not necessarily." Vicky swiveled to the keyboard, brought up another screen, and pressed the print key. She waited while the printer spit out three pages, then handed them across the desk. "Another case is in the federal appeals court, asking for clarification of the term 'Indian Country.' If the court finds that the term applies to all land within the boundary of a reservation, then nothing will prevent the tribes from selling water to Riverton. They would be on solid legal ground."

"The court hasn't handed down the decision yet." Adam flipped through the pages and tossed them onto the desk. "The decision could go either way. I think we should recommend that the tribes put any plans to develop and sell water on hold."

"I disagree," Vicky said. Silence fell over the desk like a low-hanging cloud. "I've checked with the federal clerk's office. The decision isn't expected anytime soon. But the *U.S. Code* defines Indian Country as all land within the limits of a reservation, and there's no reason to think the court won't uphold the code. I believe the tribes should go ahead with plans to offer water to Riverton."

Adam got to his feet and leaned over the desk. "The tribes don't want two different legal opinions, Vicky. We have to be united on this." He spun the pages into the middle of the desk with his index finger, as if he were shooting marbles. "Let it rest for a while, okay? We'll talk about it again Monday. Let's knock off early and go to Jackson for the weekend. I'll get on the internet and find us a nice condo. We can snowshoe, go cross-country skiing, relax, talk about something other than law."

Vicky looked away from the shadows of pain and pleading in Adam's eyes. She studied the piles of papers on the desk, the buttons lined in rows on the keyboard. She had been thinking about getting away. Going to LA to visit Susan for a few days. She hadn't seen Susan in more than six months. Six months and so many changes in her daughter's life. A new job at a company that created visual effects for the movies; a new man—somebody named Brett. She had told Susan she would fly out to LA the first chance she got.

"Shall I make the reservation?" Adam asked, still leaning close. She focused on his hands flattened against the desk, the sharp outlines of knuckles popping through the dark skin. What he had said was true. She wondered why it had gone that way between them, where it seemed that all they had in common was the law.

"Why not?" she said.

Adam swept one hand along the desk, as if he might sweep away like so much dust any problems lingering between them.

The door cracked open, and Annie Bosey, the secretary, leaned around the edge. "I was wondering if I might leave a little early," she said. "Got a lot of cooking to do this weekend."

Adam turned toward her. "Is there a feast on the rez we don't know about?"

"At the mission," Vicky said, and Adam looked back. "A welcome-home feast for Father John."

"You didn't tell me he was back."

"He arrived earlier this week." Vicky shrugged.

"Okay if I leave?" Annie said.

Vicky gave a little wave, and Annie stepped backward, pulling the door closed behind her.

"I didn't think it was important," she said. The pain in Adam's eyes was so intense that she had to force herself not to look away.

"Not important? The man who . . ." He let the rest hang between them.

"We were friends for a long time," Vicky said. "We worked together on a lot of cases. You know that."

"You don't think it's important that your friend has returned?"

"I meant the feast isn't important." Vicky could feel herself stumbling over the words. There was no reason not to have mentioned that John O'Malley was back. She had been waiting, she realized, not for the right time, exactly, but until she had sorted out the feelings coiled and knotted inside her like a rope. He had been gone six months. She had been angry when he left, but that had made no sense. She had always known that one day he would leave. Gradually the anger had given way to something else, like the stages of grief. Anger and finally acceptance. She had come to accept certain things: a part of her life had ended, but a new life was waiting to begin. A life with Adam that had been on hold. The office six days a week. Dinner two or three times a week, and he sometimes spent the night. There were the out-of-town business trips that Adam took: Casper where he had rental properties, meetings in Montana and South Dakota with the Crow and Cheyenne and Lakota tribes on various cases. It was always Adam who wanted to attend the meetings. He liked moving about. It meant nothing, the way he always wanted to leave, she had told herself. We are traveling people. The Lakota, the Arapaho, all the Plains Indian people liked to move about. She had almost convinced herself that she and Adam Lone Eagle could have a life together.

And now, John O'Malley was back.

"Do you want to go to the feast?" Adam said. "We can leave Jackson early."

Vicky was about to say yes, that she would like that. It surprised her, the sound of her own voice saying, "It's not necessary."

3

THIS WAS THE surprise. Pickups and cars nose to tail around Circle Drive, bumping over the snow-packed field that the drive wrapped around in search of parking spaces. People streaming down the alley between the church and the administration building, heading toward Eagle Hall with covered dishes and bulky brown paper bags cradled in their arms. Little kids running ahead or trailing behind, coats unbuttoned and thrown open in the crisp, cold sunshine. Father John stood on the stoop outside the front door of the church and watched the parade.

Ten o'clock Mass had been packed, people smashed in the pews, lining the side aisles and piled in the vestibule. Looking out at the brown faces turned up to him, the rightness of it washed over him. This was the destination he had been going toward all of his life. This was where he belonged. Yet he couldn't shake the uneasy feeling nipping at him like a wild dog at his heels. If he gave himself over again to the people and the place, how could he ever leave?

The feast would be held this morning, and he would act surprised, as if he had never guessed. Odd how the parishioners were determined to celebrate his homecoming, as if he were back to stay after having wandered about and gotten lost for a while. His own celebration would be different. Not because he was here to stay, but simply because he was here now.

After Mass, he had stood outside in the cold, parishioners gathering around, roughened brown hands grasping his own, enveloped in a chorus of voices: "Glad you're back, Father. Glad you're back." Finally he managed to extricate himself and head back into the church. Silence had settled over the pews and the aisles. The faint odors of snuffed candles mingled with the leftover scent of damp coats and wet boots. He hung his vestments in the sacristy, then retraced his steps outside and headed toward Eagle Hall.

The doors stood wide open. Groups of men huddled outside, puffing on cigarettes cupped in their hands, cowboy hats pulled low against the glare of sun and snow. He could see people milling about in the half light inside. The buzz of conversations mingled with the odors of coffee and bacon drifting past the doors.

"Must be some pretty good donuts this morning," Father John said, playing along with the surprise.

"Baked 'em ourselves," one of the men said. Amusement flickered in his black eyes. They knew that he knew.

Father John was aware of the hush that had come over the hall, like an expectant pause. The moment he stepped inside, the noise erupted—clapping and shouting his name: *Father John. Father John. Father John.* A huge white banner with red letters floated above the crowd: Welcome Home. Hands rose in the air, waving him forward. He lifted his own hands and waved back, aware that a little boy had wrapped himself around his legs. He scooped up the kid—Howie Black Bear, about five years old now, with black hair that stood straight up, a round brown face and white teeth; he had baptized Howie the day he was born, when the doctors didn't think he would live. He set the boy on his shoulder and, holding on to him with one hand, began making his way through the hall, dodging the round tables and metal chairs, shaking hands, aware of the sound of his own voice: thank you, thank you. What a surprise! So glad to be back with you. So glad to be back. Howie was as light as a leaf on his shoulder.

"This way, Father." Elena's voice behind him. He turned halfway around and saw the housekeeper marching through a tunnel of people and nodding him toward the long table at the end of the hall. He swung around and went after her. Groups of elders sat at the tables around the periphery of the hall, paper plates stacked with food in front of them. Elena and the other women had seen to it that the elders were served first. Now it was his turn to fill a plate of food—he was the guest—then everyone else would line up to help themselves.

The table was filled with platters of sandwiches and bowls of stew with steam curling around the rims and plates of cookies and brownies and cakes. Eric Black Bear had appeared at his side and was trying to coax Howie off his shoulder. Father John handed the boy a cookie and set him in his dad's arms. Then he went about fixing himself a plate. All familiar, the chunks of beef, potatoes, carrots, and onions in the thick gravy, the bologna tucked between slices of white bread, the array of desserts—the comforting food of home. He poured coffee into a cup and carried the plate and cup toward the tables where the elders sat.

He spotted Andrew Wallowingbull and made his way over, smiling at the other elders, nodding in respect. "Okay to join you?" he said. Two other elders were also at the table: Martin Running Horse and Robert White Plume, wearing plaid shirts with silver bolo ties at the collars and tan cowboy hats pushed back from gray hair and brown faces. The cowboy hats nodded in unison, and Father John set the paper plate and coffee cup on the table and dropped into the chair he'd nudged over with his boot. He started on the stew and took part in the usual pleasantries, beginning with the weather. This was the in-between, Robert said, the sunny days that fell over the vast expanse of plains between the winter storms. The stew was hot and delicious, and even the bologna sandwich tasted good. "More snow coming," the elder went on. "Feel it in my bones. Arthritis kicking up before the next snow."

"You like Rome?" Andrew asked. The others sat very still, and Father John could see the answer they longed for in the dark, watching eyes. Rome was interesting, he told them. An ancient city, layers of civilization beneath your feet, the past all around you, but it wasn't the reservation. What could he say? He shrugged. It wasn't home. They smiled at that, as if he had confirmed what they had known all along.

When Robert went for more coffee and Martin turned his chair to talk to the elders seated nearby, Father John leaned across the table toward Andrew. "I saw Kiki the other day," he said, an opening gambit. He hadn't been able to get Kiki Wallowingbull out of his mind: a young Arapaho riding the rails to Los Angeles. Yet there was every possibility that Kiki hadn't told his grandfather he was going to California, hadn't wanted to worry him. "Gave him a ride on Seventeen-Mile Road. Looks like he's trying to straighten out his life."

Andrew set his elbows on the table and rubbed his hands together, pulling at his fingers, as if he wanted to restore the circulation that for some reason had stopped. "We been worrying about the boy." He nodded toward his wife, Mamie, gray-haired and tight-lipped, bustling about the food table with the other grandmothers. There was a commotion in the corner where the drum group was setting up. A microphone squealed. The strong smell of fresh brewed coffee filled the air. "Been through some rough times last few years. Got himself mixed up with a bad bunch, drug gang selling drugs to the people. No good, those guys. Got Kiki sent to prison for two years. He's done with all that now. He's not messing with drugs anymore, Father."

"Hope he stays out of trouble," Father John said. Kiki was probably in Hollywood now, he was thinking. A drug user just out of prison, venturing into a place he didn't know, looking for a past he didn't understand.

"Got to let go of the anger first," Andrew said. "That boy's been eaten alive with a powerful anger he's been carrying around since he was born. He came screaming into the world filled with anger."

The old man was quiet for a moment, staring off into space, arranging something in his mind. Father John waited. Finally, Andrew said, "Came out of the past. Gathered itself up and settled inside my grandson, like a weight on his heart. Always talking about how the people need justice. We gotta get what's due us from everything that we lost. All the land gone, all the old ways gone. Makes him feel helpless, 'cause he can't do anything about it. Festers inside him, eating him alive. I told him, Grandson, you gotta let it go. The people had to let it go. We gotta go on and live. Everything that killed us in the past, it'll keep on killing us if we don't let it go. Step out ahead of it, I told him. Get on with your life." Andrew picked up his foam cup and drained the last of the coffee. He looked old and weathered, yet there was something sturdy about him, like one of the old cottonwood trees around the mission.

Father John offered to refill his cup, but Andrew shook his head. "He tell you he was heading to California?"

Father John nodded.

"Crazy idea he could go off to Hollywood and find out what happened to my father. Charlie was his name. Went out there a long time ago to be in the movies. You heard about how Arapahos and Shoshones were in the movies?"

He'd heard a little about it, Father John said.

"Movie people wanted real Indians, so they came to Wyoming and talked to a cowboy named Tim McCoy. Sometimes Arapahos got cowboy work, whenever the government agent said they could leave the reservation. Couldn't go nowhere without the agent saying it was okay. Couldn't even go to town to buy groceries. Not that it mattered none. Most of the stores had signs up that said no dogs or Indians allowed. Couldn't go see the relations in Oklahoma or Colorado. Couldn't even ride the ponies off the reservation without soldiers or the sheriff throwing them in jail. Only time the agent gave permission for the boys to go cowboying was when people were starving. Sometimes they'd round up wild horses in the Red Desert outside Lander and drive 'em onto the trains that came through Arapaho. Sometimes Indians got work on the big ranches owned by white men. That's how come some Arapahos got to cowboying with Tim McCoy. You heard of him?"

"Kiki mentioned him," Father John said.

"Cowboy star, made lots of movies. Good man, McCoy. White man with a good heart. When he was cowboying around here, he treated Indians like everybody else. Even learned the sign language so he could talk to the old buffalo Indians that came from the Old Time and remembered how it used to be. Came to the reservation for celebrations. Camped with the people, got to be like family."

Andrew slid his hand across the table, took hold of Father John's hand, and gripped it hard. "White man like yourself," he said. "People trusted McCoy. Pretty soon he had his own spread up in the Owl Creek Mountains. He was a big man when the movie people came around looking for Indians, so they asked him, did he know any Indians wanted to be in the movies? Well, he knew Indians that wanted to work. Indians that wanted to put food in their kids' mouths. So he told the movie people, he'd get the Indians, and he seen to it they treated Indians fair, same as white men. They had to pay Indians more if they brought their own ponies and tipis."

"They agreed?"

Andrew nodded. He was smiling at the memories. "McCoy talked three hundred Arapahos and Shoshones into going to Hollywood. First, he had to talk the agent into letting them go. Three hundred of 'em rode the train to Milford, Utah, to be in *The Covered Wagon*. That was 1922. My father went with them. Still a young pup, wasn't even married yet, but he wore his hair long, and movie people wanted longhairs. Said they looked like real Indians. All they had to do was be themselves, ride ponies, live in tipis, whoop and holler like white folks think Indians do, look like they were attacking wagon trains."

"He must have returned to the reservation after that," Father John said.

"Came home after the movie was finished, got himself married. The next April he went to Hollywood with other Shoraps, camped in a place called Cahuenga Pass and put on an Indian show at the theater where they showed the movie."

"Kiki said your father didn't come back."

Andrew slumped backward, as if a weight had crashed down on him. "They all come home, 'cept for him. That's how come I never knew my dad. Some of the Indians tried to get my mother to believe that he ran off. Just didn't show up for the stage show one night. They said he must've gone off to Mexico 'cause he didn't want to be a prisoner again on the rez. My mother never believed it. Besides, they was just saying what the movie folks told them. Charlie Wallowingbull was just another Indian. Nobody was too bothered about what might've happened to him. So the movie folks said he disappeared."

"What about Tim McCoy?"

"Oh, he was bothered plenty, 'cause he come to the rez to see my mother. That was after McCoy was a big movie star himself. Told her he'd never stop trying to find out what happened. He raised a lot of hell, kept pushing for the truth, but he never could find out anything. I got a letter he wrote us. Said he'd tried his best, even went to the police, but there wasn't any record of a dead Indian that April. I showed the letter to Kiki. 'Listen, Grandson,' I said. 'If a big movie star like Tim McCoy didn't find the truth back then, what makes you think you're gonna find it now?'"

Father John took a moment before he said, "Why would Kiki think your father had been killed?"

Andrew stared off into space. The buzz of conversations filled up the quiet. A blur of kids circled the tables, laughing. "Mother knew the truth in her bones," Andrew said, his voice barely a whisper. "That's how it is with the truth. You can't push it away, cover it up, and pretend it isn't there. It takes hold of you and never lets go."

"Have you heard from Kiki?" Father John said. "Did he get to LA okay?"

"Kiki's not one for telling things 'til it's time for them to be told." Andrew was shaking his head. "Said he was goin' to Hollywood to talk to folks, find out what happened. Figure it'll take him a few days to find out that nobody cares. Then he'll come on home. That's what his grandmother"—he tossed his head again toward the food table—"keeps saying is gonna happen."

"Let me know when Kiki gets back," Father John said. Lord, let it be soon, he was thinking.

He spent a few more minutes chatting with Andrew and the other elders, finishing the stew and draining the last of his coffee. The drums had started, and the singers' voices rose over the soft, rhythmic thuds. Finally he excused himself and started around the tables, thanking people for coming, tousling the black heads of the kids. And all the time, he realized—visiting with Andrew and the elders, joking and laughing at the tables—he had kept an eye on the door. Vicky had not come.

4

October 1922

THE GIRL WAS trouble. Anyone could see that trouble followed her like a pony sniffing after a cube of sugar. All in white, the girl. A gauzy white dress that moved in the breeze and turned pink and orange in the sunset, white stockings and white shoes with little bows on top. And a face as white as the piece of porcelain he'd seen in the shop window in Riverton that day the agent had told him to take the Ford Runabout into town to pick up parcels his wife had ordered at the dry-goods store. Like porcelain, the white arms and little white hands drifting with the folds of her dress. Her eyes were violet. She was about the most beautiful girl he had ever seen. Curly yellow hair flowing over her shoulders as she looked around at the tipis and the campfire giving off little bursts of fire and smoke. Like a queen. He could feel the uneasiness creeping over him like the wind.

"What's she doing here?" William Thunder dropped down in the space between Charlie Wallowingbull and James Painted Brush. The smells of burning sage and the dry dust of the desert mingled with the faint whir of voices. Goes-in-Lodge and the other buffalo Indians sat cross-legged on the ground close to the campfire. The white men were lining up on the other side. Tim McCoy—you could spot him a mile away in his white cowboy hat—had already positioned himself where he could see the Indians and the movie people.

"She's Missy Mae Markham," Charlie said. "She's a big star in a lot of moving pictures."

"I'm gonna get me one of them box cameras and take her picture." Painted Brush was leaning so close to the fire that William could see the red fingers of light licking his face.

"She's nobody in *The Covered Wagon*," William said. Here she was just one of the players, like the Arapahos and Shoshones—five hundred of them counting the other Shoshones that came from Idaho, all camped in the middle of the desert for four weeks now, next to the tent city with a couple thousand white movie folks, the nearest town a place called Milford with a few horse-drawn wagons and crank-up Fords on the Main Street. Except that the Indians were important. Couldn't make the photoplay without them, not with the white players crossing Indian country in covered wagons, practically begging the Indians to attack. Just like in the Old Time, the buffalo Indians said.

The important people stood shoulder to shoulder now, staring across the fire at the buffalo Indians. The director, Mr. Cruze—McCoy called him Jimmie—and J. Warren Kerrigan standing real close to the pretty black-haired woman, Lois Wilson. They were the most important players, near as William could tell. Seemed that a camera was always pointing their way. On the other side of the black-haired girl was Alan Hale, the guy that played the bad man. By the end of the photoplay, William guessed, Kerrigan would win the pretty woman. He had heard that when white people went to a fancy theater to see a moving picture, they hollered and stomped their feet until the good guy finally won.

But what William couldn't figure was why the girl was always hanging around. Why did she have to come to camp every evening to talk about the next day's shooting?

Bunched up behind the director were Mr. Cruze's assistants, the production manager, and three cameramen. Mr. Cruze always insisted on having the cameramen at the evening meetings. They could smell tomorrow's weather, he said. They knew the best time to shoot different scenes. "What do you think?" he would ask them before the meetings ended. After they gave their opinions, he would tell the elders what time in the morning the Indians should be ready.

And the girl in the Indian camp for every meeting, drifting around the Indians like a white wisp of smoke. She had a way of tilting back her head and gazing up into the eyes of each man, making promises. "She's nothing but trouble," William said. He could feel his lips pulled tight, the words pushing against his teeth. Behind him, he could hear other Indians wandering over, moccasins scuffing the hard-packed earth.

"We shoot the attack tomorrow." Mr. Cruze's voice bellowed into the evening quiet. The breeze had picked up, and the girl patted her dress around her legs. Her gaze ran over the Indians, as if she were trying to locate someone. Red and gold lights from the campfire lit up her face. Her eyes were like purple glass.

"Biggest scene in the photoplay, civilization against savages, march of progress across the West. You understand how important the scene will be?" Mr. Cruze started walking up and down, flapping his big arms, the collars of his white shirt standing out around his thick neck. He had on his usual floppy hat with the beak that crowded his face. Everything about the man was big—as if he owned the desert.

McCoy's hands were flying about, translating everything the director said for the buffalo Indians. They came from the Old Time when all the tribes used sign language. No need to learn other languages. Everyone knew what was said. They had never learned to speak English. Trouble was, nobody except the old men used signs anymore. McCoy had learned signs so he could talk to them. Whatever he said with his signs, they would believe. He spoke the truth.

McCoy himself had come to the reservation and talked the old buffalo Indians into going to the desert to be in the moving picture. Then McCoy had gone around talking to the young men who kept their hair in long braids. The movie people only wanted longhairs, he said, 'cause they looked like real Indians. William had decided to go even before McCoy had finished with all the particulars. He had convinced Charlie and Painted Brush to come along. Even though they had gone to the St. Francis Mission school and learned to read and write English, figure numbers, make computations, and think about things, they still kept their hair in long braids, a way of holding on to something of themselves, William guessed. McCoy said they could help the others adjust, explain the way whites think, reassure the old buffalo Indians when they got to longing for the reservation.

William saw it then—the way the girl's eyes lit up when she spotted Charlie. "Don't pay her any attention," William said. He could see Charlie watching her, as if even the director walking back and forth couldn't block her from view. "You been seeing her, haven't you?" William said.

"Don't see how it concerns you," Charlie said.

"Soon's I get a camera, I can get a real good picture of her and take it back to the rez," Painted Brush said, and William realized that he was also watching the girl.

William leaned close to Charlie. "Concerns all of us. You take up with a white girl, and they'll send both of us home. We came together, and they'll send us back together. Painted Horse, too. Even McCoy won't be able to change things."

Mr. Cruze had turned around to talk with the cameramen, who were tossing their heads to the east and west, as if they could see the weather and the light coming tomorrow. Finally the director swung back and faced the buffalo Indians. "We shoot the attack scene at eight o'clock sharp." McCoy's hands and fingers danced about. "Gotta take advantage of the overcast before the sun breaks through. Everybody clear on the positions? Warriors attack through the boulders over there." He lifted his big arm and jabbed a hand in the direction of the rock outcropping in the hills about a mile away. "You'll be naked except for breechcloths. Bands on your arms. War paint on your faces. Bring your bows and arrows, whatever you got. Anybody doesn't have a weapon, stop at the supply tent thirty minutes before the shoot. Everybody's gotta be armed. Understand?"

McCoy's hands stopped moving, and William realized he left out the last word. Goes-in-Lodge and the others would be insulted. Then he saw that the girl was still smiling at Charlie, lifting her eyebrows in that promising way she had, turning sideways, and looking over one shoulder. Charlie didn't take his eyes from her, but he was nervous, William could tell. Clasping and unclasping his fists, the muscles of his arms bulging through his cotton shirt.

Mr. Cruze made a raspy noise and spit on the ground. "One more thing," he said. "We're gonna get a panoramic shot of the Injun camp in the first light. I want the tipis in a circle, openings facing the center. Shouldn't be too tough to move the tipis around tonight so we'll be ready tomorrow."

William could see McCoy hesitate. He looked hard at the director before he started making the signs. A stillness came over the Indians huddled close to the campfire and flowed through the Indians standing in back. The old buffalo Indians in front were nodding. It would not be polite to argue or refuse; it was polite to nod. But William knew that tomorrow morning, all the tipis would still face the east and the rising sun, the way it had always been in Arapaho and Shoshone villages. And McCoy knew it, too, judging by the embarrassed look on his face, like a shadow lengthening beneath the brim of his cowboy hat.

"Nobody here is going to change tradition for a photoplay," William said. "Mr. Cruze must've figured if he just blurted it out, McCoy would have to sign the words." The director looked satisfied with himself. It hadn't been a problem after all. Look at those old Indians nodding.

"Questions?" Cruze bellowed. "Everything understood? Good. Be on time tomorrow, eight o'clock sharp." He swung around and started back through the white men scrambling to get out of his way. The cameramen jumped in behind him, then the others fell into step, the whole group walking past the Indians standing about, past the tipis and small campfires crackling into the quiet.

Charlie started to scramble to his feet. William grabbed at his arm, but Charlie shrugged free and headed around the campfire to the girl. She looked up at him with that tilted head, those raised eyebrows and said something she must have thought funny, because she started laughing and the sound was like bells tinkling in the corral. Charlie took a couple of steps backward, but the girl moved in closer, set a small hand on the sleeve of his cotton shirt, and said something else that sent her into squeals of laughter.

William started over. He wanted to tell her to go away, that a white girl with violet eyes and porcelain skin was trouble for an Indian. Except that he would not tell her that. A white girl would know many ways to bring him and Charlie trouble. They needed the work, needed the money. Charlie, with Anna White Bull waiting for him to get enough money to buy the lumber and nails and build them a little house so they could get married. And he, wanting to start his own herd. A couple of cows, a bull. Maybe he'd have a ranch of his own someday and wouldn't have to beg the agent for permission to go off the reservation and work on the white ranches.

He saw the white man out of the corner of his eye—like a locomotive puffing through the groups of Indians, retracing his steps, as if he had just realized he had left something behind. He was tall and skinny, with curly brown hair and squinty eyes. One of Mr. Cruze's assistants, always hanging around, running errands, telling somebody what to do. He had heard the rumors that the skinny man was the girl's bodyguard. The man lurched forward, grabbed the girl's arm, and spun her around, nearly lifting her off her feet. She would be as light as air, William thought.

"You heard what Mr. Cruze said. Time to go." He pushed the girl in the direction of the others.

She stumbled a little, then gave Charlie a backward glance. "See you later," she called in that tinkling voice tinged with laughter and regret. Something not quite right with her, William thought. Something out of whack, off-kilter. Rumors had run through the Indian camp— there was whiskey and cocaine over in the tent city. Much of it as you wanted. Couple of Indians had gone to tent city and come back drunk and sick. Couldn't work the next day. Mr. Cruze had fired them, and McCoy had arranged for them to catch the train at Milford and ride back to Rawlins. They would be shamed, coming back with no money for their families.

After that, McCoy had come over to the Indian camp and talked in signs with the elders. Better keep the young bucks out of tent city. No good for them there. Best they concentrate on work. The old men had called everybody together and told them in Arapaho: *wo:to' niwatha.*

Stay away from the whites.

Now there was the girl.

The white man turned toward Charlie, fists clenched. "Leave her alone," he shouted. Little specks of saliva flew from his lips. "She's not for some Indian. Got it? The big man hears what's going on, you're all gonna be gone."

Charlie didn't say anything, but William could feel him pulling himself upright, tensing his muscles. He could kill the white man with one blow.

"Nobody here is interested in her," William said.

"Like hell you aren't. I seen you Indians watching her every minute. No dumb Indians are gonna get in the way óf Mr. Cruze's movie."

Charlie stepped forward, and William moved with him. The white man stepped back. Then he swung around and stomped after the girl.

"She's no good," William said. "Won't cause us anything but trouble."

"Problem over here?" William glanced around. Tim McCoy was making his way through the groups of Indians that had gathered about.

"Tell the white girl to stay with her own," William said.

McCoy drew in a long breath that puffed out his chest, then let it out. "Near as I can tell, nobody tells Missy Mae Markham to do anything, 'cept for Mr. Lasky. But what she tells him could stop the movie. Mr. Cruze didn't want her here, but she wanted to come. Always wants to be in the movies, see her face on the screen. Gonna be in another lead role that Mr. Lasky has lined up, but the filming won't start for a couple months, so he ordered Mr. Cruze to put her on the extra payroll."

"Why's she coming around us?" William's voice was tight with anger.

McCoy shook his head. "Conquest," he said. "Just looking for another conquest. I don't have to tell you . . ." He let the thought trail off, but William understood, and so did Charlie, nodding beside him.

The beautiful white girl was not for Indians.

5

RIVERTON SPRAWLED ACROSS the flat plains in the eastern part of the reservation. A town of wide streets and peaked-roof bungalows that squatted behind giant old evergreens and cottonwoods. There was a white-hot glare of sunshine on the snow-covered lawns and streets. On the west, the peaks of the Wind River range floated like ice caps in the blue sky. Except for the pickups, trucks, and SUVs lurching down Federal, Vicky thought, it was likely that not much had changed since white settlers had pulled up in horse-drawn wagons in 1906, settled on land that the government had purchased from the Arapahos and Shoshones, and founded a town where tribal councils and courts and Indian justice had no jurisdiction. She turned into the asphalt parking lot in front of Wal-Mart and drove toward an empty space.

Odd, the way the tan truck had turned behind her and stayed close on her tail down the rows of parked vehicles. She had been so preoccupied, her mind full of the opinion she had delivered to the tribes almost two weeks ago with Adam's thin-lipped agreement. Riverton was encircled by the reservation, which made it part of Indian Country. And tribes had the right to sell water within Indian Country. They had advised the tribal water engineer that another case concerned with the definition of Indian Country was in federal court, and that the decision would be months away. They had made it clear that the tribes had the option of proceeding or waiting for the decision. They had decided to go ahead. Development plans would be under way, a lot of money would be spent, all based on her opinion that the court would affirm that Riverton was in Indian Country. Lately she found herself wide awake in the middle of the night, the alternate scenario loping through her mind. If the federal court decided otherwise, she would be responsible for a large financial loss to her own people. The realization had left her stumbling out of bed in the mornings feeling headachy and queasy. Adam was more experienced in natural resources law. She should have listened to him.

She glanced in the rearview mirror. The truck was still behind her. A man behind the wheel: large shoulders hunched forward, big hands with puffy gloves gripping the top of the steering wheel, dark knit cap pulled around his face. It was hard to make out his features, but she could feel his eyes burning into the back of her head. She swung right into a vacant spot between two sedans and waited until the truck had passed and the sound of tires crunching the snow had faded. Then she got out. Odd to feel so jumpy and uncomfortable. Just a man going to Wal-Mart, she told herself as she hurried around the parked vehicles toward the automatic glass doors at the entrance. Dozens of men drove into the Wal-Mart parking lot every day.

The warm air inside slapped at her face. She made an effort to return the smile of the greeter in the navy blue shirt, yanked a cart free, and started toward the office supplies. Everything normal. God, had she spoken out loud? The young blond woman pushing a cart with a toddler in the front gave her a strange look as she passed. She had to relax, stop second-guessing herself. It was the water case that had made her so jumpy. Adam had stood behind her, and for that she was grateful.

But it wasn't only the case, she knew. She walked past the cameras and electronic games and turned into the row of envelopes, clipboards, and legal pads. Everything had been thrown upside down and out of place lately. Just when she had felt herself settling down, relying more on Adam, adjusting to a new life and a more certain future—John O'Malley had returned from Rome. He should have stayed away, she thought. He should just stay away. He had been back two weeks now. She hadn't seen him yet. She had made a point of avoiding the mission. She stuffed the packages of yellow legal pads, pencils, pens, blotters, and brown envelopes in the cart and swung back into the main aisle.

She saw him then. The man from the truck: the large shoulders and the knit cap pulled down to his eyebrows. Arapaho, she thought, but no one she knew, and young, not more than thirty. There was something desperate in the stiff-backed way that he stood, bulky gloves dangling at his sides, head pivoting slowly about. Something desperate and determined. He was looking for her!

Vicky wheeled the cart into a side aisle and huddled against the display of women's purses. Her heart was hammering. A heavyset, gray-haired woman glanced at her as she pushed her own cart past. This was silly, she told herself. There was no reason to suppose that the man had followed her into the store. He was only looking about, getting his bearings, trying to decide which section to shop in. And yet, he had turned into the lot and stayed close on her tail, as if he hadn't wanted to lose sight of her. *The prey can always sense the hunter.* She could hear Grandfather's voice.

She pushed the cart back into the main aisle and started toward the cash registers. He was still there, holding his place at the edge of her vision. Then she felt the laser eyes looking directly at her. He took a few steps toward her, as if he intended to stop her, have a little chat.

She swung her own cart in his direction. She would go to him, ask what he wanted, surprise him. *The prey must hunt the hunter.* He jerked his head backward. The gray-haired woman and her cart lumbered between them, and in that instant, he turned around and ran past the doors. Vicky watched until he had vanished into the sea of parked vehicles.

She was still watching for him, she realized, as she waited in the line at the cash register and paid for her purchases. She gathered the bulky plastic bags against her chest and hurried outside, scanning the lot, half expecting the tan truck to drive up, the big-shouldered man to jump out at her. She had felt the desperation in the startled way he had looked at her before he'd run outside. But there was something else, something pent up inside him threatening to explode. She had encountered clients like that in the county jail. Desperate to be released, to have the charges dropped. Ordering her to see that it happened.

She drove out of the lot, watching everything—the side-view mirrors, the rearview mirror, the vehicles parked on either side of the road, the road ahead. There was no sign of him, and she felt herself begin to relax as she drove south on Highway 789. Ahead on the right was the road to St. Francis Mission, and she realized that she had slowed down. Chances were that Father John O'Malley would be in his office in the administration building. How well she knew the place; she'd been there so many times. She could picture him behind the desk, bent over the piles of papers, the red hair going gray at the temples, the freckles on his hands and the long fingers, the eyes like blue agates. The phone would be ringing, and Arapahos would be coming and going—his parishioners. So many things that had brought them together: the DUIs and adoptions and divorces. The Arapahos who had been murdered, or charged with murders they hadn't committed. He had cared about her people as much as she did, this white man. Perhaps that was what had drawn her to him.

But that was over, and she meant to leave it behind her. She was part of Holden and Lone Eagle, Attorneys at Law, specializing in natural resources on Indian reservations. The criminal cases went to the assistant in the office, Roger Hurst. She pressed down on the gas pedal and sped up. If John O'Malley wanted the firm's help on what Adam always referred to as the minor cases, even when they involved felonies, he would have to call Roger.

THE OFFICE HAD the atmosphere of a busy law office in the business district of some big city, phone jangling almost nonstop, Annie talking into the little black mouthpiece that jutted from behind her ear and tapping on the keyboard at the same time, the door to Adam's office closed, which meant he was either with a client or on the phone, and Roger emerging from his office, waving a clutch of papers to get Annie's attention. Vicky stood inside the entry a moment watching the charade unfold. So this was who she had become: the partner in a very important law firm with offices reached by a steel-and-glass stairway or a steel elevator, carpeting thick enough for boots to sink into, and the bronze plaque: Holden and Lone Eagle, Attorneys at Law—on the front of a fancy brick building on the Main Street of Lander, a white town.

Now her clients were the Arapaho and Shoshone tribal councils and other Indian tribes in places like Montana and Utah and Nevada and Arizona. Enough people from the rez found their way to the office to keep Roger busy, just as the trickle of clients had kept her busy in a one-woman law office before she had teamed up with Adam. But there were a couple of new lawyers in the area with small offices in converted stores. She wondered how many of her people turned to them, too intimidated by the fancy brick building and the word on the moccasin telegraph—oh, it carried all the news—about the important cases she and Adam handled. And maybe that explained the Indian in the tan truck: someone who needed a lawyer but preferred to talk to her in a parking lot or inside Wal-Mart rather than inside a fancy building.

"Vicky! There you are." Annie pushed the black mouthpiece to the side, so that it resembled a thick strand of hair springing from her head. Roger had set the papers onto the corner of the desk.

Vicky gripped the bulky plastic bags in each hand, conscious of the way they were both staring at her. "Ran a few errands." She blurted out the words, wondering why she felt the need to explain. She had taken a long lunch, that was all, except that she had forgotten to eat lunch. What she had wanted was to go to the reservation, find a piece of herself, she supposed, and she had found herself driving on Rendezvous Road, then Seventeen-Mile Road. Past the mission, but slowing down for a half moment, just as she had slowed down later, before speeding up. She had turned onto 789 and headed into Riverton. Well, Wal-Mart was there. The office always needed supplies.

Roger took the bags out of her hands. He had to lean over to drop them on the floor next to the desk. He stood half a head taller than she was, with sandy marine-cut hair and tiny frameless glasses that made his eyes look like the green eyes of a giant grasshopper. He was smiling at her, but there was a wariness in his smile. "Everything okay?" he said.

"Everything's fine," Vicky said.

"You got three phone messages." Annie's pink fingernails clicked over the keyboard. She had shoulder-length black hair that shone like a mirror under the fluorescent lights, and dark, intent eyes that stared at the monitor. They might have been sisters, Vicky thought, they were so much alike: two Arapaho women, divorced and determined to make it alone. That was why she had hired her; she had seen herself standing in the doorway. "I've come about the secretary's job you advertised," Annie had said. No prior phone call, no appointment, just Annie, standing in the doorway, determination in every muscle. She had two kids to raise, she said, and Vicky had seen herself: Lucas and Susan, living with her own parents on the reservation while she was in college and law school in Denver, waitressing thirty hours a week and sending most of her earnings to her mother for the kids. It never left her mind that her children had grown up without her.

And there was Annie, raising her kids herself, in need of a job. She had hired her on the spot. She was an excellent secretary, and she was pushing for more responsibility. Recently, Vicky knew, she had helped Roger investigate several cases.

"Call from Lawson Newman at the tribal engineers' office." Annie didn't take her eyes from the monitor, and Vicky could sense the electricity between her and the man standing next to the desk. They were discreet, and Vicky appreciated that. One personal relationship in the office that everybody knew about was enough. "Adam took the call. And some other guy called twice. Wouldn't give his name, just said he wanted to talk to you. I sent the calls to Roger."

Vicky looked at the assistant. "Who was he?"

"I don't know," Roger said. The thin brown eyebrows darted together in puzzlement. "The first call, the line was dead when I picked up. The second, I could hear him breathing at the other end. I asked how I might help, and he hung up."

Vicky started toward the closed door of her own office. "Adam's been looking for you." Annie called. "Shall I let him know you're here?"

"By all means," Vicky said, letting herself through the door. She hung her coat in the walnut cabinet that occupied the wall behind her desk—an expanse of shelves and doors that held a collection of legal books and photos and a few mementos from what used to be her life. For a moment, her eyes fell on the pinecone that Lucas had found when she had taken the children on a hike in Sinks Canyon. He was about nine at the time, and Susan was six. He had carried the pinecone all the way home, a treasure, he called it. A small bracelet that Susan had beaded for her when she was about ten. She had kept them. She wasn't sure why, memories of the precious moments she had spent with her children, she supposed. She felt a pang of loneliness for the kids, grown up now and on their own. Lucas working in information technology for a corporation in Denver, and Susan, making her way at a visual effects company in Los Angeles, excited by a man named Brett who had come into her life. She would have to make time to visit Susan soon.

Even before she turned around, she could sense Adam in the office. She stepped over to the desk and dropped into her chair. "What's going on?" she said.

"Annie could have gone to Wal-Mart." Adam walked over and perched on the end of one of the upholstered armchairs she kept for visitors. He had on a white shirt, the sleeves rolled almost to his elbows and the collar open. She could see the blue vein pulsing in his neck. His black hair looked mussed, as if he'd been combing his fingers through it.

"You wanted to see me?" she said.

Adam shifted back in the chair, set his elbows on the armrests, and made a tipi with his fingers. "The water consortium has sent a notice that they intend to contest the tribal water plans. They plan to file suit in district court. Based on the Bighorn rulings handed down in the state courts, of course."

"We knew that might happen." Vicky could feel the knot tightening in her stomach.

"It will delay things for months, maybe years. In the meantime, the tribes have borrowed several million for the infrastructure to deliver water to Riverton."

"The Tenth Circuit Court of Appeals will decide the Indian Country issue, and that will supersede the Bighorn rulings."

"Maybe not soon enough."

"We shouldn't second-guess ourselves," she said. God, she had been telling herself that for the last two weeks.

"Our reputation's on the line here, Vicky."

"If you didn't agree with my opinion, you shouldn't have gone along."

Adam shook his head. "The tribe isn't paying us for conflicting opinions."

Vicky swung her chair sideways. He had left the rest unspoken, floating silently between them. *Do what I say! I'm the one in control.* She felt as if she had stepped back for a moment into that other life with Ben Holden. He was always in control. She stared at other mementos from that life lining the shelves. The porcelain doll with long black hair in the traditional Arapaho clothing: the beaded deerskin dress with fringed sleeves, the beaded possible bag and knife pouch. She had given the doll to Susan on her eighth birthday. When Susan had moved to California, she had asked Vicky to keep the doll safe for her.

"I've been thinking about taking some time off." Vicky turned back.

"Time off?" Adam slumped against the chair and let his hands dangle off the end of the armrests. A little smile started at the corners of his mouth. "We'll spend a week in Jackson."

"I was thinking," she began—the smile froze on his face—"that you could handle things around here."

"I see. You want to go somewhere alone."

"California, maybe." The phone buzzed. "It's been a while since I've seen Susan."

Adam didn't say anything. Finally he pushed himself to his feet. "I got a call from a friend on the Crow reservation," he said. "The tribe wants to develop coal on the reservation, and they're going to need good legal advice. I think he was sounding me out as to whether we might be interested."

"What did you say?"

"Advising tribes on the legal issues of developing their natural resources? That's what we do, Vicky. I told him that if they wanted the best firm, they should call us. It would be another major client."

The phone buzzed. Vicky reached toward the plastic box at the edge of the desk and pressed the speaker key. "What is it?"

Annie's voice cut in as clear as if she were seated in the vacant chair next to Adam. "That caller's on the line again. Won't give his name."

"Won't give his name?" Adam sat back down. "Roger can take the call."

"Put him through," Vicky said. She could see the man with big shoulders and bulky gloves driving the truck behind her and standing at the entrance at Wal-Mart. Looking for her. One of her own people, needing a lawyer that he could talk to in a parking lot or a box store, not in a fancy building.

"Vicky, this is the kind of call . . ." Adam hesitated. "These are the cases we've agreed that Roger will handle. We've got enough to keep us busy, and you just said you wanted to take some time off."

"He asked for me." Vicky lifted the receiver and pressed it against her ear. "Vicky Holden," she said. She could hear the sharp intake of breath at the other end. It was a half second before Adam got to his feet and walked out, closing the door firmly behind him.

"How can I help you?" Vicky said into the sounds of breathing. She could almost feel the presence of the big-shouldered man at the other end of the line.

"I didn't mean to do it." The voice was so low that Vicky held her own breath to listen. "You gotta help me. You're Arapaho. I figure you're gonna understand."

"What happened?" she said. "What are you talking about? I can't help you unless I know what this is about."

The man was crying now, deep, shuddering sobs that broke down the line. "Listen," she said. "Whatever it is, I'll do my best to help you." She waited a moment, listening to the sounds of sobbing. When they seemed to quiet, she said, "What is it that happened?"

"I didn't mean to kill him."

Vicky pulled a yellow pad across the desk and found a pen in the drawer. "You had better come in," she said. Manslaughter, she was thinking. "I can help you." She realized that she was talking into a vacuum and that whoever had been at the end of the line had hung up.

She replaced the receiver, got to her feet, and went into the outer office. Adam's door was closed. It loomed like a barrier between them. The clack of the keyboard stopped, and Annie looked up.

"What's the news on the moccasin telegraph?" Vicky said. If someone had turned up dead, Annie would have heard about it before the news could make its way to the radio or newspaper.

Annie gave a little shrug. "I don't know," she said. "June Nestor left that no-good husband of hers, and . . ."

"Any kind of an accident? Anyone been killed?"

Annie rolled her eyes toward the corner of the office. "Two weeks ago, Cliff Many Moons drove into the river . . ."

"Lately," Vicky said. "The last day or two."

Annie shook her head, and Vicky went back into her office, sat down, and stared at the phone. On the other end of the line, there had been an Arapaho probably not much older than Lucas, with big shoulders and a tan pickup who needed a lawyer.

6

THE WIND BLEW a wave of snow off the prairie and across Givens Road. Fists of snow hit the windshield. Father John peered past the wiper into the glistening whiteness. It had snowed off and on during the past two weeks, alternating days of blizzard whiteouts with days of sunshine so bright he found himself squinting most of the time. The sun was beating down hard this morning, the sky the clearest blue. Every mile or so, a small house, snow piled on the roof, rose out of the whiteness. He'd driven past when he saw the turnoff, nothing more than a gray indentation on the white prairie. The rear wheels slipped and balked as he backed up, then lurched into the right turn. He tried his best to stay on the narrow road that led to the house, but it was hard to tell where the edges dropped off into the borrow ditches that ran alongside.

He had taken the call an hour ago: Mamie Wallowingbull, voice tight with worry. "He's not doin' so good," she'd said, launching into the reason for the call. There was no time for the usual pleasantries:

How are things going, Father? You like being back in winter? He had known immediately she was talking about Andrew.

"Would you like me to stop by?" he had said.

"Could you, Father? His heart's been acting up, racing like crazy. He's so worried about the boy. You know they was always close." She paused. "When Kiki was a kid, before he started getting into trouble."

He had told her he would be over this morning.

The front door at the faded green ranch-style house was open before he had turned off the engine. As he got out, he saw Mamie peering past the edge. The wind whipped the snow into his face. Pellets of snow showered his shoulders and fell into the creases of his jacket. He hurried up the wood steps, slick with ice. The door flew open and Mamie waved him inside.

"How are you, Grandmother?" he said, using the term of respect for the old woman. A cloud of moisture seemed to be rolling off him. Dots of snow fell from his jacket onto the gray vinyl floor. Mamie patted at the fronts of her blue sweater, then started rubbing her hands together. A small woman, a fragile look about her. She came only to his shoulder. He could see the pink circle of scalp in her gray hair.

"He's been resting," she said. "Come with me." She turned herself around—slow, jerky movements—and took a couple of steps across the small living room with the Indian blanket spread over the sofa, the imprint of Andrew's thin body in the recliner, and the TV on, the actors of some soap opera talking and gesturing in silence, like the actors in a silent movie.

He followed the old woman down the short hallway, past closed doors that, he suspected led to a bedroom and bath, and into another bedroom. Andrew lay stretched on the bed, dressed in blue jeans and plaid shirt, arms folded across his chest. For an instant Father John wondered if he were breathing. Then the old man's head turned toward him.

"That you, Father?" he said, straining to push himself upright against the pillows piled at the headboard. "Wasn't expecting visitors."

"Don't get up." Father John placed his hand on the old man's shoulder. He could feel the knobby bones, the paper-thin skin beneath the plaid shirt. "Just dropped by to see how you're doing today."

"Doin' okay, I guess." Andrew let himself lie flat again. "For an old man."

"I hear you've been having some heart trouble." Out of the corner of his eye, Father John could see Mamie hovering near the doorway.

"Moccasin telegraph say so? Don't miss much, I guess."

"Can I get you something to drink, Father?" Mamie asked.

He could sense she was anxious to get away and let them talk, as if Andrew were more likely to talk freely if she weren't there. "Coffee would be great," he said.

"You better sit down, take a load off your feet," Andrew said, giving a little wave toward the wooden chair in the corner.

Father John nudged the chair toward the bed and sat down, conscious of the sound of Mamie's footsteps retreating down the hallway. "I understand you've been worried about Kiki," he said.

Andrew gave a bark of laughter that sounded as if it had erupted from a hollow drum. "The old lady never could keep a secret," he said.

Father John waited. He could hear the clinking of metal and glass in the kitchen, the swooshing sound of water moving through the pipes in the wall somewhere.

After a moment, Andrew went on: "Haven't heard from Kiki since he took off on that crazy mission of his. Goin' off to Hollywood, looking to find the past. Keep thinking all the bad things that could happen to him, Indian like Kiki wandering around out there where he don't know anybody and nobody cares if he lives or dies. You heard anything, Father? Any news on the moccasin telegraph that nobody wanted to send our way?"

Father John shook his head. "Was he planning to stay with anyone?" He was thinking that if he had a name—any name—he could make some inquiries. He wished he had asked Kiki where he planned to stay.

The old man started coughing. He twisted sideways and pulled a crumpled blue rag out of the back pocket of his jeans. He held the rag against his mouth and coughed into it for a few seconds, hands trembling, chest heaving.

Father John was on his feet. He slipped an arm under the old man's shoulders and lifted him up a little. Still it was a moment before the coughing subsided. Andrew lay back on the pillow, breathing hard. Father John sat down and waited.

"You know the boy," Andrew said finally. "Don't tell you more than he wants you to know. Been shut up inside himself ever since he was six years old. Mamie and me had to go to his house and get him that night his folks got killed, our boy Edward and his wife. Both of 'em drunk. Two o'clock in the morning when the cops and the mission priest—name was Father Peter; I'll never forget him—knocked on our door. Got some real bad news, the priest said. You could tell he didn't want to tell us, but he did. Took hold of both our hands and said he was sorry, so sorry."

Andrew pushed the blue rag against his mouth, and for a moment, Father John thought the coughing would start again. Instead, he saw that the man was trying to stifle a sob. After a moment, Andrew said, "Father Peter asked if we knew where the boy was. Said he stopped by Edward's place. Nobody answered.

"'Kiki?' I said. Then I knew they'd left Kiki home alone and gone out drinking. Oh, I knew Edward did that, and I gave him hell for it. Didn't change anything. The boy knew not to open the door. Little guy he was, real small for his age, but he knew he had to take care of himself. I said to Mamie, 'We gotta get to the house.' All the pain we was feeling just went out to the boy. We knew we had to take care of him. So we drove over to the house. Let ourselves in with the key Edward give us, like he knew we were gonna need it some night. There was Kiki, hiding in the closet. Shivering with fright and cold. Wouldn't say anything, even then, that he didn't think we oughtta know. I said, 'Come on, son. You're goin' home with us now. You're gonna be our own boy.'"

Andrew ran the blue rag over his lips and closed his eyes. He was quiet for a long moment, as if he were watching some image play across the inside of his eyelids. Father John waited, and finally the old man opened his eyes and fixed him with a look filled with an enormity of loss. "He has a good heart," Andrew said. "He wanted to be a good boy, but there were demons in him and secrets he couldn't get out. They stayed inside and twisted him up."

"He went to California because he wanted to do something for you," Father John said.

"See what I'm telling you? He has a good heart. Got himself into rehab in prison. He's done with drugs. Wants to know the truth about our family, find out what happened to my father." Andrew rubbed the rag over his cheeks and forehead. He dabbed at his eyes. "My father went off to Hollywood and never came back. What if Kiki don't come back, Father? That's what keeps goin' round and round inside me, never leaves my mind. It's tearing me up."

"What about his friends on the rez?" Father John said. "Maybe he told someone what he planned to do. Might have mentioned the name of somebody he planned to look up."

"That girl won't help us." Mamie stood in the doorway, a coffee mug in each hand. Rivulets of coffee ran down the sides. "We called her lots of times, left messages. Said we had to know if Kiki told her anything that could help us. Asked her to call us back, but she never called back."

Mamie handed a mug to Father John. "Poured a little milk in it," she said. "I remember that's how you like it."

Father John thanked the old woman and took a sip of coffee. Hot and fresh and familiar, more delicious than any coffee he'd had in Rome. "Who's the girl?" he said.

Mamie set the other mug on the bedside table. "This is for you when you're ready," she said, brushing Andrew's hair back with her hand. "White girl he took up with after he got out of prison." She dropped onto the bed and shifted toward Father John. Her legs dangled over the edge, the toes of her brown shoes barely scraping the floor. "Never brought her around, 'cause he knew we wouldn't approve. We heard she likes drugs, likes to go out drinking. She's no good for him. How is he gonna stay off drugs with her around? The parole officer finds out he's hanging around with somebody like her, and Kiki goes back to prison. Andrew told him, 'You think she loves you? You think she gives a damn if you get locked up again?'"

"He didn't want to hear it," Andrew said. He let his head roll over the pillow a moment. "He was always stubborn. Couldn't tell him nothing, like he already knew it all. Even when he was a kid. Went around like a little old man that had already seen everything and knew everything, his mind permanently made up."

"What's her name?" Father John said. He took another drink of coffee. He would be sorry to finish it, he thought. And how was that possible, out of all the things in this world, to want to hold on to a last sip of coffee?

"Dede somebody," Mamie said. "Don't think Kiki ever said her last name, and we never asked. Been hoping she'd go away." Mamie looked down at the thin figure prostrate on the bed. She patted Andrew's hand a minute. "Kiki's the one that went away."

"They been staying at a place over in Riverton on Adams Street," Andrew said, a sudden burst of energy in his voice, as if he had grabbed onto a lifeline tossed out of nowhere. "Little white house, paint peeling off. Looks like a shack. We drove over a couple times, once we seen she was never gonna call us back. Knocked on the door—real nice blue door. Door's probably the best part of the house. We was hoping we'd catch her there. Didn't have any luck."

Father John drained the last of the coffee and got to his feet. He set the mug on the bedside table next to the other mug and placed a hand on the old man's shoulder, the bones as fragile as those of a bird. "I'll see if I can locate her, Grandfather," he said. "Maybe she's heard from Kiki."

Mamie slipped off the bed, grabbed his hand and held on for a moment, squeezing his fingers. "I got something for you," she said, motioning him to follow her down the hallway.

In the living room she sat down and rummaged through piles of newspapers on the little table next to the recliner. "It's here somewhere," she said, as if to reassure herself. Then she had it. A DVD envelope in the middle of the papers. "Kiki brought over a player so we could watch this," she said, nodding toward the black box on the television stand across the room. She handed the envelope to Father John.

On the front, in thick yellow print against a black background were the words *The Covered Wagon. James Cruze Production.* Below the title were the figures of a cowboy sitting on a black horse and an Indian with a feathered headdress greeting each other with lifted arms. Except for a breechcloth, the Indian was naked, the muscular body washed in yellows and reds. White clouds of dust rose around the horses' hooves. Above the title was a line of white type: *Out where thrills began.* And at the bottom of the envelope, in black cursive, were the words *A Paramount Picture.*

Father John turned the envelope over. On the back was the image of a covered wagon winding across the golden prairie, a red balloon sun floating in the sky. A pair of grizzled emigrants, rifles slung over their shoulders, walked at the head of the wagons. Looking close, he could make out the shadowy figures of women and children in the first wagon.

He could almost hear Kiki's voice: "Three hundred Shoraps went off to be in *The Covered Wagon.* My great-grandfather never come back."

"We watched the movie, and Andrew seen his father riding by on a pretty pony," Mamie said. "He was sure it was his father, 'cause he has an old picture that his mother give him. The movie's precious to Andrew 'cause his father's alive in it." She jabbed a finger at the DVD. "Could you watch it, Father?"

He told her he would like to see the movie.

"Kiki watched this movie a dozen times. Maybe after you see it, you'll know what he went off to Hollywood for."

FATHER JOHN SPOTTED the house a half block away. The wind had picked up, and gusts pummeled the pickup and blew the snow sideways across the street. The house stood close to the curb, lost for a second in a whirlwind of snow, the blue door jumping out. A black sedan with a rusty dent on the trunk stood in the driveway. He pulled up at the curb, the *Rigoletto* tape playing softly. The DVD was on the passenger seat next to the tape player, a burst of red and yellow against the gray upholstery. A movie filmed almost ninety years ago, and yet something in it had sent Kiki Wallowingbull to Hollywood, certain that he would find out what had happened to his great-grandfather. He got out and made his way through another gust of wind and swirling snow to the blue door.

The bronze knocker, the top screw missing, limped to one side. He lifted the knocker carefully and let it drop a couple of times. It made a dull thud, almost lost in the whoosh of the wind. He pulled up the collar of his jacket, hunched toward the door, and waited, the wind beating against his back. There were no sounds inside. The house had the vacant feeling of a tomb.

He lifted the knocker again, this time letting it hit the door hard several times. A long moment passed before he heard the footsteps scrambling on the other side. Then a woman's voice, high-pitched with impatience: "Yeah? Who's there?"

"Father O'Malley from St. Francis," he said, leaning in close. "I'm looking for Dede."

The door started to slide open, squeaking on its hinges. The face of a young woman with straw-colored hair and tired green eyes appeared in the opening. "You a priest?" she said, incredulity working into the voice.

He nodded. "Are you Dede?"

"Oh, God." The door swung back. "You better come in."

Father John stepped into a living room smaller than his office, with various pieces of worn-looking furniture pushed against the walls and a red blanket with the geometric designs of the Arapaho spread over the middle of the green vinyl floor. Taped onto the walls everywhere he looked were movie posters from the silent movies, all in faded reds, blues, yellows, and oranges that had probably been bright once. *D. W. Griffith*, Way Down East, with the lonely figure of a man riding a horse across steep bluffs. *Zane Grey's* The Vanishing American. An Indian sat bareback on a horse. There were crowds of Indians in the background and the sense of people moving away. *Hal Roach*, Call of the Wild, *based on the famous dog story by Jack London.* Here was a shaggy-looking brown-and-white dog with a wolf howling in the background. The Winning of Barbara Worth, *starring Ronald Colman.* A cowboy and cowgirl floated above cowboys and Indians and a wagon train. Another cowboy stood next to a white horse and aimed a rifle at the gold-printed letters: *Merton of the Movies.*

Plastered on the wall across from the door were posters from movies starring Tim McCoy, wearing a wide-brimmed white cowboy hat, black shirt, and white scarf tied at his neck. Bold black type leaped off the posters: *Metro-Goldwyn-Mayer presents* Winners of the Wilderness, *starring Col. Tim McCoy. Tim McCoy in His Latest and Greatest Outdoor Romance,* Two-Fisted Law. *Tim McCoy in* Silent Men.

Father John couldn't take his eyes away from the poster in the center. All of the other posters looked as if they had been arranged around it. A cowboy on a black horse was on the right, and on the left, a naked Indian in a feathered headdress riding a white horse. Colors of orange, bloodred, and black washed over the poster, giving it a sinister look. *Out where thrills began. James Cruze production* The Covered Wagon.

"Hideous, aren't they?" the girl said.

"They must be Kiki's."

"I hate 'em. I wish he'd take them down. I swear, one of these days, I'm gonna rip 'em off the walls. I'm sick of looking at them." She stepped over to a table and found a pack of cigarettes among the clutter of papers and empty foam cartons. She lit a cigarette, blew a trail of gray smoke toward Tim McCoy, and pivoted around. "All right. Give it to me. Kiki's dead, right?"

"Why would you think that?" Father John said.

"Why else would they send a priest around? Go give his girlfriend the bad news, okay? Isn't that what you do? I mean, like some kind of ghoul showing up whenever somebody's dead?"

Father John unzipped his jacket halfway. The house was warm and stuffy and smelled of rotten food and cigarettes. "I don't have any bad news," he said.

"So he's not dead?" The girl twisted her head and blew another stream of smoke toward the posters. "Makes me sick, all this old movie stuff. Crazy sonofabitch. Watching them stupid silent movies all day and night. Goin' off to Hollywood, like he was gonna find out anything. Who cares what happened to some old Indian a thousand years ago?"

"It was the 1920s," he said.

"Yeah? Well, how long ago was that? I mean, it's over and done with, right? Who cares?" She flipped the ash into a Coke can. "Look, I gotta get to work. I got a great job at that new nail place on Federal and I'm not blowin' it 'cause of Kiki. What are you doin' here, if he's not dead?"

"I'm looking for him," he said. "Do you know where I can reach him?"

"What do I look like? His keeper?" She gave a snort of laughter and tossed her head toward the posters. "Keeper of the stupid, freaking movie posters, that's what I am.

"His grandparents are worried. They haven't heard from him since he left for California."

"Oh, no, you don't. You're not laying that guilt trip on me. I told him they been calling. I gave him all the messages. Not my fault if he didn't go see 'em."

"Go see them? Wait a minute." Father John took a step forward. "Are you saying he's back from California?"

"Look," she said. "I don't know anything about this. I don't know what games Kiki's playing." She dropped the cigarette into the Coke can and started pawing through the tangle of clothes on the sofa, finally pulling out a black, high-heeled boot. "I gotta get to work, okay?" she said, hopping around on one foot, pulling the boot onto the other.

"When did he get back?"

"Last week sometime." She went back to tossing the clothes about until she had the other boot. She flopped onto the edge of the sofa, stuck her other foot into the boot, and went about pulling up both zippers. "Showed up out of the blue, never bothered to call all the time he was gone, let me know if he was alive or dead. Just left me alone, like I was nobody, didn't mean nothing to him. So he shows up. Didn't say sorry or how you been? Nothing. Just talking about how the answers he wanted was right here all the time. Didn't need to go to Hollywood after all. But how was he gonna know that if he didn't go? And a lot of other stuff that didn't make sense. I said, don't get me involved in your crazy world, okay? That's all I wanted, for him to stop talking about the fricking past all the time and just, you know, live today."

She jumped up and did a little dance step—one foot out, then the other—glancing down at the boots. Then she patted at her skirt and ran her fingers through the long yellowish hair. "You know what I mean? Live in the now."

"Where can I find him?" Father John said.

"Try the bars. How the hell do I know? Kiki's out of my life. I've had enough, okay?" She took a minute, her jaw rigid with anger. "We got into it last night. He's going on about Great-grandfather Wallowingbull getting killed out in Hollywood and somebody was gonna pay, and I said, shut the hell up! What do I care about some old man a million years ago? He tried to hit me, but he got a big surprise 'cause I threw a glass at him. Cut him on the forehead. He was bleeding like a pig. I told him to get the hell outta here, and he took off. Guess he didn't go back to Grandma and Grandpa. Maybe he went back to Hollywood." She tried for a laugh that came out like a sob. "I don't ever want to see his crazy face again. You find him, tell him come get his stupid posters."

She pivoted about and climbed up onto the sofa. Jamming the high heels into the cushions and piles of clothes, she started ripping the posters off the wall and throwing them onto the floor. *Winners of the Wilderness. Two-Fisted Law. Silent Men.* "Tell him they're in the trash where they belong," she said. "Tell him to drop dead."

"What bars?" Father John said.

She swung around and stared down at him, struggling for her balance, *The Covered Wagon* crumpled in her hands. "What bar d'ya like?" A steely calmness had come into her voice, as if all the anger had leaked out. "From what I hear, Kiki wasn't ever particular where he drinks or shoots up. Maybe he went to that place on the Little Wind River for some hits. Maybe he got high and fell into the river. I could hope, right? All I know is, he ain't never coming back here."

Outside Father John started the engine and thought about where Kiki Wallowingbull might have gone last night. Cold air spurted from the vents. The sun glistened on the skin of snow that lay over the hood. There were a couple of bars in town where he had heard Arapahos hung out. Murphy's. The Drop-In Tavern. A place called Tracers. He could start with the bars, see if anybody had talked to Kiki or knew where he might have spent the night. He could be hungover, possibly still drunk. It was never easy to come off a drunk. The memory of some of the drunks he'd been on made him wince. All those mornings when, head throbbing, stomach turning over, he had stumbled into one of his American History classes, sunk onto his chair, and ordered the smartest kid in the class to give his impressions of the

American Revolution or the Civil War or the conquest of the West, any subject that would run out the class time.

He stared at the snow tumbleweeds and tried to push the memories away. He didn't want them. He forced himself to think about what the girl had said, and what she might have left out. It was possible that not only was Kiki drinking, he could still be using. Yet, somehow, he had convinced Andrew and Mamie he was clean. There had been so much hope in Andrew's eyes at the welcome-home feast two weeks ago: *He's not messing with drugs anymore, Father.* But if he was still using, it would explain why Kiki hadn't called or gone to see his grandparents after he got back from California. And it also explained why Kiki had seemed so jumpy and distracted the morning he had given him a ride.

Father John shifted into forward and started to pull into the street. The rear tires spun and howled a second before the pickup lurched free. There was a remote spot along the banks of the Little Wind River where drug deals came down. From time to time, the *Gazette* ran articles about the drug arrests there. He turned onto Federal and drove south toward the reservation. Kiki might have stopped at one of the package stores and bought a bottle, but if he was using again, chances were good that he had headed to the river to buy drugs.

7

FATHER JOHN FOLLOWED the snow-packed ruts on Rendezvous Road to where the Little Wind River curved close to the southern edge of the reservation. He had passed the last house about a mile back. All around was nothing but great expanses of snow sparkling in the sun. Bursts of wind skimmed off the surface and tossed white streamers into the air. He parked about fifty feet from where the banks jogged to the northeast. There were no signs of recent activity, no tracks or footprints in the snow.

Blowing snow pelted his face as he headed for the riverbank. He could see the ice protruding around the edges, the narrow stream bubbling over the boulders in the middle. A fool's errand, he was thinking, and he laughed out loud at that. A fool's errand in search of what Dede called a crazy man. With all the articles in the newspaper, the drug dealers had probably moved onto a new location.

He stood on the riverbank and peered through the blowing snow that whipped at his jacket and bunched around his boots. He might have been the only man in the world, he thought, stranded on a cap of ice and snow after some global catastrophe. He turned around and, squinting into the glare, started retracing his tracks back to the pickup. He was about to get inside when the wind died back and the swirling snow dropped out of the air. It was then that he saw the ruts and tracks about fifty feet along the bank from where he had been standing. Then another sweep of wind and snow, and the view was gone.

He turned back and set out on a diagonal toward the area. Despite the bright sunshine, cold had penetrated his jacket and blue jeans. He flexed his fists inside his gloves to work the circulation back into his fingers. Each time the wind stopped blowing, he was able to see more: a double set of faint tire tracks running toward Rendezvous Road, a churned area where a vehicle had backed up. Only one set of tracks, he thought, one vehicle coming from the road and heading back. He could make out traces of boot prints. Kiki could have driven here last night, expecting to meet someone. He might have waited a while, stomped around in the snow, impatient and angry, drinking out of a bottle in a brown paper bag, reliving the fight with Dede. Why didn't she understand he owed his grandfather everything? Waiting for someone to come with the magic that would give the illusion of calmness and make him believe that things made sense.

Here was something: boot prints dug deep into the snow, as if whoever made them had been carrying something heavy. The prints ran toward the rise above the river, then looped around and disappeared into the churned snow. Father John walked alongside the boot prints and stopped where they stopped. The bank sloped down through mounds of snow and boulders to the river about five feet below. There was a peaceful sound to the flowing water.

Then he saw the body wedged between boulders and chunks of ice. The bulky dark blue jacket, the strip of dark skin between the bottom of the jacket and the top of the blue jeans, the arms thrust outward, fingers clawlike, stopped in space. Father John started down the slope, moving from one snow-slicked boulder to the next, stopping to get his balance, then going on. He knew it was Kiki even before he worked his way around the body and crouched down close to the face. Something about the blue jacket, like the one Kiki had on when he had given him a ride.

A half-inch cut gaped in the purple lump on Kiki's forehead. The brown eyes were half closed, as if he were staring downward. The jacket was unzipped part way, exposing the front of a purple-colored plaid shirt. The skin of Kiki's throat looked grayish in death. There were little cuts and abrasions on his hands, the nails torn and dirty.

Father John reached out and brushed back the piece of black hair that had fallen over Kiki's forehead. "What happened to you?" he said out loud, and yet he knew part of it. Whatever had happened, someone had driven here, carried Kiki's body to the riverbank, and thrown it down the slope. It might not have been discovered until spring.

He closed his eyes and listened to the sounds of the water and the wind whistling over the snow. "God have mercy on your soul, Kiki Wallowingbull," he said.

FATHER JOHN SPOTTED the fed, Ted Gianelli, as he came up the slope and headed in his direction. Six feet tall with broad shoulders, black hair flecked with snow, everything about him seeming intentional and measured. Twenty minutes after Father John had called 911 from his cell phone, a police car had careened down the road. It had pulled in next to Father John's pickup, and Father John had waved the two Wind River police officers over to the riverbank above the body. He had been sitting on a boulder, keeping watch. The stone's coldness had seeped into his thighs and run up his back; his fingers felt like ingots. Still he hadn't wanted to leave the body alone and wait in the pickup.

The officers had called the FBI office in Lander. An unexplained death on an Indian reservation; this was a federal matter. Another forty minutes before Gianelli's white SUV had parked behind the police car, but by then there were three other police cars and the coroner's van. One of the officers had staked yellow tape around part of the area where remnants of tire tracks and boot prints had escaped the blowing snow. Yellow tape marked a half circle at the riverbank where Kiki's body had been thrown. Other officers were moving about, examining the tire tracks and boot prints. A man in a red jacket bobbed about taking photographs. The coroner and his assistant had sidestepped down the slope and were hovering over the body.

"What brought you out here?" Gianelli said when he was still a couple of yards away. He had the quiet, intense look of the Patriots linebacker he had been twenty years ago.

"I was looking for Kiki," he said. "I heard he might have come here last night."

Gianelli waited with the patience honed on the field—watching for the snap of the ball before springing into action.

Father John went on: "I saw his girlfriend this morning. Her name is Dede. She said they had a fight last night and Kiki took off." Gianelli was nodding. He wasn't telling the fed anything he couldn't have figured out for himself. "She thought he might have come here to buy drugs," Father John added.

Gianelli lifted his chin a moment and glanced around at the sky. "What a waste," he said. "When I heard the state had paroled Kiki Wallowingbull, I knew we hadn't heard the last of him. He was going to be back into trouble, the only question was how soon. What did it take? A few weeks to turn up dead? Couldn't lose the habit or the lousy people he hung out with. Selling drugs to their own people, getting kids addicted. Real pieces of work, these bastards, and Kiki was one of them."

"His grandfather says he was off drugs," Father John said, and he told the fed that Kiki had gone through rehab in prison. He had been thinking about all of it, the cold working its way up his spine. Nobody knew Kiki Wallowingbull better than Andrew and Mamie, and they believed he was through with drugs. "Maybe he didn't come here to buy drugs," he said. "There was only one vehicle, and there isn't any abandoned vehicle around. Kiki didn't drive himself here and throw himself down the slope."

Gianelli studied him a moment, dark eyes narrowed into slits. A gust of snow swirled between them. "I was just about to say that." He threw a glance over at the officers peering down at the tire tracks. "You ever want to come to work for the FBI, let me know," he said, smile lines creasing his face. "I'll give you a good recommendation." He made a half turn toward the body below. "Coroner says he was probably beaten, but he can't say for sure that he was dead when he was dumped here."

"You're saying Kiki froze to death?"

"We won't know until the autopsy."

Dear Lord! Father John watched the coroner balancing himself on a boulder close to Kiki's body. "Why bring him here?" he said.

"You want a theory?" Gianelli snapped his gloves together. "A lot of drug deals have taken place here. Somebody was sending a message."

"So if I hadn't come along . . ."

"Exactly," Gianelli said. "Eventually some drug dealer or his client would've stumbled on the body and gotten a message loud and clear. Might not have been until spring, but it would've happened." He lifted a gloved hand. "I know Andrew and Mamie Wallowingbull want to believe Kiki was done with the drug crowd. They're good people. From what I've heard, they did their best for that boy, and they're going to spend the rest of their lives crying for him. They always believed what he told them. Wasn't in their nature to doubt him. Why were you looking for him?"

Father John made a fist and blew into the tunnel of his glove. The warm air drifted over his chin. Then he told the fed how Andrew and Mamie were worried, how they hadn't heard from Kiki since he'd gone to Los Angeles.

"Los Angeles?"

"Hollywood," Father John said. He explained that he had picked up Kiki hitchhiking two weeks ago, taken him to the café in Riverton for breakfast, and left him on the highway to catch a ride to Rawlins. "He was looking for family history. Wanted to know what had happened to his great-grandfather when he was working in the silent movies. I think he stayed about a week."

"Family history?" Gianelli gave a cough of laughter. "Just when I think I've heard it all, something else pops up." He took a step closer and—his voice low—said, "We know that meth and cocaine are shipped from Mexico to Los Angeles and from Los Angeles, the drugs come right here." He jabbed a gloved finger toward the snow. "But there are stops along the way in either Salt Lake City or Denver."

"What are you saying, Ted? That Kiki went to Los Angeles to buy drugs directly?"

Gianelli shrugged. "I'm saying the stakes would be high, maybe worth the danger of blocking out the couriers in Salt Lake or Denver. He could have brought in the drugs himself and pocketed the profits. They could have come after him."

"Except that when I saw him, he was obsessed with finding his great-grandfather."

"A week in LA?" Gianelli shook his head, pulled a small notepad from inside his jacket, and started clicking a ballpoint pen. His black gloves were flecked with snow. "Where can I find the girlfriend?"

"I don't know her last name," Father John said. Then he told him the rest: a small girl, blond hair, about twenty-five, living in a house on Adams Street in Riverton, working in a nail salon on Federal.

Gianelli scribbled something on the pad, then slipped the pad and pen back inside his jacket. "Will you tell the grandparents?"

Father John nodded. What was it the girl had called him? Some kind of ghoul, knocking on doors, following death around? The bearer of news nobody wanted to hear. He could picture the old man, swallowed in the pillows propped against the headboard, Mamie fussing over him, both of them worrying about Kiki, fearing the worst. Now he would be the one to tell them the worst had happened.

IT WAS A long moment before Mamie answered the door. He could hear the muffled sound of her footsteps padding down the hallway and across the vinyl floor in the living room, then the rattling doorknob. Finally the door inched open and the old woman's face slid around the edge. Surprise registered in the brown eyes. "You forget something, Father?"

"I have to talk to you and Grandfather," Father John said. He could hear the solemnity in his tone that had seemed to come of its own accord, the tone of a funeral oration.

"Please," she said, pulling the door all the way open and waving him inside. The look of dread had started to work into her features. "What is it? What's happened?"

Father John stepped inside. Drapes had been pulled across the window, throwing patterns of light and shade across the sofa and recliner. He could hear the ragged breathing of the old woman beside him.

"He's dead, isn't he?" Andrew had materialized at the end of the hallway and was leaning against the edge of the wall.

"Oh!" Mamie clasped her hand over her mouth. For an instant, Father John thought she would topple over. He reached out, took hold of the woman's arm, and guided her down onto the sofa.

"Come sit down, Grandfather," he said stepping over to Andrew. He slipped his arm around the man's shoulders and led him to the recliner. "How did you know?" he said. Still the solemnity in his tone. He pulled over a straight-back chair and sat down in front of the old couple.

It was a moment before Andrew said, "They killed him, just like they killed my father." Mamie had shifted around, her eyes fastened on the old man. Little lines of moisture ran down her cheeks.

"I knew they was gonna do that." Andrew shook his head, a gesture of such futility and hopelessness that Father John could feel his own heart sink. "Tried to tell him not to go to Hollywood. No good was gonna come of it. I was scared when he walked out that door"— he lifted one hand toward the front door, then let it flop back onto the armrest—"that he was never gonna come back."

"He was killed here, Grandfather," Father John said. "I went looking for him after I spoke with his girlfriend. I found his body down by the Little Wind River."

Mamie dropped her face into her hands. Tears bubbled between her fingers, her narrow shoulders were shaking. "Tell us," she said, her voice muffled and tear-soaked. "What did they do to our boy?"

Father John hesitated. Truth was so hard to tell, and so hard to take. Yet the old couple had the right to know. "The coroner thinks he was beaten," he said. "He won't know the exact cause of death until the autopsy."

"Beaten," Andrew said, as if the sound and the taste of the word might make it comprehensible. "Here. They followed him here and killed him."

"Who? Grandfather, who do you think could have done this?"

"They did it. Hollywood people. Same kind that killed my father. How long's he been back?"

"A few days, his girlfriend said."

Mamie lifted her face and dabbed at her eyes with her knuckles. "I don't believe her. Kiki would've come see us if he was back. We left messages on her phone. If he was back, he would've called us. He was always worrying over how we was doin'." She leaned over toward Andrew. "Wasn't that so? Wasn't he always worrying about us?"

"She said she gave him the messages," Father John said.

"She's a liar."

Andrew slumped like a rag doll against the recliner, chin tilted down. His voice was muffled against his chest. "They come here after him. He must've found out the truth."

Father John sat back. He'd seen this type of reaction before, the wild lunge for an explanation, the need to make sense out of the sense-less in order to keep from being swept away in a river of grief. He gave the old couple a minute before he said, "The FBI agent, Ted Gianelli, will be handling the investigation. He's a good man. He'll find whoever did this and see that he's charged."

He had meant to try to reassure them that in the midst of loss and grief there would be justice. He knew he'd made a mistake by the slow way in which Andrew lifted his head and stared at him out of black, watery eyes. "Won't bring Kiki back, will it?" he said.

"I'm sorry," Father John said again.

"Need to give the boy a proper burial. You'll take care of it, Father?"

Father John assured them that he would make the arrangements. And everything would have to be done in the next three days, so that Kiki's spirit could go to the ancestors and they would recognize him and take him into the spirit world. That was the Arapaho Way.

It was mid-afternoon before Father John left the old couple, and by then, the moccasin telegraph had done its work. Relatives and neighbors and friends had filled up the house, piled plates of food on the kitchen counter and started the coffee brewing. He could still smell the odor of fresh coffee clinging to his jacket as he drove down Seventeen-Mile Road to the mission. He hadn't told the old couple all of the truth, and it weighed on him, like a task that he'd put off, yet knew he would have to take care of. But it had seemed cruel—after telling them their grandson was dead—to tell them Gianelli believed Kiki had gone to LA to buy drugs.

And yet—here was the irony—Gianelli and Andrew had arrived at the same theory, but for different reasons. He could hear their voices in his head: Gianelli saying that the drug dealers could have come after Kiki. And Andrew saying, "They must've come after him."

8

ROGER HURST SPRAWLED on the chair and drummed his fingers on the yellow legal notepad balanced on one thigh. "He wants to talk to you."

Vicky leaned back. He was talking about Troy Tallfeathers, one of her former clients, always in trouble of one sort or another. On parole from the state prison after being convicted of dealing drugs. And now he had assaulted the tribal police officer who pulled him over for drunk driving.

"How have you advised him?" she said.

"Plead guilty, throw himself on the mercy of the court, ask for rehab."

Vicky nodded. These were the types of cases that she and Adam no longer handled. All the DUIs, domestic disturbances, accidents, assaults, all the desperate, pleading brown faces that she had once interviewed and tried to advise and console—their cases went to Roger. And Roger was doing a great job. Rarely did he knock on her door,

plop down on a chair, and ask advice. But even the few times that occurred were too often for Adam. "Let him figure it out," he'd told her.
"The clients are putting pressure on him to confer with you. They
want to know you're handling their case. They have to learn to trust
Roger."

Adam was probably right. They had enough on their plates, as he
put it. Major cases, like tribal water rights. The consortium that had
been supplying water to Riverton wouldn't sit still for competition
from the reservation. Roger had knocked on her door while she was
drafting a response to the civil suit filed by the consortium's lawyers.

Roger blew out a puff of air. His skin was so light, it looked pink,
and that made his short-cropped sandy hair look darker. Annie thought
he was handsome, and Vicky supposed that he was—in a quiet way.
Not the black hair and dark eyes and strong chin of Adam, but handsome enough.

"The federal judge is going to throw the book at him," Roger said.
"The tribal cop pulled him over on Plunkett Road. Weaving all over
the road. Failed the sobriety test, threw a couple punches at the cop.
Eventually the cop got him up against the truck, handcuffed him, and
hauled him to the county jail. His parole will be revoked for sure, and
he's looking at federal charges."

"Why does he want to see me?" Vicky said.

"He won't tell me."

Vicky glanced at the black text on the monitor. She had planned to
spend the next hour or so finishing the response, then going over it
with Adam. It should be filed with the court first thing tomorrow
morning. Roger was an excellent lawyer; there was no reason for her
to get involved in Troy's case. Except that Troy had asked for her. "I'll
try to get away later," she heard herself saying. She wasn't sure how
she would manage it.

She expected Roger to get to his feet, but he remained seated,
working his jaw sideways a moment, as if he were gathering together
more words. Finally he said, "We have somewhat of a problem. Most

of the clients I see aren't happy to see me. They call the office expecting to see you. They hear my voice, and I hear the disappointment in theirs. Like the guy that hung up yesterday."

"He hung up on me, too," Vicky said. She folded her arms on the desk and leaned forward. "Don't take it personally, Roger. My practice used to be the kind of cases you handle. Change is hard, but eventually people get used to it." God, she had become a recording of Adam's words. "You're part of this firm, and you're doing a good job for the clients."

"Okay." Roger spread both hands, then got up and headed across the office. The door had just closed behind him when the phone rang. "It's that man again," Annie said, and in the cautious tone of her voice, Vicky knew who she was referring to.

"Put him through." She pressed a button and said, "This is Vicky Holden."

The breathing was quick and uneven, as if the man on the other end were jogging. He didn't say anything.

"You're the man in the tan truck, aren't you," Vicky said. "Talk to me. If you killed someone by accident, I can try to help you."

Something changed. She could sense the change at the other end of the line, the quick breaths becoming long and jagged. He was crying.

"Talk to me," she said again. There was a small clicking noise, and she knew that he was gone.

Vicky set the receiver in its cradle and went into the outer office where Roger was leaning over Annie's desk. Whatever he was saying, Annie gazed up at him with all the rapt attention she might have given some new and wonderful phenomenon that had sailed across her horizon. Roger gave a little nod in Vicky's direction, then disappeared behind the closed door of his own office.

"What did the caller say?" Vicky said.

Annie bit at her lower lip a moment, as if she were trying to reconnect with the office. Her hair had that just-brushed look, shining under the fluorescent light. Her eyes were shining, too, and that was nice,

Vicky thought. Whatever Roger had brought into her life, it had made her happy.

"Same thing," Annie said. "Let me talk to Vicky Holden. Only this time he said, 'Don't put on that other lawyer. I'm not talking to anybody else.'"

Vicky glanced at the closed door to Adam's office. Adam would be at his desk, drafting an explanation for the tribes about the civil suit that had been filed. In thirty minutes or so, he would expect her to walk in and sit down with her response. They would go over both, make additions and subtractions, make sure they were in agreement. They were a team. Except that there was a man in a tan pickup who needed a lawyer and was too upset or scared or angry to talk to her.

She started for her office, then turned back. "What's new on the moccasin telegraph, Annie?" It was amazing how the telegraph ran into the office. News of anything that happened on the rez sped like lightning to Annie's desk. "What have you heard? Is there anything going on?"

Annie lifted her chin and gave her a blank stare of incredulity. "You mean you haven't heard about Kiki Wallowingbull?"

"What about him?" She was thinking that trouble stalked Kiki Wallowingbull like a bobcat, ready to pounce at the slightest invitation.

"He's dead." Annie gave a series of rapid blinks, as if the news was so obvious she had assumed everyone already knew. "They found his body yesterday down along the Little Wind River."

"What was it, a drug deal?"

"That's what everybody's saying, except for Kiki's grandparents. Moccasin telegraph says they claim Kiki's been straight ever since he got out of prison." Annie shrugged. "Shows how much they loved him. They're never gonna say anything else. You could probably show them a video of Kiki shooting up and they'd say it must be somebody that looked like Kiki, 'cause Kiki didn't do that anymore."

"How sad for them," Vicky said, standing still, staring at the blue-and-gold photo of the plains and mountains on the wall behind Annie's desk. Flashing through her mind were images of her own kids: Lucas at ten years old, all brown skin and black hair racing past on the Appaloosa pony that her father kept for him, and Susan at eight, soft-eyed and fragile-looking, cross-legged on the sofa with the Indian doll in doeskins and beads cradled on her lap. She had worried over what would become of them, how they would make it—parents divorced, mother in Denver most of the time working her way through undergrad and law, grandparents getting older and more frail every year, doing their best to raise them. Even after they were grown, the worry never left her. Sometimes in the middle of the night she would sit up in bed, drenched in sweat, shaking. How easily they might have drifted down the same road that Kiki Wallowingbull had taken.

"When was Kiki killed?" Vicky said, the caller's voice pushing into her mind: *I didn't mean to kill him.*

Annie gave another shrug. "Night before last, looks like."

And yesterday, the man in the tan truck had followed her into the Wal-Mart lot. The same man, she was certain, had been calling the office. "Does the fed have any leads?"

"You know the gossip on the telegraph," Annie said. "People are talking about all kinds of leads. Anybody that's been arrested for drugs is gonna be questioned, that's what I heard."

"Who found the body?" Drug user or dealer, Vicky was thinking. Drug deals went down at the river.

"Father John."

Vicky kept her eyes fastened on the secretary longer than she meant to. She had to pull her gaze away. "What was he doing there?" she said, trying for a casual tone, the same tone she might have used no matter who had found the body.

"I heard he was looking for Kiki," Annie said. "The grandparents were worried. You know Father John. He's always trying to help the people."

Vicky gave a little nod. Then she went into her office, shut the door, and leaned against it. Yes, she knew John O'Malley. Back on the rez now how many days? Twenty? And already back in place, helping the people. Oh, how she had missed him. That was what made his coming back so hard to accept, just when she had started to accept the fact that he was gone. She went over to her desk, printed out the draft she had been working on, and took it into Adam's office. An hour later she was in the Jeep, driving through the snow that swept across the wide streets of Lander.

The Fremont County jail was located in a beige brick building that resembled a fortress behind the snow-packed parking lot. Vicky parked between a truck and an SUV and let herself through the glass door into a concrete entry the size of a closet. Behind the window on the left, an officer in a tan uniform was curled over the papers on a desk. "Help you?" He spoke into a microphone without looking up. He sounded as if he were underwater.

She leaned into the metal communicator that protruded from the glass. "Vicky Holden, here to see Troy Tallfeathers."

The officer nodded. He had black hair trimmed short around big ears that stuck out, prominent, ruddy cheeks, and slits of black eyes that were now trained on her. *Moon* was typed in black letters on the badge clipped to his tan shirt. "Hold on," he said.

Vicky stepped back and waited.

After several minutes, the door next to the window swung open. "Ms. Holden?" Another officer—wide shoulders and the kind of physique that came from hours in a gym—stood in the opening. Behind him, she could see the concrete corridor of the jail. "Follow me," he said.

Down the corridor, through a series of doors that clanged shut, the sound reverberating around the concrete walls, and into the jail itself. The visiting rooms were on the right, and Vicky could see the bony outlines of Troy Tallfeathers's orange-clad knees sticking out beyond one of the doorways.

"In there." The officer waved her into the visiting room. "I'll be right outside, if he gives you any trouble."

Troy was stumbling to his feet as Vicky stepped inside. The door slammed behind her. "Don't get up," she said, taking the chair on the other side of the small table that divided the room.

"'Bout time you come to see me." Troy sank back onto his chair. He was tall and rangy-looking, with shoulders that rose above the back of the chair and elbows that jutted to the sides. He had the light complexion of a white ancestor, but the dark eyes and sculptured face were Arapaho.

"Roger said you wanted to see me," Vicky said.

"Roger." He spit out the name. Specks of saliva lit on the metal table. "I thought you were my lawyer." He leaned close, lacing the long knobby fingers on the table. His breath was like a blast of garlic and hot peppers coming toward her. "How come you sent him over? I don't want to talk to him. All he says is throw myself on the mercy of the court, ask for rehab. You know what they do in rehab? Talk you to death. Shoot you up with drugs that are supposed to get you off drugs. No, thank you."

"You're looking at time in a federal prison," Vicky said.

Troy turned his head away and scratched at his ear. "Maybe not. Might be something I know that the fed don't."

Vicky sat back and studied the young man across from her a moment. Close to Lucas's age, most likely. And Lucas was sitting in a cubicle in some skyscraper in the Denver Tech Center, thank God.

"Are you looking for some kind of a deal?" she said. "You have information about a crime?"

There was no hesitation, no half beat of consideration. "Oh, yeah. I got what you might call information, all right."

"What do you have? Is it about drugs? You know something about who's dealing drugs?"

"What are you? One of them therapists, asking dumb questions? It's just what I said, okay? I got information. Tell the fed that. Tell him I can make a lot of his troubles go away if he gets me outta here."

Vicky took a moment before she said, "The fed is not going to make any sweetheart deal with you. You assaulted a federal officer. It's a serious offense. If you cooperate by giving information on another crime, maybe the judge will give you a lighter sentence. There are no guarantees."

"So you're not goin' to the fed and get me a deal?"

"I just told you . . ."

"So what do I need you and that white lawyer for?" Troy pushed himself to his feet. He loomed over her like a flagpole, and Vicky stood up. "I'm looking out for number one, you got it? I'm firing both of you."

The door swung open. "Everything okay?" the officer said.

"We're finished here," Vicky said, brushing past him and starting back down the corridor. A waste of time, she was thinking, and maybe that was why she and Adam no longer practiced this kind of law. Clients who didn't want advice and wouldn't listen. Troy would find another lawyer. What difference did it make who the lawyer was? But a law firm that helped Arapahos and Shoshones use their natural resources, including water, to build better roads and schools and health clinics made all the difference.

She walked out of the building, steered the Jeep through the lot, and out onto the street. Oh, yes, she and Adam had made the right decision.

9

A LOUD CLANGING noise sounded somewhere. Vicky pulled herself upward out of a black well and tried to register whether the clanging came from the doorbell or the phone. Adam, she thought. Standing downstairs in the late-night dimness of the entry to the apartment building, pressing the buzzer next to her name on the metal plate. This afternoon, Adam had told her that he planned to spend the evening researching the development of coal on Indian reservations in the West. She had things to do, too, she had told him, and he hadn't asked what they might be. She had picked up a turkey sandwich on the way home and eaten in front of the TV, barely registering what she was watching.

And now Adam was here, wanting to talk, close the distance lengthening between them.

Except that it wasn't the buzzer ringing. Vicky fought her way out of a tangle of sheets and comforter and walked her fingers across the bedside table to the phone. Green iridescent numbers glowed on the clock: 1:32.

"Hello," she said.

She knew immediately by the silence on the other end that it wasn't Adam. *He* had found her home number. Was there anything unavailable on the moccasin telegraph? "Who are you?" She could hear the sharpness in her voice. "What do you want?"

"You gotta help me." The same voice as before, thick with alcohol or drugs or sleep. Or grief. For an instant she thought he would burst into tears.

She sat up and turned on the lamp. A puddle of light settled around her and pushed the shadows back along the dresser and chair, her white robe draped over the armrest. "Tell me how I can help you. Don't hang up. Just talk to me."

"I didn't mean for it to happen. I didn't mean to kill him. He made me do it."

Vicky waited, half-expecting the line to go dead. But he was still there, the raspy breaths, the choked sobs at the other end. "Who?" she said finally, barely breathing the word. "Kiki Wallowingbull?"

Silence. And in the silence, Vicky knew that she was right.

"Look," she said. She was awake now; had she been asleep two minutes ago? "Come to my office tomorrow." She stopped. That was the problem: the shiny, modern, and intimidating building on Main Street. "I can meet you wherever you say. You'll have to tell me everything that happened. You have to trust me."

Another rasping noise at the other end, then a long coughing spell. Finally he said, "Now."

"What?"

"Right now. I gotta talk to you right now."

Vicky yanked open the table drawer and withdrew a notepad and pen. She propped the pad on her knees. "Start by telling me your name."

"Not on the phone," he said. "You gotta come here."

"I'll meet you in the morning."

"I'll be dead then."

"What are you saying?"

"I got a gun. I been staring at it all night. I been thinking all I have to do is pick it up and stick it in my mouth and pull the trigger. I been thinking it'll be real easy, and there won't be nothing but blackness. Except I heard a teacher say once that, you know, when you get shot in the head, you hear a big explosion first before the blackness comes. You think that's right?"

"Where are you?" she said.

"Ethete. The house at the far end of Yellow Calf Road."

SNOW HAD STARTED falling sometime in the night, and a thick blanket of new snow lay over Highway 287. Vicky peered past the wipers that scrubbed a half arc on the windshield. There was no sign of life, no other traffic, and the few houses that she had passed were nothing more than dark shadows floating at the side of the road. Except for the hum of the engine and the sound of the tires grinding through the snow, the quiet was deep and pervasive, almost like its own kind of sound. She realized she was following the beams of her own headlights—long yellow lights spilling over the snow—and that the headlights could take her into the ditch. She forced herself to concentrate on the edge of the road, but it was difficult to tell where the edge melted into the borrow ditch and the white prairie that ran away under the moonlight. She gripped the steering wheel hard, her fingers curled stiff inside her leather gloves.

A beam of light shone ahead, then gradually dissolved into two headlights weaving toward her. She slowed a little, holding her breath as the truck lumbered past. Great gusts of snow lifted off the rear tires and plastered the windshield, plunging her into darkness, as if she had suddenly gone blind. It was a moment before the wipers pushed the snow to the side and cleared small half circles. She stared into the white world that stretched into the gray metallic sky.

Hi sei ci nihi, the grandmothers had named her. Woman Alone.

How appropriate, she thought. She was absolutely alone. Nothing but a truck that had passed and was probably a mile down the road, a few houses scattered here and there, all of them dark and quiet, as if the inhabitants had picked up and left one day, along with everyone else, and no one had thought to tell her. She could feel the lightness of the pepper spray she had jammed into her coat pocket as she'd left the apartment. A last-minute thought. She was already in the hallway, and she'd had to let herself back into the apartment and rummage through her desk drawer for the small metal cylinder. And all the time, Adam's voice playing in her head—it was still there—*Are you nuts? Going to the rez in the middle of the night, in a blizzard to meet a killer? Alone? Don't be foolish. Don't go!*

She had been trying to compose a response, something that made sense, the kind of explanation a rational person would have. But there was nothing. Nothing except the desperate, halting tone of the man's voice and the image of the muzzle of a gun jammed into his mouth. An Arapaho, like herself, in some kind of terrible trouble and needing her help. Wasn't that the reason she had chosen law school? So that she could use the white man's own laws to help her people?

Adam would never understand, she realized, but the irony was that she understood him. It wasn't anyone's fault, the rift growing between them. It was just that he had a different idea of how they should help Indian people. And he was right; that was the thing that gnawed at her and made it impossible to come up with any explanation that made sense. Of course he was right. Using the law to make certain that the tribes had the right to manage their own resources, like any other Americans, was the real way to help their people, not driving off in the snow alone to meet an anonymous Arapaho who threatened to kill himself.

She should have called the cops, Adam would say. She could almost see him: beet red with anger, pacing up and down the office. What was she thinking? She had an obligation . . .

It was stupid not to have called the cops—she shuddered at the truth of it. She'd started to dial 911, then had hung up. He would be in the house, waiting for her—the lawyer he counted on to help him— and the suicide prevention team would show up, surround the house, and who knew what might happen? He could put the gun in his mouth and pull the trigger. She couldn't shake the image.

She slowed down for the turn onto Blue Sky Highway, the tires slipping and finally digging into the snow. After a half mile, a pickup came around a bend, headlights dancing toward her. She squinted hard trying to see through the lights and snow as the pickup passed. Coming over the horizon was the faint glow of lights in Ethete.

She had to pump the brakes to keep from sliding through the red light and into the main intersection. Then, lightly pushing on the gas pedal to ease the Jeep back into motion, she drove past the Sun Dance grounds—snow weighing down the branches of the cottonwoods and more snow falling. She turned left, then took another left into the tire tracks that ran up a short driveway to a small house washed gray in the moonlight. The front windows gaped black. A tan truck stood next to the house.

She parked behind the truck and waited, engine whining, warm air blowing from the vents and barely keeping the cold at bay. Her arms and legs felt numb. Surely he had heard the Jeep's engine. He was probably watching from the edge of a window, waiting to see what she would do. The lights would flick on in the house, the front door would open, and he would wave her inside. Everything normal. She would simply meet with a client who needed help.

The lights didn't go on. No movement, no sound, nothing but the unfathomable silence. Vicky waited another minute, then, leaving the motor and the headlights on, she got out. Snow piled around her boots as she followed the yellow glare of the headlights to the door. She stumbled over the stoop hidden under the snow and grabbed at the air to right her balance. Snow ran like fire down the inside of her boots. She knocked on the door, then dipped her chin into her scarf and stomped about for warmth. Her boots made a thudding, muffled noise. No sounds from inside, nothing but the faint gusts of wind and the silence of vacancy and desertion. She knocked again, waited a couple of minutes, then tried the knob with her left hand, her right hand wrapped around the pepper spray inside her pocket.

The door squealed open a few inches. "Hello!" She leaned close and shouted into the shadows. The faint light from the headlights ran across the vinyl floor. "It's Vicky Holden. Are you here?"

No answer. She found herself stepping a little ways inside, snow dripping around her. "Hello!" she shouted. Still no sounds, and yet there was something—an ungraspable sense of another presence. She started backing out to the stoop, conscious of the snowy outline of her boots on the dark vinyl. Madness. The voice on the other end, the threat of suicide—all a ruse to get her here alone in the middle of the night. Someone wanting to harm her, maybe the relative or friend of a client she hadn't been able to keep out of prison. Somebody wanting revenge.

Then another thought; he could already be dead. And it was all another kind of ruse, a macabre pretense to lure her here so that, for some perverse reason, she would be the one to find the body.

"I'm going back to my car," she heard herself shouting into the vacancy, her own voice booming around her. "I'm going to wait for two minutes. If you don't come out . . ." She stopped herself from saying, I'll know you're dead. "I'll drive away," she said. And then what? she was thinking. Call the cops, explain why she had come to a vacant house in the middle of the night instead of reporting a suicide threat?

She swung around and, chin still tilted into the freezing folds of her scarf, followed her own footsteps back to the Jeep. He was dead, she was certain of it. She could feel death around her, seeping out of the house, permeating the air. She pulled her cell out of her pocket as she crawled behind the steering wheel and slammed the door.

"Don't move!" He was in the backseat of the Jeep, so close she could feel the rush of his breath on her cheek. "I said, don't move!"

Vicky stayed still, the cell clasped in her gloves. The pepper spray—

God, the pepper spray was still in her pocket, her coat folded around her. She could feel the lump of the metal cylinder against her hip.

"Don't turn around," he said. She could hear the shaky desperation in his voice. Out of the side of her eye, she caught the slightest glint of the gun in his glove.

"Who are you?" she managed. Her own words sounded forced and breathless.

"I told you, it don't matter."

"I can't help you if I don't know who you are or what you've done." So brave sounding now, she thought, as if she were in her own office and in control, not in the Jeep with a man with a gun.

A rustling sound of movement, as if he had slumped back against the seat. "Something happened that shouldn't have happened. I didn't start it, but I had to finish it." His voice was tentative, laced with fear and uncertainty and the desperation that, she knew, had brought her here. "Next thing I knew he was dead, but I didn't mean for it to happen. I didn't mean to kill him."

"Kiki Wallowingbull," she said.

He had moved in close again, and she had the sense of his size—a large man with broad shoulders looming behind her. She had seen him in Wal-Mart, cap pulled low around his face, collar pulled up. "He was crazy. I didn't mean it to happen."

"What do you want from me?" she said.

"I need assurances."

"Assurances?"

"They're gonna put me back in prison and throw away the key." There was a sobbing note in his voice. "I can't go back there. I'm gonna be dead first. I'm not gonna die inside like some rat in the toilets."

"If it was an accident or self-defense . . ."

"Don't turn around," he shouted, and she realized that she had shifted sideways. She righted herself and stared straight ahead at the snow that had covered the windshield, locking her into the Jeep with a madman. She realized that he had adjusted the mirror upward so that she couldn't see into the backseat. The warm air coughed and rattled in the vents.

"What kind of assurance are you talking about?" she said.

"I'll go to the fed, I'll tell him everything that happened. First you get his word there won't be any charges. I'm gonna walk outta his office a free man. He'll have what he wants, the truth about what happened. That's all I'm asking."

"That won't work," Vicky said. "He'll have to investigate. He'll want the details. Names, dates, places. Look"—she caught herself before she'd shifted again—"you have to level with me. Give me the particulars."

The man made a choking noise, as if he were strangling, and she realized he was choking back the sobs. "I got a little boy. I gotta take care of him. I can't go back to prison and leave him. You gotta help me."

"I understand," she said. "You have a child; you want to be able to raise him." And something else, she was thinking. The man was on parole.

"Easy for you, ain't it. You and that Lakota with all your education, sitting in your big fancy offices, talking to the chiefs all the time, doing the big cases. Win a few cases, lose a few. Money keeps rolling in, no matter what."

"It's not like that."

"Oh, yeah? You think there's any Arapaho around that don't get the picture?"

"Then why did you come to me?"

He didn't say anything for a long moment. Then, something changing in his tone, the fear and grief that she had heard on the phone creeping in: "I heard you were good. If I'd had a decent lawyer, I wouldn't have gotten dumped into the sinkhole I was in. You know how many Indians are dragging themselves from the cell block to the mess hall to the yards, wishing they were dead? All because they had lousy lawyers the court give 'em? Takes money to hire a lawyer like you. I don't have money."

"We do pro bono work," Vicky said, and yet, there were so few pro bono cases she and Adam had time for now.

"You gotta make it happen," he said, the sound of tears breaking against the words. "You gotta go to the fed, get me some assurances. If you don't . . ." He left the thought hanging behind her. The rear door opened, cold air swooped into the Jeep.

"How do I reach you?" she said.

"I'll reach you." There was a rustling noise and the door slammed shut, sending a rocking motion through the Jeep. She flipped on the windshield wipers and watched the large figure—hunched forward, the same black cap pulled low—getting into the truck. Then the growl of a cold engine turning over, the black exhaust spitting into the snow, and the truck was making a U-turn. She hunched forward trying to make out the license, but the numbers were indecipherable behind the snow and ice on the plate. He drove past, shimmying over the icy ridges. She straightened the rearview mirror and watched the truck turn left and vanish on Yellow Calf Road before she shifted into reverse and backed down the drive.

10

"WHAT IS THE meaning of this?" James Cruze looked like a gigantic creature upright on hind legs, William thought, silhouetted against the red sun rising out of the east. Next to him was Tim McCoy, tall, slim, dressed all in black, except for the white Stetson. "I gave the order," Cruze shouted, his voice drumming through the quiet groups of Arapahos and Shoshones gathered around the food table. "All tipis should face the circle. The cameramen are ready to shoot, and look at the sunrise!" Cruze turned his massive bulk around and waved both arms overhead, the creature about to lift himself off the ground. "Perfect for the shot I want, but the damn tipis still face east. I'm paying you to deal with these Indians."

William waited until a band of the old buffalo Indians had helped themselves to the bowls and coffee mugs stacked at the end of the table and started down the line, heaping the bowls full of the oatmeal steaming in kettles, filling the mugs with coffee. He took his place in the line and tried to ignore the white men about thirty feet away. An old Indian trick. Watching and listening, invisible, and all the time taking in everything whites said and did.

Cruze shouting about the wasted time and money on setting up the cameras early, and McCoy—voice calm and firm—saying the Arapahos and Shoshones had been facing their tipis toward the rising sun since time immemorial, and they weren't about to change for a moving picture.

"I'm paying them to do what I say!" Cruze, still shouting.

"They're doing a good job," McCoy said, and that was the end, because Cruze hoisted himself around and marched off toward one of the cameras mounted at the edge of the Indian camp on wooden platforms with wheels that Cruze called carellos.

From halfway down the table, William could smell the hot, sweet odors of oatmeal and fresh coffee. McCoy had walked over to the elders at the far end of the table, hands gripping bowls and mugs. McCoy's hands were flying, his fingers dancing. William caught part of what he said: they shouldn't worry, Cruze would get over it. He wouldn't send them home. What would he do without them? Hire a bunch of white men, paint them brown, and put long black wigs on them? Teach them to ride?

The elders started laughing. Laughing and making their way toward a stretch of ground where somebody had spread a canvas blanket. Other Arapahos and Shoshones had already gone through the line and were seated cross-legged in little groups. The early birds, William thought. Every meal, first at the tables. Diving into the fantastic spread of food. More food and more kinds than they had ever seen— pickled herrings, deviled eggs, potatoes bubbling with cheese, fish that had been baked, boiled, or cooked in green herbs, lamb and pigs roasted with apples in their jaws. The first day in the desert, they had stood back, not daring to believe it was all meant to be eaten. Mr. Cruze had urged them forward. Still they had stayed back until the director had motioned McCoy over, and McCoy had said the food was for all the players, including the Indians. And that was also fantastic, the fact that they were treated like the white people.

James stood a little way off, bent over the black box camera that McCoy had given him, peering into the lens that was pointed toward the food table. He was taking pictures of everything. For the people on the rez, he had told William. "They're not gonna believe what they see."

William filled his own bowl with oatmeal, sprinkled on some raisins and brown sugar, and poured cream over the top. They had helped themselves to the food ever since, he was thinking. The tipis were stuffed with sacks of fruits and vegetables and cans of food—leftovers and discards the Indians picked out of the trash barrels—that they meant to take back to the reservation for the winter. Sometimes there was hardly anything to eat, but this winter, the families would have food.

He topped off his mug with the hot coffee and started toward the circles of Indians. The sky was getting lighter, bands of oranges and pinks and magentas fading into the faintest blue. It was still cool, but there was a hint of October warmth in the air. So much of the desert reminded him of home: the way the sun lifted itself out of the east, glowing red and yellow, the campfires flickering here and there, giving off little circles of light, the field of white tipis set apart from the city of tents where the whites stayed, like the white towns around the reservation. Most of all, the quiet of the Indians hunched over bowls of oatmeal. Heat from the campfires licked at his legs as he passed.

No sign of Charlie anywhere, and that was odd. Charlie was always one of the first in line for meals.

The old buffalo Indians had formed a circle of their own, sitting cross-legged on the canvas blankets, voices low and confidential, speaking Arapaho. Discussing the attack scene today, no doubt. In the Old Time, there would have been buffalo robes to sit on, soft and warm. They would be discussing the day's hunt, where the buffalo herds could be found, which they knew by the odors in the wind and the faint tremors in the earth made by hooves.

William spotted Matthew Lone Bear, Mike Goggles, and James Painted Horse seated just beyond the elders. Members of the younger generation, like himself and Charlie. Not as mature and wise as the elders—would they ever be so wise? As he started toward them, he saw the old man, Goes-in-Lodge, turn his head and give the slightest lift of an eyebrow, almost imperceptible, William thought, but there nevertheless.

He veered sideways and dropped down on his haunches next to Goes-in-Lodge. "What is it, Grandfather?" He used the term of respect, speaking quietly, words meant only for the elder's ears.

"The other warrior with you," Goes-in-Lodge began, jaws chewing on each word before he spoke. "Most the time, he eats with you." Concern rang through the old man's voice. Anything might happen out here in the white world, surrounded by whites, whites in charge. Arapahos and Shoshones had to stay close. "Maybe he's sick, couldn't get outta his blanket."

William nodded. Steam curled off the bowl and mug in his hands. "I'll find him," he said, pulling himself upright.

He went over and dropped down next to James. "Seen Charlie this morning?" he said.

James shook his head, tilted his bowl upward and drained the last of the creamy oatmeal. He had the brown skin, the black hair slicked back behind his ears, and the hooked nose of a full blood. Chest caved in a little. Tuberculosis as a child, William had heard. Maybe he still had it. No one talked about it. "Not here yet," James said, wiping his lips with the back of his hand. "You ask me, he better be coming. White man starts on white time. Getting ready now." He glanced in the direction of Cruze, loping past the campfires toward another camera, arms flailing as if he could part the air ahead. "Charlie's gonna get us all sent home, if he ain't careful."

William set his oatmeal and coffee on the ground. He could feel the hard lump forming like a rock in his stomach. "He with the girl?"

"Heard him leave the tipi in the middle of the night," James said. "Heard his footsteps going toward the white tents."

William stopped himself from asking if James was sure. Of course he was sure. James could track a deer through the forest by the sounds of hooves scratching the rocks and twigs and branches snapping off the ponderosas.

William looked around at the other Indians finishing breakfast, some carrying bowls and mugs back to the table where a couple of white men dressed up in white shirts and pants would plunge the dishes into tubs of hot water before stacking them in the wood cabinets a few feet away. Still no sign of Charlie.

"Listen, players!" James Cruze's voice burst through the quiet. The sun was a blurred globe in the overcast sky, but already the air was warmer. A perfect day to make the moving picture. "Fifteen minutes call for the attack scene. Everyone in place! Indians, no clothes but breechcloths for you. Bare skin is what I want, so you look like savages. Terrify folks when you start crawling down the rocks toward the wagon train. That's what I want—terror. Don't forget your weapons. Bows and arrows, hatchets, spears. You know how to handle them. You done it in real life." He gave a growl that might have been an attempt at laughter.

Fifteen minutes, William was thinking. He got to his feet and started weaving through the players—Indians and whites—milling about, some of them heading in the direction of the rock outcroppings where the filming would take place. Others headed toward the corral. A lot of the Indians would ride across the desert to attack the wagon train. Everyone seemed to be talking. Conversations buzzed around him like a hive of bees. He could see the cameras set up on the carellos. Another camera was up on top of the rocky ridge, like a gnarled tree backlit against the sky. He went in the opposite direction, keeping an easy pace so that he wouldn't draw attention.

In a moment he was walking down the narrow dirt streets in tent city, past the rows of tents with flaps closed and waves of dust around the lower edges. Smoke trailed out of the dead campfires that had burned in front of some of the tents. He headed toward the area where Mr. Cruze and the big movie players stayed, not sure which tent was hers. It would be close by, he thought. They would want to keep an eye on her. What was it that McCoy had said? Mr. Lasky's girlfriend, here on a lark because there was nothing else to do, and he couldn't say no to her?

The whirring sound of voices had died back; silence as heavy as a buffalo robe hung over the dirt paths and tents. William passed the director's tent and slowed down, listening for the smallest sound or motion that disrupted the silence. He had moved past two other tents when it came, the faint ring of her laughter, like a bell tinkling nearby. He followed the sound, making his own footsteps soft so that his moccasins didn't scratch the ground. The tinkling noise came again, and he veered across the path and stopped in front of the tent.

"Charlie," he said. His own voice slapped at the silence.

A rustling noise, faint and hurried, came from inside. Then the flap pulled back an inch, and Charlie peered out with one eye. "What're you doin' here?"

"It's starting," William said. "We have to get to our places."

"A few minutes." The flap fell back into place.

"Now, Charlie." William said. "You have to come right now before Mr. Cruze sees you're missing."

The girl was laughing, an outburst of gaiety and lightness that floated out into the dusty path. What did it mean to her? Nothing. A bunch of Indians sent back to the rez without money for their families, and she would go on playing in the next moving picture, the Big Man's girlfriend, with lots of money, and food always on the table.

"Now," he said again, rattling the flap. "Come out now or I'll drag you out."

The flap opened and Charlie stepped out. William caught a glimpse of the girl, huddled on top of a narrow bed that stood on metal legs, blue blanket wrapped around the curves of her hips and chest, long blond curls straggling over her face and white shoulders. She was beautiful.

Then something else: boots thudding the earth, coming down the dirt path. In a half breath, the boots would intersect with the path they were on. "Missy!" The man's voice boomed like the shot of a cannon. "Where are you!" William grabbed Charlie's arm and pulled him around to the back of the tent. Still pulling him toward the path that paralleled the one with the boots, walking fast yet quietly. And Charlie was walking quietly, too.

"Get out here!" The cannon voice again.

"Leave me alone." There was a mixture of defiance and amusement in the girl's voice. "You don't own me."

"The Big Man owns you. I'm looking out for his interests, like he pays me to do. Get outta bed. Cruze wants you on the set. You gotta be in the wagon train, so the Big Man knows you weren't in bed with one of the Indians."

"Leave me alone," she shouted, and there was something new in her voice: notes of panic and fear.

"Get up!" he shouted. There was the whack of a palm against flesh.

Charlie swung around. It took all of William's strength to grip him hard enough to keep propelling him forward. The food table was just ahead, and beyond, the crowds of players, the wagons pulled into a circle, and Indians already in their places up in the rocks.

"None of our business," William said.

"Let me go." Charlie wrenched his arm free.

There was a view of his naked back, the knots of bone and ropes of muscle, the brown legs starting to kick into a run as William hurled himself against the man, knocking him to the ground. He sat on top of him and lifted his fist like a hammer. "I'll kill you," he heard himself say, a hissing noise erupting out of his clenched teeth. "You'll ruin everything. For what? The girl means nothing to you. You got a woman waiting for you on the rez. What are you doing?"

He could feel Charlie start to relax, his muscles dissolving into the earth. A kind of terror came into his eyes, then he closed them. "Let me up," he said.

William shifted his weight and got to his feet. Leaning over, he gripped Charlie's arm and pulled him upright. Charlie opened his eyes and stared at the crowds and commotion beyond the food table a long moment, then he ran the palm of his hand over his forehead, smearing the sweat into dark wavy lines. "I'm not going back to the rez," he said, starting toward the tables.

"Not goin' home? Are you crazy?"

Charlie stopped and turned toward him. "It's not what you think. It's the dream."

"What dream? You're not making sense."

"I had a dream. It was all darkness around me in the tipi, and people running around outside, lots of crying and yelling. I could hear Anna crying. All the people were crying. That's how I knew I was dead."

William bit at his lower lip. Dreams were power; the spirits came in dreams. Dreams told the truth. "Maybe you didn't understand," he said. "Don't think about it."

"I think about it all the time," Charlie said. "This is it right here. This is all the sun and the blue skies, this is all the earth I'm gonna get. She's the last woman I'm gonna have. This is life, and I'm taking what's left for me."

William threw a glance behind them, half-expecting the bodyguard and the girl to appear in the path. There was no one. "Come on," he said, grasping Charlie's shoulder. "We got to get to our places."

HE WAS HIGH on the rock-strewn hill that erupted out of the desert, like a bulge in the earth. All around was nothing but the expanse of dusty earth studded with prickly cactus and dried brush rolling into the horizon. The sky had settled into a deep blue; the sun was white in its slow arc overhead. The whole hill was crawling with Indians. At the base of the hill was the wagon train pulled into a circle, the defensive position Mr. Cruze called it. And there was Mr. Cruze himself, stomping about, arms waving. The white players scurried into place inside the circle.

He spotted Kerrigan sitting on his horse the way McCoy had taught him. He looked like a real cowboy. Walking along one of the wagons in that fluid way she had, gray dress billowing about her, was Lois Wilson. Dark hair shining in the sun, the open, trusting look on her face. More beautiful than the yellow-haired girl, he thought, with a sense of power about her that was all her own. Untouchable, while everything about Missy Mae Markham begged to be touched.

The cameras on the carellos at the base of the hill creaked and groaned in the breeze. He could see the cameramen standing spread-legged, trying to balance themselves. One camera was turned uphill, but two others faced the wagon train. The cameramen leaned in close, pulled back and looked around, then leaned in again.

Charlie crouched behind one of the rocks about twenty feet below, and that was good, William thought. He could keep an eye on him. When Charlie turned sideways, he could see the dark bruise spreading across his chest where he had hit the ground. The fool—willing to throw everything away, and not just for himself. For all of them. Oh, Mr. Cruze would send them home if he found Charlie with Missy Mae Markham. Maybe the director would keep the buffalo Indians, less likely to get into trouble. Maybe a few of the younger generation, but most would be sent packing. And painted white men with black wigs would take their places. And they would look like fools falling off their horses. McCoy had made a joke of it, but it would happen. The yellow-haired girl belonged to the Big Man.

He felt his muscles tense, his fingers tighten around the hatchet. The girl was inside the circle of covered wagons, tossing her head about, the blond curls flying in the breeze. She had on a blue dress that fell off one shoulder and draped along a white arm. The white skin gleamed. She swung her shoulders about and looked around at the other players moving into place, smiling and laughing. Then the body-guard moved close to her wagon, said something into her ear, and yanked the top of the blue dress over her shoulder.

William could see Charlie start to haul himself upright, the spear in his hand rise overhead. He started around the rock, planting his moc-casins one after the other in the slow, deliberate movement of attack. Leaning forward now, the muscles in his back and down his legs fo-cused on a single intent.

"Easy!" William called. He found himself moving downhill at the same pace. Focused and deliberate. When Charlie started running, he would run. He would stop him.

"Places, all you Indians!" Mr. Cruze shouted through a bullhorn, his voice reverberating around rocks.

Charlie stopped in place. Below, Missy was leaning out of the wagon, pointing a rifle at the Indians about to attack over the hill. The bodyguard huddled with a group of white men, all of them holding rifles. A long moment passed before William sank back into place. Charlie turned and climbed back up the rocks.

"Cameras!" Cruze shouted.

Everyone started moving. Hundreds of Indians racing ponies across the desert, spears and bows and arrows lifted high, clouds of dust swirling about. Other Indians jumping from the rocks, running down-hill through the brush, hollering and yelping, swinging hatchets over-head, pointing bows and arrows at the wagons. The buffalo Indians were in the lead, just like in the Old Time. William ran after them, his moccasins pounding the rocks and hard ground, something free and wild in it, something real and honest.

11

THE DRUMBEATS THUDDED into the quiet. The three musicians hunched over the drum at the foot of the gravesite, beating out the rhythm meant to call the *hi nono eino* to the cemetery. A little crowd huddled around the rectangular grave that three of the volunteers had dug yesterday, breaking through the layers of wind-crusted snow into the hard, frozen earth. The canopy overhead snapped in the wind. Andrew and Mamie sat in the front row of the folding chairs arranged on one side. A few other mourners—mostly old people—occupied the other chairs.

Father John could feel the cold biting through his vestments, shirt, and blue jeans and into his skin. Clouds had built up over the mountains, the sun breaking through for a few moments before disappearing. He had said the funeral Mass for Kiki in the church this morning. Afterward a line of vehicles had wound out of the mission grounds and onto the bluff where St. Francis cemetery was located. He had half-expected Dede to show up, but she hadn't appeared. He removed the prayer book from the backpack he'd brought to the site and glanced over the group of mourners, brown eyes turned up to him, shoulders hunched inside bulky jackets, gloved hands clasped together. Then he read: "In those days, I heard a voice from heaven saying, Blessed are the dead who die in the Lord. Let them rest from their labors, for their works follow them."

He let the words hang in the frigid air a moment before sliding the book into the backpack and pulling out the small pottery bowl and the bottle of holy water. He poured the water into the bowl—the eyes following him, the air heavy with silence. He found the sprinkler at the bottom of the backpack. Sprinkling the holy water over the coffin, he said, "Dear God, we ask for your mercy so that Kiki and all our relatives who have passed out of this world may enjoy everlasting happiness. Through our Lord Jesus Christ, who lives and reigns with You in the unity of the Holy Spirit, God, world without end."

Then he stepped back and waited. After a moment, Ernest White Eagle and Thomas Willow, two of the Holy Old Men—the elders who preserved the Arapaho spiritual beliefs for the next generations— walked over to the grave. The smoke of burning sage drifted out of the pans they carried. They lifted the pans overhead, allowing the smoke to waft across the grave, then over the crowd. Last night, at the wake at Eagle Hall, the Old Men had saged Kiki's corpse as well as the mourners. Then they had painted circles of sacred red paint on Kiki's face and on the V-shaped patch of skin that showed past the top of his shirt. Marking him for the ancestors, so they would recognize him and take him into the afterworld.

"*Ichjevaneatha Nesteed hichjeva nau vedawu,*" Ernest White Eagle said, his voice low and clear in the cold. He was as tall as Father John, nearly six feet four inches, stoop-shouldered and thin-looking inside the massive down jacket. Thomas Willow barely came to his shoulder, with a wrinkled, calm-looking face and eyes accustomed to looking at sadness.

"Jevaneatha nethaunainau, Jevaneatha Dawathaw henechauchau-nane nanadehe vedaw nau ichjeva, Kiki Wallowingbull."

There had been so many wakes and funerals in the nine years Father John had spent at St. Francis Mission. Some of the Arapaho words were familiar, and he could guess at the rest. *God is the Maker of heaven and earth. His spirit fills everywhere on earth and above us. Go to the Creator. Go with the ancestors, Kiki Wallowingbull.*

The Old Men placed lids on the pans. Smoke smoldered about the edges for a moment, then vanished. They set the pans on the earth and took seats on either side of Andrew and Mamie. The three men who had dug the grave yesterday—volunteers he could always count on to help at funerals—began turning the crank that let the coffin down. The drums started up again, thumping into the squealing noise of the crank. One by one, the mourners began filing past, dropping items onto the coffin. Pieces of hair tied in a ribbon—a sign of life. Slips of folded paper with prayers written on them. Messages for Kiki to convey to relatives in the afterworld. And other items, all of them gifts: a keychain, Father John thought, by the metallic clink it made against the coffin, a book, and a red scarf. Finally Andrew got to his feet. He carried a brown cowboy hat over to the grave and let it drop. Kiki's favorite thing. It would go with him into the afterworld.

The drumming stopped, and slowly the mourners began walking toward the pickups parked on cemetery road, boots scraping the snow. Andrew and Mamie huddled together a moment before starting after the others. After everyone had left, Father John spent a few moments praying over the grave. Kiki's hat and the other items were scattered over the top of the coffin. "May you find peace and rest." He spoke out loud, as if Kiki were there—in a counseling session or stopping by to say hello after Mass. He couldn't remember Kiki ever coming to Mass. Maybe when he was a kid. It was hard to connect a thirteen- or fourteen-year-old kid with the prison-hardened and jumpy young man he had picked up on Seventeen-Mile Road.

He gathered up the backpack and started toward the pickup, the only vehicle still parked at the cemetery. Red taillights flickered in the gray daylight as the last vehicles turned out of cemetery road and headed back toward the mission.

"THEY'RE TAKING IT pretty hard," Elena said. Father John glanced over at the table where Andrew and Mamie sat with some of the other elders. The rest of the mourners were scattered around the other tables, and several grandmothers were setting out plates of food at the long side table. The smell of fresh coffee filled Eagle Hall, and other smells were coming at him: the pungent odor of simmering stew—beef, potatoes, and carrots—the smells of hot apple pie and bananas in a cake.

"Andrew's waiting to talk to you," Elena said. He felt her fingers on his arm, nudging him toward the table. "I'll get you some coffee."

Father John took off his jacket and hat, set them on top of the jackets piled over a chair, and headed across the hall. Andrew caught his eye and started to get up—a halting, stumbling motion. For an instant, Father John thought the old man would topple over. He sprinted toward him, knocking over a folding chair that thumped against the floor, but Andrew seemed to find his own balance. He moved sideways toward a vacant table and eased himself onto a chair.

Father John sat down beside him. "This must be very tough for you," he said.

The old man balled his fists, then ran the back of his fingers over his cheeks. Moisture glistened on the knobby knuckles, a fact he seemed to realize because he folded his hands together and hid them under the table. "I gotta be strong for Mamie," he said. "That boy was all the relatives we had. I'll be going with Kiki soon, and she's gonna be alone. Oh, the people won't forget her, stuck out in the house alone." He threw a glance around the room. "They'll see that she's got fuel for the winter, some food in the cabinets. Won't be anybody that loves her like family."

"I'm sorry, Grandfather," Father John heard himself saying. The words sounded small and unimportant, like leaves tossed into a river of grief.

"Can't stop thinking about the boy," Andrew went on. "Nothing left of him on this earth now, except for the kind of boy he was, his reputation. All a man has is his reputation." He leaned sideways, bringing his face close. Father John glimpsed the pink scalp showing through the thin, white hair, and the little tufts of white hair in the old man's nostrils. "The fed come to see us yesterday," he said. "Not much we could tell him, 'cept we want him to find the SOB that killed Kiki, Mamie and me. Our time to go, we want to know there was justice for Kiki."

Elena appeared, set two mugs of coffee on the table, then moved away. Father John took a sip from one of the mugs—steam rising off the top, the odor so strong it made him realize how hungry he was, the coffee itself infused with cream.

Andrew took a couple of sips, then wrapped the mug in both hands and stared at the coffee. "All the questions the fed asked. When did we see Kiki last? How could we be sure he was clean? Maybe he was using drugs and we didn't know it?" The old man lifted his eyes. They were rheumy and tear-filled. "Wanted to know who Kiki hung out with since he got out of prison. What about Jason Bellows? I told the fed that maybe Kiki used to hang around with the likes of Bellows, but not anymore."

Father John didn't say anything. He had never met Bellows, but he had heard of him. There probably wasn't anybody on the rez who hadn't heard of him: gang leader, drug dealer, but he was like a wisp of smoke blowing across the plains, gathering in the arroyos and on the riverbanks, selling meth or pot or cocaine—whatever the customer wanted—and vanishing. Customers and other dealers knew how to find him. Kiki had been one, and he ended up in prison. But Father John had never heard that Bellows had been arrested.

"Trouble is," Andrew said, "I'm worried the fed's not ever gonna find the guy that hurt Kiki and left him to die at the river like a dog 'cause he's already convinced himself that Kiki was dealing drugs and that's how come he got killed."

Father John took another drink of coffee and waited. In years of counseling, he'd learned to recognize the signs. Andrew hadn't told him everything yet; there was more to come.

"Everything's gonna be taken from Kiki," Andrew said finally. "First his life, and now the man that he was. Just like what happened to my father. Went off to Hollywood to work, get some money and food for his wife and the kid he was gonna have, and they took his life. Then they took his reputation. Said he ran away from his wife and kid. But my mother carried the truth here . . ." He balled up a fist again and thumped at his chest. "In her heart she knew what kind of man he was. He wasn't never gonna leave her and his kid, unless he was dead."

The old man leaned in close, moisture glistening in the furrows of his cheeks. "Somebody out there," he said, waving a hand toward the window and the expanse of snow and gray sky, "don't ever want people to know what happened. Kiki found out the truth, and that's why he got killed." The muscles in the old man's jaw clenched; the cracked lips came together in a tight, pink line.

Father John leaned back against the chair; the rungs pressed against his spine. It seemed preposterous—an old man stuck in the past, a lifetime spent trying to understand why his father had left him, and a grandson hanging onto the family stories, maybe trying to come to terms with the fact that his own father had driven off a cliff. Yet Kiki had messed up and gone to prison. Then he had gotten off drugs. Maybe he had seen his chance to redeem himself in the eyes of his grandparents. There was power in the need for redemption, Father John thought. He had been trying to redeem himself for nearly ten years—trying to stay sober, honor the vows he had taken, bring a gift to all those who had believed in him, all the people he had let down—the provincial and the other superiors, his colleagues, his own family. Wanting to say, "I've changed. I'm not the man I used to be."

He said, "Do you think Kiki found something in Hollywood that brought him back to the rez?" It was what the girl, Dede, had said. The truth had been here all the time.

Andrew nodded, a look of gratitude suffusing the old eyes. "Hold on." He leaned on one hip and extracted something from the back pocket of his jeans. "Here's the letter I told you about." He held out a worn, frayed envelope that looked as if it had been opened and closed a hundred times. The address was in bold, black handwriting: *Mrs. Wallowingbull. Indian Reservation. Wyoming.* In the upper left corner, the same bold handwriting: *Tim McCoy, Ambassador Hotel, Hollywood, California.*

"This come for Mother," Andrew said. "Was at the agency for months, and nobody told her. Day came she had to go see the agent about getting seeds for our vegetable plot, and the agent says, 'You got a letter here, Anna. How come you ain't come to get it?' I can picture her standing at the counter, real small and quiet. Hard for an Indian lady, not having a husband to look out for her. So the agent pulls this envelope out of a box and throws it across the counter. She didn't know how to read, and he knew that, but he let her stand there, looking at the envelope and not knowing what to do. He was enjoying himself, thinking she was stupid. She said he laughed when she asked him to read the letter to her."

Father John slipped the letter out. The paper was yellowish and brittle, cracking a little at the fold. He was afraid it might fall into pieces in his hand. It was the same handwriting on the envelope, with large, swooping letters, as if the writer had taken his time, thinking his way through the message.

Dear Mrs. Wallowingbull,

I am writing about your husband, Charlie. He was a very fine man. Everyone connected with The Covered Wagon *thought highly of him. I have spent many hours in an attempt to deter-*

mine where Charlie might have gone. He did not appear at the Egyptian Theatre on the evening of April 10 to participate in the prologue show for the premiere of the motion picture. His friend, William Thunder, went to Cahuenga Pass to find him and reported that he was not in his tipi. His horse, Ranger, was in the corral. When Charlie did not appear the following morning, a search was gotten under way. The other Indians and I spent several days walking through Cahuenga Pass on the supposition that he might have gotten lost. I am sorry to report that we have found no trace of him. However, I have checked with the police and there are no reports of an Indian being found dead. I tell you this to keep up your spirits. I am sure that the studio is very concerned about the disappearance and will do everything to locate your dear husband. I myself will not give up the search.

My best wishes to you,
Tim McCoy

Father John slid the letter back inside the envelope and handed it to Andrew. A connection to his father, he was thinking. "Kiki saw this?"

Andrew nodded. "Showed it to him lots of times. Told him what McCoy said when he come here . . ."

"You met McCoy?"

Andrew looked away and frowned at the memory. "I was maybe ten years old when a pickup drives up our road and a big, tall man, dressed in black and wearing a white Stetson gets out. Says he's Tim McCoy. He'd been in lots of movies by then and everybody knew who he was. Moccasin telegraph was full of news that a movie star was on the rez. I remember the way he walked up to my mother with his big hand out to shake her hand. She just stood there, looking real small and scared, like she knew he was bringing bad news. We all went inside and Mother give him some coffee. He made himself comfortable and looked me up and down. 'Look just like your dad,' he said. Then he told Mother he was real sorry he never could find out what happened. He stayed a little while, drank some more coffee, like there was lots of things he'd been thinking about that he wanted to say, but he didn't know how. Then he got up and said his good-byes. That was the last we heard about my father."

"You think McCoy knew what happened?'

Andrew took a couple of seconds before he said, "He knew, all right."

Father John drained the last of his coffee. It was possible that Kiki had found whatever it was that McCoy knew, and it had brought him back to the reservation. *The truth was here all the time.* It would explain why Kiki hadn't gone to see his grandparents after he got back. He was looking for the rest of it.

"I can make some inquiries," he said. He could see the hope running through the old man, the light coming on in the dark, watery eyes. "I can try to find out who Kiki might have talked to after he got back. Maybe I can learn something that would convince Gianelli to take a different tack."

The old man slid the envelope across the table. "Take this," he said. "Might help you some way." Then he took hold of Father John's hand. It surprised him—the strength in his grip. "Let Kiki have justice," he said. "It would be a gift."

12

"LET ME GET this straight." Ted Gianelli leaned back behind a desk stacked with an array of papers and file folders. He crossed his thick arms over his chest. Bushy black eyebrows started to lift, creating fissures in his forehead. The flat-faced buildings on Lander's Main Street floated in the window behind him, snow pillows on the roofs. There was the muffled sound of traffic working through the snow-clogged streets. "You have a client who admits he killed a man."

"Just someone who talked to me." Vicky tapped the ballpoint against the notepad on her lap. She had climbed the narrow black steps to the second-floor offices of the local FBI, conscious of the hopelessness, the ridiculousness of her mission. Reaching for a confidence she didn't feel, she said, "He says it was self-defense. He didn't mean to kill anyone. Last I checked, taking another life in an act of defending oneself or someone else is justifiable. What evidence do you need that it was self-defense?"

"We're talking about the death of Kiki Wallowingbull?"

"It's possible." She tried for a stone face.

"What's his name, this client of yours?" Arms on the armrests now, a more expansive, open look, as if he might consider her request. The fronts of his black leather vest fell open over a gray, Western shirt with silver buttons. Wisps of black hair curled over the cuffs. On one hand was a silver ring in the shape of a bull's head. Vicky could still picture the feds on the rez when she was a kid: dark suits, white shirts, and blue ties, riding around in SUVs that the people called G wagons. You could spot them a mile away. Everybody scattered ahead, hiding, refusing to talk to them.

"Technically, he's not a client. Just someone I'm trying to get information for. I can't give you his name," she said. She didn't know the name—the reality of it hammered in her head. All she knew was a voice on the phone, a man in the shadows. She kept her features still, hoping Gianelli wouldn't read her thoughts. "He's scared," she went on. "He has priors."

"Of course he does." Another lift of the eyebrows. "Let me guess. Any other charges, and he's back in prison for a long time."

"He has the right to be heard on his own terms. The right to tell his story about what happened."

Gianelli leaned forward, laced his hands over a pile of papers, and said, "Bring him in. I'll interview him, same as any other person of interest in the case."

"He won't come," Vicky said. She jotted the words *no success* on the pad. "Not without assurances that you will consider the fact it was self-defense."

"Your job . . ."

"I know my job, Ted." Vicky smiled, an effort to soften the tone lingering in the air. "Advise him to come in, submit to an interview, tell the truth, and take his chances. We're not talking about the average white guy in an SUV out there . . ." She tilted her head toward the window. ". . . who thinks the law is always on his side and can't imagine any innocent person getting dumped into prison. We're talking about an Indian who's been in prison. He knows what can happen. He won't take any chances, and frankly, I wouldn't advise him to."

"Nice speech, Vicky. We both know it's crap. No matter what your guy claims, I would have to match it to the rest of the evidence, see if it makes sense. These things take time, and there are no assurances until the investigation is over and all the pieces are in place. Would help to get things started if your client said where this act of self-defense took place."

"I heard Kiki was killed at the river."

"Don't believe everything you hear on the moccasin telegraph. I need to know where it happened. Bar? House? Barn? Outdoors? Where was it? Forensics would have to examine the site, see if what they find supports the story. Something else . . ." He leaned over the desk, pressing a fleshy stomach into the edge. "If your man took him to the river and left him to die, it's a whole different ball game. He'd be looking at conspiracy, aiding and abetting . . ." He moved his hands apart, as if he were holding a ball over the desk.

Vicky scribbled on the pad, gaining time. Here was something that the moccasin telegraph hadn't broadcast, or if it had, Annie hadn't thought to include it in her daily report of the news. "Are you saying he froze to death?"

"Big problem right there," Gianelli said. "Autopsy says Kiki was alive when somebody took him to the river. He had a concussion. There was a laceration on his forehead and a more serious linear laceration at the back of his skull. No drugs in his system." He waited a moment, watching for a reaction, she thought. Then he went on: "Either your guy assumed he was dead and tried to dispose of the body, which could send him back to prison. Or he knew he was still alive, took him to the river, and left him to freeze to death. Either way, he has some explaining to do." Gianelli sat back in his chair and regarded her for a long moment. "If drugs were involved . . ."

Vicky held up a hand. "You just said there were no drugs in Kiki's system."

"Doesn't mean drugs weren't involved."

Vicky stuffed the notepad and pen in her bag and got to her feet. "Thanks for your time," she said. And what would she tell the man in the tan truck the next time he called or showed up in the backseat of her Jeep or—God, here was a thought—pulled her into an alley somewhere? That she hadn't gotten anything? What would he do, this man with a gun who preferred to die rather than return to prison. Decide she should die, too? He had already killed a man.

Gianelli came around the desk. "What do you really want? You knew I couldn't give you any assurances. What are you after?"

Vicky faced him for a moment, not saying anything. How to explain to this white man? An Arapaho, one of her own people, desperate—*crying* with desperation. And she a lawyer, sworn to help desperate people. "I'll tell him what you said," she managed. "I doubt you'll hear from him."

"We'll find him, Vicky. You know that. We're talking to a lot of people on the rez, and sooner or later, some guy with his own problems will want to make a deal. He'll give up your guy. We'll go to his house and arrest him, and there won't be any assurances."

"You think there were witnesses?"

Gianelli shrugged. "Nothing ever takes place in total obscurity. Somebody always knows what happened. It just takes time to find that person."

Vicky turned around and started down the narrow hallway lined with all types of books—legal books and manuals and bound files— conscious of the sharp clack of Gianelli's boots on the floor behind her, his arm reaching past her to the doorknob. Before he could open the door, she said, "How come Father John found the body?"

"You didn't hear?"

"Moccasin telegraph didn't mention it."

"The grandparents were worried about Kiki, so Father John went looking for him." The door swung open, and Vicky stepped out into the hallway. "Lucky guy," Gianelli said, leaning against the doorjamb.

"Saw *Giselle* at the Caracalla Baths. I'd give this," he said, making a sawing motion across his forearm, "to hear an opera sung there. Good to have him back, isn't it?"

Outside, Vicky started the Jeep, then waited a moment. She would go to St. Francis Mission. She would pretend that nothing had changed, as if he had never left.

"FIVE CALLS THIS morning while you were at the funeral." Lucy set the message slips on the desk. "You should be three men," she said.

Father John fanned the slips and glanced over them. The usual calls. Janice Birdsley wanted to set up counseling appointments for her and her daughter. Kate Swifter resigned from the religious education committee. *Needs time for elderly mother*, Lucy had scribbled across the bottom of the slip. *Could you visit the old lady?*

Here was a message he didn't want. He stared at the swings and curlicues of Lucy's handwriting. *Father Bill Rutherford. Please return his call.* Lucy must have noticed what he was looking at because she said, "That's your boss, right? The provincial? You should ask him to send another priest."

"I'll think about it. Anything else?" Father John looked up at the girl hovering about the desk. She had settled into the job, as if it had been hers all along, waiting for her to claim it.

"You like that movie?" She nodded at the DVD of *The Covered Wagon* on the corner of his desk. He had watched the DVD last night, lost for a couple of hours in the sweep of the black-and-white prairies, the long line of covered wagons rolling against the sky, the headlong clash of emigrants and Indians. He kept looking for familiar faces among the Arapahos and Shoshones, and at one point, he was sure he spotted Goes-in-Lodge, the old Indian playing the role of chief. He had been one of the leading men who had brought the Arapahos to the reservation in 1878. There were photos of him around the rez—in the schools and the convenience stores.

"It's pretty good," he said. "You like silent movies?"

"Silent? You mean like no talking? Like in the olden days?"

"They didn't have to talk," he said. "They used their eyes and their expressions. They could talk with their hands." He picked up the DVD and handed it to her. "Arapahos are in this one."

"You're kidding."

"You might like it," he said. Then he told her that it belonged to Andrew Wallowingbull, and he would have to return it.

"Arapahos in the movies?" She lifted a skeptic eyebrow and stared at the yellow-and-red-and-black DVD cover a moment. "What the heck." She tucked the DVD against her. Looking as if she were about to leave, she said, "You had a visitor this morning. That lawyer came around."

"Vicky Holden?" Father John sat back in the chair. So many things in Rome he had wished he could share with her—the way the rain glistened on the pavement in the narrow streets, the skylight illuminating the face of Bernini's *St. Theresa in Ecstasy*, the old lady plucking at his black suit jacket, begging him in Italian to pray for her, the wealthy parishioners insisting that English tutors give their children a proper British accent. All of it, she would find interesting. But she hadn't come to the welcome home feast; she hadn't stopped in to say hello. He had known with the certitude as strong as steel that she hadn't wanted him to return. "What did she say?"

"She'll be back." Lucy hesitated a moment before she went on: "I heard about her going off to be a lawyer and coming back. Works in a fancy office in Lander. How long did she go to school?"

"A long time. Would you like to be a lawyer?"

"No way." Lucy gave a quick shrug. "How about you?"

"Do I want to be a lawyer?"

"How many years did you go to school?"

"After high school? About fifteen. Thinking about becoming a Jesuit?"

"Yeah, right." She shook her head, rolled her eyes, and pivoted about, her sneakers padding down the corridor.

He picked up the receiver and dialed the provincial's office. An interim appointment, Bill Rutherford had said. One month, six months, a year. He hadn't been back three weeks; it never occurred to him that a permanent pastor might be found so soon. A man picked up at the other end, a priest assigned to the provincial's office, and Father John said he was returning Father Rutherford's call. "Sorry, Father," the priest said. "You just missed him. Care to leave a message?" There was no message, Father John told him.

He had pressed the cutoff button and started to return the next phone call when he heard the thrum of an engine on Circle Drive, the sound of tires plowing through the snow. All vehicles had a similar sound, he thought. And yet he knew that it was Vicky's Jeep. He heard the door slam, a dull thud softened by the freezing temperature, and her footsteps coming up the steps. Cold air swooshed across his office as the front door opened and closed. There were footsteps in the corridor, then Vicky stood in the doorway.

Father John got to his feet. "Vicky," he said, walking around the desk. It was like the first time he had seen her: standing in the doorway, surveying his office, her dark eyes finally settling on him. *So you're the new priest everyone's talking about.* Her voice a mixture of hardness and softness, and that had caught his attention. He had known who she was—the Arapaho lawyer he had heard about. He had expected her to be tough. It was the softness he hadn't expected, or how beautiful she was. No one had thought to mention that fact to a priest.

"It's good to see you." He crossed the office, thinking he would take her into his arms—a welcome embrace between two old friends. But something about her stopped him, something forbidding. A gulf that he couldn't bridge.

She had already moved past him, unbuttoning the black coat she was wrapped in. A green fuzzy scarf was tied at her neck, and she loosened it so that it draped over the front of the coat. "You're looking good," she said. "Rome must have agreed with you."

Father John stepped back and motioned her to a chair, but she wouldn't take it, he was certain. She would pace the floor unable to sit still until she had talked out whatever had brought her to the mission.

"Coffee?" He kept his voice light and noncommittal, as if she were just another parishioner who had stopped in. "It's pretty good. Lucy made it."

"No, thanks," Vicky said. "I had a long chat with Lucy earlier. Your new assistant?"

"Helps to keep the place running." Father John walked over and leaned against the edge of the desk. He stopped himself from asking how things were going at the law firm. She would decode the real question: How were things between her and Adam? At any rate, he could sense by the way that she strolled over to the window, then walked back into the center of the office that the preliminaries were over.

"So you went looking for Kiki. What sent you to the river?" she said.

He told her that Kiki's girlfriend thought he might have gone there.

"To buy drugs?"

"Andrew and Mamie say Kiki was clean."

"The autopsy report confirms that," she said. "Somebody took him to the river and left him to die." Vicky threw up one hand in a gesture of helplessness. "Maybe Kiki went somewhere else to buy or sell drugs, ran into trouble, went on the attack for some reason. Look . . ." She spun toward him. "I've talked to someone who says that's what happened. He says he had to defend himself. The problem is, I don't have the slightest idea of who he is. No name. No references. Nothing. Just a voice on the phone and . . ." She hesitated a moment. "In the darkness."

"You believe this man killed Kiki?"

"He expects me to work miracles, get Gianelli to agree not to press charges because it was self-defense. He's scared and he's not thinking straight. He's suicidal. I have to find him."

Father John took a moment. He was getting the picture. Whoever the man was, he had chosen to remain anonymous. He had called Vicky and, somehow, managed to see her. And he had reeled her in. He was desperate. "He's Arapaho, isn't he?" Father John said. Vicky would do everything possible to help one of her people.

She gave him a half smile and quickly looked away.

"He'll get back to you," he said, trying to reassure her.

"It will be on his terms. I have to find him first, talk to him face-to-face. It's the only way I can convince him to come forward. Adam . . ." She paused and headed back to the window. "With our firm behind him, he would have strong representation. There's every chance we can see that he's exonerated."

She swung around and walked toward him again. "I figure he must have been part of Kiki's circle. Maybe he dealt him drugs, or maybe Kiki was the dealer. What do you know about Kiki? Who are the people he associated with? The girlfriend, what's her name?" She moved so close that he caught the faint smell of sage in her hair, and the freshness of snow and cold. "What do you know?"

Father John put up the palm of one hand to still the questions in her expression. Then he told her how Kiki had spent a week in Hollywood hoping to find out what happened to Andrew's father back in the 1920s. "Charlie Wallowingbull," he said. "One of the actors in *The Covered Wagon*. After the movie was made, he went to Hollywood to promote it. That was in April 1923, and he never came back to the rez. The family has always believed he was murdered."

Vicky turned her head and stared into space. "My grandfather used to talk about how his father had been in the movies," she said, pulling something new out of her memory. "Arapahos and Shoshones were the real Indians in some of the cowboy-and-Indian films. One time, when I was a kid, he took me to the movie theater in Lander to see one of those old movies. Part of Indian heritage week." She gave a little shrug. "The place was packed with more Indians than came to Lander in an entire year. Everybody was excited. They clapped and cheered when the movie ended. I remember how proud I felt."

She looked back at him. "Could be an excuse Kiki gave the old people. You know, a trip to Hollywood to look up the past."

"Gianelli's working the drug angle," Father John said. "He thinks Kiki went to LA to buy drugs, bring them back to the rez, and cut out the usual distributors. It could have gotten him killed."

Vicky started patrolling the worn carpet again. "So this guy could also be involved in drugs. Even if he was protecting himself against Kiki, if the assault occurred during a drug deal, he would still be looking at serious charges. Purchasing and distributing controlled substances. Maybe felony murder. It explains why he wants to remain anonymous. And why he wants assurances up front from Gianelli before he comes forward."

She stopped pacing and faced him. "What do you think?"

Father John took a moment. It all made sense in a rational, logical way. Kiki's body dumped at the river—a place where drug deals went down, where other drug dealers would find the body. An example of what happens if anyone tries to sidestep the usual way of doing business.

And yet the logic couldn't shake the uncomfortable feeling that had taken hold of him. The sound of Andrew's voice kept running through his head: *He's clean now. Making a new life. He's sorry for messing up, trying to make things right. All a man has is his reputation.*

"According to his grandfather, Kiki was through with drugs," he said. "He was trying to straighten out his life."

A kind of knowing smile came into Vicky's expression, as if she were smiling to herself. "That's the problem with kids like Kiki," she said. "They can always convince the people who love them the most. It works for everyone. The kid can keep dealing drugs and his family can remain in blissful denial. Don't tell me you haven't seen it before."

He had seen it before, he was thinking. He tried to return her smile, but he couldn't shake the discomfort. Something different about Kiki's case. Kiki was trying to *do* something for his grandfather, right a wrong somehow in the past, bring Andrew the truth about his own background, get some kind of justice.

"What's the girlfriend's name?" Vicky said.

Father John leaned over the desk and pulled a pad and pen out of the drawer. He wrote down the name and the address of the little house. "She works at a new nail salon in a strip mall on Federal," he said, tearing off the sheet and handing it to her. The touch was swift, her hand as soft as silk. It was so good to see her again.

"Be careful," he said. "Seems like I've said that to you before." He shook his head and smiled at that. He might have saved his breath. Vicky would do everything she could to help her client. Her own safety? She would think about it later, if she thought about it at all.

He watched her slip the sheet of paper inside her bag and fling the scarf around her neck. She stood still. "How long will you be here?" she said.

Father John spread his hands. "For a while," he said. For a long time, he would have liked to say. But Bill Rutherford would call back.

"It's good to have you here." There was something forced in the words, he thought, as if she had decided it was something she ought to say.

Then she was gone. Boots clacking, the swooshing noise of the front door opening, and the blast of cold air floating through the office before the door thudded shut.

13

1922

"MOVE IN, MOVE in!" James Cruze stomped past, shouting into the black megaphone. Waving an arm at the cameraman behind the rectangular, boxlike camera made of smooth-looking wood—mahogany, perhaps, but William wasn't sure—with brass fittings that gleamed in the sun, a crank on the right side and two reels of film on the top. A round lens protruded like a giant eye from the front. Another lens jutted from the right, above the crank. The cameraman dipped forward and peered with one eye into the side lens. His other eye was wrinkled shut. The camera stood on a tripod, which made it almost the same height as the cameraman. A clicking noise started up, like the noise of a bird leaping about, as he turned the crank.

So many lessons to learn about white men. And now this: the way they melted into their machines, became a single force. All of it—camera, tripod, man—stationed on the carello. Other men stood like guards on each side of the carello, which they pushed back and forth, whatever Cruze said, while the camera remained steady. If the camera moved, William realized, the players would look jerky up on the screen, like jackrabbits jumping about.

"Get the eyes when the old man comes out!" Cruze's voice burst from the megaphone, a force large and deep. A man in a black cowboy hat standing to the side lifted a violin and started playing a fast-paced melody that, William knew, was meant to help the players move quickly about. "Action and emotion in the eyes," Cruze said. William had heard the director say that before, and always the carello had rolled closer to the players, the way it was rolling now toward Fort Bridger.

William was at his place outside the fort with a couple dozen other Indians. Charlie stood a few feet away, looking like he'd missed his best shot at a buffalo and wouldn't eat for a week. "Fort Indians!" Charlie had scoffed last night when Cruze went over to-day's shooting. William had felt the familiar knot tighten in his stomach. Charlie might refuse to play one of the drunken Indians that hung around the forts in the Old Time begging food and whis-key, mostly whiskey. Trading buffalo robes, trading their wives and daughters for whiskey. "So that's what they think of us," Charlie had said.

William had spent most of the evening trying to convince Charlie that it was just a story. An untrue thing. Just like the building that looked like Fort Bridger wasn't true. Yet if William hadn't seen the white men putting up the walls, he would have believed the impossible—that they had moved Fort Bridger from the banks of the Platte River in Wyoming to the Nevada desert. But that was another lesson about white men. There was no limit to what they might do. They had found photographs of the real Fort Bridger and constructed another fort, so true that the buffalo Indians who used to trade at the fort wouldn't have known the difference, if they hadn't seen the imposter rising in front of their eyes.

Except that the untrue fort was nothing more than a single wall with a wooden door in the middle, which made it all the more fantastic because it seemed to be so much more than it was. He'd spent some time yesterday watching the carpenters build a wooden platform behind the wall. And now the platform had been turned into a room at Fort Bridger, with a wooden table, chairs, and narrow beds piled with buffalo robes. Muslin curtains hung on rods at the sides of the room. The cameramen had pulled the curtains this way and that, testing the amount of light and shadow that fell over the platform.

One wall, a platform, open air, and curtains. It wasn't true.

"You don't understand," Charlie had said. "Stories are true. I'm not goin' be a fort Indian."

William had gone to find McCoy. He was in his own tent, light glowing in the canvas, reading a book, a gas lamp on the table. And McCoy had gone running to the Indian camp, long legs stretching out like the legs of a yearling. William had run after him. Any trouble and the Indians would be sent packing. That was the way McCoy had put it.

William had waited outside the tipi, listening to the low rumble of voices. McCoy's voice firm with sympathy. Charlie's voice angry at first and finally sinking into a low mumble. McCoy gave him a nod when he came out, and William knew that McCoy had reminded Charlie that in two weeks they could collect their money, ride to Milford, and board the train. They could go home.

Now Cruze lifted the megaphone to his mouth. "Bridger! Open the door and step out. You've heard the wagons rolling in. You haven't seen white people in months. You're excited and overcome with joy. Let's see excitement and joy in your eyes. Crank 'em!"

The cameraman started turning the crank. The violin music got faster, like the music speeding up at a powwow, and the door at the fort swung open. The old man playing Jim Bridger leaped outside, throwing both hands in the air. A smile stretched across his face, eyes wide with excitement. He stepped forward, bowlegged and stiff-legged at the same time, as if he weren't used to moving about without a horse. The player looked so much like Jim Bridger, Goes-in-Lodge had said when he first saw him, that he was sure the old trader's ghost was walking the earth.

"Good! Good!" The voice blasted out of the megaphone. "Keep moving. You are greeting the emigrants. They've come a long distance, suffered many hardships, and now they will be safe for a time at your fort. Let us see the safety you offer. Cut! Perfect!"

Cruze swung around and waved at the cameraman. The carello rolled backward and the camera swiveled about so that the lens now turned on the wagons lined up in front of the fort. "Emigrants! You are finally at Fort Bridger. You have hungered for the sight of this outpost of civilization for hundreds of miles. You are exhausted from the long trip, yet now you are overcome with joy and relief. Show us the exhaustion and the joy. Eyes! Eyes! Let us see the feelings in your eyes."

The pretty woman with black hair, Molly Wingate in the story, climbed down from a wagon. She looked tired and dusty, shoulders drooped in weariness. He must have been twenty feet away, yet William could see the tears welling in Molly's eyes and the mixture of relief and joy shining through her expression. She lifted her head, drawing from a well of inner strength and started forward.

Cruze shouted, "The eyes. The eyes. You see Indians hanging around the fort. You do not trust them." Molly's eyes became rounded in fear. "The fort is your refuge. You trust only Bridger. Let us see the trust and fear." Molly stumbled past Goes-in-Lodge and two of the other buffalo Indians seated cross-legged around a pile of buffalo robes and threw herself into the arms of the old trader. Shining out of her eyes was a different spirit from the one William had seen at breakfast this morning. She had been Lois Wilson then, relaxed and chatting with the hero, J. William Kerrigan, as they moved down the food table, helping themselves to bacon and eggs and oatmeal.

Kerrigan jumped out of another wagon and went after Molly, but now he was Will Banion, in love with Molly, looking out for her. And yet this morning he had left Lois Wilson at the food table and gone over to eat with Cruze and two of the cameramen. It was the same with the other players, William realized. Shape-shifters, all of them. Jostling one another as they dished up food, sitting in the shade next to a wagon, looking tired and bored. Then shifting into emigrants, weary and determined, frightened and courageous, driving the oxen, walking in clouds of dust next to the wagons.

"Get the wide angle." Cruze walked about, gripping the megaphone and flapping his other arm like a lopsided bird trying to lift off. Another camera stood nearby on a tripod fixed to the ground. The cameraman who had been standing about came to life and hunched over the lens.

Cruze swung back to the fort. "Indians! I need menace, surliness. You are drunk, beaten down. You know your ways have ended. You hate the emigrants who took your lands. Show us the bleary, drunken hatred in your eyes. Whiskey bottles are everywhere. You are drinking out of bottles." He bent his head and peered around. "Where are the bottles?"

McCoy stepped out of the crowd. White cowboy hat pulled forward, shading his face, black shirt sweat-smashed against his back. He walked over to the director. "I thought we settled this." His voice cut through the hush. "Indians went to the forts to trade. Look!" He nodded in the direction of Goes-in-Lodge. "They've brought buffalo robes to show the way they traded."

"The audience wants to see drunken Indians." Cruze waved him off. "Get the whiskey bottles!"

"It will look like Indians were drunks. That isn't the truth."

"What do I care about truth? We give the audience what they want, and they want drunken Indians."

William saw Goes-in-Lodge push himself to his feet. The other buffalo Indians stood up beside him. Straight-backed, all of them, heads high, staring out beyond the line of wagons toward the expanse of brown desert. Then they started walking in the direction of the tipis. The others fell in behind. Two and three at first, and finally groups of Indians walking away. William hung back.

"What the hell is going on?" Cruze's voice was hoarse and strained. "We're not done shooting."

"They were traders," McCoy said. "You've turned them into drunkards."

Cruze started pacing, carving out a wide circle. Little clouds of dust rose around his boots. "All right! All right! Get 'em back here. They can be goddamn traders. But I want some drunks, you understand? The audience expects drunks."

McCoy swung about and hurried after the Indians. William watched him push through the others until he had caught up with Goes-in-Lodge. Hands were flying: McCoy first, then Goes-in-Lodge and some of the other old men. Finally they turned around. It was like watching a herd of buffalo starting back.

"Indians!" Cruze spit out the word. He was still pacing about, muttering something about Indians being more trouble than they were worth. He stopped pacing, lifted the megaphone, and shouted, "Places everyone. We don't have all day."

William moved to his place near the fort and watched the others trailing back and dropping cross-legged onto the ground. A prop man scattered whiskey bottles about. Goes-in-Lodge and the buffalo Indians settled themselves around the pile of buffalo robes. Charlie was standing back. Finally he came toward William. The prop man cut across his path and tried to hand him a whiskey bottle, which Charlie stared at for a moment. Then he took hold of the neck and threw the bottle high into the air. His face was red and puffed. The bottle arced toward the fort and crashed against the wall, making a loud popping noise. Pieces of glass shimmered in the dirt.

"Great!" Cruze shouted. "Get the broken glass. It will look like the Indians had a drunken orgy outside the fort."

William could read the signs that McCoy made toward Goes-in-Lodge. "Two more weeks and you can go home."

An air of resignation dropped over the buffalo Indians, William thought. Hunched over, eyes on the pile of buffalo robes, as if all they cared about was making the trade, bringing food home to their families. They would have looked the same at Fort Bridger in the Old Time. William could feel the truth of it in his bones. He had heard the grandfather stories all his life. How the warriors rode for days, the sun hot on their backs, the packhorses straining and snorting with the weight of the buffalo robes. How they waited in front of the forts to bargain with the white traders and soldiers coming and going. They drove hard bargains, the whites used to say. The old men would laugh at the memory.

Until the last days, when the buffalo were disappearing and the warriors had no robes to trade. Only beaded necklaces and pieces of extra clothing and worn moccasins spread on the hard ground. Finally the warriors had stopped going to the forts. But the fort Indians went, the beggars with no dignity, driven mad by the white man's whiskey and the hunger in their bellies.

William watched Goes-in-Lodge, waiting for the old man's expression to change. He stayed stone-faced. All the buffalo Indians, stone-faced with resignation. It would be up to him and Charlie and the rest of the younger generation, he realized, to show the anger over all that was lost.

William made himself look menacing, crouching alongside Charlie and some of the others, as if they were ready to attack the wagons drawn up at the fort. The violin squealed at a faster tempo. The camera clanked over the sound of boots on the ground, the whoosh of air parting as the players moved about. Molly threw herself again into the arms of the old trader. Will Banion was right behind, hovering over her. The woman he loved. He'd gotten her safely to Fort Bridger.

Then William saw the beautiful white girl, huddled in one of the wagons, cradling a doll that resembled a baby. Her blond curls fell around the folds of the dark shawl pulled about her shoulders. A pioneer woman, crossing the plains, wanting only a new and better life for her child!

William could feel himself changing the way the other players had changed. He was someone else, a warrior in the Old Time with everything slipping away. It was like the vision quest he had made last year. Alone on the cliff, with no food or water, only the little campfire of burning sage. On the third day he had seen a man approaching. The man had shifted into a bear, and he had known that the bear would give him bear's gifts of courage and determination. It was the bear that had been true, not the shape of the man, and William wondered which shape was true for the players. Which shape was true for himself, the friendly, helpful Indian or the menacing warrior waiting for a chance to kill white people?

"Cut!" The director's voice broke through his thoughts. "Indians, that's all for now. Wait by the tables."

William saw that the carello had been moved all the way around the set so that the camera now faced the inside room. One of the cameramen yanked a curtain partway across the rod, and sunshine and shadow striped the room. Cruze yelled something at Bridger and Molly Wingate, who stood near the table. The camera started whirring, then settled into the familiar clacking noise as William started after Goes-in-Lodge and the others. Almost everyone was moving toward the food tables, whites and Indians alike. He could see the plates of donuts, the silver coffee urns.

"Did you see her?" Charlie stepped beside him. "She looked worried."

William kept his eyes straight ahead, not saying anything. He knew who Charlie was talking about.

"They could hurt her."

"They wouldn't do that." William kept his voice beneath his breath so that the others wouldn't hear. He spoke out of the corner of his mouth. "She makes money for them. White people love money. Why would they hurt her?"

"She loves an Indian."

William stopped and faced the man. The other Arapahos and Shoshones flowed past—a few buffalo Indians hurrying to catch up, the younger generation sprinting ahead. Moccasins made a rhythmic scuffing sound against the ground, and little clouds of dust rose around their tanned-hide trousers. "She doesn't love anybody but herself," he said.

William saw Charlie's hands ball into fists. He forced himself to seem relaxed, unconcerned, but inside he felt himself get ready to stop the fists from crashing into his face. Indians fighting on the set. They would all be sent back to the rez without paychecks. "You're different, that's all. She's been amusing herself."

A fist came up then, but William lifted his arm and knocked it back. "Take it easy," he said. "Remember who you are. Arapaho. We came here to do a job. We keep our word."

Charlie seemed to think on this because the fist dropped. He began to relax into himself, shoulders sagging, arms hanging at his sides. "I never met a woman like her," he said. The other Indians were slowing down, staring at them as they passed, and William could see the worry coiled in their eyes.

He said, "They'll probably send her back to Hollywood. McCoy said she's gonna be a player in another movie. She never should've come here." He was thinking that if Mr. Lasky heard about her and Charlie, he would order her back to Hollywood.

"Remember what McCoy told us," he said, but he realized Charlie

wasn't listening. He was looking toward tent city. There she was: floating down the narrow street between rows of tents, the white dress
swaying around her legs as she moved in the direction of the tables.
The sun shone through the curled blond hair that lay over the white
shoulders. The shawl she'd had on was gone. William realized he
was holding his breath. He could never have imagined a creature so
beautiful.

Everyone was staring at her, Indians and whites alike. Time
stopped, then started up again as people twitched back into motion.
The wind blew up a cloud of dust, which made her seem blurred and
out of focus and unreal, as if she existed in a dream.

"She isn't hurt," William heard himself saying, but he knew it
wasn't true. Something about the way she gazed into space a moment
before she thrust a white shoe past the hem of her dress, set one foot
on the ground and propelled herself forward. Then she stopped and
gazed about again before taking the next step.

"She's drunk," William said.

"They must've given her cocaine," Charlie said. "They give her cocaine and Orange Blossoms that are nothing else than gin and ver-
mouth in orange juice, much of it as she wants. They shouldn't give it
to her. I'm gonna tell 'em . . ." He lurched forward.

William grabbed his arm and pulled him back. "Not your business," he said. Out of the corner of his eye, he saw the skinny white
bodyguard burst from the crowd around the tables and run toward
the girl. He grabbed hold of her shoulders and spun her about. She
was staggering, the white shoes sliding over the ground, and for an
instant he thought the white man would let her fall. Let her grovel, the
beautiful white face in the dust. It wasn't right. Still, he grabbed Charlie by the shoulders to hold him in place. But Charlie twisted hard, and
William felt the hard blow of a fist in his chest, the shock of a foot
stomping on his own.

"Stop it!" James was between them, brown arms taking hold of
Charlie.

Past the crowd of Indians and whites, William could see that the girl and the skinny man were gone. The narrow street that divided the tents was empty, as if she had been a ghost that had vanished when the white man appeared.

"She's gone," he said.

Charlie stood still, and James stepped back. William felt his own hands relax on Charlie's shoulders. "Let's get coffee," he said.

14

FATHER JOHN FINISHED the fried chicken and mashed potatoes Elena had left in the oven, washed the dishes, and stacked them in the draining pan. He refilled his coffee mug and walked down the hallway to his study across from the living room, Walks-On scuttling ahead. The dog had already settled onto his rug by the time Father John sat down at the desk. Something deserted about the residence, he thought, with only Walks-On and him rattling around and the silver night bunching at the windows. He missed having an assistant. Even those assistants who had spent most of their days at St. Francis trying to land an assignment somewhere else had been company.

"Just you and me, buddy," he said, patting the dog's soft fur. Walks-On shifted around and licked at his hand.

The house was a bit like the residence in Rome, he thought, a thing of the past, holding on to its place. Except that the residence in Rome had started as a palace, not a two-story house faced with red bricks looking out on a drive that circled through an Indian mission. A palace from the Renaissance, fifteen-foot ceilings with fancy moldings and gold paint peeling from the chandeliers, black-and-white-tiled floors and faded frescos and bellpulls that no longer connected to anything. At least there were three other priests at the residence, a human presence in the corridors in the mornings and evenings. "Have a good day." "Arrivederci." Sometimes, when he was awakened in the middle of the night by the clack of footsteps on tiled floors, he had wondered if it was one of the other priests or a visitor from the Renaissance.

He opened the laptop that Father Ian had left behind. The streetlight outside cast a yellow glare on the monitor. He moved the laptop a little, sipped at his coffee, and waited for the machine to go through its usual gyrations and flashing screens.

All a man has is his reputation. He hadn't been able to get Andrew's words out of his mind. Late this afternoon, at Riverton Memorial, visiting Marcia Nolan in intensive care from a burst appendix and Lewis White Robe going through detox, then back at the office returning phone calls—the old man's voice had been thumping like a drum inside his head.

Illogical in the extreme, as one of his philosophy professors used to say. It made no sense to believe that Kiki Wallowingbull had learned something in Hollywood that had led to his death on the rez. Logic dictated that Kiki had died in some kind of drug feud. Gianelli was working on the drug angle—whoever had beaten Kiki unconscious had left him to die in a place where drug deals came down, an example to anyone else who might break whatever codes existed among drug dealers.

And Vicky went along with Gianelli's theory, and why wouldn't she? Father John closed his eyes a moment, trying to push away the image of her this afternoon. How glad he had been to see her—almost like reconnecting with a part of himself, the part he had left behind when he went to Rome. In the instant she had appeared in the doorway, the world had seemed round again. And yet there was something sad about her, and unforgiving. He had felt as if he were trying to reach her across a great chasm.

He took a drink of coffee, then typed in *The Covered Wagon* and *Arapahos*. A list of websites materialized on the first of twenty pages. He read through the descriptions. *Silent Films. Jesse Lasky—Famous Players. James Cruze, Director. Locations. Western myth in cowboy and Indian movies.* This could take hours. He clicked on to the next page.

And here was something. *Indians Featured in First Epic Western.* He went to the website and watched the advertisements materialize at the side and, finally, the lines of black text from a newspaper dated November 5, 1922:

Three hundred Arapaho and Shoshone Indians from Wyoming and 200 Shoshones from Idaho, along with their tipis and horses, are camped in the desert on the border of Utah and Nevada while they play themselves in The Covered Wagon. *The Indians are among 3,000 people at work on the moving picture. Actors, technicians, carpenters, cameramen, the director, and assistant directors are housed in what is called a "tent city." The Indians have erected their own tipi village nearby. Meals are served in three shifts. "We have created our own metropolis," says James Cruze, the director.*

According to Jesse Lasky, vice president of production of Famous Players–Lasky, The Covered Wagon *will be the first epic Western to capture the hardships of emigrant wagon trains. Marauding Indians intent upon destroying innocent people accounted for much of the hardships. The studio has assembled 500 wagons for scenes depicting the train winding over the vast and barren prairies. So far the $500,000 budget for* The Covered Wagon *has risen to almost $800,000. "The Covered Wagon will be the greatest moving picture ever made," Lasky said.*

"Jimmie Cruze will take his place among Hollywood's most celebrated directors."

One scene features an Indian attack on the 500 wagons camped in a box canyon. The Indians crawled down the rocks wielding their horrible weapons, such as hatchets, spears, and bows and arrows, and emitting bloodcurdling screams to launch the surprise attack. Cameras captured the action and the horrible expressions on the Indians' faces, as well as the fear on the faces of the innocent white emigrants.

Among the Indians are "buffalo Indians," old men from the time the tribes survived by hunting buffalo and attacking white wagon trains. "Filming this picture brings back their old memories," Lasky said.

Col. Tim McCoy, a rancher who served in the Great War, rounded up the Indians and convinced them to play themselves in the movie. "The colonel drove a hard bargain," Lasky explained. "Indians get paid $5.00 per day, same as white players. They get extra pay for the horses and tipis."

Father John drained the last of his coffee and read through the next paragraphs:

The filming has taken place in all kinds of weather from blistering sun to snow and blizzards. Dust raised by hundreds of oxen, horses, and the covered wagons lay over the entire location. Lasky said that the cameramen film through the dust, which adds a sense of authenticity.

Premiere of The Covered Wagon *will be April 10 at Grauman's Egyptian Theatre in Hollywood. Some of the Indians will be on hand to help promote the film.*

Father John read through the last sentence again. Charlie Wallowingbull had been among the Arapahos and Shoshones in Hollywood.

An Indian, running into some kind of trouble, stepping on someone's toes, disappearing. There was logic here after all, he thought. The disdain and prejudice toward Indians at the time seeped through the article like a bad odor.

He went back to the list of websites. On the fourth page, he found a site with Arapahos in bold letters and clicked on it.

Col. Tim McCoy enlisted his friends, the Arapahos, for the movie The Covered Wagon *in 1922. McCoy later went on to become a major Western actor who starred in more than a hundred films. Many of the Indians he had recruited for* The Covered Wagon *appeared with him in subsequent films, including* Spoilers of the West *and* End of the Trail.

The silent so-called cowboy-and-Indian films solidified the Western myth for Americans. Cowboys were seen as lone champions of civilization bringing decency and law into a primitive society. Indians were cast in roles of ferocious savages intent upon killing whites and, by extension, civilization itself. Little attempt was made to present the Indian view that they had the right to protect their lands and way of life from the encroaching wagon trains. Yet the Indian actors were willing to play such roles for the money and food they received, much needed on the reservations of the 1920s.

Father John closed the site and perused the rest of the list. Nothing to suggest what may have happened to an Arapaho in Hollywood in the spring of 1923. Except the prejudice that existed, the stereotypical views of savage Indians, and the fact that the movies were more real than life and that most Americans had encountered Indians only in the movies. The thought sent a chill along his spine. Anything might have happened to Charlie Wallowingbull.

He typed in *Grauman's Egyptian Theatre, The Covered Wagon premiere*. Another list of websites, shorter this time but all of them looked interesting. He opened one of the sites and read that Tim McCoy and fifty Arapahos and Shoshones had put on a show with Indian dances, drums, and demonstrations of roping and sign language every evening before the movie was shown at Grauman's Egyptian Theatre. The Indian show took place for eight months.

A small photo on the website showed the lobby bill for the performances. Black type splashed over the images of Indians in feathered headdresses and beaded shirts and dresses: *Real Indians present authentic Indian culture. Ancient dances and songs. See Indians "talk" sign language.*

The Indian show was a hit, according to the website, helping to turn *The Covered Wagon* into one of Hollywood's most successful films of the 1920s. A decade later, the film was still ranked among the top five movies in earnings.

Father John navigated to another site, and this was what he wanted, a photo of the Arapahos and Shoshones who had gone to Hollywood. Most were wrapped in blankets. A few wore feathered headdresses. They all wore moccasins. They stood huddled together, staring without expression into the camera, except for three young men standing a little apart on the right. It looked like Goes-in-Lodge in the center, the reserved place of honor for the leading man. He didn't recognize anyone else. There were no identifications.

He studied the three young men on the right. Possibly Charlie Wallowingbull, William Thunder, and James Painted Brush. It was logical—three friends, standing apart.

"What happened to you, Charlie?" he said out loud. The sound of his voice came back to him out of the silence in the house.

ELEVEN PARISHIONERS AT Mass this morning, scattered about the pews, kneeling, hands clasped over the top of the next pew, jackets unzipped. Old faces and old friends, Father John thought. He had offered the Mass for the soul of Kiki Wallowingbull, and everyone had nodded.

Most of the old people who regularly came to daily Mass—pickups banking around Circle Drive in fantails of snow, headlights blinking in the gray light—would be praying for Kiki anyway. The same generation as Andrew and Mamie, mourning their own losses through the years.

He lifted the chalice for the consecration: *Take this and eat. This is my body.* He held the chalice over the altar, then genuflected. This was always the moment that brought him to himself, the heart of the matter, the reason he had become a priest. He had fought against a vocation. Two, three years spent fighting. The priesthood? It was not his plan. His plan was a doctorate in American history, a teaching position at a small New England college, a wife, and a bunch of kids. His life had stretched in front of him, content and fulfilled.

But always this moment at Mass: *This is My Body. You are not alone. I am with you.*

He had finally accepted that there was another plan for him, one he had known nothing about and never would have chosen. Working at an Indian mission that he had never heard of, with people he hadn't known anything about before he had arrived almost ten years ago. Odd how the mission had become his home, the people his family. We go in the way we know not, St. John of the Cross had said.

This is my blood. He lifted the chalice of grape juice that recovering alcoholic priests consecrated in the place of wine and took a sip. *Do this in memory of me.* Black heads bowed and nodded over the pews. The quiet of early morning invaded the church. He prayed silently: *Have mercy on Kiki's soul.*

THE ODORS OF hot bacon and fresh coffee filled the entry as Father John let himself into the residence. Walks-On came running down the hallway. He patted the dog's head, hung his jacket on the coat tree, and went into the study where he found the photograph he had printed out last night sitting on top of a pile of papers, dark faces staring out of the past. He followed Walks-On back to the kitchen where Elena was at the stove turning strips of bacon, humming softly to herself. Strands of her short, gray hair sprang free from the beaded barrettes she had inserted in the back. She stopped humming and, without glancing around, said, "Help yourself to coffee."

He filled a mug, poured in enough milk to turn the coffee a caramel color and took a chair at the round table in the center of the kitchen. The *Gazette* lay folded next to a knife and fork. He pushed the newspaper aside and smoothed out the photo.

"What's this?" Elena set down a plate of bacon, fried eggs, and toast.

"I was hoping you could help me," he said, sliding the photo in her direction. Elena dropped onto a chair, picked up the photo, and held it close to her face.

"Some of the old Indians that were in the movies," she said.

He told her it was a photo of the Indians who had spent eight months in Hollywood promoting *The Covered Wagon.*

She nodded. "I heard about that. Lived in tipis up in a canyon. Rode ponies to Hollywood every night. Made good money, I heard." She spun the photo across the table. "This about Kiki going off to Hollywood?"

Father John gave her a little smile, took a bite of egg and bacon, and washed it down with coffee. "You must be reading my mind."

"Kiki got himself killed here 'cause of what he was up to. Selling drugs to his own people. Trouble is, Andrew won't ever accept the truth, so he says Kiki must've gotten killed 'cause of something in Hollywood, just like his father. Only everybody knows that his father ran off and left everything behind. The rez wasn't good enough for him once he got a taste of Hollywood ways."

She leaned forward and bit at her lower lip a moment. "I wasn't gonna say anything, 'cause you shouldn't say bad things about the dead." She glanced across the kitchen, a mixture of sympathy and disapproval working through her expression. "You know the way grown-ups talk, then shut up when they see the kids? Well, I heard my father talking with some of the old men that went to the movies. They said that Charlie Wallowingbull didn't know his place. Come close to getting all of them fired and sent home. They said he got mixed up with one of them white women. A big star, I guess. Somebody no Indian had any right to fool around with."

"What was her name?"

Elena lifted both shoulders in a weary shrug. "Just some movie actress. I don't remember her name."

"Did they say what happened to Charlie?"

"Up and left one day. That's what I heard. Andrew should just leave it alone, and so should you. Won't get you nowhere, stirring up a lot of painful memories."

Father John took another bite of toast and egg. Mixed up with a white woman, he was thinking. No Indian had that kind of right. Then it occurred to him that Charlie might have run off with the white woman. He dismissed the notion. If she were an actress, there probably would have been a lot of publicity and everyone would have known what happened to Charlie.

Then a new thought crept like a shadow at the edge of his mind: What if there had been publicity? Articles in the movie magazines of the time, mentions in the gossip columns. It wouldn't have been something the Arapahos would have talked about; it would have been hushed up, everyone trying to protect Anna Wallowingbull. Better to let her think Charlie had just walked away alone. Sometime today he would try to find a couple of minutes to check the internet again.

He pushed the photo toward her. "Recognize any faces?" he said.

"Goes-in-Lodge." Elena set an index finger on the figure in the center. "Those three over here"—she moved her finger to the side—"I'd say Charlie's one of 'em. The other two are probably William Thunder and James Painted Brush. I heard they was real close."

"Any idea who Kiki might have talked to on the rez?" he said.

Elena had gotten to her feet and was leaning over, refilling his coffee. She had the same look that came over his mother when she was running out of patience with him. She turned her back on him and jammed the coffeepot into the brewer. "You think he was going around pestering people about what happened to his great-grandfather way back then?"

"Arapahos have long memories." Father John ate the last bite of eggs and took another drink of coffee.

She had turned around and was smiling at him—the kind of I-give-up smile his mother broke into when he had finally worn her down. He half-expected Elena to throw both hands into the air. "All the same, folks wouldn't've liked getting asked about stuff that happened before they got born. If Kiki bothered them, nobody's talking about it. Now that he got himself killed, nobody wants the fed out on the stoop every time they open the front door, asking a lot of useless questions."

Father John tapped his index finger on the images of the three young men. "Kiki might have gone to see some of Thunder's or Painted Brush's descendants. Any idea of who might have been willing to talk to him?"

"No Thunder descendants around here." Elena sat down and peered at the photo again. "Thunder family left the rez a long time ago. They're Oklahoma Indians now." She chewed at her lower lip a moment. "I heard somebody named JoEllen Redman is living around here. She's supposed to be a Thunder, but I never met her. Never comes to the get-togethers or celebrations. But there's dozens of that Painted Brush clan. No telling which ones Kiki might've bothered." She pushed the photo his way. "You ask me, the only one that might've heard anything is Ella Morningstar. If I was looking for one of my ancestors, I'd go see her. Makes it her business to know everything about everybody."

Father John got to his feet. "Would you mind putting out the word on the moccasin telegraph that I'd like to talk to JoEllen Redman?" he asked.

She shrugged. "Won't do any good if she don't wanna talk to you."

"Thanks," he said. She would get the word out anyway. He picked up the photo and looked at the image of the elderly Goes-in-Lodge, the man everyone else would look up to, even confide in. He folded the photo and slipped it inside his shirt pocket. Then he thanked Elena and headed down the hallway. He knew Ella Morningstar. She was a descendant of Goes-in-Lodge.

15

IT WAS MID-AFTERNOON—the temperature a frigid twenty-eight degrees, the sky a gunmetal gray, and snow drifting down—before Vicky left the office. They had spent the morning, she and Adam, working on the tribal water case. The water consortium had asked the court for an injunction to prohibit the tribes from selling water to Riverton until the civil case could be heard. All of which meant more documents requesting that the injunction not be granted and reams of paper to protect the rights of the Arapahos and Shoshones to sell or giveaway or do whatever they wished with the water resources on their own reservation.

And Adam's calm demeanor, the firm set of his jaw, steadying her somehow, as they had worked out the wording in the documents he would file this afternoon. This was what they did best—he hadn't expressed the thought, but she could see it moving behind his eyes. This was the kind of case that mattered.

The pickup ahead belched black smoke that lay like an oil slick over the snow on Rendezvous Road, the rear wheels spitting back clouds of snow that splattered the Jeep's windshield. Vicky peered past the wipers and followed the pickup onto Seventeen-Mile Road, past the sign breaking out of the gray light—St. Francis Mission—past the white spire of the church floating among the bare branches of the cottonwoods, past the cemetery.

At the intersection with Highway 789, the pickup turned south and Vicky drove north toward Riverton. Trailer parks, warehouses, and garages flickered past the windows, her thoughts on John O'Malley. He was the way she had remembered, as if six months had melted away and he had never left the rez, never gone to Rome. But it was August then, and now it was winter, and everything had changed. Still, she was so glad he was back. She could be glad for a little while, she told herself. Later, when he left again, she would have to figure out how to be.

She fit the Jeep into the traffic along Federal, passing a truck with a horse trailer that swayed behind, her eyes searching both sides of the street for a nail salon. There were a number of salons. She wasn't sure which one was new. It could take a while to find the salon where a girl named Dede worked. A strip mall stretched ahead on the left, and she slowed down to read the small sign close to the curb: Pizza, Coffee Shop, Beauty Products, Star Nails. A banner that said New was plastered next to Star Nails. She pulled into the turn lane, waited for three oncoming cars to pass, then turned into the parking lot. It took a moment before she spotted the small shop with a neon-lit star on the plate-glass window. Above the star, in large black letters, was the word Nails. She took a vacant place in front and made her way through the falling snow across the sidewalk that had been shoveled to a thin layer of ice.

The nail salon was a narrow slot fitted between a take-out pizza shop and a shoe repair shop. Inside the odors of hot cheese and spicy tomato sauce mixed with the faint chemical odors of leather and fingernail polish. A glass-fronted counter divided the small entry from the series of stations that ran down one side all the way to the back. Two women with gray hair and sparkling rings sat at the middle stations, hands flattened on white towels. Hunched toward them, stroking red polish on their nails, were two girls who looked about eighteen with big, blond hair, tight tee shirts, and dangly earrings. One of the girls was chewing gum.

Vicky had the feeling that they hadn't heard her come in, or if they had, they chose not to acknowledge her presence. Finally the girl with the gum looked up, red lips parting in a practiced smile: "Be with you in a few minutes. Pick out your color." She nodded toward the rack of polishes on the wall next to the counter.

"I'm looking for Dede," Vicky said.

Both girls stopped polishing and stared at her long enough for the gray-haired women to look around, annoyance creeping into their features.

"Babs!" the girl with chewing gum shouted. The other girl concentrated on the polishing task.

"Babs! Somebody here about Dede."

A rustling noise came from the back, followed by the sound of a chair scraping a hard floor. A door flung open. An older woman, probably in her fifties, trim and fit-looking in blue jeans and white shirt with stylishly cut dark hair and the air of "manager" about her came down the line of stations. Her cowboy boots rapped out a sharp staccato on the floor.

"You looking for Dede?" Pinned to the woman's blouse was an orange badge with *Babs* scribbled in thick black ink. "Haven't seen her in three days. Leaves me with just two girls. No thank-you, no see-you-around, just doesn't show up. Like she dropped off the face of the earth. Who are you? A bill collector?"

"I'm an attorney," Vicky said. She pulled a business card out of her bag and pushed it across the glass countertop. "Vicky Holden."

"Jesus." The woman stared at the card a moment. "So she is in trouble. What happened to her? Is she dead?"

"What makes you say that?"

"Wouldn't surprise me," the woman hurried on. "Kind of jerks she hangs around with. Boyfriend got himself killed. A prize jerk, you ask me. Somebody had it in for him." She gave a halfhearted shrug at the inevitability of it all. "You hang around with guys like that and you could end up dead, too. That's my opinion."

"You try calling her?"

"Oh, yeah. Left four or five messages. Basically, I said, 'Dede, where are you? Got appointments waiting here.' Never heard from her. Thanks I get for taking her on when we opened up. I should've known by the looks of her that she was gonna be trouble."

"What's her number?" Vicky said.

The woman pulled a long face and stared at Vicky a moment through narrowed eyes. "I don't know about giving out numbers to anybody that walks through the door."

"I understand," Vicky said, "but if Dede's in trouble, I might be able to help her."

Babs turned sideways and ran her glance over the bottles of polish sitting in the wall cabinet. Long orange fingernails tapped out a nervous rhythm on the glass countertop. "Hold on," she said finally.

She walked back to one of the vacant desks, picked up a cell, and tapped a couple of keys. Then she jotted something on a notepad, tore off the page and walked back. "Don't tell her where you got this, okay?"

VICKY PRESSED THE keys on her own cell, her fingers stiffening in the frigid air trapped inside the Jeep. The buzzing noise sounded far away. She held her breath. There was a chance the girl would answer, and Vicky would introduce herself, say she was trying to find someone who knew Kiki. *The man who killed him.* Could she meet her someplace?

The girl's voice was at the other end, high-pitched and rapid: "Hi.

Sorry I can't talk right now. It's partying time! Leave your name if you want and stay cool."

"This is Vicky Holden," Vicky said. "You don't know me." Then she launched into the rest of it and left her cell number and the office address. She doubted Dede would find her at the top of the steel-and-glass staircase on the second floor of the modern building in Lander.

She turned on the ignition and glanced at the clock: 4:12 blinked red on the dashboard. The manager didn't say she had gone to Dede's place to look for her. A few phone calls had been all. If Dede were home, she would have answered the phone. But that wasn't necessarily true. There were evenings and weekends in the apartment when she tried to let the calls go to the answering machine, wanting time away from the voices on the other end, pleading for help. *My boy got arrested last night. He's in the Fremont County jail. DUI. Can you help us?* But it never worked, because she always found herself listening to the messages, calling Roger and passing them on. Those were the clients he handled now.

She backed out of the spot and drove across the parking lot onto Federal. The snow made a crunching noise under the tires. A half dozen blocks, and she turned right into a residential neighborhood and headed toward Adams Street and the address that Father John had written down for her.

She spotted the small white house as she came down the block, tucked in close to a two-story frame house with a flat front and sloping porch and blinds slantwise in the windows. A farmhouse, most likely, left over from the early 1900s when white people moved onto plots of land surrounded by the reservation and proclaimed the new town of Riverton. The plots were larger then, little farms with barns and outbuildings. The house looked like one of the outbuildings.

There was a cut in the curb that, she supposed, led to some kind of driveway, but it was hard to tell. The snow was undisturbed, as if it had been painted on. There were no signs of tire marks or footprints, no sign of life.

Vicky parked the Jeep close to the curb and made her own trail through the snow, hard and crusted like concrete starting to set up. Little mounds of snow and ridges of ice covered the small stoop at the front door that was painted blue. She was about to knock when she realized that the door was open a half inch. She pushed it in a little further and leaned close. "Dede?" she called. "Are you here? It's Vicky Holden."

There were no sounds, nothing but the kind of echoing silence of a vacuum. "Dede?" she called again, her own voice coming back to her, strange and muffled sounding. She felt herself shivering involuntarily against the cold air that worked its way past her coat. Who would leave the door ajar in the winter? Unless the girl had left in a hurry, packed up and moved on somewhere after Kiki was killed, running out without bothering to pull the door tightly shut behind her.

Vicky turned around and surveyed the neighborhood, the vacant-looking farmhouse and, behind the pickups and sedans parked at the curb across the street, a row of small frame houses painted in fading pastels. She started back through the snow, stomping her boots into the depressions she had just made. Someone who might know Dede's whereabouts could be inside the farmhouse or one of the other houses.

She stopped halfway across the yard, another thought pounding in her head. If Gianelli was right and Kiki had been killed over drugs, then Dede could have gotten caught up in the same trouble. *You hang around with guys like that*—Babs's words jammed her thoughts—*you could end up dead, too.*

She swung around and retraced her steps. Across the yard and onto the stoop, stomping her boots to knock off the snow before she pushed the door open and stepped inside. "Dede?" she called again, but there was no answer. There was something about a house that was bereft of any living presence, the air totally still without any disturbance of breath. From somewhere deep inside came the faintest sound of water dripping. Dark curtains had been pulled across the window, but the faint gray light from outside floated past and ran through the shadows in the small, boxlike living room. She gripped the doorknob hard, keeping the door open while she patted the wall with her other hand. Her fingers found a protruding lever that she pushed. A lamp across the room sputtered into life.

The place had been ransacked. Sofa overturned, chairs tossed about, cushions ripped open, and trails of white cotton stuffing littering the floor. Posters had been pulled from the walls—strips of heavy paper dangled like curled ribbons. Half the face of a cowboy in a white hat and black shirt, flashing half of a smile, like a gargoyle. The name *McCoy* stood out in white letters over the hat. *Winners of the Wilderness* appeared below broken words: *Metro Goldw present.*

Vicky picked her way across the room to a doorway that led to the narrow kitchen in the back. Drawers had been pulled out and tossed about the floor among a scattering of utensils and broken dishes, a couple of dented-looking pans. Still no sign of life. In the hallway on the left, she found another light switch, but nothing happened when she clicked it. The hallway stretched ahead into shadows, a faint gray light coming through the pair of doors opened across from one another. She made herself walk toward the doors. She pushed in the door on the right and glanced about the bathroom. Drawers on the floor, broken bottles and jars thrown about, a black razor standing upright on the counter. Water dripped in a steady pulse out of the sink faucet.

She stepped backward and looked past the door across the hallway. A bedroom that might have been smashed by a truck. The dresser lay facedown, nails popping out of the back, shiny in the wave of gray light from the window. Curtains that had been torn from the rod lay on the floor in a heap. Everywhere jeans, tee shirts, high heels and cowboy boots, broken bottles, and papers. The bed sank sideways; the mattress had been stripped. A mound of blankets and pillows on top.

Then she saw it. The small silver and turquoise ring that looked as if it had slipped off a finger. It lay beside the mound of clothes, and the mound, she realized, was the shape of a body.

God. God. God. She backed out of the room and started running . . . down the hallway, across the living room, stumbling over a cushion, righting herself against a toppled chair, and lurching through the door. She slipped in the snow and went down on her hands and knees. Snow stung her hands inside her gloves and gathered in her boots. She pushed herself to her feet, wincing at the pain in her knees, and ran for the Jeep. She had to clamp her jaws together to stifle the scream erupting in her throat.

Then she was behind the steering wheel, unsure of how she had gotten there—when had she found the key in her bag, pressed the unlock button? She locked the doors and fumbled in her bag for her cell. Shivering now, her teeth chattering in the quiet, she managed to press 911.

"What is your emergency?" The operator's voice sounded calm and experienced. "Hello? Are you there?"

"I think a woman is dead," Vicky managed.

"Where? Where are you?"

"The white house at the corner of Adams. She's dead inside."

"Your name?"

"My name?" God, what did it matter? A girl named Dede was dead! "Vicky Holden," she said.

"Wait where you are. Officers are on the way."

She managed to tell the operator that she would wait.

VICKY WATCHED THE Riverton police car framed in the side-view mirror as it pulled into the curb behind her. She had started the engine after she'd hung up, and the wipers cleared half-moons through the snow piling on the windshield. Warmth poured out of the vents. Still she felt chilled to the bone and disoriented. The occasional vehicle that had driven past, thrashing through the snow, the sound of engines whining on a side street, the smoke curling past the gray-tiled roof down the block—all of it seemed unreal, disconnected to the terrible reality of a dead girl inside the house.

She rolled down her window and waited for two officers—bulky blue jackets zipped to their chins, holstered guns and clubs and mace attached to the black belts on their trousers—to walk up. "You made the call about a dead woman?" One of the officers leaned toward the opened window. Thick gloved hands wrapped over the edge. Vicky was aware of the other officer stationing himself outside the passenger door.

"Inside," she said. "I think she's on the bed."

"Your name?"

"Vicky Holden. I'm an attorney."

The officer nodded, as if he had placed her. "You saw the body?"

Vicky tightened her hands over the steering wheel and tried to still the tremors moving through her. "No," she said. "The house is ransacked and it looks as if . . ." She stopped herself, struggling to place the thoughts in a logical order. "I think there might be a body under the piles of clothes and blankets on the bed."

"Wait here," the officer said. He walked around the back of the Jeep, then both officers stomped through the snow toward the front door still flung wide open, the way she had left it.

She rolled up the window and made herself look straight ahead past the wipers. She didn't know the girl named Dede; she had never met her. Just a girl mixed up with the wrong kind of guys, and now she could be dead. The man who had killed Kiki—oh, God, her client—could have come for the girl. She pressed her gloved fist against her mouth to stop herself from crying. Her own daughter, Susan, was like that—just a girl who might meet anyone, might get into a crowd that included drug addicts and dealers. Not knowing, not realizing the dangers. She made up her mind that she would call Susan tonight. She would go to visit her soon, just as soon as she could get away.

She realized both officers were looming outside her window, and she rolled it down, wondering when they had come out of the house. "What made you think there was a body on the bed?" The first officer leaned in close. She could see black stubble on his thick chin.

Vicky shifted around, but before she could say anything, he went on: "Whatever you thought, there's no one inside, dead or alive. We checked everywhere. It's a small house, no place to hide."

Vicky felt herself begin to breathe, and she realized her breath had been stopped like a plug in her chest. "It looked like a body," she said, trying to keep her voice steady. "Buried under the blankets and clothes on the bed." None of this was making sense. She could hear the inadequacy of it in her own voice. What she had seen was the ransacked house and the body-shaped mound and the turquoise ring and she had panicked. A lawyer, trained not to panic. Trained to look at the facts in a dispassionate, considered manner and arrive at logical conclusions. At the least, she might have lifted a corner of a blanket to verify her suspicions.

She heard herself explaining—stumbling on—about how she had feared the worst when she'd seen the ring, as if it had slipped off a finger. "Her boyfriend was killed four nights ago," she said.

"You talking about the Arapaho found at the Little Wind River?"

Vicky nodded. "All I know is that the girl's name is Dede," she said, answering the questions in the officer's eyes. "I've never met her. I came here to ask her about Kiki." A thick black eyebrow shot up, the only disturbance in the officer's face, and she hurried on, "I'm doing some investigating on behalf of someone."

He stared at her a moment, then threw a sideways glance at his partner. She might as well have thrust an end-of-the-road sign in front of him—No Outlet, or Don't Proceed from Here. In the masks they pulled over their faces, she understood they had understood the rest of it, the part she hadn't said: ". . . investigating on behalf of someone who could be involved in the death of Kiki Wallowingbull."

"How'd you know where she lived?" the officer said, stepping onto neutral ground.

Vicky told him she had talked to the manager at Star Nails where Dede worked. "She hasn't shown up in three days."

The officer lifted himself upright and stared back at the house. "The girl could be in trouble, judging by the look of the house. Drug dealers like to mess up places when they're looking for somebody. People they go after usually end up dead. We're gonna want to find her fast."

The other officer hadn't taken his eyes from her. "Call us if you hear anything about her. Seems to me you lawyers . . ." He shook his head a moment. ". . . oughtta be able to find a way to keep a girl from ending up dead without compromising any clients."

"I'll do what I can," Vicky told him. She was free to go, she knew. There was nothing else she could say, nothing else she *knew*. God. She didn't even know the name of the client the officers assumed she was protecting.

She moved the gear stick into drive and pulled away from the curb, watching the officers receding in the side-view mirror until, by the time she had reached the next block, they were gone.

16

THE WINTER DUSK must have been gathering for the last hour, Vicky realized, because darkness had fallen like a blanket when she pulled into the spot in front of Star Nails where she had parked earlier. The Jeep's headlights floated in the plate-glass window. Past the window, the salon was enveloped in end-of-the-day shadows broken by the globes of light that hung over two stations. Chewing-gum girl, still seated at the nearest station, looked up from the outstretched hands of a client and blinked at the headlights. Then she was on her feet, dodging the front counter, lurching for the front door. She took hold of the sign with black letters that said Open and turned it around so that it read Closed. Then she retraced her steps and sank into the chair across from the customer. She was shaking her head.

There was no sign of Babs or the other technician, but a pencil of light stood at the base of the door where Babs had emerged earlier. Chances were the manager was still in the salon, and the globe shining over the vacant station meant that the other technician might also be there.

Vicky switched off the headlights. She left the engine running, the warm air purring in the vents. There had been light, intermittent snow all day, and now the snow was getting heavier, just like the forecast she had heard on the radio this morning. There would be blizzard conditions tonight.

She clapped her gloved hands together, making a series of muffled thuds in the quiet. She still felt on edge, as if she had found herself on the top of a steep precipice with nothing to hold on to. Waves of relief that a girl named Dede was still alive alternated with waves of dread that someone had come looking for her. And whoever it was had trashed her house. A sign of what he would do to her.

Inside, the door to Babs's office opened and the other technician stepped out. Gripping the doorknob, leaning back a moment, her other hand waving away some kind of objection. She wore a red coat that fell to her knees. A slice of white stockings showed between the edge of the coat and the top of long black boots. Hanging off one shoulder was a large black bag the size of a shopping bag. She smiled, pulled the door shut, and gave the finger to the door.

Then she headed toward the front, saying something to the other technician, who nodded without looking up. Slowing down a little—blond hair sprayed over the shoulders of the red coat—she leaned sideways as she passed her station and flipped off the dangling light. Another few steps and she was past the counter and letting herself outside. Vicky could hear the tinkling noise of the bell as the door opened and closed.

She got out of the Jeep, which seemed to startle the girl, who stepped backward. For an instant, Vicky thought she might dart back inside, but instead she pulled the black bag around in front and began digging for something. "Salon's closed," she said.

"I want to talk to you about Dede," Vicky said.

"You heard what Babs said. Dede hasn't come to work for a while. I gotta go." She put her head down and started walking past the neon words blazing in the plate-glass window: Best Pizza in Town.

"Dede's in trouble. You're her friend, aren't you?" Vicky stayed in step beside the girl. "What's your name?" she said.

The girl stopped and turned toward her. They were in front of a dry cleaner, closed for the day, the window a black sheet speckled with snow. The girl's breath hung like a little cloud between them before she said, "I don't know anything, so leave me alone."

She shrugged away and started walking again. Vicky caught up. "I went to Dede's place. Somebody trashed it pretty bad. You know that her boyfriend was killed. I think whoever did it is looking for Dede."

The girl sprinted forward, crossed in front of Vicky and headed toward a maroon-colored pickup. Vicky stood on the sidewalk and watched her jab the key into the lock and yank open the door. "Leave me alone," the girl shouted.

"She's in danger," Vicky said. "The man that trashed her house will find her eventually, and he will kill her."

The girl threw herself behind the steering wheel and started the motor. A couple of seconds passed before the motor coughed and sputtered into life. She was reaching for the door when Vicky said, "He'll come for you first, as soon as he figures out that you and Dede are friends. How long do you think it will take him? It didn't take me very long."

The girl held the door open. She was hunched over, staring at the dashboard, a gloved hand tightening over the door handle.

Vicky stepped off the curb and moved around the open door. "Tell me where she is," she said.

"I don't want nothing to do with any of this," the girl said. "I never asked her to dump her troubles on me. None of my business. Month ago, I never heard of Dede Michaels. So we worked together, so what? Sure, we went out sometimes, had a few drinks and some laughs at the bars. That's how she met Kiki Wallowingbull. I don't know why she got mixed up with that Indian. I told her it wasn't gonna come to any good, but did she listen? Hell no. Then she comes running to me, crying, wanting a place to stay. Needs protection, she says, and I said, protection from what, and she says, the guys that killed Kiki."

She lifted her head and gave Vicky a sideways look. The lines of moisture at the corners of her eyes shone black in the dim glow of the dashboard lights. "You can follow me," she said.

FATHER JOHN TURNED off Seventeen-Mile Road and drove past the sign that leaned into the darkness and falling snow: Goes-in-Lodge Road. He stared past the wipers. The whole area had once been the site of Goes-in-Lodge's camp, he knew, and some of his descendants still lived in the houses set back from the road, holding on to a small part of the land that had belonged to the family. It was easy to imagine what the area had looked like a hundred years ago—circles of tipis with flaps facing east and campfires burning in front, kids yelling and running about and dogs yapping. Horses out in the corrals behind the tipis. The Wind River rushing past the northern edge of the camp.

He had heard the stories from the elders—so many stories of when the people had first come to the rez. At the convergence of two roads— the red road and the white road—knowing they must follow the white road. "We were traveling people," old man Walking Bear had said, "and we had to settle down. We was hunters, and we had to learn to get our food out of the ground. We spoke Arapaho, and we had to learn English words and write them down in little books that we was supposed to read. We lived in tipis, and we was told to live in wood boxes." But some of the old buffalo Indians, Walking Bear said, refused to coop themselves up like chickens in boxes. So they put their ponies in the boxes and went on living in tipis. For many years, they kept their camps, same as in the Old Time, with family all around and everybody living in tipis.

Father John tried to stay in the tracks that cut through the snow.

He could feel the snow pushing against the tires. Lights glowed in the windows of most of the houses, and yellow cones of light lay over the snowy fields. The sky had turned the blue-gray color of steel. Apart from the thumping noise of the tires and the whine of the engine, a soft quiet enveloped the whole area. He had the sense that he was moving toward the edge of the world. So different from Rome, pedestrians everywhere yelling into cell phones, motorbikes revving up and squealing, cars spurting past, horns honking. The noise even managed to penetrate the thick stone walls of the former palace. And in the Vatican Library, the background noise of the city had floated over the voices of the missionary priests discussing ways to incorporate Christianity into ancient spiritual beliefs.

It was at the St. Ignatius church where he found the quiet he had gotten used to on the reservation. Sometimes in the late afternoon he would find himself in the church, he and a few elderly women scattered here and there, rosary beads tangled in their gnarled fingers, the stone columns rising overhead and the outdoor noises muffled and far away. He would pray for his parishioners at St. Francis, the old people, the younger generation, the kids. And he prayed for himself, for the strength and the courage to let them go. Then, almost four weeks ago, he had gotten a call from the provincial. Father Ian would be leaving St. Francis for a mission in Guatemala. Would Father John be interested in returning for an indeterminate length of time—however long it might take to find a permanent pastor? Of course he was interested. Strange the unexpected ways prayers were answered.

He would not have to let the people go, not yet.

The yellow, blocklike house loomed out of the falling snow. Lights shone in the front windows. The driveway had been plowed, and tire tracks ran to a small shed at the back. He could see Ella Morningstar moving about the kitchen as he drove up the driveway. He stopped close to the house and left the pickup running. She would have seen the headlights and heard the engine and the tires on the hard-packed snow. She would do whatever she wanted to get ready for a visitor. It was a couple of minutes before the door opened and Ella leaned out, waving him inside.

"ALL OF A sudden, everybody wants to talk about when Arapahos and Shoshones were in the movies." Ella Morningstar was a small woman with gray hair parted in the middle and caught into thick braids that ran over the front of her white sweater, a grandmother with children older than Father John. She had small brown eyes that lit up when she talked and reddish hands that fluttered over the table. "Kiki Wallowingbull came around a couple times asking for my grandfather's stories. He was real interested, wanted to find out about his own family. Poor guy." She shook her head slowly.

"When was Kiki here?" Father John took a spoonful from the bowl of hot stew she had set in front of him. Aromas of coffee and simmered potatoes, carrots, and beef and hot fry bread had hit him the minute he stepped into the living room. She had taken his jacket and hung it over a straight-back chair, then motioned him to the kitchen. She had figured he would need some hot food, she told him, so she had warmed up the stew, fried a little bread, and put on a fresh pot of coffee after he called and asked if he could stop by.

"A few days before he got killed." Ella took a bite of stew and chewed slowly, her eyes contemplating the bowl in front of her for a long moment. "I think he was trying to turn his life around. It's a good sign, young people getting interested in the past. Means they're starting to care about where they came from, the kind of people the ancestors were. Helps them get a hold on their own lives. He died too soon."

Father John cut a piece of beef with his fork. The beef fell into pieces. He mixed the beef with pieces of potato and carrot and took a bite. Somehow he had missed that part of it, he was thinking. Kiki had said he wanted the truth for his grandfather—a gift for Andrew, a kind of plea for redemption. But Kiki had also wanted the truth for himself, as if what happened to his great-grandfather would open the way to understanding his own life.

He realized that Ella had said something else about Kiki asking for the stories. "He was jumpy, you know. Real nervous. Couldn't sit still. I told him, you're asking for a gift. You need to ask in the Arapaho Way. Respectful-like," she said. "He said he was only asking 'cause his own great-grandfather had gone to Hollywood with my grandfather, Goes-in-Lodge, only his great-grandfather never came back. He started talking real nice then, but I didn't give him everything at first. Gave him one story and waited to see how he acted. He thanked me and didn't ask for any more. He came back the next day."

Father John set his fork down, took a bite of the hot fry bread, and leaned over the table. "Grandmother," he said after a moment, "I'm also here to ask for a gift. The fed thinks Kiki was killed over drugs, but Andrew says that Kiki wanted to turn his life around. I'm trying to find anything that might convince the fed that Kiki's death wasn't part of a drug deal." He took a moment. His own words sounded preposterous, hanging over the table between them.

The woman across from him was nodding. She gripped her coffee mug in both hands and peered at him over the rim. "The second time he came," she said, "I gave him one of my own stories. Told him about how I remembered Tim McCoy coming to the Goes-in-Lodge compound. I was maybe eight or ten, and we lived in one of the houses over there . . ." She nodded toward the window and the expanse of fields under the falling snow. "All the relatives lived in the houses nearby. I remember one of my cousins knocking on the door. Hurry up, she said. The white movie star's come to visit Grandfather. We ran all the way over to Goes-in-Lodge's house. He had a brush shade out back. You seen brush shades the way they used to make 'em?"

She hurried on, not waiting for an answer. "Poles stuck in the ground, willow branches on the roof and the walls. Real cool in brush shades, don't matter how hot it gets outside. The people used to make brush shades in the Old Time, and we keep trying to make 'em as good as they did." She set the coffee mug down, picked up her fork, and took another bite of stew. "Anyway," she went on after a minute, "we slipped inside the brush shade and sat in the corner. We made ourselves real small. McCoy was sitting across from Grandfather, and they were talking mostly in signs. It was something to watch. Hands moving real fast, and everything quiet. Except every once in a while they'd bust out laughing. They was talking about the time in the movies. I understood parts of what they said, 'cause the old people used to talk to us in signs. They was afraid we wouldn't know how to make signs when we grew up. Used to talk to us in Arapaho, too, for the same reason. That's how come some of the old people like me . . ." She gave a shrug and a little laugh. "We still talk Arapaho. We still use signs sometimes."

Father John smiled at her. So many times he had watched the elders signing across the crowd at a celebration at Eagle Hall or at one of the powwows. He could understand a few of the signs, but the elders' hands moved so quickly that it was difficult to get most of it.

"Grandfather trusted McCoy," Ella said. "He had a good heart. Looked out for the Indians when they were working in the movies. He was a big man, I remember that. Wore a black shirt and black trousers and had a white Stetson that he kept on his knee. I seen some of the old movies he was in, and he always wore a white Stetson. I remember Grandfather saying people didn't want to leave the rez. They didn't know how white people was gonna treat them. Every time we left the rez, it was bad. Signs up everywhere that said, No Indians."

She gave him a little smile and went back to eating for a moment before she said, "Only reason they went to work in *The Covered Wagon* was because my grandfather told 'em it would be okay. He trusted McCoy."

Father John finished his own stew. It was delicious. Hearty and smooth and just enough spice for the taste to linger on his tongue. The food in Italy was also delicious, yet he had missed the simplicity of fry bread and stew and strong, fresh coffee.

"I told Kiki some of the things that Grandfather and McCoy said about when they were making *The Covered Wagon*. How the Arapahos and Shoshones had their own camp next to a tent city where the whites lived. Set up just like a town, with streets and intersections. Grandfather said the dust was something awful, and it drove the whites crazy. They wasn't used to living in tents with horses and wagons stirring up so much dust, but it didn't bother the Indians, he said. It reminded them of how it was on the plains when they were kids."

Ella got to her feet. She stacked the empty bowls, took them to the counter, and picked up the coffeepot. "Grandfather and McCoy talked about how they went to Hollywood and lived in Cahuenga Pass eight months and put on an Indian show every night. White folks crowded into the theater to see real Indians, like they were aliens from another planet."

She refilled the coffee mugs and sat back down. "The Indians used to hang around the studio when they weren't working. The place looked like a barn, but out in back was a big field where they had all kinds of sound stages. There was everything on those stages—city blocks, villages, farmhouses, hotels. Grandfather said it was like magic. They used to watch the actors playing out different scenes. They had curtains they pulled around the stage to let in the light they wanted. Lot of times they used what they called klieg lights, and the actors' eyes got real red and swollen. The cameras made a whirring sound when they were cranked."

Ella worked at her coffee a long moment and stared past him into the shadows of the living room, summoning the past, he thought. A little girl folded in the corner of a brush shade, listening to her grandfather and a movie star reminisce about a fantastic world and imagining . . . what? That she might go to Hollywood one day? Be in the movies, like her grandfather?

"I told Kiki some other stories," she said, bringing her eyes back to his. "I told him Grandfather said Charlie Wallowingbull didn't like playing by the white man's rules. Grandfather said there was whispers about him and some white movie star. He said he kept going over and over in his mind what he could have done to keep Charlie from going off like he did, not telling anybody, just disappearing from his tipi one night."

Father John set his own mug down. Goes-in-Lodge was a respected elder, the man who trusted Tim McCoy and convinced the others to be in *The Covered Wagon*. One of the Indians had disappeared, yet neither Goes-in-Lodge nor McCoy had known what had happened to him.

"Do you know JoEllen Redman?" he said. "I understand she's a descendant of Thunder's." He had been hoping the woman would hear on the moccasin telegraph that he wanted to talk to her. He had checked his messages today. Nothing from JoEllen Redman.

Ella smiled at him and shook her head. "There's lots of Redmans around, but I never heard any of 'em was part of the Thunders. They went to Oklahoma a long time ago. Grandfather always said they were a strange bunch."

"Did Kiki happen to ask about her?"

The old woman pursed her lips, still shaking her head. "What Kiki wanted to know most of all was if my grandfather left any letters. I told him buffalo Indians never learned how to write. I told him, you gotta talk to descendants of the younger generation that was in the movies. They was the ones went to the mission school and learned how to read and write. Felix Painted Brush is the one he oughtta talk to. Over on Sand Butte Road where it dips south."

Father John thanked the woman. He pulled on his jacket and gloves, let himself out the door, and set his cowboy hat on his head as he made his way through the snow stinging his face. The pickup coughed a moment before it finally burst into life. Ella was peering out the window as he backed down the drive. Everything about the pickup felt frozen, the thumping tires, the steely coldness of the steering wheel through his gloves.

Charlie didn't like playing by the rules, Ella had said. He could have run off, started a new life somewhere. He wondered if Kiki would have told his grandfather the truth, if that was what it had turned out to be.

17

THE TAILLIGHTS OF the blond-haired girl's pickup blinked red in the hazy snow. Vicky stayed as close behind as she dared, giving herself enough room to grind to a stop at the stoplights. They were creeping uphill in a parade of snow-piled vehicles when a truck switched lanes and slid between the pickup and the Jeep. She tapped on the brake, the Jeep shaking around her, inched into the oncoming lane to pass the truck, then pulled back, blinded for an instant by headlights looming toward her.

She should have gotten the girl's name. If she lost the pickup, she would have to hope the girl showed up for work tomorrow at the nail salon. But by then, she would have told Dede that a lawyer was looking for her, and Dede could be hundreds of miles away. The right-turn signal ahead started flashing. The truck turned into a parking lot where neon lights from a bar flickered over rows of parked vehicles. Vicky pressed down on the gas, swung into the other lane, and passed two sedans. If the girl's pickup turned into a neighborhood, it would vanish into a driveway or garage and she would never find it.

The pickup was just ahead now. They were nearing the edge of town—blocks of warehouses, shops, and garages interspersed by open stretches of snow. The red taillights grew brighter as the lights of town fell away. A scattering of stars poked through the haze. Then the pickup made a left turn across the road. Vicky waited for an oncoming truck to pass and followed.

Fresh tire tracks shot down the road past open fields that were flat, white sheets of snow. Ahead the pickup made another turn and as Vicky drew closer she spotted the one-story house with white siding and a black roof. The pickup stopped and the girl got out. She slammed the door, a low thud that reverberated like a drumbeat. Before Vicky had pulled up, the girl was inside the house.

Vicky followed the footsteps through the snow and knocked on the door. A muffled scream came from inside, like the scream she had once heard from a coyote caught in a trap. She knocked again, louder this time.

"I told you, nobody knows I'm here!" The scream turned into loud shouting. "Nobody! You hear me! You were supposed to be my friend."

Then the other voice, quiet, cajoling at first, and finally shouting: "What choice you got, Dede?"

Vicky knocked again, then tried the knob.

"You promised, Gayle. You promised, and you broke your promise and I'm gonna be dead."

The knob turned in her hand, and Vicky pushed the door open a few inches. The blond-haired girl—apparently Gayle was her name—was saying something when Vicky leaned inside and shouted over her: "I can help you, Dede. We have to talk."

There was quiet then, the exhausted quiet after a storm has passed.

"Dede?" Vicky said.

The door swung open, and the girl facing her was barely five feet tall, with cropped straw-colored hair and smeared circles of green mascara around green eyes. For an instant, Vicky had an image of the trapped coyote as the girl threw wild, desperate looks about the room. "Who are you?" Her voice had a hoarse, strangled sound.

"I told you . . ." Gayle stood on the other side of the room that looked as if it doubled as a living room and bedroom, with blankets and pillows tossed about a black sofa.

"Shut up!" Dede swung a fist out to one side. "Nobody's talkin' to you."

Vicky told the girl her name and said she was a lawyer.

"I don't need no lawyers, okay?" Dede kept opening and closing both hands into tight fists, the knuckles popping like kernels of corn.

"I went to your house . . ."

The girl cut in. "You gonna tell me something I don't know? What business is it of yours if those guys trashed my house?" She walked across the room and sank into the pile of blankets on the sofa. She was crying silently, her shoulders shuddering. She leaned forward and pulled her arms around herself. "They killed Kiki," she said, "and now they're gonna kill me 'cause I seen 'em."

"Who are they?" Vicky sat down next to the girl. *They*, she was thinking. The man who contacted her—the choked, weeping voice on the phone, the hulking man with the gun in the backseat of the Jeep, the man who admitted that he had killed Kiki—wasn't the only one involved in Kiki's death. "I can help you if you tell me what you know."

"Help me what? Get killed? End up in the river like Kiki? I don't need that kind of help."

"Listen to her, Dede." Gayle plopped down on the armrest and reached for Dede, but the girl jerked away. "Tell her who they are."

Dede picked up the corner of a pink blanket and dabbed at her eyes. "Same guys that come to see Kiki after he moved in," she said. "Geez, I hardly knew him. Met him at Tracers the Saturday before, and we got along real good, you know what I mean? Like he was a decent guy, didn't do drugs or nothing. Sure, he told me he just got out of prison, but so what? Lot of guys do something stupid and go to prison. Don't mean they're bad people. So I asked him to move in, you know, 'cause I thought we was gonna get along real good. Sure, he was Indian, but I been with Indian guys. What difference does it make?"

"Tell her what they said when they came to the house," Gayle said.

Dede shifted around and stared up at the blond girl. "You don't want me here, do you? Why don't you just say so? What're you worried about? They're gonna come here and trash this precious dump?"

"Okay, that's it." Gayle jumped to her feet. She took a couple of steps across the room and turned back. "You know what? You're right. I don't need drug dealers in my life. I don't need them coming here looking for you and tearing my place apart. So you tell her everything, or you get outta here tonight."

Dede slumped against the sofa and studied the piece of pink blanket bunched in her hands. It was a moment before she said, "They came to the house and they, you know, wanted Kiki to work for 'em again, set up some new connections on the rez so they could sell the stuff. He told 'em he was done with all that. It wasn't his way anymore. I mean, he got serious. Told 'em to get out and not come around again. Just leave him alone, that kind of stuff. So they left."

"They left without any trouble?"

"They owed him, Kiki said, 'cause he kept his mouth shut and took the rap and went to prison. He said they wouldn't be back, and besides, all he could think about was those old silent movies. Geez, expected me to watch an old movie every night. Never went out anymore. It was like we was married. Put those stupid posters that he bought on the internet all over the walls."

"What did they look like?" Vicky said.

"What, the posters?"

"The two men."

"Indians, both of 'em. One was a big guy, had on a black leather jacket and big lace-up boots with thick soles. You know, working boots."

Vicky fought to keep her own expression neutral. A big man in a black jacket wearing working boots. It could be anyone. It could be the guy on the phone. "What about the other guy?"

"Tall and skinny, wore a puffy jacket. Looked like a clown. Both of 'em were real ugly, and I was scared. I told Kiki we should move, 'cause they might come back. He said they wouldn't come back and I should relax."

"How do you know they trashed your house?"

"She seen 'em." Gayle had taken one of the chairs at the chrome-legged table wedged near the doorway to the kitchen. She lit a cigarette, took a long draw, and blew a tail of gray smoke out of the side of her mouth.

"Shut up, Gayle. Just shut up."

"Tell me," Vicky said.

Dede closed her eyes a moment, a mixture of resignation and fear moving through her expression. Finally, she said, "I heard the truck drive up. Same light-colored truck they came in before. I grabbed my coat, ran out the back door, and got into my car. I could see 'em inside throwing everything around. I heard 'em breaking things. I took off, and I didn't stop 'til I was on the highway halfway to Casper. That's when I turned around and came here." She gave a little laugh. "I thought Gayle was my friend."

"Who were they?" Vicky said. She could feel her breath caught in her throat, the quiet enveloping the house.

Dede took a moment. "Kiki called the big guy Jason."

"Jason Bellows," Gayle said. "You heard of him? You want meth, cocaine, weed, you go see Jason."

Vicky didn't say anything. She had heard the name on the moccasin telegraph, always the same news: Bellows is killing our kids. Why don't they put him away? Why is he still walking around? But it was all about evidence, she knew, and Gianelli hadn't been able to get enough evidence against the man to bring charges.

And Jason Bellows could be the man she went to meet in Ethete.

"Kiki didn't pay any attention to the other guy." Dede spread her hands in the air. "But I heard Jason call him something like Tray or Toy or something."

"Troy?"

"Troy Tallfeathers, skinny, ugly guy," Gayle said, flicking ashes into a glass. "I seen him lots of times at Tracers with Bellows. That's where they hang out."

Oh, this was good, Vicky was thinking. A former client who might be involved in Kiki's death. "Troy Tallfeathers is in jail," she said. "I can go with you to talk to Agent Gianelli. If you tell him what you know, he can bring charges against both of them and arrest Bellows. They can't hurt you if they're in jail."

"Jail!" Dede spit out the word. "Until some judge lets 'em out, and then they'll come after me. This how you're gonna help? Get me killed?"

Vicky had to look away. She was aware of the circle of light shining over the table, Gayle blowing out a stream of smoke. Dede was right. Troy was trying to get a deal now that might get him released. He had information that Gianelli wanted, he had said, information he was willing to give up if the assault and DUI charges were dropped. It was possible he had seen Bellows kill Kiki, and maybe it hadn't happened in the way the voice had whispered on the telephone. Maybe it wasn't self-defense. Dede could identify Jason and Troy as the guys who trashed her house. She could implicate both of them in Kiki's murder.

And even if Troy wasn't released, Bellows was walking around free.

"You want to help?" Dede said. Something new in her eyes now, a soft, pleading look. "I need money to get outta here."

"Where will you go?"

"I got friends in Denver. They're not gonna find me there."

Vicky was quiet a moment. She held her breath against the wave of nausea that washed over her. Dede Michaels wasn't the only one who could implicate Bellows in Kiki's murder. If Bellows was the man on the telephone, then he had admitted to killing Kiki. She had heard his voice. She had seen him in the entrance at Wal-Mart—a big man with dark features and dark, intense eyes. She could identify him.

And yet something seemed wrong, out of sync. The man on the phone was upset, crying, and it was hard to imagine a drug dealer like Bellows crying over the fact he had killed someone. And as far as she knew, Bellows had never been in prison while the man on the phone had said he could never go back to prison.

Still, she couldn't be sure. You could never be sure of what a drug dealer—a killer—might do or say or how he might act to protect himself.

She pulled her wallet out of her bag, took out sixty-five dollars— all that she had on her—and set it on the blanket folded on the girl's lap. Dede grabbed the bills, like a starving dog pouncing on food.

Then Vicky found a business card and set it on the blanket. "I need you to stay in touch," she said. "Sooner or later the fed will arrest Bellows." Whatever Tallfeathers knew, it was probably enough for Gianelli to charge Bellows with something. "As soon as he is in custody, it will be safe for you to tell the fed what you know. If Bellows did kill Kiki, you can help send him to prison for a long time, Dede."

The girl nodded, as if this was a possibility to which she had already given a lot of thought.

THE ADMINISTRATION BUILDING at night always seemed to feel like an old building left abandoned by the side of a road. The floorboards creaking and groaning, the wind and snow pecking at the windows. No sounds of human voices or footsteps to disturb the atmosphere. Father John flipped on the switch halfway down the corridor. The fluorescent bulbs on the ceiling twitched and sputtered into life, sending dim columns of light over the portraits of Jesuits past, staring out through round, frameless spectacles, jaws set in certitude.

He found the switch inside the door to his office. The place looked as if it had been ransacked: cardboard boxes stuffed with files scattered over the floor, the filing cabinet drawers hanging open. This morning Lucy had suggested his files needed some organization, and he had agreed. He hadn't thought about the disorganization that would come first.

He worked his way around the boxes to his desk and checked the little pile of messages. Nothing from JoEllen Redman. Then he made his way back through the boxes, flipped off the switch, and headed down the short hallway off the corridor for the small, galley-like room that served as the mission library. A small table stood in the center, and shelves of books and files stuffed with old records lined the walls. He turned the knob at the top of the single lightbulb that dangled from a chain. A circle of light sprayed the tabletop, leaving the shelves tucked back in the shadows.

The records were here somewhere, the names of Arapahos who had attended the mission school. *Come and teach our children*, the old chiefs had said to the Jesuits after the Arapahos were sent to the reservation. The chiefs had taken the train to Omaha, a delegation of the tribe's leading men, hoping to persuade the Jesuits. They would mark off part of the reservation for a mission. They would help build the buildings. A school and dormitory and big kitchen, an eating hall. They would build a house for the Jesuits and a church with a steeple that could be seen for miles. Their children would learn to follow the white road. They would learn how to read and write the white man's words and figure things out with the white man's numbers.

He had found the record of that trip somewhere in the files not long after he had come to St. Francis. It had made him feel as though, somehow, he had stumbled into a job that was bigger and more important than anything he had planned for himself. He had felt connected to the old Jesuits in the portraits.

He glanced over spines of the hardback folders on the shelves: Finances, Building Maintenance, Lists of Donors, Letters from Provincials, Lists of Pastors, Lists of Assistants. There they were: a series of folders containing records from the school. For most of a century, there had been a school at St. Francis Mission. Part of that time, Arapaho kids had lived in the old school building that was now the Arapaho museum. Kids used to riding ponies over the plains had sat cramped on wooden benches, bent over slate boards and tablets of paper, fingers curled around chalk and pencils, tracing strange shapes that the priests said were words and numbers.

Father John ran his finger over the dates printed on the spines in faint black ink: 1880s, 1890s. The younger generation of Arapahos—Charlie Wallowingbull's generation—would probably have been in the mission school around 1910. He lifted out the folder with the dates 1910–1920. It was heavier than he had expected, little motes of dust escaping from the cover, brittle, brownish paper stuffed inside.

He sat down at the table, opened the top cover and began thumbing through the papers. At the top of each sheet, the date had been written in the neat, precise handwriting of one of the old Jesuits, conscious that what he wrote would belong to history. Father John started with the top sheet: 1910–1911. He glanced down the column of names on the left: Gus Yellowhair, Robert Oldman, Mary Running Bull, James Whiteman. All familiar names on the reservation, but none of them the names he was looking for.

He picked up the next sheet: 1912–1913, and here they were: Charlie Wallowingbull. William Thunder. James Painted Brush. He had to smile at the first names. Which of the Jesuits in the corridor had given out the solid English names after deciding that calling a boy Wallowingbull or Thunder or Painted Brush wasn't appropriate?

He closed the folder and replaced it on the shelf. He had the sense that used to come over him when he was doing research in graduate school on some obscure event in American history, the sense that things were beginning to fall into place. The records confirmed what he had suspected. Charlie Wallowingbull, William Thunder, and James Painted Brush—standing apart from the other Arapahos and Shoshones in the photograph he had found on the internet—were friends. They had known one another since they were kids, they had gone to work in *The Covered Wagon* together, they had gone to Hollywood together. If anyone knew what had happened to Charlie, it would be a descendant of one of his friends. And Kiki had probably talked to Felix Painted Brush.

A floorboard creaked. He had been so lost in the records, he hadn't heard the front door open. He got to his feet and walked out into the shadows of the corridor.

She stood in the doorway to his office, a perplexed look about her, as if she had wandered into the wrong building looking for someone who wasn't there. She was wrapped in the black coat, the green scarf around her neck. Snowflakes glistened in her hair.

"Vicky!" he said.

She did a little jump backward, startled out of her own thoughts. "Oh, good! You are here," she said. Her voice had a muffled quality, as if she were still outside speaking through the cold. "Do you have a minute?"

"Sure." He waved her through the doorway, stepped in behind her, and flipped on the switch. A white light flooded over the office.

"I have to talk to someone," she said.

"Coffee?" Father John indicated the empty coffeepot on the small table near the door. He could make a fresh pot in five minutes.

"Just talk," she said. "Adam . . ." She spread her hands sheathed in black leather gloves. The snow had melted in her hair, leaving a silver sheen. "He wouldn't understand," she said.

"Well, try me," he said.

18

THE GRIEVING, THE troubled, the addicted, the victims of abuse and neglect, the lonely and the confused, and the Arapahos who just needed
someone to talk to found their way to St. Francis Mission at all hours
of the day and night, the white steeple a beacon shining through the
trees, drawing them in. Father John took the chair across from Vicky
and wondered what had brought her at this hour. At least ten o'clock,
he was thinking, because it was almost 9:30 when he had started
working in the library. He didn't want to glance at his watch. Vicky
would catch the glance immediately and bolt for the door. He waited
as she settled in. Removing her gloves, unbuttoning her coat, and
throwing back the fronts.

"The guy that's been calling me may be a murderer," she said
finally. She wore a blue blouse that made her eyes look black.

"The anonymous voice on the phone? You've defended murderers
in the past."

"Of course. They all deserve the full protection of the law. Innocent until proven guilty, no matter how heinous the crimes." She shrugged and glanced away a moment. "My job used to be to convince the jury of the lack of evidence or the extenuating circumstances that forced some scumbag to rape and strangle or shoot or beat to death some victim whose name I tried not to remember and whose face I can never forget. We send those cases to Roger now, Adam and I."

"What is it, Vicky?" Father John clasped his hands between his knees and leaned forward. How well he knew her, he was thinking. The way she fidgeted when she was upset, the way her brow furrowed in concentration, the intensity in her eyes. He hadn't forgotten any of it.

"The man admits to killing Kiki Wallowingbull," she said. "In self-defense, he says. No premeditation, no intent."

"But you don't think so?"

"Now he could be threatening to kill Kiki's girlfriend. He might have trashed her house. And get this. He doesn't work alone. It turns out he's teamed up with one of the firm's clients, Troy Tallfeathers, who happens to be in jail at the moment for DUI and assault on a police officer. He's hoping to get himself a deal. He could walk out of jail and kill the girl."

"Who are they? Can Dede identify them?"

"They came for her, and she ran out the back door. So they left her a message."

"You're certain they're the same guys?"

"She saw them before she drove away. Troy Tallfeathers, currently residing at the county jail. It would be her word against his, of course. The other man is Jason Bellows."

Father John leaned back against the chair and took a moment. Jason Bellows was dangerous, with a reputation that spread like black tentacles across the reservation. Kids as young as eleven hooked on meth, their parents sitting in his office, cursing the man who floated like a ghost beyond the reaches of the law.

"Friends of Kiki's?" he said after a moment. He had wanted to believe that Kiki was clean, free of drugs, consumed with a mission. He must have misread the man somehow, missed the clues, the telltale signs. Six months in Rome, and he was losing his touch.

"Looks like it. Dede said Kiki kept his mouth shut about Bellows and went to prison. Bellows and Troy came to see him after he got out. Wanted him to get back into the business. She said Kiki threw them out." Vicky pushed herself upright and started pacing—a swing to the window, then back along the desk to her chair and back to the window—her boots tapping out a steady rhythm. "Roger asked me to talk to Troy," she said. Then she told him that Troy maintained he had information Gianelli would want. Pacing. Pacing. What Troy wanted was a deal, and when she told him that was impossible, he had fired her and Roger.

She stopped and looked at him. "I think he wants to give up Bellows. He knows how Kiki really died, and he's worried Bellows might want to make sure he never talks about it. It's his skin or Bellows's. Dede's in danger, too. She can identify both of them, connect them to Kiki, and I can't do anything to protect Dede except to give her a little money to hide somewhere in Denver and wish her good luck."

Vicky swung around, walked over to the window, and began tracing a finger around a snowflake plastered outside on the pane. "I can't talk to Adam about any of this."

"He's your partner, Vicky. Maybe you should try . . ."

"Adam is buried in drafts and memorandums and court documents on the rights of tribes to manage their own resources and technical descriptions of reservation boundaries and legalistic arguments over whether Riverton is or isn't in Indian Country." She pivoted toward him. "Do you really think he wants to hear about somebody who won't give his name or a girl on the run for her life from a couple of drug dealers?"

"I'm sorry," he said.

She squeezed her eyes shut and shook her head. "I have to take care of this myself," she said. "Kiki spent time in prison for dealing drugs. It's possible that he took up with Bellows again after he got out."

It kept coming back to drugs, Father John thought.

"We only have Andrew's word that Kiki was out of the drug business," she said. "Kiki could have gone to LA to make his own drug buy and cut out traffickers like Jason Bellows." Vicky stared across the office, considering. "The only problem is, my anonymous caller admits that he was in prison, and Bellows has managed to stay out of prison. It doesn't mean Bellows isn't the caller. He would say anything, do anything to protect himself. If it is Bellows, I can identify him. Now that he's threatening Dede, I have an ethical obligation to notify Gianelli, but first I have to be certain."

Father John stood up. "You can't go looking for Bellows. You'll never find him. He has a way of vanishing on the rez. If he hears you're looking for him, he could find you. He'll figure you know he's the one who has been calling. He won't like the fact that you know who he is. He has his own reasons for staying anonymous. It's helped him avoid getting arrested for a long time."

"There's a chance I can spot him," Vicky said. She started buttoning up her coat, gathering the scarf around the collar, tying it close. "He's been seen at Tracers."

"Hang on a minute," Father John said. He retraced his steps down the corridor past the portraits, down the short hallway, and into the library. The circle of light still flared over the table. He wondered if that was what had brought her here—the chance that he would accompany her to a place like Tracers that regularly made the police news—drunken brawls and knifings in the parking lot. Last fall, before he left for Rome, a twenty-year-old Arapaho had been shot there.

He felt a wave of relief that he had happened to be here. He might have been out on an emergency call somewhere—the hospital or a home forty miles away. But he had been here, and thank God, because otherwise, she would have gone to Tracers alone.

He shrugged into his jacket, turned off the light and went back to his office. "I'm going with you," he said.

THE SOUND OF hip-hop burst through the brick walls and shook the parking lot; outdoor lights spilled across the pickups and sedans and cast yellow streaks over the snow. Dark figures moved at the edge of the lot, four or five guys standing around, low voices working through the beat of the music. The red tips of cigarettes shone in their hands. Father John kept an eye on them as he and Vicky threaded their way past the vehicles to the front of the bar.

Inside the hip-hop blared into a fog of smoke and beer and whiskey smells. Bodies gyrated in the center under a spray of red and yellow lights that landed like coins on the floor, then evaporated. He had to lean close, his lips almost brushing her ear. "This way," he said, taking hold of her arm and steering her toward the bar. Odd, he thought, the instinct he retained for always knowing where the bar could be found.

They worked their way past the figures darting back and forth between the dance floor and the booths along the walls. A mixture of whites and Indians. Twentysomethings, some of the girls probably underage from the looks of the skinny, half-developed arms, the bud-like breasts poking from tee shirts. The men looked older, sure, and experienced. Groups of men hung back in the corners, hoisting beer bottles and watching the dance floor. Father John saw them looking at Vicky. Then their eyes registered him, and they looked away.

A guy with tattoos running up thick arms, a thick head that sat directly on his shoulders and spiked black hair sauntered over and grabbed one of the skinny girls by the arm. She threw a satisfied look toward the knot of girls she'd been huddling with as the man propelled her onto the dance floor.

"Nice place," Vicky said under her breath. He realized he was still leaning toward her, shielding her.

There was only one vacant stool at the bar, and he steered her there.

She gathered her coat around her as she sat down. "Hello, there." The man on the next stool—blond hair with big ears and alcohol-bleared eyes—shifted his weight toward Vicky and gave her a faint toast. "Buy you a drink?" Slurred and hopeful.

Before Father John could tell him to back off, Vicky said, "I'm with someone."

The man swung about on the stool and blinked up, taking him in: about six foot four, cowboy hat, serious-looking. "Hey, no offense," he said. He started to get off the stool, balancing the glass of whiskey and hanging on to the edge of the bar at the same time. "Fine-looking woman, just admiring, that's all."

Father John moved toward the stool, but the man wasn't giving up. "Didn't mean nothing. Just being polite, buy her a drink." A drunk, and drunks never knew when to stop explaining. Wasn't that what drunks did? Explain. Explain. Explain. All in the earnest hope of keeping everyone's attention focused on something else, not the alcohol-soaked shells they had become. He had been an expert at explaining.

"Take it easy," he told the drunk. "No insult taken."

"Good. That's good." The drunk started to weave away, then dipped back. "'Cause I wouldn't be insulting a good-looking woman like that. Real lady. Indian princess, I'd say."

"Maybe you oughtta find your friends."

"Good idea." He saluted with the half-full glass. The ice clinked and whiskey slopped over the top as he backed into an Indian with thick shoulders and long black hair and began another round of explaining.

"You want something?"

Father John turned around. The bartender was leaning over the bar. He looked about thirty with a shaved head and a silver cross dangling from one ear. A white apron with yellowish and red streaks was cinched around a thin waist.

"Coke," Vicky said.

Father John nodded the same.

"What d'ya want in it? Rum?"

"Just plain," Father John said.

The bartender shrugged and started down the bar, then he came back, eyes narrowed on Father John. "Don't I know you from somewhere?"

"I don't think so." He was thinking that half of the Arapahos and Shoshones in the bar probably recognized him. The moccasin telegraph would burst with news tomorrow.

The man shrugged and moved away. Father John turned slightly and glanced around the bar pulsating with yellow and red lights and hip-hop and shadowy figures moving on the dance floor. "See him anywhere?" he said.

"Everybody here looks the same," Vicky said. He had to lean close, watching her lips. "This is probably a wild-goose chase."

The bartender was back, shoving two tall glasses of Coke across the bar. "I remember now." He had a low, direct way of speaking that cut through the noise, honed through years of practice. "I seen your picture in the newspaper. You're that priest at the mission, just got back from Rome." He drew in his lower lip and bit at it a moment. "Don't know as I ever seen you here before. You planning on making this a regular stop?" He let his gaze wander to Vicky and back.

"We're looking for somebody," Father John said. "Jason Bellows. You know him?"

That stopped him. The man flinched and took a step backward, shaking his head. "Don't know who you're talking about." He stared at Vicky a moment. "What are you, a fed?"

Vicky sipped at her Coke a moment before she said, "Do I look like a fed?"

"Who knows, these days." The bartender yanked at the silver cross on his ear.

Father John stood up and pulled out the folded bills in the small pocket of his blue jeans. A twenty and a five, all the money he had. He pushed the packet across the bar. "Keep the change," he said. "If you happen to see Bellows, we'd appreciate it if you pointed him out."

The man walked his fingers toward the packet, pulled it in, and slipped it into his shirt pocket. "I don't want any trouble," he said.

"Neither do we." Father John took a drink of Coke. The music had ended, leaving the sound of wheezing voices punctuated by guffaws and a high, piercing laugh.

"Cops been watching the place. Had some trouble in the parking lot last couple of weeks, lot of hotheads around looking for trouble, picking fights with straights like you, you don't mind me saying. You better watch yourselves." He threw his shoulders around and started toward the drunk pounding an empty beer glass at the end of the bar. Other guys had moved in, crowding between the stools, shouting orders. There was a loud thud of a door slamming shut, and Father John glanced around. A group of men, Indians and whites, sauntered in, shaking off jackets, high-fiving a couple of other men. The music started up again, monotonous beats, a cacophony of sounds, and couples started bouncing through the smoky haze to the dance floor. The second circle of Dante's hell, he thought.

"Will he help us?" Vicky said, and Father John turned back.

"Wait and see."

The bartender was tending to another customer. He filled a beer mug, set it down, and came along the bar. "Big guy. Black leather jacket near the door," he said.

Vicky started to shift around.

"Don't look now!" The man's tone was sharp. Then he shot two fingers in a V toward the Coke glasses. "You want refills?"

Father John set the palm of his hand over the top of the glass. He was aware of Vicky staring across the bar at the blurred haze of figures in the mirror behind the display of liquor bottles. After a moment, he glanced around and spotted the black leather jacket: a big guy with wispy black hair, the center of attention, judging by the way the crowd parted as he approached. "Look over by the booths on the right," he said.

Vicky turned around and, at that moment, as if Jason Bellows had felt their eyes on him, he looked over. The amusement in his expression was wiped away, replaced by a look of menace. He stared at them a moment, then started over, elbowing people that didn't move out of his way fast enough. He leaned over Vicky. "Who are you?" he said.

"Tourists," Vicky said. "Checking out the local zoo."

He shifted his lower jaw a moment, hands jammed into the pockets of his jacket. Metal chains ran across the shoulders and down the sleeves, glinting in the dim light. "Funny," he said. "Never seen you in the zoo before."

Father John stood up. At least three inches taller than Bellows, and that was a fact he meant to emphasize. He set a hand on Vicky's shoulder. "Just having a drink," he said. "It doesn't concern you."

Bellows eyed him for a long moment, then shrugged and started into the crowd. Then he leaned back toward the bar. "Get me a draft," he said, still shooting his gaze their way. "How long the cops been here?"

"No cops tonight." The bartender set down a glass with a thin layer of white foam on top. "Take it easy. Enjoy yourself. Lots of beautiful girls wanting to dance with you."

Bellows picked up the glass, stood up straight, and chugged the beer. He set the glass on the bar, waited while the bartender refilled it, then sauntered back into the crowd.

"It's not him," Vicky said. A little smile of relief had started working at the corners of her mouth. "It's not the man I saw at Wal-Mart." She turned toward him, an open, frank smile lighting her face. "Let's get out of here."

FATHER JOHN SAW them as they started toward the door—two of the men who had come in with Bellows, shaggy-haired, jackets unzipped, edging their way through the crowd, eyes focused like lasers on them. He leaned toward Vicky. "We're going to have company," he said.

"What?" She blinked up at him, then she saw them, too, because she stopped in place, as if her muscles had frozen.

"Keep walking." He pulled the keys out of his jacket pocket and pressed them into her hand. "The minute we get outside, you run for the pickup. Get inside and start the engine."

"I'm not leaving you," she said. She was moving slowly, a stiff-legged gait, as if she were going to her own execution.

"Just do as I say." He opened the door and gave Vicky a moment outside before he stepped out, slamming the door behind him. She was running in and out of the shadows along the building, and he started after her. The door opened behind him just as he had expected. Curious, there were no sounds of voices, no drunken, boisterous shouts, nothing except the hurried and determined thud of boots in the snow.

He kept walking, not taking his eyes from Vicky. Let her get in the pickup. Let her be safe.

They hit him then, a hard fist in the back, another fist crashing against his arm. He swung around and managed to plant his own fist into one of the men's solar plexus before the other one had him by the shoulders, pushing him into the brick wall. In a flash he saw what would happen next: he would be stood up against the wall and pummeled until he dropped into a heap.

An engine growled into life, headlights zoomed over the brick wall.

He managed a kick sideways that landed on a shin bone. There was a sharp snap, and the guy let out a scream that punctuated the sound of boots scraping snow, the loud gusts of breath, in and out. He started to crumble as the other man dove forward and planted a hard right that seemed to carry all of his weight into Father John's rib cage. Pain erupted like fire inside him. When the guy swung for his face, Father John blocked his arm and managed to drive a fist into his nose that popped like a ketchup bottle, spewing red globs over his face.

Out of the corner of his eye, Father John saw the pickup inching forward, the headlights playing over them, like spotlights on actors stumbling about, missing cues. The guy with the nose was still coming at him, shouting obscenities now, a fusion of words gurgling past the blood in his mouth. Father John deflected another punch and connected with the guy's jaw. He staggered backward, then reared up like a wounded grizzly, spitting saliva and blood.

Father John held his place, fists raised. *Keep your fists up.* His father's voice booming in his head. *The bullies come after you, you stand your ground! Like this.* And he had demonstrated the boxing maneuvers—eleven or twelve then, learning to protect himself on the streets of Boston.

But he wasn't a kid, and the man was gathering his strength into a murderous rage that no bully had ever managed.

"Get in!" Vicky shouted, and he realized she had driven the pickup alongside and was leaning across the front seat. The passenger door hung open. "Get in!" she shouted again.

Father John took hold of the door and pushed it against the man lunging toward him. The man staggered backward, regrouped, and lunged again as Father John threw himself onto the passenger seat. As he pulled the door shut, the pickup shot forward. For an instant, he thought they would hit the guy, who had to jump back, stumbling over the other one writhing in the snow, one leg bent backward.

"You hurt?" The pickup creamed onto the street. He could feel the rear shimmying.

Father John bent over and tried to get his breath. He pressed his fingers against his ribs.

"Should I take you to emergency?" She was driving fast, weaving in and out of traffic. They couldn't get away from Tracers fast enough. "John! Answer me. Do you need a doctor?"

He managed to sit up, his breathing almost normal now, his heart no longer beating in his throat. The pain was like a knife bisecting his chest. "What have you been up to, Father?" he managed, trying for a lighter tone. "Not much. Just a friendly brawl outside a tavern."

"John!"

"I don't need a hospital." He didn't think any ribs were broken. Bruised, was probably all. He'd had bruised ribs before, the first time when he was nine and crashed his bike, the last time when he collided with a runner during a baseball game his senior year at Boston College. He was in for a long night of pain and sore muscles. The Coke was making him feel a little nauseated.

"I'm so sorry," Vicky said.

"It wasn't your fault. Bellows didn't like the way we looked."

"No. It was my fault. I dragged you into this. I had to know if Bellows was the guy that contacted me."

"And now we know," he said.

19

LIGHTS GLOWED IN a few windows of the apartment building, and the entry was lit up like an aquarium, clouds of condensation on the glass panes. Vicky pulled into her reserved place in the parking lot and watched another tenant pick her way down the sidewalk sheathed in ice and let herself into the entry. The woman bent over the elevator buttons before disappearing past the sliding doors. No one else was around. Green numbers glowed in the dashboard: 12:13. Warm air pumped out of the vents. The deep hush of nighttime and snow settled over the building and the rows of parked vehicles.

She stared up at the light in the window at the far end of the second floor. She had left the shades open this morning, and after a couple of minutes, she saw Adam stroll past the window. Waiting for her, worried. Angry, more than likely, and he had every right. She should have called this evening and let him know where she was. It was stupid to leave the office early without a word to anyone. Just run off like that, making a dash for her own freedom. Driven by what? The determination to help a man who wouldn't even give her his name? An Arapaho, like herself, too frightened of the powers of white men to trust anyone.

She turned off the ignition. The hum of the engine faded, and the vents went quiet. It was surprising how quickly the cold air started to seep inside, breaking through the cracks, drilling past the windows. Still she waited, trying to steady herself for the look on Adam's face, the disbelief and disappointment in his eyes. And what to say? How to explain? That an anonymous caller had most likely killed Kiki in self-defense, just as he claimed? That the caller was not the drug dealer Jason Bellows? Another wave of relief rolled through her. As long as drugs weren't involved, she was certain she could help the man. There was every chance he would be exonerated.

She could imagine the disappointment deepening in Adam's eyes until they resembled shiny black stones at the bottom of the Little Wind River.

Vicky got out of the Jeep, and in a couple of minutes she was riding up the elevator, sucking in the warm air and clapping her gloved hands to punctuate the confidence she wished she felt. She walked down the corridor and was about to insert her key in the lock when the door flung open.

"My God. Where have you been?" Adam invaded the doorway.

Vicky stepped past him. "Sorry I didn't call," she said.

"I thought we were going to have dinner together." His voice came from behind as she set her bag on a chair and hung her coat in the closet. This morning dinner had seemed like such a good idea. A chance to talk. Later he would spend the night. They could put themselves back together as a couple. But all of it had left her mind.

"I am sorry." She turned toward him. "There was someone I had to see in Riverton."

Adam stood still a moment, taking her in, deciding how to understand. Oh, she knew the expression well, the way he looked at a client when he was trying to sift through the half truths and fill in the rest. "Did you eat?" he asked.

She shrugged. It wasn't important.

"I picked up some Chinese," he began, but she waved away the thought. Somehow it made her stomach churn.

"We had better talk," Adam said. He stationed himself on a stool at the counter that separated the small dining room from the even smaller kitchen and nodded toward the vacant stool beside him.

Maybe you should try . . . John O'Malley's voice rang in her head. She had told herself she would never again let John O'Malley into her life. She would not go through the pain again, the kind of pain addicts endured in withdrawal that turned them inside out. Yet how quickly she had turned to him. Like falling back into a familiar pattern, a way of walking or seeing, or turning her head. She had left him at the residence and watched him walk up the sidewalk, holding on to his side. She had felt limp with guilt. It had been her decision to go to Tracers, her problem. She shouldn't have involved him. And yet, for a brief time it had been the way it used to be—she and John O'Malley working together.

Vicky slid onto the stool and locked eyes with the man next to her: black hair with traces of white shining through, dark complexion and the telescopic gaze that focused on the smallest detail. So handsome that the eyes of women trailed him in every restaurant, every store they went into. He had large, patient hands, clasped together on top of the bar, waiting. He was Lakota, the largest tribe on the plains in the Old Time, the aristocrats of the plains, some historians called them, who ruled by sheer numbers and outrageous courage. All the other tribes, her own people included, tried to avoid them, but that was difficult. They were everywhere. Mostly her people had tried to get along with them.

She smiled at the idea. Difficult to avoid, so try to get along.

"What's funny?" He didn't sound amused.

"You and me," she said. "Arapaho and Lakota."

"We were a good team."

Were. She said, "I went to talk to Kiki Wallowingbull's girlfriend. I was hoping she could help identify the caller."

Adam spread his hands flat. "I'm not even going to ask how you found Kiki's girlfriend."

"Listen, Adam," she said. Then she told him the rest of it: how Jason Bellows and Troy Tallfeathers, who had been the firm's client, had trashed the girl's house; how she had thought Bellows might be her caller and had gone to Tracers to identify him.

"My God, Vicky. What are you thinking? You, alone at a place like that?"

She told him she hadn't been alone. He got it right away. Face going lighter, almost pale, eyes narrowing into slits.

"Father O'Malley with us once again," he said. "You couldn't have come to me?"

"I didn't think you would understand."

"Well, you're right about that." He gave her a moment, then he said, "Is that it? Anything else I should know about my partner? About our firm?"

"Bellows isn't the caller, and I don't believe drugs were involved in Kiki's death. The next time the man calls, I'll try to coax him to come forward. I think he's telling the truth."

"Why do you care?"

"Why do I care about my own people?" She waited a moment, allowing the question to hang between them. "Why do I care that they get justice instead of being screwed over by white laws and white stereotypes that all Indians are drunken bums who deserve to be locked up? So what if an Indian is convicted for a crime he didn't commit? He probably got away with another crime, so it balances out. Why do I care if that's the kind of justice we've had to live with?"

"Okay, I get it. You're a big crusader, you're going to right all the wrongs. Good. Good." Adam got to his feet. "We need somebody like you, the Indian Joan of Arc, finally here to save us from the white hordes."

"You'd better go," Vicky said.

Adam opened the closet door, found his black jacket, and pulled it on. "I'm going to the Crow Reservation tomorrow," he said, calmer now. The litigator in the courtroom, calm and rational. "The tribal council is considering hiring our firm to advise them on developing the coal on the reservation. I don't know when I'll be back. I'm sure you can handle anything else that comes up with the water case."

He seemed to be waiting, expecting her to say something—zipping the jacket, pulling on his gloves. Vicky looked away, but he moved to the periphery of her vision, swinging around, yanking open the door. She couldn't be the woman, the partner, he wanted. Orbiting around him. She couldn't go back to the woman she had once been, trying to fit herself around Ben Holden's whims and demands.

The floor trembled as the door slammed shut.

THE COMPUTER SCREEN glowed in the half light of the study. Outside, snow pecked at the window and the wind banged the porch door in back—a steady tapping noise that reverberated through the residence. Father John could hear Walks-On snoring on his rug in the corner. Waves of warm air spewing from the vents alternated with the cold drafts that swept across the floor. He typed in a string of words: *Movie actress 1922 The Covered Wagon.* He sat as still as he could, waiting. The smallest movement, he had discovered, sent spasms of pain through him despite the tape he had wrapped around his ribs. Bruises the size of fists had blossomed on his skin. He had winced with the pain as he pulled his shirt back on.

Lines of black type, the keywords in bold, started to materialize on the screen. He read down the lists of websites and clicked on one that looked promising. An article by Walter Winchell culled from *Photoplay*, with narrow columns, a curlicue font, and two photos framed in black lines, like mortuary photos. A woman with long, curly blond hair and a doll-like face—cupid lips and painted eyebrows—stared out of the photo at the top of the page, looking very much alive. Posing for the photographer like an actress accustomed to taking directions, hands demurely folded in the skirt of a flimsy-looking white dress.

His mother had kept photos like this in the family album: great-aunts and three- or four–times-removed cousins, posing for some unknown relative with a box camera, the men stiff and formal in buttoned suit coats and high-necked shirt collars, gripping bowler hats over their stomachs; the women beautiful in flowing dresses and wide-brimmed hats. Frozen in time, as if they would go on forever, the sun falling over the smiling faces, the women's white arms.

He smiled at the memory. Later, in some history class, he had studied the 1920s, the era when life had changed for American women. Emancipated, free to vote at last, free to find their own way and pursue their own careers. It was the era of Prohibition and bobbed hair, and the Charleston and flaunting the law in speakeasies. And with it all came a new sexual freedom for women.

Printed in bold under the doll-like face in the photo was the caption: *Lasky featured player, Missy Mae Markham, accepts minor role in first Western epic.*

Father John read down the narrow columns:

> *Our sources tell us that Missy Mae Markham will appear as an extra in* The Covered Wagon! *Naturally, when we heard the news, we were determined to bring our readers the story. Now that story can be told.*
>
> *Our sources say that Missy Mae Markham turned down the leading role of heroine Molly Wingate on the basis that the part was beneath her. She stormed into Jesse Lasky's office in the studio at Selma and Vine streets, threw a copy of the script onto the desk, and screamed that she would never stoop to riding outdoors in the sun all day in a covered wagon. Reportedly she told*

the famous studio head he could find an unknown player for such a lowly part in a foolish movie no one would pay to see.

As you know, readers, Missy Mae Markham is rumored to have a very powerful, anonymous patron in Hollywood. Consequently, Mr. Lasky had no choice but to honor her outburst. The part of Molly Wingate was given to Lois Wilson. While not an unknown, she has not generated the enthusiasm among moving picture fans that has made Miss Markham a box-office hit. Nevertheless, Miss Wilson is a beautiful and accomplished player.

Our sources also say that Miss Markham got wind of the fine performance that Miss Wilson was delivering in the role she had turned down. She ordered her chauffeur to drive her to the desert where she notified the director, James Cruze, known to everyone in Hollywood as Jimmie, that she would play Molly Wingate after all. Faced with reshooting at great expense, Mr. Cruze telegraphed Mr. Lasky. Evidently Mr. Lasky sent a messenger to Miss Markham ordering her back to Hollywood. But Miss Markham stamped her little feet and refused to leave. She claimed the desert air was good for her lungs, and she enjoyed meeting new people. We assume she referred to the 500 Indians who are players in The Covered Wagon.

At long last, a compromise was arranged. Lois Wilson would remain in the heroine's role, but Miss Markham could have any other role she wished, as long as it did not require extensive reshooting. A press release from the studio said that "Miss Markham has generously agreed to appear in a lesser role than she usually plays to guarantee the success of The Covered Wagon.*"*

Look for the familiar blond beauty cradling a baby in the scene at Fort Bridger when The Covered Wagon *premieres, dear readers, and remember that you read the real story here.*

Missy Mae Markham. The name was familiar and unfamiliar at the same time, like other names of long-ago movie stars that surfaced from time to time in a book or magazine or in snatches of conversation: Valentino, Mary Pickford, Douglas Fairbanks, Charlie Chaplin. Father John studied the smiling, doll-like face. Eyes lit with determination and the satisfied look of a child who has thrown a tantrum, gotten her own way, and was already plotting to throw another. He wondered if Missy Mae Markham was the woman Elena had heard rumors about—the white woman Charlie may have gotten involved with.

He waited a moment for the sharp cut of pain to subside in his ribs, then closed the site and clicked on one with the words in bold type: *Trouble on Location of* The Covered Wagon. Another Winchell byline in *Photoplay* materialized. The article was shorter, like a news flash that had made the deadline.

Trouble brews on the location of The Covered Wagon. *Our sources tell us that Missy Mae Markham seems determined to call attention to herself, which can only aggravate the problems that the director, James Cruze, has encountered while shooting an epic Western moving picture on location, such as the constant desert winds, dust raised by 500 wagons and hundreds of horses, and a flood when a lake dam burst and water inundated the tent city where 3,000 people are housed. Not to mention the fact that Mr. Cruze must worry about the equipment, food, lumber, and hundreds of head of stock that had to be transported to the location. Through it all, our sources say that Miss Lois Wilson, despite the fact she suffered frostbite in shooting a scene, has behaved like a true professional.*

We are sorry we cannot report the same for Lasky's golden girl, Missy Mae Markham. It appears she has turned her attention to the Indians working as players. She has been heard declaring that Arapahos were the handsomest, bravest, and most interesting men she has ever met. (We can only surmise what her patron must think.) Our sources say this development came about after J. Warren Kerrigan, who plays Will Banion, rebuffed Miss Markham's attention. No doubt a popular player such as Mr. Kerrigan is accustomed to the wiles of beautiful moving picture stars such as Miss Markham and knows they often lead to trouble. It is unfortunate that the Arapahos seem to be unaware of the dangers.

Need we also mention that, out on the desert, there is little control over alcoholic beverages or other intoxicants with which players like to indulge themselves. Our sources say that night after night, tent city becomes a moving feast of parties, where Orange Blossoms and other stimulants flow freely.

Perhaps Col. Tim McCoy, the real cowboy hired as technical adviser for the movie, should warn his Indian charges?

Father John clicked on another site. A full-page layout of photos from *Silver Screen* magazine came up. At the top was a photo of Missy Mae Markham in a dark dress with a frayed shawl over her shoulders, huddled on a stool in what appeared to be a room in a tenement, the look of a waif about her, except for the pistol gripped in her hands. The caption below said: *Missy at work in the studio lot on her new film in which she must defend her honor. The other players need not fear! Missy is an expert marksman who learned to shoot on her daddy's ranch in Texas.*

The caption beneath the photo on the middle of the page said: *Stars arrive for premiere of The Covered Wagon at Grauman's Egyptian Theatre the evening of April 10.* The photo showed lanes of automobiles—square-topped sedans with elongated hoods, coupes, Packards, and Model Ts—stopped in front of the theater. Crowds of people stood on each side of a wide carpet that stretched from the street to the theater entrance, heads craned toward the stars walking along the carpet, men in dark tuxedos, women wrapped in furs, jewels gleaming in their hair. Klieg lights lit up the sky like fireworks.

Yet another photo showed Missy riding in the passenger seat of a light-colored, long-bodied Packard convertible, a white scarf lifting into the air. *On April 12, 1923, hundreds of fans lined the streets to welcome Missy and Mr. Jesse Lasky on their arrival in Flagstaff to scout the location for yet another moving picture.*

At the bottom of the page was another photo of Missy Mae Markham, but this one was different. A candid shot taken before she'd had a chance to assume the demure, satisfied pose of a movie star. She stood among a group of Indian men in tanned-hide shirts and trousers and moccasins, black hair tied in braids, headbands with eagle feathers that rose over their heads. She looked small, reaching only to their shoulders despite the high-heeled shoes that poked beneath the hem of the flowing white dress. The Indians looked out at the camera, but she stood sideways, laughing and glancing up at one of the men, as if he had just whispered something surprising in her ear. There was a radiance about her, a white light glowing in the center of the dark faces. The caption read: *Missy takes time from a busy shooting schedule at the studio to visit with Arapahos from* The Covered Wagon. None of the Arapahos were identified, but Goes-in-Lodge stood in the center, the faintest look of unease etched into the old man's stoic face. Other buffalo Indians stood on either side. Standing a little apart, close to the movie star, were James Painted Brush, William Thunder, and Charlie Wallowingbull.

Father John pressed the print key and waited while the printer gyrated and hummed and finally spit out the copies. He studied the photograph. Missy Mae Markham had fixed her eyes on Charlie Wallowingbull.

20

"VISITORS! VISITORS!" SHOUTS rang through the village. There was the swooshing noise of people rushing past, the rasp of moccasins against the ground. William stepped outside the tipi. Indians ran toward the covered wagons drawn up outside Fort Bridger, and whites poured out of tent city. Campfires crackled, throwing up little circles of light against the dusk. Moving over the desert in the distance was a great brown cloud that billowed against the sun dropping in a red sky.

"Visitors!" The shout came from the group of whites pushing ahead of the crowd. Six weeks in the desert, William thought, living inside a moving picture with no connection to the outside world. He could feel the sense of excitement, as if someone in the crowd had tossed him a lariat, and now he could lasso anything he wished—home, the reservation—and bring them to him.

He spotted Charlie and James standing by one of the wagons, next to McCoy. James was turning from side to side, his camera in front of his face, snapping pictures of the crowd. William made his way over.

He had a clear view past the crowd. A long tan automobile, shining in the last of the daylight, drove in the direction of Fort Bridger. The top was rolled back, and William could see the man at the steering wheel. He wore a floppy cap that bobbed up and down as the automobile rose and dipped over the dirt road. In the backseat was another man, a black bowler shading his face.

"Who's that?" Charlie's voice cut through the hushed voices of the crowd.

"Mr. Lasky!" someone shouted, and William saw Mr. Cruze dodge past the people in front and start running alongside the automobile, a couple of cameramen straining to keep up. The director had the rear door opened before the automobile had ground to a stop. "What a surprise!" He might have been shouting through the megaphone. "We didn't know you were coming."

The man in the bowler climbed out of the backseat. He was almost as tall as the director, a narrow man in a long black coat that hung close to the ground. Beneath his hat, he wore round, rimless glasses that glinted as he looked around. Then he set about brushing dust off one shoulder, then the other, and Cruze joined in, sweeping his hands over the back of the man's coat. "Great to see you!" the director shouted.

William felt an unease stirring inside him. Out of the corner of his eye, he could see McCoy shaking his head. No one had visited the location, and here was an important man in a big automobile. Mr. Cruze bent toward the man, one ear cocked to catch whatever the boss was saying. "Yes, yes," the director said, a lower voice now. A strained look had planted itself on his face.

"What's it mean?" Charlie had moved in closer. James was behind him, taking pictures. William could see the crowd gathering around the automobile.

"I heard rumors the picture's gone over budget," McCoy said. "Started out at one hundred thousand, went to five hundred, now it's nudging eight."

William caught Charlie's eye for an instant. Five hundred thousand? Eight hundred thousand? What was this, grains of sand? Stars flickering in the black sky? How could there be so much money in the world?

"Could be the boss isn't happy about spending all that extra money and has decided to shut us down. Could be he heard of problems on the set."

William glanced at Charlie, but Charlie looked away. He stood ramrod straight, nothing changing in the brown mask that was his face. It was amazing what a good player he had become. News about Charlie and the girl must have reached Mr. Lasky. There were telegrams that went back and forth between Mr. Cruze and Hollywood; several times he had seen the director's assistant set off in a black Model T for Milford where the telegraph office was.

"So that's the boss?" A tense note sounded in Charlie's voice that, William realized, had nothing to do with the moving picture. The tall, narrow man in the black coat was the man who owned the girl.

McCoy turned toward Charlie. "From what I hear over there," he nodded in the direction of tent city, "Lasky's the front man, runs the studio, gets paid to keep the money people happy back in New York. They get unhappy, Lasky has to solve the problem."

William looked from Charlie to James. Money men. White men with a lot of money who owned everything around them—tent city, covered wagons, Fort Bridger. They had sent the front man who could wave his hand and all of it would melt back into the desert as if they had never been here.

"What about our pay?" James gripped the box camera in one hand.

"If we get shut down," McCoy pushed the white cowboy hat back on his head, "I'll do my best to see you Indians get the pay you were promised."

The little group around the automobile started through the crowd, Mr. Cruze striding ahead, motioning people to the sides. Gradually the crowd began to fall away, leaving a clear pathway toward tent city. As Mr. Cruze walked past, William saw him nod at McCoy, who started after the director. The boss and his driver and the cameramen hurried behind.

William realized that James had dropped to his haunches and was drawing in the sandy earth with a stick he had found somewhere. He and Charlie hunkered down on either side. "The coming of the big white man is not a good sign," James said. The picture in the dust was the image of a bird about to lift off. William understood. The eagle was his spirit guide, and now James asked for the eagle's wisdom and strength. He had three children on the rez. He needed the pay that was promised.

William felt McCoy's shadow fall over them before he looked up into the white man's face. The features chiseled into place, the mouth barely moving as McCoy said, "You want to see the dailies?"

William pushed himself to his feet. Charlie was beside him, but it was a moment before James managed to stand up. No one said anything. The Indians had never been invited into the big tent at the edge of tent city where the white players went every evening to see the moving pictures they had made that day. "There's gonna be a special showing," McCoy said. "Looks to me like Cruze wants to convince Lasky he's making the greatest picture ever. Anybody wants to see the dailies . . ." He lifted a hand toward the other Indians gathering around. "Come with me."

McCoy swung about and started off. It was almost dark, and the white hat seemed to float over the black shirt. He veered toward Goes-in-Lodge, said something to the old man, then kept going. Goes-in-Lodge and several buffalo Indians stepped in alongside the others. An air of excitement ran through everybody, something new coming. No one had seen the moving picture. Now they would see themselves.

The large tent was crowded with whites and Indians when they stepped inside. William took a second to let his eyes adjust to the darkness. He could make out the shadowy heads of people seated in the chairs arranged in rows. Other people crowded along the sides. Halfway down the aisle was what William had once heard McCoy call a projector, and a beam of light ran from the projector to the large screen shimmering at the far end of the tent. Mr. Cruze stood up in front of the screen and squinted into the light. Then he seemed to fix on what he was looking for. He beckoned to McCoy, who started down the aisle.

Most of the Indians had gathered in the back, and William followed Charlie and James into an empty place in the far corner. Above the heads nodding on the chairs, he could see Mr. Cruze seated next to Mr. Lasky. McCoy sat on the other side.

There was a loud clap. One of the cameramen hurried down the aisle to the projector. Then a short, bald man with a pockmarked face and a big stomach stood up at the side of the screen and fit a violin under his chin. A screeching noise cut through the sounds of people talking and shuffling about. Like a wind dying down, the tent started to grow quiet, except for the clicking sound of the projector and the whine of the violin.

Black, white, and gray images began floating across the screen. Covered wagons coming across the desert, coming from the horizon. Oxen hauling the wagons, massive heads bent into the task, muscles flexing beneath the sheen of their coats. Some emigrants walked alongside the wagons, flicking whips at the oxen. The heads of women and children bobbed inside the wagons. William couldn't take his eyes away. So this was the way it had been, this was what the buffalo Indians had seen with their own eyes. Trains of covered wagons that went on and on crossing their lands. He swallowed back the lump in his throat. For a moment he felt as if he couldn't breathe.

Another scene flashed on the screen. The wagons fording the Platte River, the canvas tops dipping and swaying as the oxen stumbled forward. So like the Platte, he had to remind himself that the white men had dug out a passage so that water could flow from a lake. The river they made was as deep as the Platte.

There was Charlie on the screen, half-naked, running after the white man on the horse, demanding payment for helping to ferry wagons across the river. The violin was faster now, the tempo of a horse galloping. The white man pulled out a pistol, pointed it at Charlie and shot him. Charlie fell onto the ground.

William squeezed his eyes shut. Charlie was beside him, he knew, but he couldn't look at him. Charlie was dead now. Stories are real, Charlie had said.

The music was still fast, but joyful and free somehow. William forced himself to look again at the screen. The wagons drawing up in front of Fort Bridger, the old trader bursting out the door. Molly ran into his arms, and right behind her was Banion, just the way he had seen it happen. And there was Missy, huddled in a wagon with her doll child.

Finally the images flickered and vanished, leaving the glowing white screen. Everyone was frozen in place. Then someone started clapping, a low, steady beat, and the whole audience joined in. People jumped to their feet and raised their hands over their heads. They were shouting and cheering. "Bravo! Bravo!" Even the Indians in back, shouting, "Bravo! Bravo!" Shouting for themselves, William thought, for the other lives they had lived on the white screen, the warriors they had been.

He waited with Charlie and James while everyone filed outside. The buffalo Indians first, the other Indians crowded behind. And finally the white people getting to their feet, scattering the chairs, coming down the aisle, and stepping past the projector as if it were a strange and powerful force. After almost everyone had left, William turned to Charlie. "It's only a story," he said, but Charlie looked away.

He followed Charlie's gaze. Floating down the aisle in a white dress a few feet ahead of the skinny bodyguard was the girl. Charlie didn't take his eyes off her until she had disappeared beyond the flap of the tent. The bodyguard veered over and lay a hand on Charlie's shoulder for a long moment, warning him not to follow her. Charlie stood in place, red-faced and tight-lipped. "Bastard," he said, when the white man had ducked out of the tent.

At the edge of his vision, William saw McCoy hurry down the aisle and run outside. In a moment he was back, Goes-in-Lodge and four other buffalo Indians trailing along. He ushered the old men into the aisle, then he walked over; "Mr. Lasky wants to talk to you," he said.

William stepped out first and walked around the projector, just as the white people had done, sensing the power coming off the metal. Behind him he could hear the footsteps of the others, slow and tentative. At the front, Mr. Lasky and the director and two cameramen were seated in chairs pulled into a circle. The shadows of their heads bobbed on the screen. The instant Mr. Lasky stuck a cigar between his lips, Cruze found a match, flicked it into life, and leaned over to light the boss's cigar.

William stopped a few feet away, the others coming up beside him. A polite habit he had learned as a boy—don't push yourself; wait to be noticed. McCoy nodded them forward, and they sat down to one side of the buffalo Indians, across from the boss. In the dim light from the projector, William could see the black whiskers sprouting on Mr. Lasky's chin, the gray tufts of hair, like a nest, in his ear. He kept a hand curled over the cigar; a tiny red light glowing at the end.

So this was how it would end, William thought. Inside a tent, their own shadows flickering on the screen. They would be shamed before Goes-in-Lodge and the other old men. Shamed before their people.

"How do you Indians like the moving picture business?" Mr. Lasky seemed cheerful. He jabbed the cigar in William's direction, crossed his legs, and swung a black boot out into the circle of chairs. McCoy's hands started flying, signing the white man's words.

Goes-in-Lodge smiled and nodded. The other buffalo Indians broke out laughing. It was good, the old man signed back. *Niisini!* We have seen white men do wondrous things.

McCoy translated, and it was Mr. Lasky's turn to laugh. A bold shout of amusement that left sparks of spittle hanging in the air a moment. He jumped to his feet and began moving about, the shadow flowing back and forth over the screen. "*The Covered Wagon*'s the greatest moving picture in history. You see all those panorama shots of wagons coming across the desert? Fantastic! It'll knock the socks off audiences. All we gotta do is make sure folks come to the movie theaters. Tell 'em," he said, jabbing the cigar toward the director before dropping back onto his chair.

Mr. Cruze pushed his chair back and got to his feet. The black shadow rose across the screen. He made a noise in his throat, his eyes fixed on Goes-in-Lodge, hands clasped at his waist. William could see the white peaks of his knuckles rising out of the pink skin. "Mr. Lasky has hit upon a brilliant idea," he said. "He believes the public should be given an . . ."

"Incentive, Jimmie," the boss cut in. "I say we need special promotion." He seemed to recollect himself. "Go on," he said, flipping the cigar on the ground where it flickered and glowed red.

McCoy's hands were still flying.

"Mr. Lasky would like to hire you to take part in a prologue at Grauman's Egyptian Theatre in Hollywood that will take place each evening before the movie." He took a moment, running his tongue over his lips. "He seems to believe the public will require such an incentive to bring them to the theater. May I say"—he turned to Mr. Lasky—"that it is my belief *The Covered Wagon* will be its own incentive. I do not believe . . ."

"Yes. Yes." Lasky stood up. For an instant, he looked less sure of himself, as if he regretted getting to his feet. "*The Covered Wagon* is your masterpiece, as we are all aware. But I am aware of the expenditures." Next to him, William could see McCoy signing for the old Indians. "We are almost three hundred thousand dollars over budget. The prologue will help promote the movie. You Indians can just do what you always do. Sing. Dance around and holler and yell. You'll wear your own costumes, naturally. Keep your hair long, lots of feathers on your heads. Audiences will love feathers. We'll put big signs up all over Hollywood. Come see the first and greatest Western epic moving picture, *The Covered Wagon*. Preceded by a prologue starring real Indians."

McCoy said, "When will this take place?"

"Premiere is April 10. You go home after we finish here, see your families, and come to Hollywood first week in April. I need at least fifty Indians. Same pay you're getting now. Bring your horses and tipis. You can pitch 'em up in Cahuenga Pass." Lasky spread his hands as if the matter were settled. "McCoy, you're in charge of who's gonna come."

"I'll go." It was Charlie's voice. Then other voices: Goes-in-Lodge and the other buffalo Indians and James, all speaking up, voices giddy at the idea of more work, more money.

William turned to Charlie, took his arm, and started to walk him backward, away from the others. He tried to think what to say, how to tell him that they shouldn't go.

Charlie said, "That's where she lives. In Hollywood."

21

CENTRAL WYOMING COLLEGE spread across a hilltop on the western edge
of Riverton, swathed in snow and wrapped in a gray sky. Gusts of
wind sent snow bursts over the sculpture of dancing figures in the
center of campus. Vicky parked in the visitor's lot and made her way
along the walkways, dodging students with packs slung on their backs
and intense expressions beneath the knit hats pulled low on their foreheads. She found the building that housed the psychology department
and took the stairs to the second floor. The sounds of students moving
through the halls reverberated against the concrete walls. Professor
Jane Gorsuch had agreed to see her at 10 a.m. She was ten minutes
early.

She knocked on the door next to the professor's name on a white
plaque affixed to the wall. No answer, no sound of movement inside.
She knocked again. She had started back down the corridor toward
the chair at the top of the staircase when one of the doors opened

ahead. Jane Gorsuch stepped out, a tall woman in navy blue slacks and matching sweater, pushing a piece of gray hair from her forehead. "Vicky!" she said, walking toward her.

"I'm a little early," Vicky said.

"Come with me." The woman brushed past, waving Vicky along, an unhurried determination in her step. She used a key to unlock her office door and stepped in ahead. "Take a seat." She nodded toward a folding chair in front of a wall of books haphazardly arranged on metal shelves and sank onto a chair in front of the desk. "The criminal mind is a most curious thing," she said. "I'm not sure I can provide the insight you're looking for, but I'm also not sure anyone can."

"I appreciate your taking the time to see me," Vicky said. She had consulted with Jane Gorsuch several times in the past, when most of her cases were unimportant, except to the clients involved. Petty criminals getting drunk or high, committing assault and battery, driving while impaired, whole lives ruined in moments. Jane Gorsuch had provided valuable insight into the personalities, suggested strategies for handling the defense, and provided reasons for juries to believe the clients might be redeemable.

She had called Jane this morning, worried that the anonymous caller would never call again. If Troy Tallfeathers knew anything that might implicate Jason Bellows in Kiki's death, the caller would be free and clear. The information might be enough for an indictment against a known drug dealer who had managed to skate past any criminal charges. In the past, it had been Bellows's associates who went to prison: Kiki Wallowingbull, Troy Tallfeathers.

"How can I help?" Jane said.

"This is hypothetical."

Jane tipped her head in acknowledgment.

"I need an informal profile, your gut feeling about someone."

"Male or female?"

"Male. Arapaho."

"Hypothetical situation and hypothetical male." The woman smiled. They had played this game in the past. "Tell me about him. Any idea of his age?"

"Late twenties." Vicky shrugged. It was a guess, and she could see in the way Jane nodded that she knew it was a guess. "He admits to killing another man in self-defense, and he insists upon remaining anonymous. But he knows he needs help."

Jane gave a barely perceptible nod; her hands rested on the ends of the armrests. She didn't say anything, and Vicky went on: "He calls a lawyer several times, but refuses to give his name."

"What is his tone?"

"Frightened and tense. He weeps. He claims he didn't mean to kill the man, but he had no choice."

"He had no choice because the other man was trying to kill him?"

Vicky glanced away. She had assumed that was the case, but Kiki could have threatened him in some other way. "He doesn't make that clear," she said.

"What else does he divulge?"

"He has served time in prison. He mentions something about parole, and he's afraid he'll be charged with manslaughter or even murder and be sent back to prison. He doesn't want his son to grow up without a father."

Jane pursed her lips a moment, then she said, "That's quite a lot, you know. What does he want?"

"He wants assurances from the FBI that he won't be charged. He thinks the lawyer can convince Agent Gianelli that it was an act of self-defense."

"Based on nothing but his version of what happened? No evidence or eyewitnesses? Just his word?"

Vicky sat back and studied the black leather bag in her lap. She admired the way Jane cut into the heart of the matter. "Gianelli couldn't give any such assurances, of course. But let's say the lawyer talks it over with him anyway, so that she can tell the caller the next time he calls what the fed said. The lawyer believes the caller's story and is trying to gain his trust. She hopes he might come forward."

"What would make you believe him?" Jane said. "Hypothetically."

Vicky took her eyes away. "The sadness in his tone," she said. "The fact he was worried about his son growing up without a father. I think he believed that sooner or later, he would be implicated in the death. He was trying to settle matters ahead of time."

"A man who refuses to give his name, contacts you by telephone . . ." Jane stopped. "There's something you haven't told me?"

"He called one night and asked to meet me at a house in Ethete," Vicky said. "And I went." She waited for Jane to say the word hanging between them—foolish—but Jane said nothing, and she told her how he had gotten into the backseat of the Jeep. "He said he needed assurances before he came forward. He wouldn't let me turn around."

"So you've never actually seen this man, and you can't identify him."

"Not exactly," Vicky said. Then she told her that she was sure the man had followed her into Wal-Mart. "I got a glimpse of him, enough that I could identify him."

"You're certain it was the same man?"

Vicky was quiet a moment. She had no way of knowing whether the man in Wal-Mart wasn't just a random motorist who followed too closely on the Jeep's tailgate and went into Wal-Mart along with a couple hundred other people that day. What proof that it was the same man on the telephone? Except for the way he stood inside the door, looking about, looking for her. The air of despair and fear about him, the same despair and fear she had heard in the voice on the telephone.

She pressed her spine against the hard ridge of the chair. "I'm certain," she said. "How would you profile him?"

Jane drummed the fingers of one hand on the armrest. "Impulsive and reflective," she said, "an unusual combination. He followed you into Wal-Mart, presumably to make contact. An impulsive action, but reflection set in. He had second thoughts and didn't make contact. Better to remain anonymous and call you. He also killed a man in self-defense, he says. Another impulsive act, uncontrolled by thought. Later the thought processes set in and he realized he had created a problem for himself, one that might take him away from his son. With me so far?"

Vicky nodded. Everything Jane said confirmed her own theory. "He's frightened."

"He is motivated by a strong fear of abandonment," Jane said.

"Abandonment?"

"Not only for his son—that he could be forced to abandon his son—but for himself. Most likely his own father had abandoned him." She lifted both hands, palms up, and spread the fingers. "We don't know why, and in any case the reason wouldn't matter to a child. With respect to that trauma in his life, he holds on to the child's point of view, aware only of the pain. If he reveals too much of himself, you may also abandon him. You could let him down. That is his fear. It is much safer—an act of self-defense, you could say—to call you on the phone or contact you from the shadows. He does not trust easily. I would venture to say that he does not trust at all, especially the authorities. He needed an interface between himself and the authorities, which explains his impulse to contact you, a lawyer and an Arapaho."

"Someone else could be charged with murder in the case," Vicky said.

"Ah!" Jane shifted in her chair, both hands brushing at the armrests. "If that occurs, you won't hear from this anonymous, hypothetical person again. His fears would be banished. His son would be safe, and neither he nor his son would have to fear abandonment. He would be confident that the matter had been put to rest in the best possible manner and he would no longer fear being drawn in."

"I need to find him," Vicky said. She knew Jane was waiting for her to go on, and she said, "The truth could come out. A witness might reconsider." Troy, she was thinking, would be forced to admit on the witness stand that he hadn't actually seen Jason Bellows beat Kiki into unconsciousness. Any defense attorney worthy of the name would drive that point home to the jury. "And even if the other man is convicted," she pushed on, "the caller might still come under suspicion at some point in the future. It can take years sometimes for the truth to come out. He will always live with that possibility. And something else . . ."

Jane put up her hand. "My question for you is why you would want to find this man."

"I think he regrets what happened and wants to clear the record. I heard the regret in his voice, the need to tell the truth and make things right. I can help him, but not if he remains in the shadows. I became a lawyer to help people with no reason to trust the authorities and no hope. I want him to know there is reason to hope."

"Then I should give you the rest of the profile." The look on the other woman's face had changed, something dark and foreboding had come into her eyes. "We are discussing a man who has already killed another human being. An impulsive act because he considered himself under threat. He did what he had to do. The regret that you believe you heard in his voice is regret at the possible consequences to himself and to his son, not regret over killing a man. Should he consider himself free, he would not want to be located. He would see the possibility that you might find him, identify him, and force him out of the shadows as a serious threat to his own life. That makes him very dangerous."

"You're saying . . ."

"He could kill you, Vicky."

VICKY SAT OUTSIDE in the parking lot, listening to the motor idling, the vents humming with the first surge of warm air. Students hurried past in groups. A few trudged through the snow alone. "I have a little boy," the voice on the phone had said, and then the snuffling noise of tears

that wouldn't hold back. "I gotta take care of him. I can't leave him."
Jane could be right. If she found him, he would believe that she would
give him up to Gianelli. Kiki had threatened him somehow, and he had
killed him. He could kill again.

She shifted into reverse, backed out, then crept forward down the
rows of vehicles, the voice still running through her head like a melody
that takes hold, and the sadness in the voice, the despair and fear. She
had become a lawyer for people like this, she had told Jane. She was
aware of the numb tightness in her hands curled over the steering
wheel. He said he had killed in self-defense, and she had believed him.
She still believed him, that was the thing.

She stopped for a red light, tugged her cell out of her bag, and
called the office. "Hey, Vicky." Annie's voice on the other end. "Everything okay?"

Everything was fine Vicky told her. "I want you do some investigating."

"What?"

"You've been wanting more responsibility, Annie. I need you to get
the updated list of parolees in Fremont County from the U.S. attorney." She could sense the hesitation at the other end. The firm had no
right to the information. The list was available to law enforcement
officers, not to defense attorneys. She could call the U.S. attorney herself, but it was more likely that he would talk to an investigator from
the firm than to one of the attorneys. She pushed on: "Tell him we
have reason to believe a parolee is involved in Kiki Wallowingbull's
murder."

"I don't know, Vicky . . ."

"You can do this. Make him understand we're working on his side,
the side of law enforcement."

"Okay," Annie said after a moment. "It might take a few days." She
let another second pass before she said, "Oh, Susan called. Wants to
talk to you."

The light had changed, traffic started, and Vicky eased the Jeep through the intersection, guiding the tires into the parallel ruts in the snow. She thanked Annie and waited until she was stopped at another red light before she called Susan. The first ring and Susan picked up, as if she had been staring at her phone, waiting for her mother to call her back. "Hi, honey," she said, but Susan was talking over her. When was she coming to LA? Did she remember her promise?

"How about this weekend?" Vicky heard herself saying. And the moment she had said the words, the idea seemed obvious, as if she had been contemplating it for weeks, which she had, in a way, looking for a break in her schedule. And now it had come. Adam would be on the Crow Reservation for a few days, the court date hadn't yet been set for the civil case that the water consortium had filed against the tribe, and Troy Tallfeathers was no longer a client.

And the anonymous caller—the hopeless voice, the man in the shadows—would not call again. She would have to find him.

"Really? Are you kidding?" Susan yelling. Vicky could imagine her dancing around her desk the way she had danced around the living room as a little girl who had just gotten a piece of candy. "I can't wait for you to meet Brett," Susan said. "You'll like him, Mom. He works for a law firm, you know."

No, she didn't know, Vicky was thinking. Susan had said so little about him, yet Vicky had heard the excitement and hope in her daughter's voice with every mention of Brett. "I'll book my flight right away," she said. "You're sure this weekend is okay? You're not busy?"

"Make it a long weekend, Mom," Susan said.

22

THE PICKUP BOUNCED over the frozen ruts in the driveway. Father John hit the brake and skidded to a stop at the corner of the brown house with the front door painted neon green. Behind the house, the barn had weathered into the color of moss. An ancient pickup streaked with orange rust looked as if it were leaning against the barn. He cut the engine and waited, watching the house through the sunlight that sparkled on the hood. Felix Painted Brush would have heard the pickup coming up the driveway. If he were home and wanted company, he would come outside.

The pain had settled in, like a hot iron on his skin. He had been awake most of the night, the pain throbbing at the core of him, his ribs so sore he'd had to sit up in the living room, and his throat pinched with thirst. A shot of whiskey, two, three shots, and the pain would dull. He had contemplated going to the emergency room where the doctors would do a better job of taping his ribs than he had done. But the doctors would hand him painkillers. An alcoholic always recovering, with a fistful of painkillers! It made him want to laugh. There would be no visits to the emergency room. He would be back on whiskey within hours.

Sometime around dawn he had noticed the snow had stopped, and now the sky looked as if it had been painted blue and the sun was beating down. Still, he could see his breath on the windshield.

It was a couple of minutes before the side door on the barn creaked open and the old man's head poked around the edge. A puzzled expression at first, then—gloved hands fiddling with his glasses, pushing them against his nose—the expression transposed itself into surprise and even, Father John thought, pleasure.

He got out of the pickup and started along the side of the house, wincing with the pain that cut through him like a knife. He fingered the cut over his eye. He had plastered on a Band-Aid this morning, and he wondered how he would explain. Felix was coming toward him. A tall man in his late seventies, bone thin and bundled in a denim jacket that looked several sizes too big, thick braids of gray hair hanging down the front. A crosshatch of deep lines etched the brown face. "Hey, Father!" He raised a gloved hand and squinted into the sun. "Long time no see. What'd you do? Run into a door?"

"Something like that," Father John said. No doubt the news would be on the moccasin telegraph before long. He hurried into the polite pleasantries: How you been? Getting along pretty good. Heard there might be more storms coming. Yep. We need more snow. The old man shook his head. Missed us while you was in Rome, did you? Couldn't wait to get back to the rez?

"How did you know?"

Felix dipped his chin into the collar of his denim jacket and gave a snort of laughter. "We had bets on how long it'd take you to get back."

Father John laughed. A sharp, deep pain shot through him, and instinctively he wrapped an arm around his middle.

"I give you two weeks. Lost that bet real bad. Henry over there"—

Felix nodded toward the empty expanse of snow; Henry Lone Bull's house was at least two miles away—"won the bet. Said it'd take six months before your boss gave in, but everybody knew you'd keep pestering him 'til he did."

Father John had to swallow another laugh. He had kept up a steady stream of emails to the provincial all the time he was in Rome. How well the people here knew him.

"Come on in." Felix was smiling. He led Father John onto the path shoveled through the snow to the back door, head bent forward, back rounded into the task. Both arms swung at his sides. "Got some coffee brewing," he hollered over one shoulder. "Figured I was gonna get pretty cold stripping the stalls and laying in new beds for the horses."

"I can help you," Father John heard himself saying. He was still holding on to his side. Lord, he wasn't going to be much help.

The old man stopped and hauled himself around. Father John could see the pinpricks of light dancing in the brown eyes. It was too late to mention the broken ribs. "Don't mind saying that'd sure be great," Felix said. "Four hands are better than two. Let's get us some coffee first."

Father John followed the old man onto the stoop that had been shoveled to a clear glaze and into the small kitchen stuck onto the back of the house like an afterthought. Moist smells of coffee and something else—burned eggs and tobacco and neglect—hung in the air. Dirty dishes were piled in the sink; other dishes and pans littered the counters and spilled over onto the stove top. He could see a corner of the linoleum floor curling up, and strips of blue plastic had started to peel off the seats of the chairs. The top of the table was somewhere beneath the stacks of cereal boxes and canned food. Three years ago Mercy Painted Brush had dropped dead on the kitchen floor. He had said the funeral Mass, blessed the grave at St. Francis cemetery, and made an effort that first year to stop by every week to see how Felix was doing. But the visits had become less frequent, more haphazard. Whenever he happened to be in the area.

Felix had peeled off the denim jacket and hung it over a hook behind the door. He moved to the counter, rummaged in a cabinet a moment, and lifted out two mugs. "Make yourself at home," he said out of the corner of his mouth, his attention turned to pouring the coffee. He carried the mugs over, hands shaking as he nudged a cereal box out of the way. Coffee sloshed onto the table.

Father John waited until the old man took a seat before he let himself down on the chair, holding his breath a moment against the pain. He managed to get his jacket off and let it fall behind him, then he took in the rich aroma of the coffee for a moment before he took a sip. He could feel the old man waiting.

Finally, he set his mug down and said, "I've been looking into Kiki Wallowingbull's death." The hot coffee seemed to quiet the screams in his ribs.

Felix nodded, as if he had suspected as much. "Not that bad a kid," he said. "Came to visit an old man a couple times." He smiled at the memory, then took a drink of coffee. "Few days before he got killed."

"Andrew's worried that Kiki's death will be written off as part of a drug deal gone bad," Father John said. "Could you tell me what you told him, Grandfather?" He held his breath, hoping he hadn't sounded rude.

But the old man was shaking his head so hard that the pair of braids swung over his red plaid shirt. "The boy give up that drug life, said he learned his lesson. Didn't want nothing more to do with drugs. Lot of young fellows take a wrong road for a while. Hell . . ." He glanced up out of the corners of his eyes. "Took a few wrong roads myself. Spent a couple years in jail before the army got me. Took a bullet in the leg over in Korea. I got me an honorable discharge and come back to the rez. That's when the elders got a hold of me and said, time you grew up, got responsible, remembered you're Arapaho. You got responsibility to the people. Kiki was in that same place, seeing he had responsibilities. Wanted to do something right for his grandfather, make up for all the grief he give him. Only thing . . ." He paused a moment and sipped at the coffee. Then he said, "You could see all that anger boiling inside him. I told him he was gonna have to fix it, let it go, but he didn't listen. Didn't surprise me when I heard he was dead."

Felix moved the mug around the table in a small circle and shook his head. "The boy wanted to know about Hollywood," he said. "Sat where you're sitting and talked about how Charlie Wallowingbull and my father went off to be in the cowboy-and-Indian movies when they was young. I guess the agent on the rez give my dad a first name—James or something—but he never liked it much. Went by his Indian name, Painted Brush. Died in 1945. I was thirteen. Well, that was a long time ago."

The old man was still shaking his head. He cupped his hands around the coffee mug and looked at Father John. "Kiki wanted stories about that time. I didn't mind his asking, 'cause I knew he was wanting to find who he was and what he come from. Same for you. I don't mind your asking 'cause you're trying to find the truth, no matter what story the fed might come up with. Truth is, Kiki wanted to know how come Charlie never come back to the rez. Story was, he took off, just run away from everything. Run away from who he was. Kiki needed to know that wasn't true. Said he needed the truth for his grandfather, but you ask me, he needed it for himself."

The old man scooted his chair back, flattened his hands on the table and pushed himself to his feet. "How about a refill?" Before Father John could say anything, he had grabbed the coffeepot and was sloshing coffee into the mugs.

"I give him the stories I remember." Felix sat back down and nudged the coffeepot into a vacant spot in the forest of cereal boxes. "Wasn't a lot of 'em. Fact is, Dad didn't talk much about that time. Too busy raising a few head of cattle and keeping food on the table. Then he got TB and was real sick the last couple years of his life. That's when he told most of the stories. There was always a gleam in his eye when he talked about being in the movies. First movie was *The Covered Wagon*. Tim McCoy, you heard of him?"

Father John nodded. He could see the somber-faced man in the white cowboy hat staring out of the posters, and Kiki's girlfriend pulling the strips off the wall.

"Looked out for the Indians. Seen they got treated like everybody else."

"Did your father ever talk about Charlie?"

Felix took a drink of coffee, then held the mug under his nose a long moment. "I didn't like telling Kiki, but he wanted the truth. They was all worried Charlie was gonna get 'em sent back to the rez with no money. There wasn't a lot of cowboying jobs for Indians around these parts, and they needed the money. Charlie was one of them stubborn Indians, gonna do what he wanted. Didn't like playing a drunken Indian, the way the director wanted. Walked off the set one time. Said they didn't need the movie people telling 'em how to be Indians. Dad said that him and William Thunder took hold of Charlie and threatened to knock some sense into him."

"Did he say what happened to Charlie?"

"Just took off one night. I didn't like saying so to Kiki, 'cause it wasn't the story he needed. They was in Hollywood doing an Indian vaudeville act. Dad says there was signs all over Hollywood advertising *The Covered Wagon* and the Indian show."

Felix set the mug down and, leaning forward, laid his arms on the table in a circle and clasped his hands. "Kiki told me he went to Hollywood and found out his great-grandfather got murdered. He was gonna see that justice got done, make somebody pay."

The old man nodded, the brown eyes laced with sadness and regret. "Hold on, I told him. Nobody around here killed Charlie Wallowingbull. You can't hold somebody responsible that wasn't even born. He got real agitated at that. Everybody oughtta know the truth, he said. Then he asked me for another gift."

"Kiki asked if there were any letters, right?" Father John said.

The old man gave a smile of acknowledgment. "I laughed out loud, couldn't help it. Yeah, Dad learned to read and write at the mission school, but he never had time to do it. Out in the pasture most the time before he got so sick. Afterward, all he could do was sit on the porch and watch the fences falling down and the herd get smaller. I tried to help out, but I wasn't strong enough to make much difference. So he just watched everything he'd worked for go to hell. But there was something that kept him going for a while. Somebody had given him one of them box cameras. I kept it for a long time after he died, 'til one day I sold it at a pawn shop in Lander for money to buy feed. He loved that camera. Used to say that pictures was like their own world. They had their own truth. I think he liked making pictures of the world he wanted. So he took lots of pictures of the two old cows we had left and it looked like we had a real big herd. He took pictures of the fence where it was good. Looked like we had a real prosperous ranch. Same with the barn. With the light just right, you couldn't see the boards falling off."

"Did he have the camera in Hollywood?"

Felix nodded. "Started taking pictures everywhere. Maybe he thought he could turn into one of them movie people, except for he was Indian." The old man rocked the chair backward, stood up, and went into another room. Father John could hear drawers opening and shutting. After a moment he was back, plopping a small album that bulged with photographs on the table. "Here's the first pictures he made." He flipped back the cover and shoved the album toward Father John.

The pages were thick, black sheets, with little white triangular corners that held the photos in place. He leaned close to look at the black-and-white photos yellowing with age. Scenes of covered wagons, crowds of Indians and whites milling about, long tables covered with plates of food. A photo of a man who looked like the photo of Jesse Lasky he had found on the internet. He was getting out of a light-colored Packard. And street scenes, with old-fashioned square-shaped cars, pony carts, and horses moving past flat-faced buildings. Pedestrians dodged vehicles and strolled down the sidewalks, stopped in mid-step. In one of the photos, he could make out the faint sign on a hillside in the distance: Hollywoodland.

"See what I mean?" Felix said. "Pictures make their own world. It exists forever. When I got older, I used to look at these pictures and wonder if that's the way it was in Hollywood, or if that's the way Dad wanted it to be. Look." He flipped two or three pages until he came to a group of five photos of Indians wearing tanned shirts and trousers and moccasins. Their hair hung in braids, feathers lifted out of their headbands. "Everybody's happy, smiling, but Dad said the whole time in Hollywood, they worried about the families back on the rez. Did they get the money they sent? Was there enough to eat? In this world here . . ." He tapped at the page. "There wasn't nothing to worry about."

He turned another page and set his finger on the top photo. "Goes-in-Lodge," he said. The elder staring out of the faded black-and-white image looked strong and proud, like the leader of some undiscovered country, shoulders straight and head held high, an eagle-feathered headdress flowing down his back. "There's Charlie on the right. He moved his finger to the next photo where two Indians were seated on what looked like a wooden bench in front of a light-colored barnlike building. The black letters on the side read: Lasky Studios.

"William Thunder's on the left," he said. "William was about the only one could put up with Charlie. Always tried to calm him down, keep that temper of his from getting them all sent home."

"Looks like Missy Mae Markham here." Father John laid his hand alongside the photo at the bottom. A candid shot of Charlie and William on either side of a small woman who barely reached their shoulders. Her curly blond hair hung over the front of a dark dress. She held on to the edges of the ragged-looking shawl draped over her shoulders. Poking past the hem of her skirt were the pointed toes of tiny-looking black shoes. They stood near the corner of what looked like a barn. LASK appeared at the edge.

Father John studied the photo for a moment. Something familiar about it. The shawl and black dress were the same costume the girl wore in one of the photos in *Silver Screen* magazine. He had printed out the page and placed it in the file with the other articles he had found. He was accumulating quite a little stack.

"She's still about the prettiest girl I ever seen," Felix said, "even if she is all dressed up in costume for some movie."

"She was a movie star." Father John was still studying the photo. The girl had linked her arm into Charlie's and tilted her head back, staring up at him with wide, adoring eyes. But what had caught his attention was the way William Thunder, standing a little apart, turned halfway toward the couple, had fastened his eyes on her. What James had caught with his box camera was the look of abject and hopeless love in William's gaze.

"I never cared who she was," Felix said. "Whenever I looked at that photo, she was whoever I wanted her to be."

"Did Kiki see the photos?" Father John asked.

He nodded. "Next time Kiki come here, I showed him the album. Must've spent an hour or more sitting right where you're sitting, staring at these old photos." Felix started to lift the photo of William and Charlie and Missy Mae Markham out of the white corners. "After a while, he said, 'Thank you, Grandfather,' real polite-like and drove outta here like he was heading around the last lap of a racetrack. A couple days later I heard on the moccasin telegraph he was dead." He handed the photo to Father John. "Might want to check the back," he said. "Dad wrote some things down."

Father John turned the photo over and read the clear, precise handwriting of a man who had been a student at the mission school: *Charlie and William with big movie star Missy Mae Markham at Hollywood studio, April 10, 1923.*

"May I borrow this?" Father John said.

The old man tipped his head and gave a wave of assent, and Father John asked if Kiki had said anything about Thunder's descendants.

Felix shook his head. "None of them around these parts, far as I know."

23

A DOOR SLAMMED upstairs as Vicky let herself into the office building. The pale afternoon light washed down the walls and crept over the stairway as Roger came hurtling toward her, taking two steps at a time, balancing a briefcase under one arm and zipping up his jacket. "New charges against Troy." He spit out the explanation as he passed.

"What kind of charges?" Vicky said. She was talking to the man's back. Roger was already in the entry, yanking open the door.

"Conspiracy in a homicide," he shouted over one shoulder.

"Wait a minute, I'm coming with you." The door had already slammed shut and Roger was hurrying past the front window. By the time Vicky reached the parking lot, the black sedan had started to back out. She ran across the snow and tapped on the passenger window. The sedan rocked to a stop, and she slid inside.

"When did this happen?" she said, conscious of the breathless sound of her own voice.

"Troy called about five minutes ago. Begged us to take him back. He sounded suicidal. Said he talked to Gianelli yesterday . . ." Roger glanced over at her. "Waived his right to have an attorney present and proceeded to tell Gianelli how he had been at a house in Ethete where Kiki was killed, and how Jason Bellows killed him."

He slammed a fist into the steering wheel. "Troy figured Gianelli wanted Bellows so bad that he'd shake his hand and thank him for being a good citizen."

"What house in Ethete?" Vicky said.

"What?" Roger glanced over. A blue vein pulsed in the center of his forehead.

"The house where Kiki was killed."

"Vacant place on Yellow Calf Road. Near as I could figure from what Troy said, Bellows and his gang used the house in the past to move drugs."

Vicky stared out the windshield. The sedan ahead had turned off, leaving an empty snow-covered road running toward the county jail. The sky was the color of dulled steel, and it was starting to get dark. She could feel her muscles tightening. Despite the warm air swirling around her legs, she felt chilled. Nothing made sense. She had gone to the house in the middle of the night to meet an anonymous caller who had wept on the other end of the phone and insisted Kiki's death had been accidental, an act of self-defense. God help her, she had believed him. But Jason Bellows was not the anonymous caller.

TROY TALLFEATHERS WAS in the small interview room halfway down the corridor from the metal door that blocked the entry from the jail itself. He sat slumped forward over the metal table, hands in his lap. His black hair was shaved close to his scalp. He looked up as she and Roger stepped inside, then went back to studying his hands.

Vicky took the seat on the other side of the table next to the concrete wall. Roger dropped down beside her. "You're looking at serious charges," Roger said. It surprised her, the calmness in his voice. "Assault on a federal officer, and now conspiracy in a homicide and probably other charges."

Troy lifted his head. His eyes were red-rimmed, as if he'd been crying. "How'd I know the fed was going to turn on me? I did him a favor. You want Bellows? I told him. I'll give him to you. Now I'm going down with him."

"What did you tell Gianelli? Start at the beginning," Roger said.

"Wait a minute." Vicky leaned over the table toward Troy. "You have to understand this is only a consultation. I've been in communication with someone who may be involved, and we are no longer free to represent you." She could sense Roger's gaze boring into her. "We can recommend another firm . . ."

"Some other lawyer?" Troy stared at her a moment, then looked away. His hands were shaking.

"Anything you tell us could be used against you at some point," Vicky said.

"All I'm saying is the truth," he said. "The night Kiki got killed, I called Bellows, said we needed to talk. He said meet him at the house at midnight."

Roger took a moment before he said, "That would be the house in Ethete."

"What'd'ya wanna call it? Corporate headquarters? Business offices? Warehouse? Jason used to stash shipments there, okay? That's where we used to buy stuff from him to sell around the rez, 'til the fed got on to the place. He had to move the stuff to a house over in Arapaho where his girlfriend used to live, before she got smart and moved to Cheyenne. You might say Bellows took over the place, said he deserved it, all the grief she'd given him."

"Why did you want to meet him?" Vicky said. She was thinking that the man who called her might have gone to the same house.

"We needed to cool it for a while, with the fed nosing around. He come over to my place, tried to get me to talk, but I didn't say nothing. So I was gonna try to make Bellows face facts, you know. Move the business someplace else."

"How did he take it?" Vicky said.

Troy gave a raspy laugh. "I never told him nothing. Same time I got to the house, Lennie showed up. Said Bellows told him to be at the meeting."

"Lennie?" Roger sat back, arms folded over his chest.

"Lennie Musser. White dude hung with us, Indian wannabe. Anyway, the front door's wide open and it's freezing cold outside. I seen a light inside, like a flashlight. Right then, I said to Lennie, something's wrong. Man, I should've gotten the hell outta there. I wouldn't be sitting here now." He lifted his eyes to the ceiling. "What I did was walk real quiet to the door and look inside. That's when I seen Bellows hitting some dude in the kitchen. There's a flashlight on the counter. I seen the dude go down. I didn't know who it was at first, but I knew Bellows killed him, the way he was stretched out. Lennie seen it, too."

Vicky sat back and studied the man on the other side of the table a moment. "What did you do?"

"Bellows seen us. He says, 'Get in here and shut the door.' It was the way he said it, like he might kill Lennie and me and it wouldn't make no difference. So we did like he said, and Bellows says we got a problem with the sonofabitch trying to cut into the business. That's when I seen that it was Kiki on the floor. Bellows was going mental, stomping around the body like he wanted to kill him again, saying nobody was gonna take over his business, who'd the bastard think he was, he deserved to die. They all deserved . . ."

"All?" Roger interrupted. "Who was he talking about?"

"How do I know?" Troy shrugged. "Kiki must've been working with somebody. Bellows was going on about how Kiki went off to LA to make a buy, how he was trying to cut him out, how nobody was gonna cross him."

Troy puffed out both cheeks and blew a cloud of foul-smelling air across the table. "He said we gotta get rid of the body in case anybody comes snooping around. Like he was thinking somebody working with Kiki might show up. Every once in a while he'd kick the body. We gotta make an example outta him, he says. Anybody messes with Jason Bellows, this is how he's gonna end up. So he tells me to take him over to the river and dump him. Every meth head on the rez'll get the message, he says."

Vicky felt as if the floor were moving beneath her. If Bellows hadn't killed Kiki, why would he insist upon dumping the body at the river to send a message? Why would someone else call her and claim that he had killed Kiki? She had the sense that she had been taken in by one of her own people. She could see the amusement in Adam's face when he heard the news. She made herself concentrate on a scratch in the metal table—the solid fact of it—to steady herself. "Anything else?" she said.

"Bellows said I had to do it, like it was my job." He shrugged. "Like Lennie and him had more important stuff. Make sure you dump him over the bank, he told me. So I loaded Kiki into the back of my truck and put a tarpaulin over him and drove out to the river. It was freezing cold, snow everywhere. My truck got stuck, and I had to haul Kiki on my back. He was heavy as a horse. I had a helluva time getting him over close enough to roll him down the bank."

"Where were you when the police stopped you?" Vicky said.

"Soon as I got the truck outta there, all I wanted was to get the hell away."

"You'd been drinking," Roger said. A matter-of-fact tone.

"What'd'ya think? You ever dump a body? I smoked some weed, drank half a bottle of whiskey."

"Kiki was alive when you dumped him," Vicky said.

Troy sat back, as if she had landed a blow in his solar plexus. He kept blinking, and for a moment, she thought he might burst into tears. "I thought he was dead. I wouldn't've left him out there to die. I wouldn't've done it, no matter what Bellows said. Kiki and me used to hang together when we was in prison. Looked out for each other. He tried to get me to clean up, same as he did. Least I thought he got clean. But all the time, Kiki was setting up his own gang, gonna do his own business. Didn't surprise me none that Bellows killed him." He stopped. He was still blinking, as though he had to get around a new reality. "What's gonna happen?" he said, his voice barely audible.

"You agreed to testify against Bellows?" Roger said.

"I gotta get outta here."

"We're going to call another lawyer for you. Maybe he can get the prosecutor to drop one of the minor charges. No guarantees."

Roger got to his feet, and Vicky stood up next to him. Her legs felt wobbly. It was possible Troy was telling the truth. Possible that she had been wasting time, worrying about an Arapaho who was nothing more than a shadow, a whispering voice, probably on drugs, confessing to a murder he didn't commit. She didn't believe it.

They left Troy alone in the interview room, the guard waiting to take him back into the cell block. Outside, Vicky strode ahead of Roger, wanting a moment to sort it out.

"What's going on?" Roger said when they got into the car. He had switched on the defroster, and a little half circle began to clear at the bottom of the windshield. The engine made a low rumbling noise.

"If I represent the man who's been calling me . . ."

"He's not your client, Vicky."

"There could be a conflict of interest. I'm sorry, Roger, but we can't take the chance." She let a beat pass before she said, "Troy could be lying."

Roger gripped the steering wheel and stared through the half circle of cleared glass. He made no effort to drive away. "You think your guy killed Kiki, and Bellows happened to stumble on the body and decide to send a message of his own?"

"Why would the caller admit to killing him if he hadn't done it?" Vicky took a moment, aware of the sound of her own breathing. "I think he called me because he got worried that Gianelli would connect him to Kiki somehow, which means he is connected to Kiki. He wanted to get ahead of the game, claim it was self-defense."

"Okay," Roger said. "Let's say you're correct and it wasn't Bellows who killed Kiki. It doesn't mean that Kiki wasn't setting up his own drug business. Your anonymous caller could have been in on it. Maybe he and Kiki had a falling out, and Kiki's death wasn't self-defense after all."

Roger waited a moment, and when Vicky didn't say anything, he shifted into forward. The tires whined and spun before getting purchase in the snow. They drove back through town to the office building, and Vicky got out in the parking lot. It was dark now, the parking lot sheathed in ice and snow. The Jeep felt like an icebox when she slipped inside. The motor groaned and sputtered before turning over, cold air blasted from the vents, and a country song drifted out of the speakers.

Vicky drove down Main Street and turned onto the side street that ran in front of her apartment building. She wished she could shake the sound of the voice at the end of the line saying that he had a kid, that he didn't mean to do it.

VICKY HAD PARKED behind the apartment building and was picking her way across the icy pavement when she saw the bulky dark figure rise up between two parked cars and start toward her. Lights glowed in the entry and tentacles of light reached into the parking lot. There was no one else around.

She gripped her bag, a thousand impulses firing. Run back to the Jeep? Run to the entrance? She made herself keep walking. It was still early in the evening. A man in the parking lot didn't mean anything.

Probably another tenant, except every part of her knew that was not the case.

Up the curb onto the sidewalk, the soles of her boots sliding a little. Walking deliberately now, every step considered, the bag gripped in her hand like a weapon. The man stepped onto the sidewalk about twenty feet ahead, still coming toward her. She recognized him now, the swagger in his walk, the bulky shoulders leading one after the other, the head thrust forward. A man who acted on impulse, Jane Gorsuch had said. He had killed once, he might kill again. Vicky could hear her heart pounding in her ears. She felt as if her muscles were fused together.

He was closing the distance between them.

"I've been hoping you would call again," she said, trying for the calm and matter-of-fact courtroom voice.

He stopped and put up one hand, a traffic cop warning her not to come closer. "You got the deal?"

"Why don't we go to a coffee shop and talk," she said, her heart still pounding. She threw a quick glance around the parking lot. Nothing but the dark hulks of parked vehicles. "If you killed Kiki in self-defense, I can help you get the matter cleared up."

"All you had to do was tell the fed what happened."

"I need you to come forward."

"Just tell the fed what happened."

Vicky took a moment. They were getting nowhere. "I need details. Give me something the fed can check out, make sure you're telling the truth."

"I'm telling the truth!" he shouted. Then, almost a whisper, "They're gonna throw me in prison and toss the key. I got a little boy. I gotta take care of him. I can't leave him. I don't want him growing up knowing his old man's in prison. It'd be better if I was dead. You know what I'm talking about?"

"Where did it happen?"

"What?"

"Where was Kiki killed?"

"What the hell difference does that make?"

"I need the details," Vicky said. "I need something concrete. Give me something Gianelli can verify."

He looked away at that, and Vicky studied his profile backlit by the entry lights. The hooked nose, the high cheekbone of her people.

Finally he turned back. "Kiki called, all upset, agitated-like. Wanted to meet me at a place in Ethete."

"Where?"

"What does it matter?"

"The details matter."

"House on Yellow Calf Road. I figured the fed must've been smelling around something that happened a long time ago before we got sent to prison. I figured there was some kind of trouble, so I went."

Vicky was aware of the sharp sound of her own breathing. It was the same house where Kiki had been attacked. "What kind of trouble?" she said.

He threw up his arm again. "Enough. You got your details. Tell the fed to check out the house. He'll figure out what happened."

"What about Bellows? Was he at the house?"

"Bellows? Why would he be there? Didn't have nothing to do with him."

"I think you're lying," she said. "What I can't figure out is why."

He stared at her out of narrowed eyes, his face dark and pinched beneath the knit cap. "What are you talking about?"

"There is a witness who says that Bellows killed Kiki at the house." A pair of witnesses, she was thinking. Lennie Musser would back up everything Troy said. "Bellows is bound to be indicted for homicide in the next day or so."

He staggered backward, as if he had been struck by an unexpected force. It was a second before he seemed to get his bearings, then he swung around and headed down the sidewalk.

"Where can I reach you?" she called, but he was running now, weaving through the parked cars, another shadow melting into the shadows of the trees at the edge of the lot. She was certain now that she would never hear from him again.

24

LATE AFTERNOON, AND the sun dropped behind the rounded peaks of the Wind River Range, leaving a leaden sky and long dark shadows that reached across the white plains. The air was filled with the stillness that gathered before a blizzard. It would snow again tonight, Father John thought. The sign for St. Francis Mission rose out of the shadows ahead. He slowed down and turned into the mission. Lights shone in the windows of the administration building, and he could see Lucy's blue sedan parked in front.

He had planned to return sooner, and he felt a wave of gratitude toward the girl for staying on. It had taken a couple of hours to muck out the stalls and lay new beds in Felix's barn—he moved slower than the old man. The barn was like an icebox. Still he'd found himself sweating like a workhorse, the pain in his ribs gathering into a white heat, as if a branding iron had been strapped onto him. Now the pain had subsided somewhat into a numbness that, at least, made it easier to breathe.

He parked next to the blue sedan and, using the door for support, managed to lift himself out. Lord, he was too old for brawls in parking lots. Fighting the likes of Bellows's gang—he could've gotten himself killed. He gripped his side and made his way up the ice-slicked concrete steps. A wall of warmth mixed with the smells of old wood and plastered walls fell over him as he stepped into the corridor.

Strange, the rhythmic thumping noise, followed by a series of thuds. He followed the noise to the doorway of his office. Lucy was across the room, leaning over an opened drawer of the filing cabinet. She slammed the drawer shut and pulled out the next drawer. The red-tipped fingers started flipping through the tabs on the folders, as if she were counting out dollar bills. Cardboard boxes were scattered about the floor, but some of them were empty. "Surprise," she said without turning around. "I'm almost done getting you organized. About time, too, I'd say." She shoved the drawer closed and pivoted about. "Got the files organized in the top drawers. I'll start on the others tomorrow."

"Organized!" Father John managed to get his jacket off and hung over the coat tree. The pain was crawling across his back. "That will be a first," he said. He had intended to sort through the files, discard and straighten and make some kind of sense out of them for the last two or three years. There never was enough time.

"What brought on this burst of activity?" He walked over and lowered himself onto the chair behind his desk.

"Didn't you ever get tired of not being able to find things?"

"One time that I remember," he said.

"Right." She looked around. "What's wrong with you anyway?"

"Wrong with me? Let's see?" He swiveled slowly toward her. "I'm a busy man?" Then he realized he was still holding on to his side. "A little soreness in the ribs," he said, but each breath brought a new stab of pain. "It's nothing."

"You know what I heard on the moccasin telegraph?" The girl flounced over and sank into a side chair. "You went to a bar last night and got into a fight. I mean, look at you. You're hurting and you got a Band-Aid above your eye. I mean, geez, Father, what am I supposed to tell people when they wanna know what happened?"

Father John started to lean forward, but he had to wait for the sharp pain to pass. Whatever he said would be on the telegraph about five minutes after Lucy left. She would be on the cell phone as she drove out of the mission. "Tell them I went to the bar because I was looking for somebody." They were there together, he and Vicky, and that would be on the moccasin telegraph, too. "A couple of goons jumped me in the parking lot," he said.

Which wasn't going to satisfy the girl's curiosity. He could see it in the unblinking way she stared at him.

"Look," he said. "Vicky Holden and I are both trying to find out what happened to Kiki Wallowingbull. You can put that out on the telegraph. Anybody who has any information can call me here at the mission."

Lucy jumped to her feet. "I'm not just some gossip with nothing better to do, you know. You think my friends care about some druggie that got himself killed?"

"That's the point, Lucy." Father John inched forward and braced his arms on the desk, which seemed to provide a little support for his ribs. "It's possible that Kiki wasn't involved in drugs and something else led to his murder. I'm trying to find out what it could've been before the fed files it away with a lot of other unsolved drug deaths. And I don't think you're a gossip. I think you are a very bright girl with enough initiative to take on the world's worst filing cabinet. You should think about going back to school."

Lucy threw her head back, let out a puff of air, and examined the ceiling a moment. "That's why my mother got you to hire me, isn't it?" she said, leveling her gaze at him. "She figured you'd convince me to go back to school." She walked around to the front of the desk and rapped her knuckles on the edge. "What did school ever do for you?"

Father John waved toward the office. "Gave me all this," he said.

She rolled her eyes and started for the door. "I loved history," he went on. "I loved learning about the past, how people lived, what they did. It was interesting to see the way the past influenced the present, made it the way it is. I think that's the best part of school—the chance to understand something you love, make it a part of you."

She was holding on to the door frame, looking back. "My mother told you to say that, didn't she?"

"Not exactly," he said. "Not in those words. Any messages this afternoon? Did JoEllen Redman call?"

"Check the folder." She swept a hand toward the new metal rack on his desk. "Who is she, anyway? I heard you're looking for her."

"Somebody I'd like to talk to about Kiki," he said.

She shrugged at that, then she was gone, the sound of blue jeans swishing together and boots clapping down the corridor.

He pulled over the rack, selected the folder with *Today's Messages* printed on the tab and started going through the small pile of message sheets. Nothing from JoEllen Redman. He spent the next two hours returning calls, making appointments for baptisms and counseling, lining up a substitute religious education teacher for Helen Loneman, who had gone to Denver to care for an elderly relative. At some point, Lucy had hurried past the door, wrapped in a jacket and scarf, and hollered, "See you tomorrow."

Beyond the window, the sky had deepened into blue black, and the streetlamps around the mission had switched on. The familiar hush of early evening began to settle in. Early evening and early morning—his favorite times of the day, when the stillness was complete and he could get some work done. He used to go looking for the stillness in Rome, but even in the early morning, there was always noise and bustle out on the streets, and the evenings were filled with the sounds of belching motorcycles and the clamor of horns. He would work until the AA meeting at seven, he decided; Elena would put his dinner in the oven.

An hour and a half later, he glanced at his watch—6:45. He liked to get to Eagle Hall a few minutes early to help set up the chairs, although he doubted how much help he would be tonight. He assembled the messages into the folder along with notes he'd made, and set the folder back in the metal rack. A place for everything, he supposed, and his teenaged secretary would expect everything in its place. It still hurt to breathe, but not as much. As soon as he stood up and started across the office for his jacket, the pain came roaring back. He could see Vicky behind the steering wheel—the dashboard light bathing her face—shouting *Get in! Get in!* The belt of pain tightening around his ribs as he'd thrown himself onto the seat, and not really feeling the pain, he realized. Thinking she was safe.

He flipped the light switch, went into the corridor, and turned off those lights. Darkness fell into the stillness of the building. He let himself outside, locked the door, and headed down the steps, which seemed even slicker than earlier.

He had reached the alley between the administration building and the church when he heard the engines gearing down, the vehicles plowing through the snow. AA members arriving a little early, he thought. They could help him set up the chairs.

He was about to start down the alley toward Eagle Hall when he saw the two trucks racing across the grounds, clouds of snow swirling about, darting in and out of the circles of light around Circle Drive. He could make out three men in each truck, bulky shoulders squeezed together. The passenger window in the lead truck dropped, and an Indian leaned out, yelling and hammering a fist against the door. The engines growled as the trucks skidded to a stop next to his pickup. The men jumped out. Bellows took his place in the center, the others shadowing him. One of the shadows carried a metal baseball bat that glinted under the streetlamp.

"You should be satisfied, Bellows," Father John shouted. They were about thirty feet away, but closing the distance, heavy looking boots digging in the snow. "You gave me a couple of bad ribs. That ought to be enough for you."

"How about a broken head?" the Indian with the bat yelled.

"What do you want?" Father John kept his gaze on Bellows, making a point to ignore the others. Bellows was the man he had to deal with. He could almost hear his father's voice in his head: *Look for the leader of the pack. Take out the leader and the rest will turn tail and run.* But he had been twelve years old, and his father had been giving him tips about bullies on Commonwealth Avenue, not a hardened druggie like Bellows. They were no more than six feet away now, squinting at him, readying themselves for some choreographed maneuver. It was almost comical. He swallowed back the guffaw rising in his throat. He could see the sweat on their foreheads. Odors of whiskey and something else that he couldn't identify drifted toward him.

"Snitches deserve punishment," Bellows said.

"What are you talking about?"

"You come into Tracers looking for me." Bellows held up a gloved paw. "You and that Rap lawyer. Troy told her I was at the house in Ethete, ain't that right? So you and her come looking for me, make sure I match the description that bastard give her. Don't think I don't know where to find her." He swung his head back and forth and let out a raspy laugh. "Now ain't that funny. You a priest."

Father John didn't say anything. He kept his eyes on the man.

"Over at Tracers with the lady. Your parishioners know what you're up to in the evenings, Father?" he said, drawing out the word.

"Get to the point."

"You paid off Hun at the bar to point me out. Well, Hun ain't gonna be pointing at nobody for a while. You seen what you come for and you went running to the fed, ain't that right?"

"Your name never came up, Bellows."

"I'm supposed to believe that, you lying priest. You'll say anything to save your neck. How come the fed started coming around, asking stupid questions? Pulling in Lennie here." He lifted an eyebrow and looked slantwise in the direction of the guy with the bat. "Trying to get him to rat me out. Where was I the night Kiki got offed? Why'd I do it? Says the federal grand jury's gonna indict me for murder one, and the boys are gonna be accessories, so they'd better save their own skins."

"Kiki Wallowingbull was a friend of mine." Father John said, his gaze still on Bellows. At the periphery, he could see Lennie inching forward. And beyond, headlights turning into the mission, weaving through the cottonwoods.

"So what?"

"So I wanted to make sure you weren't the guy that killed him." The headlights bounced over Circle Drive.

"You snitched me out . . ." Bellows balled his fists and dropped his head, like a bull about to charge.

"Hold on." Father John made himself stay in place, holding Bellows and the bat guy in his gaze. Thinking, he would have to take out the bat guy. The instant the bat lifted, he would deflect it with his arm and throw his weight into the guy. Playing all of it out in an instant, like a silent movie racing in his head. The others would be all over him, but he'd have a couple seconds. The headlights splashed around them. "I don't think you killed Kiki," he said.

The guy with the bat did a sideways turn into the headlights. "We got company."

"Get him now!" Bellows lurched forward. Father John felt the blow rip through him like a cannonball. He managed to land a fist in the man's windpipe that put him off balance, but then the others were on him. Someone ripped his arm back and started shoving it toward his shoulder. He was floating in a blaze of klieg lights, dark figures stumbling around, actors all of them.

He was barely aware of the thwack of a door shutting and a man's voice shouting: "Back off, you sonsobitches!" There was the crack of a rifle shot.

The figures around him froze in place. Father John felt the pressure ease off a little but his arm was still immobilized. He couldn't move. It was all he could do to stay on his feet.

"Let him go!"

Bellows straightened his shoulders and turned toward the dark figure gripping the rifle, backlit by the headlights. "What're you gonna do, old man? Shoot all of us?"

"Nah, Bellows!" It was Lucky Meadows, one of the AA regulars. He took a step forward and lifted the rifle. "I'm just gonna shoot you."

Bellows stayed still a moment. "Let's get outta here," he said finally. He made a marching move, and the others shifted toward him. Father John realized his arm was free.

"You ain't goin' nowhere." Lucky kept the rifle pointed at Bellows's chest. Father John was thinking that the man had slogged through the jungles of Vietnam with a rifle on his back. He could bring a bighorn sheep down with a bullet in the heart from across a mountain.

"Nobody moves 'til the cops get here."

"You crazy, old man?" Bellows shouted. "You know who you're talking to? Maybe you don't like living."

Father John managed to work his arm down. It felt like a log, numb and stiff with pain circling at the edges. Thank God, it wasn't broken. He headed past the Indians, rubbing his arm, trying to coach the circulation back.

"Called the cops on my cell soon's I seen what was goin' on," Lucky said when Father John moved in beside him. "On the ground," he shouted. "Facedown!" The rifle was still trained on Bellows.

"Do what he says," Bellows shouted.

They started to drop, one by one. Knees and toes of boots digging into the snow. Then they were stomach down, faces turned sideways. Sirens had started out on Seventeen-Mile Road. Lennie coughed into the snow.

"You're next," Lucky said to Bellows.

"This ain't got nothing to do with you." Bellows raised both hands, palms outward in the Plains Indian sign of peace. "You let us get outta here, I won't forget it."

"I killed better men than you. You got one second to get on your face."

Bellows got on his knees, eyes locked on Lucky, anger and hatred shooting out of the black pupils. Sirens blasted through the quiet. "You're gonna pay, old man," Bellows said, his voice filled with menace.

Then he was on his stomach, setting the side of his face into the snow as two police cars slid to a stop, blue, yellow, and red lights flashing on the roofs. Wind River Police shone on the doors. The sirens cut off, leaving an echo hanging in the air.

The doors flung open, and four officers emerged. Gripping black pistols, they came forward in a phalanx. "What's going on, Father?" one of them said.

"Goons tried to kill Father John," Lucky said. "I got here just in time. Had my rifle in the truck."

"Okay. Drop the rifle," the officer said, and Father John realized that Lucky still had the rifle on Bellows. He leaned over and set the rifle in the snow.

Other vehicles turned into the mission, and a line of four pickups started around Circle Drive. Engines ground to a stop; doors snapped open. "Stay back," one of the officers shouted. "Police business. Best you drive on out of here."

Parishioners all of them. They stood their ground, arms folded, watching, just as Father John knew they would. St. Francis belonged to them. They wouldn't leave until they knew everything was okay.

Another officer had pulled out a radio. "Disturbance at the mission," he said, the radio close to his mouth. "Six Indians involved. Need backup."

"Is it true, Father?" The first officer stepped forward while the others took up positions around the men spread-eagle on the ground. "They came here to kill you?"

"They wanted to teach me a lesson," he said. His body was on fire.

"They were beating him up when I got here," Lucky said.

"You need an ambulance?"

"No ambulance," Father John said. No ambulance and no hospital and no painkillers to take off the edge and bring the old thirst for whiskey crashing over him, washing him away. He would have to push through this.

"I'm going to need a statement."

"Right," he said.

25

FATHER JOHN SPOTTED the Jeep in the rearview mirror as he turned into the mission grounds. A few car lengths behind, and long shadows of cottonwoods falling over the snow-packed road between the Jeep and his pickup. Vicky was behind the steering wheel, holding on tight, he imagined, her expression hard set with whatever was racing through her mind. He had been gone six months, yet in the moment she had walked into his office, he had felt as if he had never left, everything about her exactly the way he remembered.

He drove around Circle Drive and slid across an icy patch of snow into his parking place below the window of his office. He lifted himself out in a blur of pain and waited until Vicky had pulled in alongside, then opened her door. She gathered up her bag on the passenger seat and dropped out of the Jeep.

"Do you have a few minutes?" she said.

He waved her ahead, then took her arm to steady her on the ice, although he was probably the one who needed steadying, he realized. Her arm felt small and thin beneath the sleeve of her black wool coat. He moved ahead up the icy steps that he had sprinkled with salt earlier and flung open the massive wood door. Lucy had turned the light on, and a column of light flowed out of the corridor and into his office on the right.

"I can make a fresh pot of coffee," he said, leading the way. The stale smell of coffee permeated the office. What was left of the coffee he had made earlier this morning looked black and thick in the pot that sat on the table next to the door.

"No. No." She waved away the suggestion. "This won't take long." She had set her bag onto the chair and was already patrolling the office. It always made him want to smile—her way of handling things was so different from his. No sitting at the desk, pondering, thinking, attempting to create perfectly logical syllogisms—in the Jesuit way. Sometimes logic had nothing to do with the truth.

He hung up his jacket, then he went over and half sat against the desk. "Tell me what's bothering you," he said.

She stopped pacing and faced him. "Jason Bellows was indicted for homicide this morning. I have to find the man who's been contacting me."

He understood immediately. "Your anonymous caller doesn't have any reason to be found."

"Exactly," she said. "He'll live the rest of his life waiting for a knock on the door. I can help him clear up this whole matter. He'll have his life back."

"Vicky . . ."

She swung toward him and put up one hand. "I know," she said, and that made him swallow a smile. How was it she knew that he was about to tell her it could be dangerous to locate a man who believes he had gotten away with killing another man?

"I've met with Professor Gorsuch. She has already warned me."

Vicky turned and went back to carving out the circle on the floor. "I heard the sorrow in his voice, the remorse. I heard the fear that he would be taken from his child, that his child would grow up without a father."

"How do you expect to find him?"

"The same way Kiki did. I'm going to LA to see Susan this weekend, and I intend to stay a few days and see if I can learn what it was that Kiki found. I need your help. What did Kiki do in LA? Where did he go? Who did he talk to? You've been talking to people on the rez, haven't you?"

He nodded, and this time he did smile. How well she knew him. "I haven't come up with much. Nobody I've talked to mentioned anything about Kiki in LA."

"Whatever he came up with out there, I think it could have led to his death." She started around in the circle again. "The caller has never told me what made him kill Kiki, just that it was self-defense. Now Jason Bellows has been indicted and he'll probably be convicted. Drug dealer, gang leader. Assaulted anybody that crossed him, including you." She stopped again and swung toward him. "I heard about last night," she said. "How are you?"

He shrugged. "A little stiff and sore." Not quite the truth, he was thinking.

"Bastard." She spit out the word and went back to pacing. "Bellows belongs in prison all right, but not for a murder he didn't commit. God!" She pushed her hair back, letting the thick black strands run through her fingers. "Gianelli and the U.S. attorney have been waiting for a case with enough evidence to convict him, and now they have it. Troy Tallfeathers, one of our former clients"—she threw up both hands and lifted her eyes to the ceiling—"happened to go to the house at Ethete where Kiki was knocked out. He'll testify that he saw Bellows hitting him. One of Bellows's gang members, Lennie Musser, will back him up. It was Troy who dumped Kiki's body at the river on Bellows's orders."

Father John had to look away. He could still see the barren snow-scape along the banks of the Little Wind River, the snow lifting in the wind. The image of Kiki's body, thrown down the bank, legs bent and arms askew, eyes fixed on the sky, and the surprised expression frozen on his face. The image would never leave him. Left there to die by a man named Troy Tallfeathers.

Vicky had stopped pacing; something had gone out of her now, some spark. She looked small, huddled inside the big black coat. "Bellows wanted Kiki left where other druggies—anybody who might consider moving into Bellows's territory—would get the message. But he was wrong. I think Kiki went to the house to talk to somebody about what happened to his ancestor and ended up dead. I can't prove it unless I find the caller."

Father John leaned across the desk and rummaged through the folders that Lucy had set in the metal rack. He lifted out the folder with the articles, photos, and notes he had been compiling and thumbed through the pages until he found the photo of Arapahos and Shoshones taken during rehearsal in Hollywood for the Indian show. "Charlie and his friends William Thunder and James Painted Brush are on the right," he said, handing the photo to Vicky. He told her that all of the Arapahos and Shoshones had returned to the reservation when *The Covered Wagon* was finished. Then fifty of them had gone to Hollywood in the spring of 1923 to promote the movie. "Charlie and Anna were married while he was home," Father John said. "She was pregnant with Andrew when he left for Hollywood."

Vicky studied the photo, shaking her head. "Imagine," she said. "Ancestors prancing around a stage in Hollywood, roping plaster cows, wearing skins and moccasins, talking with their hands. I'm sure the audiences were amused." She waited a beat before she asked when Charlie had disappeared.

Father John flipped through the file folder and pulled out the letter from Tim McCoy that Andrew had loaned him. "The evening of April

10." He handed her the letter. "Charlie didn't show up at the Egyptian Theatre for the premiere, and William rode up to Cahuenga Pass where the camp was. He wasn't anywhere around. McCoy checked with the police. There were no reports of a dead Indian. There's more," he said, and he gave her the copies of the articles on Missy Mae Markham from the movie magazines and the photo James Painted Brush had taken.

Vicky took a moment to scan through all of it. Finally she looked up. "You think there was something between a movie star and Charlie? White woman and Indian? That would have caused trouble, all right."

"She's looking at Charlie," Father John said, "but William is looking at her."

"Oh, my God." Vicky slapped the little pile on the desk. "A love triangle."

Father John slipped the papers back into the folder. "Missy Mae Markham earned millions for the studio," he said. "A public scandal involving an Indian would have destroyed her at the box office."

"Maybe they ran off together. Disappeared. Charlie and the movie star."

Father John tapped the folder. "One of the photos shows her in Flagstaff with Jesse Lasky after Charlie disappeared."

Vicky walked over to the window and looked out. The gray daylight cast a silvery sheen on her hair. She could hear a truck gearing down on Seventeen-Mile Road. Finally she turned around. "Did Kiki see the photo of Charlie and William with Missy Mae Markham?"

Father John nodded. Then he told her what Felix Painted Brush had said, how Kiki had studied the photo a long time. "Kiki was looking for the truth," he said.

"The truth!" Vicky walked across the office, picked up her black bag, and dug out her cell phone. "Whatever the truth is," she said, tapping on the keys, "Kiki got hold of the man who has been calling me." She made a half turn toward the door and tilted her head against the cell. "Dede, this is Vicky Holden," she said. "Jason Bellows has been indicted and he's in the county jail. Call me. I need your help." She closed the cell, slipped it back into her bag, and set the bag over her shoulder. "I have a plane to catch," she said.

26

CHARLIE SWUNG THE rope overhead then snapped it down over the wooden calf at the far corner of the stage. In an instant, the calf clattered across the floorboards, and Charlie pulled the rope into a tight circle. The crowd standing around burst into applause. Actors and actresses, big stars some of them, William had heard, rehearsing and shooting moving pictures on the studio's backlot. Beyond the stage, he could see cameras set on tripods in front of the other stages. Except it looked like the shooting had stopped and most everybody had come over to the rehearsal stage to watch an Arapaho lasso a wooden calf. Charlie was good at it. He could rope a calf running five horses' length ahead, but nobody on the reservation ever came around to clap and cheer. It was a job, cowboying.

Trouble was, there weren't so many jobs lately, so he and Charlie and the others had gotten back on the train at Rawlins and ridden all the way into Los Angeles with their ponies and tipis in the baggage cars. They arrived in LA two days ago. Everything looked different.

Palm trees growing along the streets, pepper trees and lemon trees and orange groves running over the hillsides, and motorcars driving up and down alongside carts pulled by horses and red streetcars screeching on iron rails. They rode their ponies all the way to Hollywood, with the big white sign on the mountainside that said Hollywoodland. A policeman stood on a box at one of the intersections and directed the traffic. They rode down Hollywood Boulevard and on out to Cahuenga Pass where Mr. McCoy said they should set up camp. "No telling how long we're gonna be here," he had said.

The longer the better, William thought. The pay was good, and all they had to do was put on an Indian show every night at the Egyptian Theatre. And tonight was the moving picture premiere. They had been rehearsing three hours now. Charlie was swinging the rope high and kicking the heels of his boots against the plank floorboards. He let the lasso fly and, this time, caught a tree stump that toppled sideways and came clanking toward him. Another roar of applause went up. The crowd started stomping their feet on the dusty ground, and out of the corner of his eye, William saw Missy Mae Markham standing a little ways off, the blond head cocked to one side, a sad, shrunken look about her. She was all in black: black dress with a black shawl around her shoulders. Still she was beautiful, her skin and hair all white and golden. Charlie had seen her, too, because he was looking her way as he yanked the rope off the stump, wound it into a thick circle and slung it over his shoulder.

The crowd was still cheering as Charlie came down the steps at the side of the stage. William watched him cut a straight line toward the girl. In the four months they had spent on the reservation, it seemed as if Charlie had forgotten about her. He and Anna got married; he was going to be a father. Missy was in the past.

Except that she was here in Hollywood. Charlie leaned in close, saying something to her, and she gazed up at him with the soft, trusting look of a deer.

"Excellent!" Mr. Lasky strode over to Charlie and thumped him on the back. The girl seemed to dissolve into the air, floating toward the other stages in her ragged black dress. "You'll wow 'em. Get 'em in the mood for the moving picture. Sign language people, you go on next." He waved toward Goes-in-Lodge and McCoy standing near the steps.

Charlie was looking around, surprise fixed in his expression, as if he expected the girl to still be nearby. The surprise started to fade into something else, William thought, a mixture of disappointment and relief. They had ridden down from Cahuenga Pass early this morning, he and Charlie. People out on the sidewalks had stopped and stared, then shrugged and kept going, and William had understood that it was all part of the moving picture business. Anything might come down the street. A few drivers had blasted their horns and waved for them to get out of the way. Most had driven past without turning their heads.

They left the ponies in the sheds out behind the backlot where Cecil B. DeMille himself left his horse, McCoy said, and spent an hour walking around the stages. All kinds of rooms—living rooms and dining rooms with thick carpets and polished tables and velvet chairs and mirrors with golden frames; nurseries with rocking chairs and cradles and toys on the floor; doctor offices with white lace on the chairs and magazines stacked on little tables, newspaper offices with typewriters and telephones on the desks. And all of it so real—all the stories the white men were making. It was hard to get his bearings, William thought, between what was true and what seemed to be true.

Goes-in-Lodge and McCoy were on the stage now, hands and fingers flying, making words out of signs. Goes-in-Lodge had on his best deerskin trousers and the shirt with fringe down the sleeves and beaded designs that his wife had sewn on the front. He wore his eagle feathered headdress, the feathers hanging down his back, each feather earned by an act of courage or generosity. William had seen the old buffalo warrior dressed like that at a hundred celebrations and ceremonies. They were the clothes he had worn on the plains, part of who he was. Now he lifted both hands and worked his fingers into signs that made McCoy burst into laughter.

"Translator! Translator!" Mr. Lasky paced in front of the stage. "Nobody knows what's going on. We need somebody to translate. You there." He flapped a small hand toward William. "You stand up on the stage and tell the audience what the hell's going on. You understand Indian signs, right?"

William nodded and made his way up the steps. He moved to the front corner of the stage where he could see both McCoy and Goes-in-Lodge. McCoy's fingers were dancing, and William said, "What do Indians like best about white people?" Then Goes-in-Lodge's fingers started moving. "Arapahos like white people's coffee," William said.

McCoy signed again, and William said, "How do you take your coffee?"

Back to Goes-in-Lodge, whose hands never seemed to stop moving. "We drink coffee half and half," William said.

McCoy made another sign, and William said, "Half coffee and half cream?"

Goes-in-Lodge tipped his head and ran his fingers up the air, and McCoy laughed. "Half coffee and half sugar," William said.

Mr. Lasky stopped pacing and gave a bark of laughter. "Half sugar!" he shouted. "Oh, that's good. Make sure you leave that in."

William translated the rest of the conversation, all about the buffalo days and how the Arapahos had lived on the plains. Nothing about the days on the reservation, which, back in the desert, Mr. Lasky had said sounded boring. When Goes-in-Lodge and McCoy finished, William followed them down the steps. Within minutes the musicians had hauled a large, round drum onto the stage, and the air filled with a low, steady thud-thud-thud that mingled with the high-pitched voices of the singers.

"Dancers get ready!" Mr. Lasky shouted. "You go on next."

William started for the tent where the trunks filled with regalia

were kept. The earth seemed to vibrate with the drumbeats. Most of
the dancers were already dressed in breechcloths and beaded vests and
moccasins. They wore feathered bustles and beaded bracelets, the fin-
est things they owned, faded and worn-looking, passed down from
the buffalo days. Most had roaches made of porcupine hair on their
heads, but a few wore long, flowing feathered headdresses. He found
his own regalia and started to get dressed when, past the opening of
the tent, he saw Charlie standing close to the girl. She tilted her head
back and looked up at him. There was something desperate in the way
she reached for his arm.

William tossed the regalia aside and ran out of the tent, passing the
dancers who had started to form into little groups. The girl lifted a
hand and let it flutter in the air like a white handkerchief, and William
saw James start toward them. He held the little black camera in both
hands.

"Take our picture," the girl called. Her voice sounded like the tinkling of a cow's bell in the emptiness of the plains.

William hurried over. He could hear Charlie murmur something
about not wanting any pictures.

"Nonsense," the girl said. Her arm was like white silk draped over
Charlie's brown arm. "Everyone wants a picture with a movie star! Go
ahead," she said to James.

A mixture of confusion and wariness seemed to freeze James in
place. He stood a few feet from Charlie and the girl, the camera gripped
to his chest.

"Go on," she said.

"No, Missy," Charlie said. He was attempting to remove his arm
from hers. "We have to put on the regalia."

"Regalia, schmalia." The girl let out a lilting laugh. "Take our picture."

William stepped next to the girl. Charlie was married now, and pictures could tell true stories. He and Charlie with the girl would be

better than Charlie alone. William stood as close as he dared, but the girl seemed unaware of his presence. She was more beautiful than he had realized. The smell of lavender floated around her.

"Go on," she said again, tilting her head sideways and lifting her chin. She held herself perfectly still.

Charlie gave an almost imperceptible nod, and James lifted the black box and squinted with one eye into the lens in the back. There was a clicking noise, and he lowered the box. The girl gave out another laugh and said, "See? Was that so bad? Really, Charlie," she said, folding both white arms around his. "Do you know how many men would give their lives to be in this picture?"

The skinny bodyguard, when he appeared, seemed to come from nowhere, as if he had dropped out of the sky. He wedged his rail-like shoulders between Charlie and the girl and looped an arm around her waist. "You're wanted on the scene, Missy," he said, pulling the girl away.

"Leave me alone," she said.

"I'll call Mr. Lasky."

"Go to hell!" She tossed her head and shrugged out of his grasp, but something had left her—a spark of fire snuffed out. She whirled about and headed back toward the stage across the lot where two cameramen waited, arms draped over the top of the cameras. One of them puffed on a cigarette.

"Let's go," William said, nodding toward the tent. James was already ahead, and they set out after him, reluctance in Charlie's step, William thought, as if he hadn't wanted to be free of the white arms wrapped around his.

William waited until they were alone in the tent, pulling on the last of the regalia, tying the feathered bustles around their waists. The thud of the drums was muffled by the canvas walls. William could hear the dancers moving about outside, lining up for the grand march onto the stage.

"Did you tell her?" William said.

Charlie was fixing a roach on top of his head. He stood in front of a small mirror propped on a trunk. He didn't say anything.

"Did you tell her you and Anna got married? Did you tell her about the child?"

"She doesn't care about that," Charlie said. He had the roach in place, and he swung around and pushed back the flap. Sunshine flared across the tent.

"All the same, you have to tell her."

Charlie hesitated in the opening. "Maybe you wish you was me," he said. "Maybe you wish she was coming around you."

"For godssakes, Charlie. She could've gotten us all sent home from the desert. She can still get us sent home. Mr. Lasky hears . . ."

He was talking to Charlie's back. He went out after him and joined the line of dancers marching up the steps and onto the stage, a whirl of headdresses and bustles and feathers, bright colors winking in the sunshine. The drum was beating loud and fast. William moved close behind Charlie. "If you don't tell her," he said, "I will have to."

"Stay out of my business." Charlie spit the words over his shoulder.

"We need the money, Charlie." William could sense the stiffness and anger in the way Charlie pounded his feet to the thud of the drums and the way he swung his head about. "I'm not gonna let you take it away from us," he said.

27

VICKY SPOTTED SUSAN coming through the crowd at the baggage carousels at LAX, the long legs striding forward, the black hair flying behind. Her smile looked joyful and free. It was the first thought that came into Vicky's mind—*my daughter is happy!*—as she hurried to meet her, dodging the luggage piled on the floor and the people moving about, her own bag clacking behind. She held on to Susan for the longest moment; she could feel the moisture on her face, or was it the moisture on her own? Finally she stepped back and, still holding her hands, said, "You look great, honey!"

"I am so glad you're here." Susan tossed her head back and let out a peal of laughter. "We are going to have such a good time. I have everything planned." She went on about the Getty Museum and the beach and a string of restaurants Vicky had never heard of, and Vicky realized that the sandy-haired, serious-looking young man a couple of feet away was with Susan.

"Oh, Mom," Susan said, following Vicky's gaze and letting go of her hands. "This is Brett. Brett, meet my mom."

The young man stepped forward and held out his hand. His grip was firm and confident, but the serious look had dissolved into a boyish grin. "I've heard so much about you," he said. An unruly strand of hair strayed over his forehead. There were tiny laugh lines at the corners of his light blue eyes. "Susan's been looking forward to your visit."

"We'll fill you in on the details over dinner," Susan said. They made their way around a couple of kids who were sprawled on pieces of luggage while the parents tried to fit other suitcases onto a cart. Vicky realized that Brett must have taken her bag because he was pulling it along, leading the way out of the area, down escalators, and into the parking garage.

He drove a slate-colored sedan, and they surged out of the lot and into a stream of traffic eight lanes wide with overhead signs that steered the lanes in different directions, and all of it flowing as if a million cars going different places at the same time were normal. It was almost dark, and the crazy patterns of headlights jumped like pieces of glass in a kaleidoscope. Susan leaned back from the passenger seat and talked on about her job in visual effects, the crazy boss, but the boss was leaving for a new position soon, and too bad for the new people she would be managing.

Vicky found herself holding her breath in the roar of traffic and the blur of vehicles as they changed lanes, finally settling into the far right lane that veered off the freeway and down a ramp. The freeway traffic zoomed past above. Another moment and they were driving along a boulevard lined with palm trees and mounds of red, yellow, and purple flowers. Behind the flowers were parking lots and shops and restaurants. She wondered what it was like when the Arapahos had come here? Orange and lemon groves spread over the hillsides? Palm trees lining the dusty roads? Probably not many vehicles, yet more than they had ever seen on the reservation, and the Pacific Ocean roaring in the distance.

Brett swung into a parking lot, and Vicky could see a slice of the beach and the boardwalk framed by the buildings. She and Susan got out at the entrance to a restaurant and headed up the wood steps. Behind them, the tires of the sedan scraped the asphalt as Brett peeled away to find a parking place.

"Isn't he great, Mom?" Susan said. Vicky held the heavy wooden door open, then followed Susan inside where Susan told the woman behind the high desk that they had reservations for three. Holden was the name.

"Well?" Susan said. "What do you think?"

"He seems very nice," Vicky told her as the woman ushered them across the restaurant and out to a vacant table on a deck with small heaters set among the tables. She placed three menus in red-leather folders on the white tablecloth and told them to enjoy dinner.

"You're okay that he's white?"

"I'm okay with Brett as long as you are," Vicky said.

"White men and Indian women—that's always been okay, right?" Susan took the chair with the back to the railing and waved Vicky to the chair with the best view of the white-capped waves rolling toward the beach under a silvery sky. "But an Indian man with a white woman? That was a no-no. I mean, it could get the Indian killed. Why do you think that was?"

"It was the times," Vicky said. She hadn't been able to shake the image of the beautiful white girl staring up at Charlie Wallowingbull, the white arms folded around the brown arm, and the dark shape of William Thunder hovering above her. "Times have changed," she heard herself saying, but Susan's words clanged in her ears: *It could get the Indian killed.*

She looked out at the ocean. It always took her breath away, the swells of the waves, the vastness, like the plains, stretching into the sky. People strolled on the beach, some barefoot, dancing in and out of the waves, slacks rolled to their knees. It was comfortable on the deck, but people outside wore light jackets, backs blowing out in the wind.

A stream of bikers and in-line skaters moved through the overhead lights along the boardwalk. The muffled shouts and laughter and the roar of the waves mingled with the violin music on the sound system.

"Brett's very serious, you know," Susan said.

"Serious about you?" Vicky looked back at her daughter.

"Oh, Mom, come on." Little red blotches appeared on Susan's cheeks, the way they had blossomed when she was small and embarrassed about something. "Serious? Does anybody even talk that way anymore? I mean, besides mothers?"

Vicky laughed. "You like him, I can see that."

"I meant he's serious about his career. He's with Bridges, Stanson, and Hughes in Westwood. Ever heard of them?"

Vicky nodded and took a sip from the water glass the waitress had filled. One of the major law firms on the West Coast. Adam had spent several years with a similar firm before he moved to Wyoming to concentrate on Indian law. No doubt Adam would know some of the lawyers at Brett's firm. She didn't say anything. She didn't want to bring up the subject of Adam.

She watched Brett weaving his way past the other tables. He took the seat on Vicky's right, but leaned in close to Susan and gave her a smile of accomplishment. When the waitress reappeared, they ordered salads, grilled shrimp, crab cakes and pasta, iced tea, and bread that, when it came, steamed the white cloth on top of the basket. They made small talk for a long while—the polite preliminaries, Vicky thought, just like on the rez. What was Susan working on? Big project, long hours with a lot of overtime, creating a visual train wreck for a Western movie. "You know how they used to film train wrecks?" Susan said. "They set two trains on the track coming at each other, and the engineers jumped off just before the crash. Locomotives reared up in the air, cars rolled off the tracks. Now we do it with graphics: smoke, steam, fire, the whole works. It's all make-believe. Not like the old days."

After the waitress had delivered the plates of food, Susan asked how Vicky's practice was going, a kind of vacant politeness in her voice, as if she felt an obligation to ask, even if the answer didn't really interest her. The law was what had taken her from Susan and Lucas when they were kids—all those years of school to become an attorney.

"I manage to stay busy," Vicky said, keeping the answer vague. She took a bite of pasta and realized her cell was ringing. "Excuse me." She got to her feet and pulled out the cell as she walked to the entry. "Hello," she said, pushing through the door. The cool breeze off the ocean and the damp air worked their way through her light sweater.

"You sure Bellows is in jail?" It was Dede's voice, filled with suspicion and defiance.

"Thanks for getting back to me," Vicky said. Then she heard herself assuring the girl that Jason Bellows was in custody and that, she was sure, bail would be set high enough to insure he would not be set free. "I need your help," she said.

"Bellows killed him," the girl said. "Why don't you just accept it?"

"Because the autopsy showed that Kiki was free of drugs, and I think somebody else killed him." Vicky gave the girl a second to understand before she went on. "What did Kiki do in Hollywood? Who did he talk to? Where did he go?"

"How would I know?"

"You're the only one who does know, Dede. Think! He must have told you something."

"What are you? Bellows's lawyer? He deserves to rot in prison. I'm not gonna help you get him free."

"I'm not his lawyer. I'm trying to get to the truth. The fed thinks Kiki was killed in a drug deal, and the prosecutor will make a strong case that Kiki tried to move in on Bellows's territory. Everybody on the rez will remember Kiki as a druggie that got what was coming to him. You know that isn't the truth, Dede. You told me Kiki was clean. Please tell me anything you can remember. Where did he go? How did he get around LA?"

"He drove, of course. Isn't that what people do out there?"

"He rented a car?"

"Used up most of his money on an old wreck, he said. Kept break-ing down on the freeways and he had to get out and jiggle wires or something. He was good with cars, Kiki was. Lived in the wreck, he told me. His own Motel 6. Parked in the Wal-Mart lots at night and ate dollar burgers. He got by."

"Did he look up any old records?"

"Records?" A sharp guffaw came over the line. "You mean like go-ing to the library or something?"

"I mean police records."

"Kiki wasn't going around any cops, if that's what you're getting at. All I remember him saying is that he talked to some old people."

"Old people?" Vicky said. A jumble of questions in her mind now. "Were they connected to the movies? Who were they? How did he find them?"

"You know what?" The old cynicism and resistance were back. "I didn't ask him all them questions 'cause I didn't care. And you know what else? I still don't care, so you got all I know and I'm gonna hang up now."

"Wait," Vicky said, but she was talking into a dead phone.

She walked back through the restaurant and took her chair. "Sorry," she said. "A call about work." She was immediately sorry she had said it, because Susan's head snapped back and a wary expression flooded her eyes. "About Kiki Wallowingbull." Vicky hurried on, a weak attempt to explain. "Did you happen to know him?" They were close to the same age, she was thinking. There was every chance Susan might have run into him.

"Kiki's your client?" Susan said. "He's a loser, Mom. Into drugs big-time in high school. I heard he dropped out sophomore year. What are you doing with clients like that? I thought you and Adam were handling Indian law."

"Kiki was killed a week ago," Vicky said. "He was off drugs."

Susan spread both hands over the traces of salad left on her plate. "I get it. You're representing the guy that killed him."

Vicky took a bite of the crab cake and washed it down with a drink of tea. She wasn't hungry; a storm of butterflies had erupted in her stomach. "It may have been self-defense," she heard herself saying. "I'm trying to get to the truth. Just before he was killed, Kiki came here to find out what happened to his great-grandfather when he was working in Hollywood in 1923."

"He was in the movies?" Brett said. "Susan told me her people were in some of the old Westerns."

Vicky nodded. "Charlie Wallowingbull disappeared from Hollywood," she said. "The family has always believed he was killed. Kiki came here to find out what happened."

"Nineteen twenty-three." Susan shook her head. "This is a now place, Mom. I mean, all anybody cares about is what's happening today."

"I think Kiki found something," Vicky said.

"Police records?" This from Brett.

"It's possible, but his girlfriend doesn't think so." And yet, there was no telling what Kiki might have done or where he might have gone. "One of the old movie stars, Tim McCoy, tried to find out what happened," Vicky said. Then she explained that McCoy hadn't been able to locate any police records.

"A lot of records weren't open back then," Brett said. "It wasn't easy for a curious citizen to get access to police records. The Hollywood division can confirm if any exist. It can take several weeks to get copies, but I've got a friend in records. He might be able to cut through the red tape."

Vicky looked at the young man. The boyish grin, the eagerness, replaced now with an earnest, professional manner in the way he had straightened his shoulders and lifted his head. *He's serious,* Susan had said. "I couldn't ask you . . ."

Brett held up his hand. "I do it all the time."

"Brett's an investigator," Susan said.

Vicky sat back, her eyes still on the young man. "I see. You are an investigator for the law firm."

"Soon to be a lawyer, I hope," Brett said. "I'm in my second year of law school. Evening classes. I'd be glad to see if there's any records from 1923 on a missing Indian male. Do you know where he was staying?"

"Cahuenga Pass."

"You're kidding," Susan said.

"They camped in the pass and rode horses into Hollywood every day."

Susan tossed her head back and laughed. "A surprise every minute in this town," she said.

"What else did this Kiki Wallowingbull do out here?" Brett said.

Vicky told him that all she knew was what Kiki's girlfriend had said. "He told her he talked with some old people, but there can't be any movie people around who were old enough in 1923 to know what happened."

"Their kids might know," Brett said. "And they'd have to be pretty old."

"Thing about the movie business, Mom"—Susan leaned over the table—"is that it's a family business. Kids follow Mom and Dad into the movies. I know best boys and grips and makeup artists whose great-grandparents were in the movies."

"How would Kiki have gotten in touch with anyone who had worked on *The Covered Wagon*?"

"I know what I would do," Brett said. "Check out the retirement homes for movie folks."

"But you're an investigator. Kiki was an Indian from a reservation."

"All he had to do was Google retirement homes for movie people. My bet is he found somebody willing to chat with him."

Vicky gave the young man a smile and thanked him. Then she caught Susan's eyes. "I'll look into that on Monday," she said. "After we've enjoyed the weekend."

Susan leaned forward and scooted herself even closer to the edge of the table. "Let's check it out tomorrow," she said. "I'd like to hear about the old days out here. I mean, it would be interesting."

28

THE FREEWAY WOUND through the hills, then straightened out past stretches of shopping centers, car lots, and blocks of houses with tiled roofs and garages that jutted toward the street. But there were stretches of wilderness, too, the way the landscape had once been, Vicky thought. Palm trees waving overhead, and trees with red and blue flowers, indigo lilacs and sage bushes with apricot blossoms, and wild grasses tinged purple. Wisps of white clouds scudded across the pale blue sky. Everything so different, so unlike the plains.

"Not much farther," Susan said. She was a good driver, gearing down for traffic stops ahead, settling into a steady pace when the highway opened up. She had a small, light-blue sedan with a clicking noise in the engine that gathered energy whenever the car slowed down. Still it drove smoothly enough. She went on about the friend she worked with who had a house in Malibu with great views of the ocean from the pool. "Her parents are in the business," she said.

They crested a hill, then started dropping into what looked like a valley of rooftops and swimming pools intersected by asphalt grids, except for the wide, green open place that looked like a park off to the left. The grounds of the retirement home, Vicky suspected. This morning, she had checked the internet while Susan was still asleep and gotten the telephone numbers of three retirement homes for people in motion pictures. Later, on the way to the Getty Museum, she had called the offices, given her name—Vicky Holden, attorney from Wyoming—and said she would like to visit the people Kiki Wallowingbull had talked to two weeks ago. No record of a Mr. Wallowingbull on the visitor lists at the first two homes, but on the third call, the woman at the other end had hesitated before asking her to hold on. Vicky could hear the click of a keyboard and the rustle of paper. Finally the woman was back. Yes, Mr. Wallowingbull had spent time with two of the residents.

"Would it be possible to see them?" Vicky had asked. Oh, yes, it was possible. All the residents loved visitors, and Norma Brown and Hugh Caldwell had so enjoyed chatting about the old days with Mr. Wallowingbull. This afternoon would be a good time, around three o'clock.

Susan slowed down, and the clicking noise gathered into the fast rhythm of a pendulum in an old clock. They made a right and drove through two brick columns onto the grounds of what resembled a college campus. The lane curved around manicured lawns with walkways past flower gardens and topiary trees. Small groups of people strolled along, men in khaki trousers and windbreakers, women in capris and pastel jackets. Ahead, set back from a circular drive, was a sprawling, one-story white stucco building with a bloodred tiled roof.

Vicky glanced at her watch. A quarter to three. The engine clicked faster as Susan turned into the drive and parked in front of a sign that said Visitors. They walked across the drive to the large porch in front of the leaded-glass door. Inside was all white marble tile and dark, polished tables with vases of flowers. The entry flowed into a corridor that ran toward the rear where a leaded-glass door mirrored the door in front. The blond-haired woman at the desk across the entry was getting to her feet as they walked over.

"You must be Ms. Holden," the woman said, holding out a hand. She looked about thirty, only a few years older than Susan, but there was an air of confidence and authority in the way she grasped Vicky's hand. She had a warm, practiced smile and blue eyes that matched the blue sapphire pendant at the base of her neck. "I'm Lilly Harrison, assistant manager," she said.

Vicky introduced Susan and the woman shook her hand. "I can't tell you how excited Hugh and Norma are to have other visitors interested in the old days. Would you mind signing in?" She pushed a registry across the desk.

Vicky signed in first. She was thinking that Kiki would have signed the same registry, and what he had learned here could have killed him. After Susan had signed her name, Lilly Harrison said, "They're waiting out on the lawn." She came around the desk and started down the wide corridor to the leaded-glass door in back.

They followed her across the marble-paved patio outside and down a grassy hillside to where a stand of bushes and gnarled trees separated the parklike grass from the beach. The sound of crashing waves came from the distance, and the soft sea breeze tugged at Vicky's slacks and sweater. The woman stopped in front of an elderly couple sitting in white wooden chairs that slanted backward. Beside them were two vacant chairs.

"Norma. Hugh. Here are your guests," she said, waving Vicky and Susan closer. "Vicky Holden, the lawyer I told you about, and her daughter, Susan. They're friends of Mr. Wallowingbull."

"Hugh Caldwell," the old man said, lifting his hand. In his eighties, Vicky guessed, with gray hair and a little gray goatee that gave him a rakish look despite the folds of wrinkled skin and the thick eyelids that drooped over his dark eyes. His palm was soft, but his grasp was surprisingly firm. "Pardon me if I don't get up," he said. "The ups and downs these days are no easy matter."

"Oh, Hugh," the elderly woman said. "You're as strong as a horse. You just don't want the bother." She looked from Vicky to Susan. "My, your daughter is beautiful like you," she said, holding up a limp white hand with gold–and–diamond rings on the fingers. "I'm Norma Brown. Perhaps you've seen my movies? Late-night television? A little diversion for insomiacs?" Vicky smiled and took the woman's hand. Then she stepped back so that Susan could greet them.

"I'll leave you to chat," Lilly Harrison said. She was already backing up the hill. Then she pivoted about and hurried toward the marble patio, long strides, arms swinging at her sides.

"Do sit down." Norma flecked ringed fingers in the direction of the vacant chairs, as if she were brushing dust out of the air, and Vicky perched on the edge of the chair close to the couple. Susan sat back in the other chair and crossed her legs as if she were settling in for a movie.

"So you are friends of that nice young Indian," Norma said. "He came all the way out here to talk about the past. Not many young people give a hoot about the old days. Too much going on too fast, you ask me."

Hugh gave a loud snort and looked slantways at Norma. "You forget how fast everything was in our day? Every generation has its own craziness. How's Kiki doing, anyway?"

Vicky took a moment, and in that moment, both of the old people seemed to understand that something had changed. They shifted around, walking their feet in her direction, and leaned on the armrests. She could hear the tension in the rhythm of their breathing.

"Kiki was killed a short time after he returned to the reservation," she said.

They stared at her, slack-jawed, eyes wide, as if they were waiting for the rest of it, something more to explain the inexplicable. Vicky heard herself saying that Kiki had gotten into an argument and was killed in self-defense. All of it supposition, based on words whispered over the telephone, uttered in the shadows.

"The poor boy," Norma said. "He told us he was looking for his great-grandfather, but I think he was looking for himself."

Vicky let the sound of the breeze fill up the space around them for a moment before she said, "It would help his family to know what he learned. It might help them to understand why he was killed. Can you tell me what you told him?"

"It was a long time ago, 1923." Hugh pulled at his goatee, working it into a neat triangle. "I was born that year, so I couldn't give him a blow-by-blow account of what might've gone on. Same for Norma here."

"Of course I wasn't born until much later," Norma said, gazing in the direction of the ocean, patting the silver hair into place, and Vicky suspected that much later was no more than a year or two. "Naturally I have no memories of my own from that time."

"Rumors were all we could give the boy," Hugh said.

Norma laughed. "Oh, how this town thrives on rumors and gossip. Always has." She brought her eyes to Vicky's. "We're in the story business. We live on stories. All we could tell that nice young man were stories we heard when we were kids."

Norma smiled. A far away look came into her eyes. She might have been lost in a movie playing in her head. "Mother did the makeup for big stars," Norma said. "Mary Pickford, Douglas Fairbanks, Charlie Chaplin, Joan Crawford, Mabel Normand. Lois Wilson. Missy Mae Markham. She used to hear a lot of juicy gossip. Who was sleeping with whom, that kind of thing. I used to sneak down the stairs and hide in a little alcove and listen to her and Dad talking. Dad was a cameraman. Karl Brown. You heard of him?" She hurried on without waiting for an answer. "That's how they got together, a whirlwind courtship on location for *The Covered Wagon*. Lots of Indians in that movie. Kiki said his great-grandfather was there."

"Did your parents talk about the movie?"

Norma nodded, still intent on the scenes in her head. "It was in 1939, the day Missy Mae Markham died. I remember Mother banging through the front door and shouting, 'Karl, you heard the news?' Dad was out by the pool, having a scotch and smoking his cigar. Mother marched out there, and naturally I followed. 'Missy's dead,' she said. I remember how Dad didn't say anything at first, just looked up at her like she was talking French or something. Finally he said, 'Took her a long time.'

"It was like a little earthquake running through everything." Hugh shifted forward. "Everybody remembered Missy Mae Markham. Big star in the twenties. Perfect, white complexion like you never saw. Folks said she had violet eyes that bored right into you. But drugs and alcohol got the best of her in the thirties. She had powerful patrons, but they deserted her one by one. Producers turned on her, wouldn't touch her with a ten-foot pole, couldn't rely on her showing up for work. She died of an overdose."

Norma ran the tips of her fingers over the rings on her other hand, polishing the stones. "I remember Mother poured herself a scotch and sat down next to Dad. The sun was setting and the patio turned red. Even the pool was red. Mother had a sadness about her. I remember how she sipped at her drink and started talking about *The Covered Wagon*. Just going back in her mind, and Dad nodding, like he remembered the same things. How Missy turned down the lead role, then changed her mind. Well, Lois Wilson had already been cast, but Missy went on location anyway. Mother said she hoped Lois would fall off a horse, and Cruze would have no choice but to put Missy in."

"My father had a lot of respect for Jimmie," Hugh said. "Made the A-list after *The Covered Wagon*. Dad said he learned everything he knew from watching Jimmie work. Didn't make much difference. Dad directed a slew of forgettable movies and never made the A-list, but he liked palling around with big names." Hugh leaned over and set a hand on Norma's arm. "But I digress," he said. "Better get to what you told the boy."

"What I told Kiki"—Norma turned to Vicky—"was what Mother said. Missy was Jesse Lasky's girlfriend, so she got pretty much what she wanted. Missy wanted him to fire Lois, but Cruze said he'd quit the movie, so Lasky had to tell her no. Made her real mad. She caused a lot of trouble on location. Even took up with the Indians," she said, her voice almost a whisper, "just to cause trouble."

"Gossip said she took up with Charlie Wallowingbull," Hugh said. "Turns out he was the boy's great-grandfather."

Norma pursed her lips together and nodded. "Charlie was real good-looking, Mother said. She worked on the Indians' makeup, too. Gave them big, black eyebrows and used rouge to highlight their cheekbones. She said everybody talked about Charlie and Missy, and Mother tried to warn him that she was Lasky's girlfriend. Told him no good would come from an affair with her. Eventually the rumors got back to Lasky, because he sent a bodyguard to keep tabs on Missy."

"Did that end the affair?"

Hugh gave out a loud guffaw. "Upped the ante with that woman," he said. "Tell them the rest of it."

"One Indian wasn't enough for Missy. Pretty soon the gossip was about the other Indian she was flirting with, Charlie's best friend."

"His best friend?" Susan scooted to the front of the chair. "She took up with his best friend?"

"She always had to be in the spotlight." Norma shook her head. "If one Indian didn't get her enough attention, she would have two. Cruze was beside himself. If the public heard that Missy Mae Markham was sleeping with Indians, well . . ." She held up both hands and spread her fingers. The diamonds and rubies flashed in the sun. "It would have ended Missy's career and cost the studio a lot of money. The body-guard must've gotten word to Lasky, because one day, Missy was gone from the location. She went on as usual for a while, starring in one movie after the other. Probably never gave another thought to Charlie or his friend."

"What did Kiki say when you told him all of this?" Vicky asked.

"Didn't say anything at first," Norma said. "Just stared out at the ocean. Then he asked me what I thought happened to his great-grandfather. I told him what I heard Mother and Dad talking about the day Missy died. One night, Charlie didn't show up at the Egyptian Theatre for an Indian show. I remember how Dad took a long sip of scotch. The sun had set, and the pool and patio were in shadows. It was eerie the way he said, 'Poor fellow got himself killed, and nobody's ever gonna know about it.'"

"What made him think that?" It made sense, Vicky was thinking. It was what Kiki had believed. He had come to Hollywood looking for Charlie's killer.

Norma drew her red lips into a thin line, the wrinkles in her brow deepened. "That's all Dad said. He knew how things were around here." She turned to Hugh. "Tell them what you told the boy."

Hugh cleared his throat, eyes narrowed in concentration. An actor preparing for the scene. "About 1933, my folks threw a big party by our pool. Everybody was there. Clark Gable, Carole Lombard, Jean Harlow, Claudette Colbert, Ron Colman, the Marx brothers, Bill Hart, and Tim McCoy. McCoy was a big star in Western movies then. Jimmie Cruze put in an appearance, and right in the midst of the merriment, McCoy and Cruze got into a shouting match. Dad ran over and tried to separate them. Naturally I got up close to the goings-on. McCoy accused Cruze of knowing what happened to his friend Charlie Wallowingbull ten years before. Cruze told him he was crazy. The Indian had walked off, that was all. But McCoy wouldn't give up. He said Charlie's family had the right to know the truth. 'Tell them he went to Mexico,' Cruze said. Took Dad and two other guys to pull McCoy off him."

Vicky took a moment, letting the pieces fall into some kind of order. Finally she said, "McCoy thought the director knew something."

Hugh shook his head and pulled on the goatee. "Never thought about it until that young man came around asking questions. But McCoy probably felt responsible somehow. Everybody knew he talked the Indians into being in the movies. Charlie was the only Indian that ever disappeared, and McCoy was the kind of man who wanted answers. My guess is he never stopped asking questions." He leaned back, rested his elbows on the armrests and made a tipi of his hands under the goatee. "You have to understand something," he said. "The studios controlled everything back then. Newspapers. Police. District attorney. Anything that could cause a scandal and hurt the box office was hushed up. There was a code of silence. McCoy was beating his head against a brick wall. Nobody was ever going to break the code."

29

GIANELLI WAS AT the top of the steps when Father John walked over to the administration building this morning. He made a fresh pot of coffee, filled a couple of mugs, popped in a *Favorites of the Opera* CD and spent a half hour answering questions. Yes, Bellows and the other guys had taken a few swings at him the other night, but he had landed a few himself. Gianelli didn't laugh. What about the parking lot at Tracers? Father John said he wasn't certain he could identify the two men who attacked him. Every few minutes Gianelli stopped to listen to Placido Domingo singing "La donna è mobile."

"First performance of *Rigoletto* took place where?" he said. It was an ongoing trivia game between them. Father John said that if he ever knew, he had forgotten, and Gianelli slapped his thigh and gave out a loud guffaw. "Teatro La Fenice. Venice," he said.

Father John shrugged. The steady, dull pain in his ribs was so familiar, it might have always been part of him. The man on the other side of the desk knew more about opera than he did, a fact that he hated to admit. "How did you know about Tracers?" he said. The front door opened and slammed shut, and he waved at Lucy as she passed his office.

"Come on, John." Gianelli had on blue jeans and boots and a leather vest over a white shirt. "I've been investigating Bellows for months. You and Vicky at a bar? You get attacked in the parking lot? That's the kind of news people like to talk about."

Father John explained how Vicky had wanted to see if Bellows was the one who had been calling her, and he had gone with her.

"The caller with no name. Claims he killed Kiki in self-defense." Gianelli took a drink of coffee, then swung the mug in the air, conducting Verdi. "Bellows hasn't managed to stay out of prison by making anonymous phone calls. You could have gotten yourself killed at Tracers. Looks like Bellows and his gang came here to finish the job." He got to his feet and set the mug on the table. Then he pulled on the jacket he had hung over the coat tree. "I don't need your help solving Kiki's murder. And I sure don't need you or Vicky getting yourselves killed. You run the mission, and I'll handle my job. We got a deal?"

"Look, Ted." Father John stood up. "Kiki wasn't mixed up with Bellows anymore. He was out of the drug business."

Gianelli threw out both hands as if he had just watched the other team make a touchdown despite his best efforts. "You ought to get the CD with Joseph Calleja. Different interpretation of the Duke of Mantua's character," he said, hauling himself around and disappearing into the corridor.

The instant the phone rang, Father John picked it up, conscious of the surge of hope in his chest. This could be JoEllen Redman finally getting back to him. Each time the phone rang over the last couple of days, he had tried to grab the receiver before Lucy had the chance. She would still pick up. "St. Francis Mission," he would hear her say, not realizing he already had it. He would hear the click as she hung up.

"Father John," he said, the sense of hope making a fire cut through him.

"Oh, Father." He recognized the voice of Lucinda, Lucy's mother. He listened for the familiar click, but it didn't come. "I just wanted to see how Lucy's doing?"

"She's quite the manager," he said. He could hear the faint noise of Lucy's breathing. "Answers the phone and greets people who stop by, makes sure I get all the messages. Organized my filing cabinets for the first time. I would say she's doing great."

"What about school? Has she talked about going back to school?"

"Not exactly," he said. But it was better that way, better to talk around the subject.

"I worry about her all the time, Father. I keep praying for her."

"That sounds better than worrying," he said. Then he spent a few minutes trying to explain how kids sometimes had to work things out in their own way and how that could take a while. Lucy was bright; he was confident she would make a good decision. The click came seconds before he told Lucinda good-bye and hung up.

Lucy was in the doorway, as if she had floated down the corridor on a silent conveyor belt. "Who was that?" she said, mischief and innocence working through her tone.

"Just a mother with a troublesome daughter." He sent her a smile.

"Oh, thanks a lot," she said. "You said I was bright."

"You are bright, Lucy."

"And I can make my own decisions."

"I said I think you'll make good ones."

"You do?" She stayed still a moment, then propelled herself across the office. "What's the name of that woman you've been waiting to hear from?"

"JoEllen Redman," he said. Such a weak rope he had grabbed onto—Andrew Wallowingbull's belief in his grandson. The fact that a drug gang leader had been arrested for Kiki's murder wouldn't shake Andrew's belief.

"I seen an Arapaho over at the bank named Redman this morning," Lucy said.

"What?"

"Yeah, I don't remember the first name, but Redman was on her badge. I seen her the other day when my mom made me go to the bank and get a savings account, now that I'm making so much money." She paused, and he gave her the smile she'd asked for. "Anyway I thought it was pretty cool the teller was Arapaho. I told her so. I asked her how long she went to school." She stopped, as if she realized she had stepped onto a slippery slope and there was no going back. "Two years at some college in Oklahoma," she said, her voice almost a whisper.

"There's something else I should have told your mother." Father John had gotten up from the desk and was pulling on his jacket. He grabbed his cowboy hat off the coat tree. "How observant you are," he said. Then he told her he'd be back in an hour or so.

FIVE CUSTOMERS IN line for the tellers at Western Bank. Two tellers behind the counter, and from his place at the back of the line, Father John could make out the name Redman on the badge of the teller on the right. She looked Arapaho, with prominent cheekbones and black, serious eyes and straight black hair going gray tucked behind her ears. Fast, confident hands counted out a small stack of bills. The customer stuffed the bills in her bag and walked off. Four customers in line now, then three when a cowboy headed toward the door.

At one point, JoEllen Redman had let her eyes run over the customers behind the black belt strung between metal stands. She had spotted him, he was certain—the quick blink, the almost imperceptible flinch—then looked back at the new customer on the other side of the counter. When it was his turn, he stepped to the side to let the woman behind him go to the teller next to JoEllen. He waited until her customer departed, then walked up to the counter.

"I'm Father O'Malley from the mission," he said.

"I know who you are." Her eyes flitted toward the glass cubicles at the end of the tellers' stations. "What can I do for you?"

"I'd like to talk to you. Do you have a few minutes?"

"I'm working." For the first time, she lifted her chin and locked eyes with him. "If you don't have any bank business, you'd better move along. There's other customers."

"It's about Kiki Wallowingbull," he said. "I'm trying to find out what happened to him. It's for the old people, Andrew and Mamie. They want to know the truth."

"God," she said. "I don't want anything to do with this."

"Did you talk to him?"

Her eyes were on the glass cubicles again, and something new in them—a spark of fear. "You have to go," she said. "I can't be having personal conversations on bank time." She drummed her fingers on the countertop, and when he didn't move, she said, "I'm working a short day. I'll be off in twenty minutes. There's a coffee shop across the street."

FATHER JOHN HUNG his jacket over the back of the chair at a vacant table in front of the plate-glass window. He went to the counter, ordered coffee with cream, and carried the mug over. A border of frost ran around the edges of the window, but he had a clear view of the entrance to the bank and the side door that opened onto the parking lot. The row of vehicles at the far end of the lot, he suspected, belonged to employees. He watched customers emerge from the front and make their way around clumps of snow on the sidewalk to the pickups and sedans parked in haphazard rows around the lot, as if they had slid into place.

He sipped at the coffee—slightly bitter and so hot it burned the tip of his tongue. The shop was getting full, the door opening and closing, customers stomping snow off their boots, and odors of wet wool mixing with the smell of fresh coffee. The window had started to steam up, and he reached over and wiped a clear spot with his shirtsleeve. The reaching made him wince with pain, like needles driven into his ribs.

Four customers exited the bank and headed into the parking lot, except for the short man in a bulky jacket who hoisted himself into a truck parked at the curb. Black exhaust burst out of the tailpipe as the truck pulled into the street ahead of two pickups, and he realized he had almost missed her. JoEllen Redman, hunched forward in a long beige coat, hurrying from the side door that was still closing toward the vehicles parked at the back.

Father John grabbed his jacket and yanked open the door. He managed to pull on his jacket as he crossed the street and hurried through the lot, wincing with the sharp jabs of pain, dodging a couple of pickups, not taking his eyes off the woman unlocking the door of a red sedan. She had dropped behind the steering wheel and was about to pull the door shut when he reached the car.

"I promise to take only a few minutes of your time," he said, as if this were the place they had agreed to meet.

"I don't know anything," she said. "Leave me alone."

"You're descended from William Thunder, right? Are you his granddaughter?"

"What difference does it make? Kiki Wallowingbull was in a gang, and he got killed. End of story. Why should I get involved? I don't know anything about it."

Father John waited a moment before he said, "Jason Bellows has been arrested."

"So I heard." There was the hint of a smile at the corners of her lips. "He killed Kiki."

"That's what the indictment says."

"Then it's all over." She tried to pull the door shut, but Father John kept one hand on the edge. "Let me go," she said. "What's his murder got to do with me?"

"Did you talk to Kiki?"

She stared straight ahead, holding on to the steering wheel. He could see the muscles of her jaw clenching. "Listen, JoEllen," he went on, "Kiki was trying to straighten out his life. That's the way his grandfather wants him remembered. He thinks Kiki died because of what he learned about his great-grandfather. I'm trying to help him find the truth."

"Maybe his grandfather doesn't like the truth. Maybe he sent you on a wild-goose chase."

"Maybe, but I don't think so. It would help me if you told me what you told Kiki."

JoEllen shifted around and looked up at him, her face frozen in a mixture of fear and resolve. "I don't know anything about it."

He tried for a smile of reassurance. "I've talked to better liars than you, JoEllen," he said.

She jerked her head around and went back to staring out the windshield. A gust of icy wind blew a piece of paper over the snow between her car and a pickup parked a few feet away. "I could scream, you know," she said. "Someone would hear me and come over here. How would that look? I could claim you attacked me. You'd be arrested."

"What are you afraid of?" Father John said again. "Are you afraid that whoever killed Kiki might come after you?"

She gave a little sob and bent her face into her hands. He could see her shoulders shaking. "Please," she said, the words muffled in her gloves. "We don't want any part of this."

"We?"

She hesitated, then dropped her hands and looked up at him again. "You come around, taking up time at my station, asking questions that don't have anything to do with the bank. What do you think my supervisor's gonna say? I saw him in his cubicle looking over at me, wondering what the mission priest is talking to me about. What're you gonna do next? Sic the fed on me? My supervisor sees the fed holding up the line, asking a lot of questions . . ." JoEllen shook her head and let out a laugh that sounded forced and painful. "I'd get fired five minutes after he left. You heard about Indians, last hired and first fired. I've got a son and he's got a kid, okay? I need this job."

She sunk inside her coat, looking up at him over the folds of the collar. "Whatever happened a hundred years ago in Hollywood doesn't matter anymore. Leave me alone. I need this job, Father," she said again, a quiet, pleading note in her tone.

Father John took a second, then let go of the door and stepped back. The door slammed shut, the engine turned over, and the sedan backed out, lurching past him over the ridges of snow. He watched the sedan pull around, jump forward, and bounce across the lot and out onto the street, JoEllen bent over the wheel. He saw her raise a gloved hand and wipe at her cheeks.

He walked back across the lot, got into the pickup at the curb, and headed in the direction JoEllen had taken, but the sedan had disappeared in the traffic lumbering down the street. A woman, terrified of what? Losing a good job at the bank with family to support? That was part of it, but he couldn't shake the feeling that there was something else. *I've got a son,* she said. *He's got a kid.* And the man who called Vicky said he had a son. The man said he had killed Kiki.

He drove south on 789, past the warehouses and tire stores and trailer parks, past the package liquor stores, and turned onto the reservation. JoEllen Redman knew the truth, but she would never admit it. She would protect her son. It kept coming back to that, the way the needle on a compass kept pointing to true north.

30

A BELL RANG in the darkness somewhere. Insistent and annoying, growing louder and louder. Vicky struggled into consciousness, gradually aware of the gray light slanting past the window shades. She started to reach for the phone on the table next to the bed, then realized that it was her cell ringing. She pushed herself off the bed and over to the chair where she had left her bag. It was a moment before she located the cell and pressed it against her ear. "Vicky Holden." Her voice sounded sleep-logged and tentative. Her tongue felt like glue.

"Vicky, it's me." Annie's voice came from a thousand miles away, another world. "I didn't wake you, did I?"

Vicky cleared her throat and said that she was fine. "What's going on?"

"The office has been hopping all morning." The words were like a gust of wind blowing through the apartment. "Lawyers from the water consortium called this morning. They are withdrawing the civil suit. They want to negotiate."

Vicky perched on the chair. An object inside her bag bit into her hip. She threw her head back and closed her eyes, allowing the news to settle in a moment. Then she heard herself asking Annie to set up a meeting in two or three days—as soon as possible, before anyone had a change of heart.

"Meeting Wednesday or Thursday." Annie said, enunciating each syllable, and Vicky knew she was writing a memo to herself. She heard the faint rustling noise of paper, then Annie saying that Roger wanted to talk to her.

There was a clicking noise, then Roger's voice: "Hey, Vicky," he said. "Soaking up some California sun?"

Vicky glanced at the gray, overcast light blooming behind the window shades and wondered why everyone thought California was always sunny. "Not exactly," she said. "How are things with Troy?"

"He's got a new attorney. Stan Smith over in Riverton. My bet is he'll testify against Jason Bellows."

"He'll be lying."

"You're still thinking about the caller, aren't you? Adam said the caller isn't your client. You don't know who he is. He hasn't hired you to represent him."

Vicky wasn't sure when she had gotten to her feet, but she was pacing the small bedroom, marking out the space between dresser, window, and bed. "You spoke to Adam about this?"

"He called this morning, and I told him."

She made herself take a breath before she said, "I'll be back tomorrow." She was flying out late this afternoon—a two-hour flight to Denver and another two hours in the airport before she caught a nineteen-seater that would skim above the snow-crusted plains and land in Riverton about eleven.

She was about to close the cell when Roger said that Annie had something else.

"Did you get the email I sent this morning?" Annie's voice again, laced with elements of excitement and pride. "I convinced the U.S. attorney's office to send over the updated list of parolees."

"Good work," Vicky said. Then she thanked her, closed the phone, and stared at the inert object in her hand a moment before she dropped it back into her bag. She was awake now, her heart pounding in her ears. She went into the living room looking for Susan, but there was no sign of her. The apartment was quiet except for the sound of a filmy curtain billowing in the breeze. On the kitchen counter, she found a note scrawled in Susan's handwriting: *Went for coffee and muffins. Back soon.*

"Back soon," Vicky said into the silence. And wasn't that the way it had always been between her and Susan? Always going away from each other somehow. A weekend planned just for the two of them, yet they had spent yesterday talking to two old movie people about nothing that had anything to do with Susan. They would spend most of today together, Vicky had promised, doing whatever Susan wished. Walk the beach, eat lunch at that little restaurant Susan loved down by the marina. But it was Susan who had said, "Let's go to Hollywood. We can walk around, see the sights, have lunch. Come on, Mom. You're dying to see where Charlie and the other Arapahos were. Admit it."

Vicky had burst out laughing. "Okay, I admit it," she said, and that made Susan laugh. Then Vicky had gathered her into her arms and held her close and whispered that she was sorry work was interfering with their weekend.

"You can't help it," Susan said. The old sharpness gone, a kind of resolve and acceptance in her tone. "You're always working."

Now Vicky sank onto the chair in front of Susan's laptop and typed the keys that eventually brought up her email. She scrolled through the usual junk until she came to the line that said Holden and Lone Eagle. Subject: *parole report.*

She opened the message and read down the list—a mixture of familiar Arapaho and Shoshone names mixed in with names like Regan and Hillard and Harris from Riverton and Lander. The name Kiki Wallowingbull jumped out from the middle of the list and stopped her for a moment. Then she read on. Close to the end was the name, Will Thunder Redman. Arapaho, twenty-nine years old.

She hit the reply key. *Good work, Annie,* she wrote. *Now I need the address for Will Thunder Redman from the county department of probation and parole. Tell them we're trying to solve a crime. Let them know we're working on their side!*

Vicky sent the email, then wrote down the name of Will Thunder Redman on the back of a stray envelope she found on the desk. She drew sharp, black lines under the name of the caller.

THEY TURNED OFF the Hollywood Freeway and started into Cahuenga Pass—Cahuenga, the Place of Little Hills in the language of the Gabrielino Indians who had once lived here, according to the LA guide that Vicky had picked up in the bookstore a half block from Susan's apartment. The guide lay opened on her lap. Outside the slopes rose in rugged clumps, covered with dried brush and occasional eucalyptus trees. Houses were tucked at the far end of driveways that spiraled upward. Scrub brush and prickly pear grew here, the guidebook said. Stands of cottonwoods and eucalyptus trees, with red-tailed hawks circling overhead.

"I wonder where the tipis were," Susan said, glancing out her window. "Imagine what the neighbors thought. A camp of Indian tipis and a horse corral."

"Not too far up the pass," Vicky said. It was a guess. She doubted anyone knew where the actual site was. She could picture the white tipis shining in the moonlight, little campfires glowing. Horses, carriages, and cars rattling past on a dirt road.

"Charlie could have stepped off a cliff or something."

"Someone would have found his body."

"Suppose nobody wanted it found."

The same thought had been moving at the edge of Vicky's mind since they had spoken to Norma and Hugh yesterday. *The studios controlled everything*, Norma had said.

"What a scandal!" Susan pushed on. "I mean, Indian jumps to his death after getting dumped by movie star. Wouldn't have been good for the box office."

Vicky stared at the clumps of scrub brush and sage with yellowish blossoms flashing past. Even worse would have been a murder. Arapaho kills another Arapaho in jealousy over a movie star named Missy Mae Markham. What would the fan magazines have made of that?

"If there's anything in the police records"—Susan gave her a quick sideways look—"Brett will find it. He's good."

"You like him," Vicky said. She watched Susan for a moment, studying the shape of her profile, the little bump at the top of her nose, the light and shadow playing over her cheekbones, the straight black hair cut in angles around her face. Somewhere in this grown-up and confident young woman was the image of the little girl with shy black eyes that Vicky carried in her heart.

"Oh, more than *like*," Susan said, throwing another sideways glance. "I think Brett's the one."

Vicky didn't say anything. She couldn't remember when Susan had seemed so happy. She tried to concentrate on what Susan was saying, something about how Brett would meet them for lunch and how Vicky would love the restaurant they were going to.

HOLLYWOOD WAS A twenty-minute horseback ride from Cahuenga Pass in 1923. It took almost forty minutes to drive down, thread into the traffic on the freeway, and follow the stop-and-go traffic down Hollywood Boulevard and onto Vine Street, the engine making the familiar clicking noise. Parked cars lined the curb. Susan pulled in alongside a sedan and stopped, ignoring the honking horns and squealing brakes. "Selma and Vine," she said.

There was no trace of the old studio, yet the guidebook said that the Jesse L. Lasky Feature Play Company had occupied a yellow barn on the corner. The studio backlot spread across two complete blocks—an area now filled with shops, offices, restaurants, parking garages, traffic-clogged streets, and blasting horns. At some point, the barn had been moved. Susan started down Selma, turned onto Highland and pulled into a parking lot adjacent to the original yellow barn with green doors and a white sign on the roof that said Hollywood Heritage Museum.

Stepping past the green door, Vicky thought, was like stepping into the past. They strolled along the plank floors, past displays of photographs and props, clothing and makeup, and old cameras. Vicky stopped in front of an exhibit with *The Covered Wagon* splashed in black foot-high letters across the back wall. Arranged in front were tanned and beaded hide shirts and moccasins, rifles and pistols, a wagon wheel, a large mahogany camera with brass fittings set up on a tripod. Among the items were photographs of covered wagons coming across the desert, an old building that looked like a fort. Another photo showed Indians with naked chests, clutching hatchets and spears, climbing down the rocks of a canyon toward the wagons pulled into a circle.

She was aware of Susan at her side. "The ancestors," Vicky said, holding out a hand toward the photos. "Charlie, William, James, Goes-in-Lodge, and the buffalo Indians. They're all there."

They remained in front of the exhibit for several moments, held by the mementos and the photos and something else—the sense of the people. Touching the past, Vicky thought, the way things had been. Finally she walked over to the life-sized cardboard figures set up along the opposite wall, conscious of Susan beside her. Above the figures was a banner that said Stars of the Past. Mary Pickford and Douglas Fairbanks and Charlie Chaplin, stopped in a smile or a nod or a wave, frozen in time. And here was Missy Mae Markham, a childlike figure with golden hair and a white dress, smiling demurely over one shoulder. Standing together were the cowboy stars Bill Hart and Tom Mix and Gene Autry and, taller than the others, with a stoic face beneath the brim of a white Stetson, dressed in black, was the figure of Tim McCoy.

Outside, Vicky pulled her camera out of the jumble in the bag and walked around the building until she found the shot that James had taken all those years ago near a corner of the barn. In the photo, the name Lasky was visible on the sloping roof. There were black shadows falling down the wall. She stared into the viewer and tried to imagine Charlie Wallowingbull and William Thunder on either side of the beautiful white woman with long, curly blond hair.

She snapped the picture, then took a picture of Susan, a strip of sunshine on her face, the breeze blowing her skirt against her legs. Susan fell in beside her, and Vicky was aware of the rhythmic clack of their footsteps on the sidewalk, the thrum of traffic as they walked back to the car.

They drove toward Hollywood Boulevard, parked in a garage, joined the other pedestrians crowding the sidewalk, most of them tourists in jeans, tee shirts, and walking shoes, cameras bumping against their chests. They dodged the tourists peering in windows of the souvenir shops that lined the block. Vicky could see the crowds bunched in front of Grauman's Chinese Theatre, the pagoda-like roof sheathed in copper lifting overhead.

Groups of people wandered about the forecourt, bent over the concrete panels with the signatures, foot- and handprints of movie stars. Vicky found herself staring down at the prints of Douglas Fairbanks and Mary Pickford, then Charlie Chaplin and Clark Gable and Marilyn Monroe. She realized that Susan had wandered to the other side, engrossed in other signatures and prints. There didn't seem to be any order, just a juxtaposition of names from different eras—Tom Mix in one place, Roy Rogers in another. There were prints of John Wayne's fist and Betty Grable's legs alongside their signatures.

It was then that she caught a glimpse of the signature carved into the cement a few feet away: Tim McCoy. The prints were large—the wide handprint, fingers outstretched and generous somehow; the long boot print that seemed to have been made with determination. She stooped over and ran her hand over the prints and the signature.

"Mom!" Susan's voice cut past the conversations around her. She looked up and saw Susan waving her forward. She worked her way around the tourists hovering over Marilyn Monroe's slab to where Susan was standing. At her feet was a looping, childlike signature that looked as if it had been scribbled with some difficulty: Missy Mae Markham.

"Do you think she cared about either of them?" Susan said.

Vicky bent over and set her own hand over the print. Such a small hand, a child's hand. The footprint was also small. "I don't know," she said.

They followed the Hollywood Walk of Fame—the bronze stars set into the sidewalk, an entertainer's name engraved on each star—to the Egyptian Theatre a short distance away. There were fewer tourists milling about the gray-and-brown concrete panels in the forecourt. Palm trees swayed overhead.

Vicky opened the guidebook and read out loud: "Imitation of an Egyptian temple. Completed in 1922. The Egyptian was the site of many motion picture premieres, among them *The Covered Wagon*, the first epic Western. A long line of limousines drew up in front of the theater. Stars, producers, directors, and other celebrities stepped out beneath the klieg lights and strolled the red carpet to the entrance. Crowds gathered outside hoping to catch a glimpse of the movie's stars, Lois Wilson and J. Warren Kerrigan, as well as such beloved stars as Missy Mae Markham. Prior to the screening each night, Arapaho and Shoshone Indians performed on stage."

Vicky bought tickets at the box office, and she and Susan stepped into a theater that was larger than she had expected, with rows of velvet seats and a gilded sunburst above the screen. According to the guidebook, there had been a large proscenium in front of the screen where the Indian show took place. She wondered what Charlie and William and the others had done to entertain the white audiences. Performed traditional dances? Roped wooden steers? Pranced around with hatchets and spears, hopping and hollering because that was what the audience expected?

She had to get out of the theater. The weight of the past was heavy; the indignities and the lack of respect they had endured, white audiences howling with laughter and clapping for more.

She hurried across the forecourt, past the crowd bunched in front of the box office, conscious of the tap-tap of Susan's footsteps behind her. Nearby was the Musso & Frank Grill where Susan had made reservations earlier. "I figure we should lunch where all the stars lunched back then," she said.

The restaurant was like a set piece from a 1920s movie, with wall lamps that glowed against the dark paneled walls. Circles of light swept over the red leather booths. They were shown to a booth at the front, near a paned-glass window. Outside the traffic lurched past and people strolled by, like props and actors in a silent movie. Beyond the tourists with baseball caps and jeans and cameras, beyond the parade of compact sedans and oversized SUVs, Vicky could almost see Arapahos and Shoshones riding down the boulevard on their way to the Egyptian Theatre.

"We're expecting someone else," Susan told the waiter just as Vicky spotted Brett hurrying across the street, dodging the traffic. He took long strides, looking about, arms swinging at his sides. In his right hand was a large manila envelope.

31

VICKY HELD HER breath, not taking her eyes from the brown envelope as Brett slid into the booth. In the top left corner, in neat black handwriting were the words *LA Police Records*. There was a small bulge in the middle. He had found something.

She took a sip from the water glass that the waiter delivered and tried to will her heart to stop jumping. Brett and Susan had entered their own little world, she realized. She might as well have been seated on the other side of the restaurant. Holding hands—Vicky could see their clasped hands just below the edge of the table— leaning in close and smiling at each other. Not speaking, just engrossed in some conversation with their eyes. She was surprised at the pang of regret that shot through her. It should have been like that with Adam, instead of the push-pull relationship they had fallen into. Her fault, she knew, attempting to push herself into the relationship, then pulling herself free. Afraid of the control, not wanting it.

And yet, with John O'Malley, they could drive across the rez, sit in his office, hardly speaking at all and yet each knowing what the other was thinking. When they did speak, they could finish each other's sentences. He would tell her to be careful; he never told her what to do. She blinked hard and pushed away the images.

"Oh, sorry, Vicky." Brett squared himself at the table, directing his attention to her. "Didn't mean to be rude. It's just that I haven't seen Susan since Saturday and . . ."

"It's okay." Susan patted his arm. "Mom understands how it is with us."

Brett leaned over the table. "I want you to know I'll always play straight with your daughter. I love her very much."

Vicky felt herself nodding, swallowing back the lump in her throat. In her head was Adam's voice: *I love you. I love you.* And those were always the times when she had pulled away.

The waiter was hovering over the table: Did the gentleman and ladies care for a cocktail this afternoon? No, they did not. Were they ready to order? Yes, they were. Salads for the ladies, a hamburger for the gentleman. Then the waiter slipped away into the soft buzz of conversations and the swooshing noise of plates being served at a nearby booth and people being shown to other booths.

Brett picked up the envelope and worked a finger under the flap. "You were right about one thing," he said. "There aren't any police reports on a dead Indian from April 1923."

Not a surprise, Vicky thought. If a report existed, McCoy would have found it. And yet, she had hoped . . .

"But I did get something from the LAPD records." Brett pulled out a white sheet of paper, a form of some kind with black type above the lines. "A missing persons report," he said, handing the sheet across the table. Vicky took in the top lines at a glance: *Los Angeles Police Department. April 12, 1923.* She read down the page: *Person Missing: young Arapaho Indian. Name: Charlie Wallowingbull. Temporary residence: Indian camp, Cahuenga Pass. Occupation: employed by Lasky Studio in show at Egyptian Theatre. Last seen at camp about six o'clock the evening of April 10, 1923. Report filed by Tim McCoy.*

"Looks like he waited for Charlie to show up before he went to the police," Brett said.

"Did they investigate?" Susan said. She was caught up in it, Vicky realized. A young Arapaho making her way in Hollywood, caught up in the disappearance of another Arapaho, as if Charlie had disappeared yesterday. But wasn't that the way it always was for her people? Whatever had happened in the past seemed always a possibility in the present.

Brett pulled another sheet from the envelope and gave it to Vicky. "This is all I found," he said.

Another official-looking form with a typed paragraph near the top, the letters ragged and smeared-looking. Vicky read out loud: *April 14, 1923, Disposition of Missing Person Report. Tim McCoy, employed by Lasky Studio, stated that he believed movie star Missy Mae Markham may have information concerning Charlie Wallowingbull, reported missing April 10. Contacted Elvin Hall, Lasky spokesman. Informed that Miss Markham has been in Arizona and couldn't possibly have any knowledge of missing Indian. Hall said that Wallowingbull was a disruptive and unreliable employee, ill at ease away from his natural surroundings on a Wyoming reservation. The studio has conducted its own investigation into his absence and concluded that Wallowingbull returned to his reservation of his own accord. Investigation closed.*

"Why didn't McCoy find this?" Vicky let her eyes skim the paragraph again.

"It was 1923, before the open records laws," Brett said. "Records could be open or closed depending upon the police chief's orders. Could be the investigation was closed because Lasky Studio wanted it closed. They gave the police a plausible explanation, something to put in the report." He nodded at the sheet in Vicky's hand. "If the studio didn't want McCoy to see the final report, he didn't see it. Sorry, Vicky." He shook his head. "I'm afraid it's not much."

Vicky smiled at the young man across from her who loved her daughter. "It's everything," she said.

1923

WILLIAM LIFTED THE breastplate carefully out of his parfleche and pulled it over his tanned shirt. The small dressing room was crowded with Indians putting on regalia from the Old Time—tanned and beaded shirts and trousers and moccasins, feathered headdresses. "Studio wants the real thing," McCoy had told them. "It's gotta be authentic."

Tonight was the premiere of *The Covered Wagon*. They had spent hours rehearsing. The theater would be filled with stars and celebrities. The Indians were quiet as they dressed, not talking much, slowly draping their bodies with precious remnants of the past. Several other Arapahos already had on breastplates. William struggled to loop the leather ties in back. The small white bones of the breastplate were cracked and some of the porcupine quills and beads had fallen off. Still it was beautiful. His father had worn it on the plains, and his grandfather before and on back—he didn't know how many generations. All of them protected from the arrows of enemies.

"You seen Charlie?" It was McCoy's voice behind him.

William finished tying the loops, then turned and faced the white man. "He's here somewhere," he said.

"He's nowhere around." McCoy had pushed his white Stetson back. His gaze switched about the room. "He ride down with you?"

William shook his head. The Indians had ridden into town two or three at a time, the way McCoy had told them. No sense clogging up the roads and getting folks riled up. The roads were already crowded with cars moving toward Hollywood Boulevard. Pedestrians jammed the sidewalks. Out in front of the Egyptian Theatre, crowds lined both sides of the forecourt, and the sky was streaked with lights from the big klieg lights that had been set up. The warm evening air was filled with a sense of expectancy and celebration.

"I figure Charlie rode down with Painted Brush," he said.

McCoy gave a quick glance toward the far corner of the room where James was fixing a roach to his head. The porcupine hair stood straight up and made him seem taller, more menacing. White folks in the audience liked the roaches.

"When did you see him last?"

"Just before I went out to the corral to saddle up."

"He wasn't with that actress, was he?"

William looked away. Not then, Charlie wasn't. Not when William had shouldered the parfleche and headed to the corral. But earlier . . . He tightened his jaw against speaking the rest of it. Late this afternoon when they were starting to pack up for the show, Missy Mae Markham had driven into camp. A silver Packard with the top down, bouncing over the hillside, scraping the brush, and her blond hair flying in the wind. Somehow she had steered around the scrub brush and cottonwoods and stopped right in front of Charlie's tipi. She had stepped out, slammed the door, and screamed, "Charlie?" Her scream, echoing over the camp, had brought the other Indians out of the tipis.

William had rushed toward her. He remembered the thoughts that tumbled through his head. He would delay her, convince her Charlie had already left for the theater, get her to turn around and drive out of there. But Charlie was ahead of him, pushing him out of the way, and he remembered something else—the arrow of anger that had shot through him. He grabbed Charlie's arm and wheeled him about. "She'll get you fired, you fool. You gotta tell her now. Tell her so she'll get out of here and leave you alone."

He could still see the expression changing in Charlie's face as if he were walking in and out of the shadows. He was fighting with himself. Oh, William knew what was inside him. This beautiful white woman, the most beautiful woman they had ever seen, and she wanted Charlie. Wanted to come inside his tipi, fling off the flimsy dress, and give herself to him. The thought had made William feel like he was choking. Because if she came for him—if she ever came for him—he would take her inside his tipi.

"You gotta tell her the truth," he said, but Charlie had already pulled away. He walked over to the woman, then led her through the camp to his tipi. William had followed. Gratitude washed over him that no one from the studio was there. No sign of the skinny body-guard. No one knew she was in camp except the other Arapahos and Shoshones. The stage show was supposed to go on for eight months. Eight months of good, steady pay. They would not say anything, but he could see the worry on their faces.

"No!" The scream burst past the tipi. The scream of a wounded animal, high-pitched and shrill as a whistle. Then the girl ran out, crashed against him, and kept running, one hand flung over her fore-head. William had felt as if he were watching a silent movie as she ran through the brush, tripping in the little white heels and lurching for-ward. The skirt of her white dress caught on a stalk of wild grass. He heard the ripping noise.

Charlie stepped out of the tipi, and they both watched her throw herself into the Packard. The motor made a coughing noise, and the thin front wheels dug into the dirt and brush. She started backing up, hunched over the wheel, the motor growling. Reverse, forward, re-verse, forward, the tires grinding down. She drove past a clump of trees, over grasses and brush that snapped under the tires. They watched until the car was lost in a cloud of dust out on the road.

"She said I promised to love her forever," Charlie said. "I never told her that. It was her story she told herself." The cloud of dust had blown away, as if the car had never been there. "I guess she's gone now." There was a sadness in the way he said it, William had thought, but now he wasn't sure. Perhaps it was his own sadness that he had heard.

"Show starts in thirty minutes," McCoy was saying. "Big audience, theater's already full. Word's gotten out there's gonna be a good prologue. We need everybody here. Lasky won't like it if we disappoint people. Go get Charlie."

William removed the breastplate and beaded moccasins. He could feel the anger burning inside him again. She had returned. It was the only thing that explained Charlie's absence. He pulled on his boots, slammed out the back door, and crossed the field to the corral. In a few minutes, he had saddled the quarter horse and was riding down Hollywood Boulevard, past the cars and the people crossing the street. Riding hard, as if the heat of his own anger drove the horse on. He could sense things, the horse. They had herded cattle together on ranches outside the reservation, and the horse always knew when to pull back, when to plunge ahead. He could sense anger; it became his own. He would have been a good buffalo horse in the Old Time, William always thought, sensing when to pull back, when to race in for the kill.

The horse galloped onto the dirt road that wound up the pass, past other cars, past a horse-drawn cart with a family inside. "Damn Indian," the driver called out as they raced by. They came around a curve, and it was then that the camp came into view, the tipis gray-looking in the fading light. He turned the horse onto the hillside and took a diagonal cut through the brush, the white heat burning inside him.

The silver Packard was parked in the same place it had been earlier. The tipis were arranged in a circle, all of them dark except for Charlie's. The white canvas glowed with the light of a lantern inside. He thought of the ranch he would buy, the small herd of cattle he would build. Charlie would ruin everything. Everything. Well, he would not tolerate it.

32

STREETLAMPS GLOWED IN the morning darkness and a fine snow drifted over Main Street when Vicky unlocked the front door of the building and made her way up the stairs. She let herself into the office and flipped the light switch. It might have been an abandoned office with side chairs neatly arranged against the walls, the polished surface of Annie's desk glowing in the light, the computer shut down, the telephone silent. The office of a firm that handled important cases that had nothing to do with an Arapaho who had killed Kiki Wallowing-bull in self-defense.

She hurried across the waiting room to her private office and shut the door, trying to ignore the feeling that she had wandered into the wrong place. She hung her coat in the closet, dropped onto her chair, and turned on the computer, forcing herself to concentrate. She hadn't slept last night. The plane had landed in Riverton two hours late. It was almost two in the morning before she got home, and she had spent the next three hours tossing about, trying to make sense out of it. It was obvious Kiki believed he had learned what had likely happened to his great-grandfather—murdered in a fit of jealousy by his friend, William Thunder, and the body disposed of, the whole matter made to disappear, by a studio making millions with Missy Mae Markham. What had Kiki done? What happened that a man named Will Redman had killed him in self-defense?

She worked through the messages and mail, then brought up the office calendar. So many important things: documents to prepare for negotiations in the tribal water case; meeting with the tribal water engineer tomorrow morning. Then she saw the note from the probation and parole department that Annie had left: *residence of Will Thunder Redman*. The second line contained the address of a house out on the plains east of Riverton.

She started reviewing the files on the water case, half aware of the office coming to life. The telephone ringing, Annie's voice filtering through the walls, doors opening and closing. At one point, Annie had knocked and pushed the door open a few inches. "Welcome back," she'd said, peering past the edge. "Good trip?"

The trip was fine, Vicky told her, glancing up from the screen. "And you are a fine investigator." Then she told her to hold the calls, and she went back to studying the files. There was another knock on the door, something hard and impatient about it. She swung around and watched Adam step into the office and close the door behind him. He jammed both fists into his trouser pockets and leaned against the door. "Just got back myself," he said.

She heard herself asking if everything had gone well, marveling at the perfunctory sound of her tone. Adam shrugged away the question and started across the office. "I think we have to talk," he said.

"I was just on my way out." Vicky pressed her hands on the desk and rose to her feet.

"Oh? This about the caller who won't give his name?" Adam said. One eyebrow lifted, which gave him a slightly off-balanced look.

"I know who he is. I intend to help him clear himself in Kiki's murder."

"Roger says our former client, Tallfeathers, has cut a deal with the U.S. attorney. The case against Bellows is as good as gold. Why can't you let it go?"

"Bellows didn't kill Kiki," she said. "My client . . ." She hesitated, realizing she had always thought of the caller as a client. ". . . killed Kiki in self-defense."

"Your client? The man has harassed you, Vicky. He hasn't hired you."

"What do you want, Adam?"

He started pacing in front of her desk, and that struck her as ironic. She was the one who paced when she was trying to work out her thoughts, place them in some kind of order, summon the words that made sense.

"What do you want?" she said again, but softer this time, trying to convey the sense that she already knew the answer, that she had been thinking about it as well, and it was okay, it was right.

Adam stopped at the far side of the desk. He looked directly at her. "This isn't working," he said. He put up a hand, as if to stop any objections, but she didn't object, and he dropped his hand. "It used to work. When we started the firm, everything worked great. You and I, on the same page. We were good together, Vicky. You know how I feel about you. That hasn't changed. You've changed. You went away."

"I went to visit Susan."

"You went away from us." He stood with his arms at his sides, the cuffs of his blue shirt rolled back over muscular forearms. They had been through a lot together. She hadn't seen it ending like this, and yet it seemed appropriate, foreordained even.

"We can dissolve the firm," Vicky said, the lawyer voice, logical, dispassionate-sounding in her ears.

"We can, but we don't have to," Adam said. "I'll be spending most of my time working with the Crow tribal council. There's a lot to get into place before they can start developing the coal deposits. I've taken an apartment in Harden. It will give us time to think. We don't have to make any hasty decisions. Holden and Lone Eagle has a reputation across the West. No sense in throwing that away."

Vicky stayed in place for a long moment after Adam had gone, the door closed behind him, the sense of vacancy that she had felt earlier sweeping over the office. He hadn't wanted to dissolve the firm, but the rest of it—the personal relationship—he had just dissolved. She had to stop herself from laughing out loud at the unaccustomed waves of relief rolling over her.

WALKS-ON BOUNDED across the drive as Father John got out of the pickup. Running on a tilt, dipping his muzzle into the snow and tossing snow windmills into the air. Father John scooped up the soft snow, patted it into a ball, and threw it. Arrows of pain shot through him. The dog doubled his tracks, chasing after the ball that disintegrated in the air. Father John stooped over slowly, cupped some more snow and threw another snowball, then he led the dog up the icy steps in front of the administration building.

Lucy appeared at the far end of the corridor when he stepped inside. Walks-On pushed ahead, shaking off his coat, sending droplets of moisture over the floor and the stucco walls. "Good. You're here," Lucy said before ducking out of sight.

Walks-On had already settled himself on the rug as Father John hung up his jacket and set his cowboy hat on the coat tree. He could hear Lucy's footsteps coming down the corridor.

"What's up?" He was at his desk when she popped through the door. She was bundled for the outdoors, jacket zipped to her chin, a scarf tied at her neck.

"Could you sign this?" She walked over, holding out a sheet of paper as if she were handing him a package in a store.

"What do we have here?" He took the sheet and read the bold type at the top: *Central Wyoming College Recommendation*. The recommendation itself had already been written. He glanced through the paragraph: *Industrious. Trustworthy. Observant. Organized. Self-starter.* The words jumped out from the lines of black type.

He laid the sheet next to the little stack of messages she had left for him. He had the sense she was holding her breath, a mute statue on the other side of the desk. "I couldn't have done a better job," he said.

She broke into a smile and took in a long breath. "I gotta turn it in today. Thought it would save you a little time if I wrote it."

"It was good of you." He selected a pen from the holder where she had corralled his pens. After organizing the file cabinet, she had proceeded to his desk, which, apart from the stack of messages, the new metal stand for folders, the phone and the pen holder, was completely clear and even dusted. He could see the pattern of grain in the wood. "But you forgot something." He pulled over the sheet and wrote: *Lucy Running Bear is an intellectually curious, hard-working young woman who will make an excellent student.* He signed his name.

"What changed your mind?" he said, handing her the paper.

"You said I'd make my own decision, so I did."

He nodded. "The college doesn't require a high school diploma?"

"Oh, that." She rolled her eyes. "I signed up for a stupid social studies class this summer so I'll get my diploma in August. I already know that stuff." She bit at her lower lip a moment. "I'm gonna do it anyhow."

"You'll like college," he said.

"Yeah? Well, we'll see about that." She spun around, started for the door, and stopped. She gave him a sideways look. "Your boss called again. I wrote down the message. Sounded a little mad, know what I mean? Are you in some kind of trouble?"

"No more than usual," he said. She gave him a little wave and vanished past the door. There was the swoosh of the front door opening and closing. He found the message in the middle of the stack: *Been trying to reach you all week. Important. Call immediately.*

Father John picked up the phone, dialed the provincial's office, and listened to the noise of Lucy's pickup belching into life over the sound of a phone ringing somewhere in Milwaukee. He could feel his muscles pulled tight around the dull throbbing in his ribs and something else—the familiar thirst coming over him. How a shot of Jim Beam would steady him, give him courage. He had been back barely a month, but what had the provincial said? A month, six months, a year?

The voice mail picked up and he had the choice of paging or leaving a message. He left a message.

He hung up and started reading through the other messages. Nothing from JoEllen Redman, but he hadn't expected her to call. She would continue to protect her son. New sounds erupted from outdoors: an engine gearing down on Circle Drive, tires crunching the snow. A door slammed. He recognized the footsteps on the steps, the smooth quickness in the way the front door opened and closed. In an instant Vicky stood in his doorway, little flecks of snow in her hair and on her black coat. Walks-On got up and went to her, and he watched her lean over and run gloved fingers through the dog's coat for a moment.

"How was your trip to LA?" he said.

"I found the name of the man who must have killed Charlie Wallowingbull." She dug through the black bag that hung over one shoulder. "William Thunder, a close friend. They were both in love with the same movie star. Thunder might have killed him in a rage of jealousy. Maybe it was even self-defense." Finally she pulled out an envelope, walked over, and handed it across the desk. "At any rate, I'm sure Kiki believed Thunder was responsible. Have a look," she said.

Father John pulled out the folded papers. *Los Angeles Police Missing Persons Report* was printed at the top of the first page. He glanced down the faint, ragged lines of type. "It's all there," Vicky said. "McCoy filed the missing persons report and suggested the police talk to Missy Mae Markham. Obviously the studio had covered up Charlie's death. I spoke with the same old movie people Kiki had talked to. There was gossip that Markham had gotten involved with Charlie while they were filming *The Covered Wagon*, and there was also gossip that she may have started up with his friend. Painted Brush got a picture of her with Charlie and William in Hollywood, which suggests she was still involved with them. But the studio would not stand for Markham's name being linked to Charlie's death. The police were probably paid to do what the studio said, and they closed the case."

Father John turned over pages of the report and the disposition and read the bold print at the top of the third page: *Fremont County Parolees*, followed by a list of names. His eyes focused on a name partway down: *Kiki Wallowingbull*. He read on. Near the bottom was the name *Will Thunder Redman*.

"JoEllen Redman's son," he said, catching the flash of confirmation in Vicky's eyes. "I spoke with her yesterday. She claims she never talked to Kiki, but she told me that Will has a son. Just like your caller."

"Kiki and Will Redman knew each other." Vicky slipped the pages back inside the envelope and waved it at him. "They served time together. Chances are they had both worked for Bellows. Kiki must have known that Will Redman was a descendant of William Thunder, and he went looking for him."

Father John tilted his head back and stretched his neck. The pain in his ribs shot upward. He could see Kiki Wallowingbull seated across from him, wiping up the syrup with a piece of pancake. Justice, he had said. It's time our family got justice. Dear Lord, he thought. What kind of justice had Kiki demanded?

Vicky said. "I'm going to see if Will is at this address." She flicked her fingers on the envelope and stuffed it back into the bag. "I can talk to him, and we can get this whole matter cleared up."

Father John got to his feet. "Will Redman doesn't want to be found, Vicky. His mother doesn't want him found. They'll deny they know anything about Kiki's death. Redman will deny that he ever called you."

"You forget that I saw him. I can identify him."

"You saw a man in Wal-Mart that you believe is the same man who called you."

"I saw him outside my apartment." Vicky threw up both hands to stall the questions in his eyes. "What are we talking about? We both know Kiki came back to the rez and out of some crazy sense of justice blamed Thunder's descendant for what Thunder did. Will Redman killed Kiki. What would you have me do? Nothing? Sit back and watch Jason Bellows convicted for a murder he didn't commit?"

"I can come with you," he said.

"It isn't necessary," Vicky said, but it struck him that she hadn't told him not to come.

33

SNOW BLANKETED THE prairie that rolled away from Riverton, criss-
crossed by narrow roads marked with the deep grooves of tire tracks.
Gray clouds edged in black hung low all around, dipping into the tops
of cottonwoods that appeared here and there. Vicky bent over the
steering wheel, trying to keep the Jeep in the ruts that stretched ahead,
aware of John O'Malley beside her, staring out the windshield, watching for signs of a house in the white wilderness.

They had driven through town in silence, past the strip malls and
box stores and warehouses that gradually fell behind until they were
out in the country. Once or twice she had started to tell him she was
glad he had come along, but she had stopped herself. She couldn't
shake the sense of misgiving that had taken hold of her. John O'Malley
had come with her to Tracers and ended up with broken ribs. Then
Bellows and some of his gang had attacked him at the mission. She
should never have dragged him into this.

"There's the house," he said, and Vicky followed the direction of his hand. A yellow, two-story house set back in a clump of cotton-woods. As she drew closer, she could see the white porch and white trim around the windows. Clumps of snow and ice hung off the porch railing and bunched on the steps. She slowed down, searching for a turn onto an access road. Then she saw a pair of tracks running like rails toward the house. She stepped hard on the brake pedal and fish-tailed into the tracks. The snow was heavier, grabbing at the tires. She had coaxed the Jeep to the edge of the trees when the tires skidded and the rear wheels seemed to lock into place. The house was about twenty yards ahead. It looked deserted.

Vicky turned off the motor. "Another wild-goose chase," she said, but Father John had already opened the passenger door. Cold air blasted the inside of the Jeep.

"Let's see if anyone's home," he said.

Vicky threw open her door and started trudging through the snow that reached for the top of her boots and dropped inside. John O'Malley fell in beside her. She was conscious of the crunching noise of their boots on the snow and the puffs of their breath running ahead. The cottonwoods cast long gray shadows, like the shadows in a forest. She felt the pressure of his hand on her arm, guiding her toward the faint traces of boot prints that made a path to the porch. Then, his hand tight around her arm, he yanked her sideways toward the trunk of a tree.

"Get down!" he shouted, and in an instant she felt herself crum-bling onto her knees, folding into the snow, the weight of his arms against her shoulders.

The gunshot sounded like a cannon that split the air and reverber-ated around the trees. The earth seemed to shift and rumble in the aftermath. "Stay down." John O'Malley was huddled next to her, nothing but the trunk of a tree between them and the rifle that now, for the first time, she saw jutting from the upper window of the house.

"Oh, God." She inched closer to the trunk and pressed her face against the front of his jacket, aware of his arms around her, reining her in. Her breath was stopped in her throat. She could hear her heart hammering next to his. The Jeep was at least fifteen feet behind them. They were ducks in a shooting gallery. "He's going to kill us," she said.

"Put the gun down, Will," John O'Malley shouted.

Vicky pulled a little away and peered around the trunk. The rifle was still balanced on the windowsill. Inside she could barely make out the shadowy figure of a man.

"Get out of here!" he shouted. His voice was heavy with rage, yet something about it was familiar.

Vicky made herself draw in a breath. "It's Vicky Holden," she shouted.

"Nobody asked you out here. Go away!"

"Put the rifle down, Will." John O'Malley's voice sounded confident, reassuring somehow. "We just want to talk to you."

"It's that priest I told you about." The woman's voice came from somewhere deep inside the house.

"Get out of here!" the man shouted.

"Will, let him help us." The woman sounded as if she were on the edge of hysteria. "Let him help us!"

"I don't need no help." The voice was muffled, as if he were speaking into a thick drapery.

"Please, Will. Please."

Vicky watched the rifle pull back from the window and the window slowly close. For a long moment the sound of breathing—hers and John O'Malley's—drifted into the silence of the snow and the trees. Then, there was the thwack of a door opening. A woman stepped onto the porch. "It's okay now," she shouted.

JOELLEN REDMAN STOOD in the middle of the small living room, clasping and unclasping her hands against the waist of her blue jeans. She looked middle-aged, with wide-set eyes, prominent cheekbones, and short, black hair fading into gray. Dark tearstains made vertical lines on her cheeks.

"You just couldn't leave us alone," she said, facing Father John. Her voice was thick with tears. She shifted toward Vicky. "Who are you?"

"I'm an attorney. Will called me," Vicky said.

Something seemed to go out of the woman, like air escaping a balloon. She stared at Vicky, eyes wide and unblinking. Then she swung around and walked over to the foot of the stairway that divided the living room from the kitchen in back. "You'd better come down here, Will," she shouted.

It was a moment before the man with thick shoulders, black hair that hung below his ears, and eyes as black and opaque as coal started down the steps that creaked and groaned under his boots. "What're you doing here?" Will Redman said, taking the last step with a little lurch. He was the man in Wal-Mart, the man outside her apartment. His was the voice on the telephone. Vicky could have sworn to it in court.

"She says you called her." There was a pleading note in JoEllen's voice.

"This whole thing's settled," he said. "I don't need no lawyers and priests coming around, so why don't you both just get out of here."

"A man may go to prison for a murder he didn't commit," Vicky said.

"I'm supposed to feel sorry for Bellows?" Will Redman listed sideways and spit out a puff of air, as if he were spitting on the floor.

"Convictions can be overturned," Vicky said. "How many people know you went to meet Kiki at the house in Ethete that night? Did you tell anyone what happened?"

"You said you told those guys at Tracers, Mickey and Rob," Jo-Ellen said.

"Be quiet, Mom." The words shot out of the side of his mouth. He

didn't take his eyes from Vicky. "I'm taking my chances. There's witnesses that say Bellows killed Kiki."

"Come on, Will," Vicky said. "Troy and Lennie are hoping to make
a deal with the feds, stay out of prison, and take over Bellows's gang.
When they realize that is not going to happen, they'll recant. They'll
tell the truth that neither of them actually saw Bellows beating up
Kiki, that Kiki was already unconscious on the floor when they got to
the house."

JoEllen cupped her hands over her mouth and gave out a sharp
sob.

Vicky pushed on. "Or let's say that Mickey and Rob start thinking
about what you told them and decide to talk to the fed. They may
even leave out the self-defense part. Either way, homicide charges
against Bellows will be dropped. Sooner or later, Agent Gianelli will
knock on your door."

"We're all done talking." Will walked over and flung open the door.
"Get out."

"Is that your son?" Father John nodded toward the photo in the
brass frame hanging over the sofa. A boy about five stood wide-legged,
squinting into the sun and leaning back a little as if he were winding
up to throw a baseball. He had a big grin and dark, trusting eyes.

"That's Matthew," JoEllen said, a mixture of pride and sadness
moving through her expression.

"Leave him out of this," Will said, but beneath the bravado, Vicky
could hear the tone of the man on the telephone, the sob-choked
words: "I got a little boy. I gotta take care of him."

"He lives in Casper with his mom," JoEllen said. "Will's trying to
get half custody. That's why he can't get involved in any of this. You
see that, don't you?"

"Is that what you want for your boy?" Vicky said. "Living in a
shadow, waiting for the knock on the door? You called me because
you wanted to be cleared."

Will kept one hand on the doorknob. He squeezed his eyes together and, for a moment, all of the bluster and determination peeled away. He was the man on the phone again, the man in the shadows who needed help.

"We can help you," Vicky said. "We know why Kiki wanted to see you. You have to trust us. Tell us what happened."

Will kicked the door shut. He walked over, sank onto the sofa, and hunched forward, dropping his forehead onto clenched fists. JoEllen sat down beside him and slipped an arm around his shoulders. She nodded toward the worn-looking upholstered chair, and Vicky sat down.

"Kiki called here," Will said. "Wanted to meet over in Ethete. Mom tried to tell me to stay away, that he was trouble, but I got to worrying what he might've gotten himself into. We used to work together." He dropped his voice to a whisper, like the whispers on the telephone. "We got arrested by the Riverton cops for distributing and spent a couple years in Rawlins. Got paroled about the same time. How'd I know he wasn't back in the drug business and wanting to pull me in again? I needed to clear things up, make him understand I was done with all that. I got my kid to think about. Mom's letting me live here 'til I get back on my feet, get a place of my own, and get my kid half the time. I got a job fixing tires at the tire shop. I had to make sure Kiki got it straight."

"What happened when you got to the house?" Father John had perched on a footstool. He leaned forward, hands clasped between his knees.

"Kiki was crazy. I never should've gone to meet him. Went crazy in prison." Will dropped his hands and looked from Vicky to Father John. "Happens to Indians," he said. "Locked up in a steel box all day, can't see the sky. We both got straight in rehab, but Kiki started going on all the time about how he had to repay his grandfather, give him something back for all the trouble he caused. His grandfather never knew what happened to his father, so Kiki was gonna find out soon as he got paroled. Well, I got to the house and he tells me he went to Hollywood and found out how his great-grandfather, Charlie, and my great-grandfather, William, were buddies. They were in a movie together. I said, Man, what's this got to do with anything? He got real mad. I seen him get mad when we were dealing drugs. Damn near beat a guy to death one time. I had to pull him off. So I got tense, you know what I mean."

He took a moment, and Vicky said that she understood. Then he went on, "He started shouting all kinds of craziness, like William killed his great-grandfather over some movie star, and the Thunders ruined his family and a lot of other junk like that. He said I had to go with him to his grandfather and apologize for all the suffering the Thunders caused him. I said, You're crazy, man. I don't know what you're talking about. I'm out of here. I turned around to leave, and that's when he hit me. Hit me hard on the back of the head. I thought I was going down. But I must've swung around, 'cause I caught him hard in the throat with my elbow and he was the one that went down. His head hit the corner of the cabinet."

Will slumped against the back of the sofa. "I'm never gonna forget the sound of his head hitting that cabinet," he said. "I knew he was dead. So I ran outta there. Got in my truck and drove away. There wasn't anybody around."

"He told me all about it." JoEllen had taken her arm from her son's shoulders and gathered her hands in her lap. "I told him to shut up about it. Nobody was ever gonna know."

The house was quiet, except for the small groan of a water pipe somewhere. "But you didn't want Kiki's death hanging over you," Father John said after a moment. "You wanted to be cleared."

"Nobody's gonna believe me," Will said. "So what if William Thunder killed his great-grandfather? What the hell's that got to do with me?"

"Could be the truth," JoEllen said. She was staring at a space across the room. "My father said his dad came back from Hollywood a week after he'd left. All the other Indians stayed for months acting in some show. Soon as he got back, he packed up everything they had, mattresses, chairs, tables piled in the back of an old truck, and they drove to Oklahoma. Nobody knew they were leaving, not even the government agent. They just got outta here. Oklahoma's where we stayed until a few years ago when Will"—she threw a sideways glance at her son—"came back to the rez and got into trouble. I moved up here to help him out, keep an eye on how Matthew was doing. My father said his dad never wanted anything to do with white people after he got back from Hollywood. You can't trust them, he said."

"Is that what you told Kiki?" Father John said.

JoEllen started nodding. Her eyes were watery and tears started down the tracks in her cheeks. "This is all my fault," she said. "Kiki came around to the bank asking for stories about the past. We went to coffee, and I told him what my father said."

"Listen, JoEllen," Vicky said. "Kiki talked to other people, too. All he had was circumstantial evidence at best. He had stories, that's all. There's no way to know for certain that your grandfather killed Charlie Wallowingbull. What we know is that Kiki believed the stories were true." She looked at Will. "What time did you go to the house?"

"I don't know."

"You have to know."

"He left here about seven o'clock," JoEllen said.

Will shrugged. "I told Mom where I was going. I guess I wanted somebody to know where I was, in case I didn't come back."

"Good," Vicky said. "You told your mom where you were going, and you told her what had happened after you got home." She nodded at JoEllen. "You can swear to the time he left and the time he returned. The thing is, Troy admits that it was midnight when he and Lennie went to the house and saw Bellows. Kiki had been unconscious for almost four hours. He died at the river where Troy left him." Vicky looked back at the man slumped sideways in the cushions. "You didn't kill Kiki," she said. "Someday your son will be glad to know that."

Will sat very still, his eyes quiet, the only movement a vein pulsing in his temple. "What difference does all this make? Nobody's going to believe this junk."

"We can confirm your story," Father John said. "We've been talking to people Kiki talked to. We know what he believed. We know why he asked you to meet him."

"You ask too much," Will said, defiance working back into his tone. "I can't take the chance the fed will believe it. I can't go back to prison. It's like Great-Grandfather seen in Hollywood. You can't trust whites."

"They can help us." JoEllen was staring at her son, eyes narrow with pain and anxiety. "You can put all this behind you, get on with things." But he was shaking his head, the bravado spreading across his features like an invisible rash. He was the shadowy figure in the window again, the man who had fired a warning shot.

"Go on." Will threw a hand toward the door.

"We'll go with you to talk to Agent Gianelli," Vicky said.

Will got to his feet, walked over to the door, and yanked it open. "The feds got their man, and they're not gonna let him off no matter how many guys change their stories. Go on, get out of here."

Vicky waited a moment—for what? she wondered. That Will Redman, a man who couldn't trust, who acted on impulse, might change his mind? Finally, she stood up, crossed the room, and walked out into the icy afternoon. The sound of Father John's footsteps echoed behind her.

They were about to start down the porch steps when Vicky turned around. "We're going to wait five minutes in case you change your mind," she said to the man holding on to the edge of the door. She could hear JoEllen sobbing.

"IT'S NO USE," Vicky said. They had been waiting at least ten minutes, the motor humming and the warm air flowing out of the vents. "He's right, you know," she went on. "Bellows will be convicted and chances are that Troy and Lennie and anyone else who knows the truth will never come forward. The case is closed." She tapped her fingers on the edge of the steering wheel.

"Maybe not," Father John said.

Vicky watched the door swing back. Will and JoEllen, bundled in bulky coats and scarves and gloves stepped out onto the porch. They hesitated a moment before starting down the steps.

Vicky found the cell in her bag and called Gianelli as they headed toward the Jeep, the snow swirling about their boots.

"I'm bringing in the man I told you about," Vicky said when Gianelli had picked up. "He struck Kiki in self-defense. He thought he was dead when he left the house."

"You know the case is wrapped up, Vicky." There was a tiredness in Gianelli's voice, a mixture of impatience and eagerness to get on with something else.

The rear door opened. JoEllen slid across the seat, and Will piled in behind her, both of them tight-lipped and silent and something else, Vicky thought: reconciled.

"We'll be there in thirty minutes," she said before she closed the cell.

34

THE OLD MAN was sleeping, legs stretched out on the recliner, a buzzing noise issuing from his open mouth. Father John hesitated inside the front door. "I can come back later," he said.

"No. No," Mamie said. Her fingers wrapped around the sleeve of his jacket and pressed into his arm. "He's just resting a little. He wants to see you."

Father John unzipped his jacket and waited as Mamie walked over and shook Andrew's shoulder. The old man seemed to spring to life. Head jerking back, boots paddling back and forth as if he were swimming. "Hey, Father!" He lifted one hand in a kind of benediction.

"He's brought us news about Kiki," Mamie said, waving Father John to the straight-back wooden chair at the foot of the recliner. "Coffee, Father?" she asked, but before he could answer, she had vanished past the doorway into the kitchen.

Father John sat down and shrugged out of his jacket. He set the file folder that contained the articles and photos on the floor. "How are you, Grandfather?" he said.

Andrew lifted a reddened, knobby hand and waved away the polite pleasantries. "You found out what happened to Kiki?"

He told him all of it then—how Kiki believed that William Thunder had killed his great-grandfather, how he had met one of Thunder's descendants, Will Redman, at a house in Ethete, how Kiki had insisted he come with him to apologize to his grandfather, and how they had gotten into an argument. At some point Mamie handed him a mug of coffee, set another mug on the table next to the recliner, and settled into the upholstered chair in the corner. "Will tried to leave and Kiki threw a punch at him," Father John said. "Will swung around and knocked him unconscious. It was an accident, Grandfather. It had nothing to do with drugs."

Andrew blinked slowly, absorbing the information. "Nothing to do with drugs." He repeated the words as if he wanted to make certain he had heard them correctly. "Everybody will remember that."

Father John took another moment before he said, "Another man, Troy Tallfeathers, took him to the river."

A soft gasp came from the corner.

"I'm sorry." Father John glanced from Andrew to Mamie.

Andrew lay his head back. His eyelids started to fall, and for a moment, Father John thought he would drop off into sleep, then he saw the tears spilling over the old man's lower lids. "The boy was a hothead," Andrew said. "All that anger he never could get rid of, like a wolf eating his insides, and he kept looking for ways to feed it. Drugs was a way for a long time before he come to his senses. Next thing we knew"—he looked over at Mamie—"all he talked about was how he was going to Hollywood and dig up the past, find out what happened to my dad 'cause it made him mad, he said, that we never knew. We had the right to know the truth, and he was gonna get it. It was like he was addicted all over again, still feeding the wolf."

Father John told them that Gianelli had investigated Kiki's death and concluded that Will Redman had struck Kiki in self-defense. The U.S. attorney had chosen not to prosecute. But Bellows, Tallfeathers, and Lennie Musser had turned on one another and faced numerous charges from aggravated assault to distribution of controlled substances. "They could be looking at twenty years in prison," he said.

The old people stayed quiet for a long while, still reconciling themselves, Father John knew, to the fact that their grandson was dead. "So Kiki found out that one of Dad's good friends killed him. William Thunder." Andrew drew out the name as if he were sampling its taste on his tongue. "Used to cowboy together before they went off to be in the movie. Dad and Thunder and Painted Brush. They always stuck together."

"It looks like that's what happened," Father John said. A shadow of disappointment moved across the old man's face, and he hurried on: "It's the most likely explanation, even though there was no police report of his death, just as McCoy's letter said." Then he told him that the police had conducted only a perfunctory investigation into Charlie's disappearance, and that the movie studio probably covered up what happened.

"Why'd Thunder do such a fool thing?"

Father John threaded his fingers together and leaned forward. This was the tough part, and yet Kiki had wanted to give his grandfather a gift of truth. He picked up the folder, slipped out the photo that Painted Brush had taken, and handed it to the old man. "It may have been over a movie star by the name of Missy Mae Markham," he said. "She was in *The Covered Wagon*. It's possible that Charlie and Thunder both fell in love with her."

Andrew brought the photo up close to his face. "She's real pretty," he said. "Dad looks good, too. He was a fine-looking man." He handed the photo back, and when Father John offered it to Mamie, she waved it away. "She must've gotten real mad when Dad got to Hollywood and told her he got married and had a kid coming."

Father John stared at the old man. He felt as if he were seeing him for the first time—the white hair tied in braids that hung down the red plaid shirt, the rheumy eyes and creased face, the arthritic hands that had just thrown a fastball into his chest. My God. There were so many hidden corners of the past, so many shadows and obscure places. It was like trying to find Orion behind a cover of snow clouds. Orion was there, you knew, but you couldn't make out the shape.

He slipped the photo back into the folder. "It's hard to know what happened with any degree of certainty," he said.

The old man was nodding. "Dad would've come back to us otherwise," he said. "Everybody said he just walked off, deserted us. Now we can say the truth." He turned his head toward Mamie. "Tell everybody that wants to know."

Father John drank some of the coffee and thanked the old couple. He got to his feet, scooped the file folder off the floor, and handed Andrew the DVD of *The Covered Wagon* that he had slipped in front of the stack of printed magazine articles and photos. "Do you mind if I keep McCoy's letter for a little while?" he said. He had meant to return the letter. And later this afternoon he had intended to drive over to Felix Painted Brush's place and return the photo, but he still needed them. He promised to stop by again soon, let himself outside, and, shrugging into his jacket, headed for the pickup. He wondered who would care about a murder that took place in 1923. Maybe some of the old people who still remembered stories from that time. Ella Morningstar. Felix Painted Brush. He doubted that Will Redman or his mother would want to be reminded, but he decided that he would talk with them again.

He turned the ignition and backed down the driveway. Then he rummaged through the papers and flashlight and tire gauge in the glove compartment, pulled out his cell, and drove onto the road. He had one message: The provincial's office. He hit the play key and steered the pickup into the snow tracks as he listened to the voice of Father Bill Rutherford. "Sorry to miss your calls." The voice sounded calm, cleansed of the usual notes of fatigue and weariness. "We seem to be playing telephone tag, John, but I do need to speak with you about the mission. Call me when you get this message."

Father John pressed the end key and turned onto Blue Sky Highway, aptly named, he thought, with the blue sky stretched over the snow-covered fields as far as he could see, the sun reflecting like fire off the hood of the pickup. He would return the call later. Now he pressed the key for Vicky's office.

It was a moment before Vicky was on the other end. "Do you have a few minutes for a cup of coffee?" he said, not knowing why he had suggested coffee. He could go to her office, and yet there was something formal and forbidding about the office. "There's something I'd like to talk to you about."

"The coffee shop off Main," she said. "Give me thirty minutes."

He told her he would meet her there, tapped the end key, and set the cell on the passenger seat. It was a good thirty minutes to Lander.

HE SAW VICKY outside the plate-glass window before the door opened and the bell clanged into the coffee shop. She gave him a little wave. The front of her black coat hung open over a white blouse and dark slacks. He could see the glint of a silver necklace against her throat as she turned toward the counter. There were a few people seated about the other tables, reading newspapers and working on mugs of coffee with foam bubbling on top. Father John set the file folder in the center of the small table he had selected next to the back wall and took a sip of the plain coffee that he had altered with three little containers of cream.

It was a few minutes before Vicky set a mug on the table and took the chair across from him. She let her coat drop over the back. "Is everything all right?" she said.

He told her that he had just visited Andrew and Mamie. She gave him a half smile of understanding, then sipped at her coffee a moment.

There was the familiar resolve in her eyes, but thinner and softer somehow.

She set the mug down. "You told them what happened to Kiki?"

He nodded. "I think there's some comfort in the fact that Kiki hadn't gone back to drugs. He was clean . . ."

"Obsessed but clean." Vicky shook her head and closed her eyes a moment as if she could shut out some of the senselessness of it. "How did he take the news about his father?" she said.

Father John shrugged. "He always believed his father had been killed. He never knew who was responsible." He opened the folder and shook out the contents. "It looks like Thunder was responsible," he said, spreading out the photos and copies of magazine articles and the copies of the LA Police Department's reports, "but something Andrew said made me think that might not be true." He looked up at Vicky. "Andrew said that Missy Mae Markham must have been pretty mad when his dad told her he had gotten married."

Vicky went still for a moment. Then she turned her head and stared across the coffee shop. Finally she turned back, picked up McCoy's letter, and read out loud: "Charlie didn't show up for the show on April 10." She dropped the letter and slid over the missing persons report. "McCoy reported him missing two days later and suggested the police talk to Missy Mae Markham. According to the studio, Missy Mae Markham was out of town and couldn't know anything about the disappearance." She pushed the sheet away. "Case closed."

Father John lifted the copy of the magazine photo of Missy Mae Markham and Jesse Lasky and studied the long light-colored Packard, the smiling, thin-haired man with the small rimless glasses lifting a hand from the steering wheel to wave at the photographer, and the beautiful woman with blond hair flying back and a white arm lifted in a languid wave. He handed the photo to Vicky. "Taken April 12 in Flagstaff," he said.

Vicky glanced at the photo before setting it down and picking up the photo Painted Brush had taken. She turned it over and read out loud the words scrawled by a mission Indian who had learned to read and write: *Charlie and William with big move star Missy Mae Markham at Hollywood studio, April 10, 1923.*

"The studio moved fast," she said, flipping the photo over the other sheets of paper. "They got her out of town immediately, before she could talk to the police or anyone else." She spread her hands and gave a little laugh. "It makes sense. If an Indian had killed another Indian, maybe the studio would have gone to a lot of trouble to dispose of the body and make it look as if Charlie had walked away. But there were other ways they could have handled it, stories their PR people could have handed out. Two Indians got in a fight at the camp in Cahuenga Pass. One ended up dead. But if one of the leading stars was the killer, the studio would certainly have done everything possible to cover it up."

"William may have known the truth," Father John said. He had been turning it over in his mind on the drive to Lander, examining the hypothesis from one angle, then the other. "He may have run into Missy that night when he rode up to the canyon. He could have found Charlie dead in his tipi." He tapped one of the magazine articles. "She always had a bodyguard, the gossip columnists said. The bodyguard probably came looking for her, saw what had happened, saw William Thunder . . ."

Vicky cut in: "Threatened him, told him to leave town and keep his mouth shut or he would swear he had seen Thunder commit the murder."

Father John nodded. It was the same scenario he had arrived at. "It explains why Thunder came back to the rez while the show was still going on. He moved his family to Oklahoma and told them never to trust white people."

"Had he stayed here"—Vicky smiled and shook her head—"there would always have been rumors and gossip, people speculating on whether he had killed his friend. In Oklahoma he could try to forget and hope people here would also forget. And everyone did, except for

Charlie's family." She paused and took another drink of coffee. "How do you think she did it?"

Father John found another page of photos and held it up. At the top was the photo of Missy Mae Markham in a dark dress, one hand clutching a dark shawl, the other holding a pistol. "Taken at the Lasky Studio on April 10," he said. Then he read the caption out loud: "Missy is an expert marksman who learned to shoot on her daddy's ranch in Texas." He set the page down. "Even prop guns can cause death at close range," he said.

"So she went to Cahuenga Pass, found Charlie in his tipi, and shot him." Vicky stared across the coffee shop a moment, as if she were watching the scene play out. Then she picked up the photo of Charlie and William with the movie star. "Do you suppose Painted Brush knew the truth?" she said. "Is that why he took such pains to write that the picture was taken at the studio where Missy was making a movie on April 10, the day Charlie died?"

Father John smiled at her. Then he piled the pages and photos together, squared the edges, and set them inside the folder. She had a way, he was thinking, of filling in so many missing pieces.

They finished their coffee and walked outside. The sky was still blue, but the temperature was falling, and he could see their breath in the air between them. He nodded at the pickup parked at the curb. "Want a lift back to the office?" he said.

She laughed at that. It was only a block away, she said, and then she was off, dodging the clumps of snow on the sidewalk. He waited until she had crossed the street. Then he got in the pickup and turned on the engine. Cold air whistled out of the vents as he opened the cell and pressed in Father Rutherford's number. He listened to the buzzing of a phone in the provincial's office a thousand miles away as Vicky disappeared past the redbrick building at the corner.

AUTHOR'S NOTE

Tim McCoy was the genuine article—a real cowboy who became a cowboy movie star with a career that spanned three decades and included more than a hundred movies. It was McCoy's name on the marquees and McCoy's likeness on the posters—white Stetson on his head, revolver in his hand—that brought audiences to the moving picture palaces. Read the fine print near the bottom of some of those posters and you'll find the words *with John Wayne*. McCoy was a star when no one had heard of Roy Rogers or Gene Autry, and it was the popularity of singing cowboys like them who stopped the action to sing a song that gradually shoved McCoy off the main stage. Real cowboys didn't let the bad guys get away while they warbled songs and strummed guitars.

It was McCoy who single-handedly brought Arapahos and Shoshones into the movies. He had spent years working the ranchlands near the Wind River Reservation and had befriended many of the people. After rising to the rank of colonel in the army cavalry during World War I, he returned to Wyoming as the state's adjutant general where he was at work the day in 1922 that the man from Famous Players–Lasky walked in and said the studio needed five hundred "real" Indians for the moving picture they were about to make. McCoy agreed to talk to his Indian friends, but he wanted assurances: Indians were to be treated like everyone else (an almost outrageous condition in the 1920s), they were to receive the same pay as other extras, plus meals, and were to get extra money for their horses and tipis.

The deal was struck, and McCoy and five hundred Arapahos and Shoshones began movie careers in the first western epic, *The Covered Wagon.* McCoy was the technical adviser on that film, but after that, he became an actor and before long, a movie star. Arapahos and Shoshones went on to appear in other silent movies, including *Spoilers of the West* and *End of the Trail.*

McCoy remained friends with the Arapahos, visiting the reservation into the 1970s and often stopping by to see his friend, Father John Killoren, S.J., pastor of St. Stephen's Mission (the actual mission upon which St. Francis Mission is based).

In the story, Father John and Vicky are the ones who must learn the truth behind Charlie Wallowingbull's disappearance in Hollywood in 1923. But I have no doubt that if an Arapaho had actually gone missing in Hollywood, Tim McCoy would have torn the town apart to get the answers. He was that kind of cowboy.